Prai...

ASIA MACKAY

'A **lethally addictive** blend of **domestic suspense and hard-driving thriller**. Set aside some time for this one – **you won't be able to put it down**'
A.L. GAYLIN

'A cracking book – **funny, thrilling, touching**. It's as if mum-lit was on crack with shades of *Killing Eve*. This is a **thrilling, original and funny** read which takes spy fiction to a new level. I loved it'
CLAIRE ALLAN

'**I ABSOLUTELY LOVED IT!!!** It's **so new** and **different** and **refreshing** and I found it **such fun** (also loved the **feminist** message)'
MARIAN KEYES

'A **riotously fun** read . . . **James Bond should retire** now: Lex Tyler shows him up for the tired, old has-been he is. **With prose as sharp as her heroine's (actual) killer heels, Asia Mackay puts the sass in assassin** as it's never been done before'
L. S. HILTON

'An annoyingly **brilliant** and **funny** first novel'
HUGH GRANT

THE
NURSERY

ASIA MACKAY

About the Author

Asia Mackay is a Chinese Scottish author and mother of four based in London. Asia studied Anthropology at Durham University, after which she started a career in television. She presented and produced lifestyle programmes in Shanghai before moving back to London, where she worked for Ewan McGregor and Charley Boorman as Project Manager on their round the world motorbike documentaries. *Killing It*, her debut novel, was the First Runner Up in Richard and Judy's Search for a Bestseller competition and First Runner Up for the Comedy Women In Print prize.

THE NURSERY

ASIA MACKAY

ZAFFRE

First published in the UK in 2019
This edition published in the UK in 2025 by
ZAFFRE
An imprint of Bonnier Books UK
5th Floor, HYLO, 103-105 Bunhill Row,
London, EC1Y 8LZ
Owned by Bonnier Books
Sveavägen 56, Stockholm, Sweden

A CIP catalogue record for this book is
available from the British Library.

ISBN: 978-1-78512-684-0

Also available as an ebook

1 3 5 7 9 10 8 6 4 2

Typeset by IDSUK (Data Connection) Ltd
Printed and bound in Great Britain by Clays Ltd, Elcograf S.p.A.

www.bonnierbooks.co.uk

For Trotts

You're fun, funny and mine
I feel lucky, I really do
But when you say I have PMT
I really want to kill you
X

'GET DOWN! GET DOWN!' I shout at the man in front of a dilapidated warehouse, as I pull up opposite him in a black van. He ducks to the ground just as a stream of bullets tear up the wall where he had just been standing.

'Your cover's blown.'

Another shot rings out.

'Lex? That you?' comes the muffled shout from behind a four-foot-high carefully ordered pile of wooden planks. We are at an old deserted gasworks in East London. Building work had stalled last year due to a bankrupted building company and retracted permissions.

'I'm here with Jake. We're going to get you out,' I shout back.

We've been ordered by Platform Eight to undertake an emergency extraction. As assassins in an elite underground branch of Her Majesty's Secret Service it's a slightly different remit to what we are used to. But the target under attack is one of our own. Simon Black has been undercover with a drug-dealing syndicate, tasked with taking out the newly appointed Head. This morning we'd intercepted communication that they knew about him.

I slide out of the driver's door, keeping low. The gunfire continues. I hear it ricocheting off the roof. Why are they aiming so high? I look up just in time to see a plank of wood come crashing down, knocking Black off his feet.

There's another burst of gunfire and in my earpiece is Jake Drummond. 'Hostiles down.'

I run to Black and pull the plank off him. He's out cold. But there is still a pulse. I drag him the few feet to the van. Jake screeches up next to us on his motorbike. He jumps off and together we sling Black into the back of the van.

'I'll call in the Clean Team. You get him out of here.'

I get into the driver's seat and accelerate fast. I just need to get back to the relative safety of the industrial park. Witnesses and CCTV should halt a further attack. I speed along the ramshackle road. Two turns and I will be at the alleyway leading back to the main road.

My phone rings through the van's Bluetooth. I ignore it. A large black four-by-four roars around the corner.

They're coming for us.

I push into fifth gear as I accelerate further. I need to somehow outrun them.

'Hi, just a quick one.' Will's voice crackles through the hands-free.

What the hell?

I must've clipped the answer button on the steering wheel. Now is not the time for a chat with my husband who remains oblivious to what exactly being a data-analyser for the Government Communication and Data Specialisation Branch really entails. He thinks the biggest danger I face in my supposed desk-bound job is square eyes from staring at a computer screen all day long.

'Can you pick up my dry-cleaning on your way home?'

I reach for the hang-up button. Just as the four-by-four rams into the side of us and I'm flung against the driver side window.

'Hello, Lex? What was that bang? Are you OK?'

I peel myself off the window and grab hold of the steering wheel and slam my foot down on the accelerator, powering slightly ahead of the four-by-four. The collision has slowed them down more than me.

'Dropped my phone. I can't really talk now. I—'

'Please, Lex, it's not that hard a question. I'm going to be stuck here until late. I'm on my last shirt and I'm so swamped I'll need to be back in the office early tomorrow.'

'I . . . just, hang on.'

I jolt forward as the four-by-four hits the back of the van. A turning is coming up on my right, I pull down hard on the steering wheel, swerving round the corner at speed. The four-by-four can't brake fast enough and overshoots it.

I speed down the road before taking another hard right. Having memorised the small network of roads back towards the motorway I know I'm close.

'You there?' Will sighs.

'Yes. I'm here.'

There is still no sign of the four-by-four. They're going to try to cut me off. But where?

'Look, I get it. You have an important job, you're busy, I'm busy, but come on, Lex.' His voice is pleading.

If I keep on this road, I just need to pass two side streets before reaching the motorway. It's worth the risk.

'I . . . I'm thinking.'

I sail past the first side road. Nothing.

I check my side mirrors; maybe I've lost them.

'Well?'

I approach the second side street just as the four-by-four roars out and slams against the van. I am again thrown against the window. I don't let go of the wheel as I pull down hard to correct our path.

'Darling?'

I try to think of my schedule for the rest of the day.

I'm drawing a blank.

'OK, yes. Fine. I'll do it.'

'Hallelujah. See, it wasn't that—' I cut him off.

The four-by-four is now rammed right up against my van – together we are careering down the road towards the small alleyway.

Only one of us is going to get through and it's going to have to be me.

I must time this just right. My foot is already fully down on the accelerator. I need to jolt the car out the way with enough time to make it through the alleyway and not hit the wall. I take a deep breath and calculate the distance ahead.

Twenty feet, ten feet, six feet and I swing down hard and fast on the wheel. The force clips the four-by-four and sends it spinning to the side and crashing into a warehouse.

I pull down hard on the wheel again and hold my breath as we speed through the narrow opening. The wing mirror breaks off as we skim the side of the wall and go full pelt through the alleyway and out into a small slip road that joins the motorway.

We are clear.

'Lex, you copy?' Jake crackles into my earpiece.

'Black is secure. Entering the A1020 now. I'll take him back to the Platform.'

'No,' Jake's voice rises, 'meet me at the service station on junction six. You're the one that needs to make the pick-up, remember? You can take my bike.'

He's right.

It has to be me.

I check my watch. I have fifty-three minutes to get to the other side of London. The recriminations if I don't are not worth thinking about. I pull into the service station and fling open the van door, getting out just as Jake screeches up alongside us. He takes off his helmet and hands it to me as he gets off the bike.

'Go now.'

'Roger that. Look after him.' I nod over my shoulder to the still unconscious figure in the back of the van.

Speeding through the busy streets of London, weaving in and out of traffic, I grit my teeth. I have to make it. I just have to.

When I finally pull up outside the main gate, I jump off the bike and look around. The large green Portakabin is just up ahead. The whole area is deserted. Not a good sign. I check my watch. Fuck. Despite the full speed and the shortcut, I'm twelve minutes late. I pull off my helmet and tear up the metal steps, the rattling thuds announcing my presence to those inside.

The door opens and there is Yvonne. Ruler of this strange kingdom with the peeling walls and air with the faint smell of sewage. She's wearing all black and her curly hair is tied back in a tight bun. Her mouth is set in a thin line.

'Sorry I'm late – had a small setback. Hope everything is OK here.'

'We've had our own problems today. Come through. I need to show you.'

I follow her into the small hallway. She reaches for the iPad on the table by the door and shows me the screen. On it is a photo of an arm with two distinctive red marks. You can just make out indentations.

'Who is this?' I ask.

'You know I can't tell you that.' She folds her arms. 'This is meant to be a safe haven, not a place of violence. We were given no warning this could happen.'

'I understand completely. You must accept our apologies. I'll sort this out.'

She nods curtly and motions towards the double doors behind her. I open them and there sits the perpetrator in a red plastic chair, fidgeting with an empty plastic cup.

With just one look at my face she comes running at me.

And into my arms.

'Mama! Mama!'

I pick Gigi up and give her a kiss on the head.

I had at least kept the promise I had made leaving the house this morning: that after weeks of hardly seeing her, I would be the one to pick her up from nursery today. The memory of her reaction – great big smile, lit-up eyes and cries of 'Hurrah, Mama, hurrah, Mama' as she jumped up and down – meant failing her would have undoubtedly traumatised me more than her.

Yvonne comes up behind me. 'I told you Mummy was coming. That she hadn't forgotten about you. She was just running a tiny bit late.'

I'm reminded that we are both in trouble.

'Now listen, Gigi, you've been very naughty. You must never ever bite anyone. You know that.' I look into her big blue eyes and silently implore her to not show me up further in front of her headteacher.

'Gigi bite.' She smiles up at me.

'No, Gigi. NO bite.' I look at Yvonne. 'Are you sure you can't tell me who it was? I'd like to apologise to their parents.'

She is already shaking her head. 'Our policy is very clear. Data protection. We never inform parents of the name of the victim or the abuser.'

I laugh. 'Abuser is a little harsh, don't you think? I mean, she's only two.'

Yvonne stares at me. 'Abuse is characterised as hurt or injury by maltreatment. And believe me, this individual was maltreated by your daughter.'

Gigi giggles. 'Bite. Aarumph.' She gnashes her teeth together.

It's very hard to not laugh. One look at Yvonne's frowning face helps.

'No, Gigi. Biting is bad. Very, very bad. And if you do it again you may not be allowed to come to this nursery. And you love it here, don't you?'

Gigi nods. 'Gigi like school.' Gigi had walked through the Portakabin door for the first time just a few weeks ago at the start of the school's autumn term. She had thankfully taken to it immediately. I was probably the only mother who had had to cart a crying toddler away from school. Looking around the rundown classroom, the grey partition walls brightened up with children's drawings and finger paintings, it was hard to comprehend just what exactly made it so magical.

I turn to Yvonne. 'So I'm hoping it's not a three strikes and you're out policy?' I try a smile.

Yvonne's face remains impassive. 'This should never happen again.'

'Of course, of course. We will make sure she understands. I really am very sorry, she's never done this before.'

'I should hope not.'

'Bye bye, Eeeyvon.' Gigi waves and grins at her. She seems immune to just how terrifying this woman is.

'Bye bye, Gigi,' says Yvonne. 'Now you enjoy your special time with Mummy.'

Mother. Secret agent. Two roles. Two lives. There are days when it's tough. Of course there are. But today is one of those winning days. Where I crammed it all in. Saved a colleague. Picked up my daughter. Whipped up some fish fingers for her dinner. Succeeded in getting her to eat three pieces of carrot. And got her to bed after only six bedtime stories and three threats of banning pudding for a week. Victorious days like this are few and far between and it's important to revel in them.

Will arrives home as I'm sitting on the living room sofa, toasting myself with a large glass of red wine.

'My dry-cleaning upstairs?'

Shit.

Part One

Bite

bite, *v.*
1. Use the teeth in order to inflict injury on.
2. Take the bait or lure.

Chapter One

A BUSKER WITH A TOPKNOT was singing about 'running' in an enthusiastic falsetto at the bottom of the escalators at Holborn tube station. I recognised it as a Florence and the Machine song. A few commuters winced. It was a little too high-pitched for early Monday morning.

I gave him a nod as I walked past him and joined the escalators up into the daylight.

The weekend had been quiet. All active missions were on hold. My orders had been to not leave London, keep my head down and await a full update at today's briefing. After two days of a husband still grumpy about ShirtGate and a daughter wielding a glue gun demanding craft time, I was ready for whatever the Platform could throw at me.

I walked up to the grey office building adjoining the tube station. I swiped my specially modified Oyster card against the double doors and entered. In the small reception area was a waiting lift. I walked in and pressed a combination of buttons that took me down to the hallowed halls of Platform Eight.

Our offices were situated in a disused underground network of rooms and tunnels coming off Platform Eight at Holborn tube station. It was a fitting location for our covert branch of the security services – we could roam all over London hidden from the all-seeing CCTV, whilst the sounds of the trains helped mask the noise from uncooperative interviewees. Only we knew the dark truth behind the seemingly innocuous tube announcements. 'Signal failures' were often caused by over-enthusiastic interrogating shorting the electricity supply and affecting the whole underground grid. A 'person on the tracks' could be a person who would rather die than answer our questions – it was a particularly effective disposal method as 'splatters' were near impossible to do autopsies on.

I entered the lift an everyday commuter and exited an underground secret agent.

This was our world. Officially we were the Government Communication and Data Specialisation Branch used by MI5 and MI6 for specialist data analysis. Unofficially we went by the catchier Platform Eight and were a covert division tasked solely with missions that left no paper trail and no target alive.

We were Rats.

We scuttled around underground doing the unpalatable work necessary to keep everyone in Britain safe.

We were the Security Services' dirty little secret.

I ran my hand against the concrete wall as I walked towards my meeting room. The division was a hive of activity. There were people hurrying up and down the corridors. Phones ringing. Shouts from office to office. Around sixty people work out of Platform Eight. Only half were Rats, the rest were Tech Support or working in departments like Surveillance, Special Projects and Research and Development. We may all have different skillsets, differing motivations, but all of us who worked at Eight shared the unfaltering belief that what we were doing was vital to national – and international – security. Sanctioned assassinations for the greater good. Saving lives by taking lives.

This was our final morning before a full lockdown. Unit leaders were calling in all Rats abroad or undercover.

Platform Eight was on high alert and we needed everyone in our network to be told.

Throughout London buskers were singing their hearts out. Today certain carefully positioned performers were singing songs specially chosen by us. Songs that had a special meaning to our undercover operatives.

In certain spots around town new graffiti would be appearing on key street corners. The homeless begging in specific alleyways would be holding signs in red.

In the days where electronic correspondence was monitored and could no longer be trusted we relied on a wide network of more simple forms of communication.

Everything usually ignored we used to our advantage.

The public – or the Sheep, as we liked to call them – wouldn't notice these tweaks. These little changes. But all our people would know the symbols, the signs, the lyrics.

Run. Watch out. You're compromised. This was what London was screaming to our operatives, to our informants.

We had got to Agent Black in time. The others might not be so lucky. There was a Snake in our midst and no one was safe. Slithering around alongside us, using their inside knowledge to hurt us above ground. None of us would be safe until this traitor was found. Until they were eliminated.

As I walked past an open office door I heard, 'I'm worried. She hasn't liked my latest photo on Instagram and I know she's been on it this morning as she liked a photo of a dog walking in snow boots.'

It may have sounded like typical office watercooler chit chat but this was important work. Tech Support were using social media to make sure Platform Eight operatives were getting the message all over the world. Key accounts posted photos of sunsets and planes in flight. Status updates like 'Time for holibobs!'. Inspirational quotes along the vein of 'Every ending is just a new beginning'. Every post was a call to get out, to get somewhere safe and hide out.

It was a flurry of activity now but soon the corridors would be quiet.

I'd been a Rat for twelve years and this was the first time we'd ever had a full lockdown.

I walked into the meeting room. The rest of my unit were already assembled around the large, grand mahogany dining table, which had been installed there for as long as anyone could remember. It had become so much a part of the fabric of Platform Eight that it was underneath this table we carved the names of all the Rats we'd lost over the years. Within London there are many memorials marking the names of those who had given their lives to serving this country. But for us – those who didn't officially exist – this was as good as it got. It was our way of honouring our fallen comrades. A small reminder that even if no one else knew, we did.

Stationed in his usual seat at the corner of the dining table was Geraint 'G-Force' Callewaert, a small bespectacled IT expert, who was our Lead Tech Support. There was nothing he didn't know about computers and he always seemed happiest plugged into his laptop, heavy metal on his headphones, tapping away at defeating yet another sophisticated security system.

Opposite him was Robin Goh, a happy-go-lucky Chinese man with a strong Scottish accent, who was still paying his dues as a Rat-in-training. Recently he had been complaining about how it was time he branched out on his own. Got his own unit. Grew up and left the nest. It was down to Jake and me to decide if we thought he was ready.

Jake had been my partner since I started as a Rat. Our history had been complicated: a veritable mess of sex and slaughter and blurred lines. A certain clarity was reached when I married Will – I took my marriage vows seriously. But there was always a question mark. And then a couple of years ago everything came to a head when Sandy White, our long-time unit leader, betrayed us all. He turned out to be a Snake, a traitor of the highest order, a turncoat, a disloyal fuckwit. On the take from the Russians and hired to tank our latest mission, Sandy had enrolled Nicola Adams, our Tech Support, to help him and together they tried to frame me and then kill me. Jake helped me stop them and it only took nearly dying for me to finally confront what was between us. The lines were now crystal clear. Partner. Colleague. Friend. Godfather to Gigi.

Sandy and Nicola's traitorous actions could have torn our unit apart. But there was no in-fighting or finger-pointing for our combined failing to spot the signs. Their betrayal brought the remaining four of us closer together. We had all been subjected to a series of intense interrogations and prolonged close monitoring. Not to mention the whispers from colleagues we had worked alongside for years looking at us and wondering if we too were dirty. Together we had had the gratification of being cleared of all wrongdoing and heralded as heroes for crushing a plot that would've given Russia an upper hand in cyberspace and beyond and taken decades to recover from.

Both Jake and I had been offered the vacated role of unit leader. Both of us had turned it down.

The broad six-foot-seven black man with the salt and pepper beard currently standing at the head of the dining table was the one who had said yes to the position. He was, as always, smartly attired in chinos and a shirt with a grandfatherly grey cardigan. The only nod to casual comfort were weathered size sixteen Nike trainers.

Hattie Goodswen had started out as a Rat thirty years ago, before moving into the army to an undisclosed position. I couldn't ever imagine he was the type of agent who would be able to simply melt unobtrusively into the background.

I had asked him about it once and he had shrugged and said how I'd be surprised how easy it was: 'I just wear a hoodie. Or look unwashed and bedraggled. People may spot me out the corner of their eye but they won't dare look at me. It's easy being invisible when no one wants to see you. All witnesses can ever remember is "big and black", all the CCTV ever shows is "big and black".' He brushed his cheek. 'This is a blessing.' Hattie was very dark – dark enough that grainy CCTV could never get a clear impression of his face. 'I was a Rat for ten years and seen walking away from the scene of a crime at least twenty times, but no one ever managed to put together an e-fit. Everyone gets so blinded by all this,' he gestured over his large bulk, 'that they never take the time to notice anything else.' Hattie always spoke softly. I often wondered about him. This misunderstood big man.

He was back at Platform Eight in his first desk job and he was proving to be an excellent Team Leader. He was a large, comforting presence. His voice had a deep, soothing tone – he never raised it. I trusted him, he was a good man and it was easy to get along with him. Although considering what I went through with Sandy, simply having a boss who didn't want me dead made for a happier working environment.

Pixie Nisbett was our other new arrival. A born and bred Londoner, she'd started with us last year as our unit's Tech Support to back up Geraint. As an expert hacker with a background in code-breaking, she was an invaluable addition. She also added a splash of colour to an otherwise grey office environment. Tall with frizzy blonde hair, she was today wearing sequined jeans and a pink jumper, which had 'Hot hot hot' emblazoned across it in red letters. Her large earrings, which jangled every time she moved her head, were fluorescent pineapples.

Pixie seemed incapable of talking to anyone without an endearment. I was pretty sure Hattie shuddered every time she called him 'sweetcheeks'. She seemed to have no internal filter – everything she thought she said aloud. It was both refreshing and worrying – I had to presume outside the office she managed to keep any work-related thoughts to herself or Special Projects would've recommended her dismissal long ago.

I took my seat at the table next to Jake. I noticed a splodge of porridge caked on the right thigh of my jeans. I scrubbed at it with a babywipe from my bag. Since having Gigi I'd never been more grateful for the Platform's relaxed dress code. Once, when Gigi had a bad chest infection and I'd been up with her throughout the night, I turned up at the Platform half-asleep wearing tracksuit bottoms, a stained top and a mum bun. Jake had asked what the undercover homeless mission I was going out on was.

I didn't bother trying to explain to him there were many different definitions of mum chic.

Hattie cleared his throat as he looked down at us all. If he stretched I was sure he could easily place both hands on the meeting room's peeling ceiling. 'We're about to go on lockdown. There's a Snake in our midst and agents and informants are dying thanks to this traitor. For the first time in Eight's history the Committee have decreed that all active missions need to be shut down.'

The Committee ran the country. A group of unknown individuals who made the decisions. The Prime Minister and Parliament were a front to give the appearance of democratic control. But they were all just puppets acting out the Committee's orders.

'What you don't know is that we will be the only unit still in operation.'

'Oh no, darlin'. Really? I just booked tickets to ComicCon.' This was Pixie.

Hattie pressed a couple of buttons on his laptop and what looked like a website homepage was projected onto the whiteboard. Against a black background was 'The Tenebris Network' written in large red font. Underneath was the tagline, 'Discreet online recruitment services for all your personnel needs'.

'This is our newest threat. Because of them we have seven dead and counting. Whistle have been tasked with locating and eliminating the Snake working for Tenebris before they undertake further damage.'

Whistle was our unit name. Hattie had renamed us this upon his appointment as unit leader. He felt 'clean as a whistle' was a fitting nod to a unit that had been tarred by our previous unit leader's traitorous actions. It was no surprise the Committee had chosen Whistle to find this latest Snake. After all they'd put us through the Committee could trust us to be clean. And we'd come up against a Snake before and won.

Robin frowned as he read the whiteboard. 'Online recruitment services? So Tenebris is a kind of LinkedIn? Although I don't get how a networking website can get any of us killed?'

'I wouldn't be so sure. Reading through CVs of people showing off about their management skills would bore me to bloody death.' Jake leaned back in his plastic chair and took a large gulp of coffee. He had dark circles under his eyes and was wearing the same shirt as yesterday. What Jake got up to on nights when he didn't get home could vary from acrobatics with one of the many willing doe-eyed, long-limbed twenty-somethings that flocked to his dark, brooding looks, to dabbling in activities that could be violent, illegal, immoral or even all three. One time we'd been called in in the middle of the night for an urgent mission, I'd had to pick him up bloodied, bruised and missing a shirt from some disused railway tracks. Jake needed to push it, he needed to be on the edge. Even being a Rat wasn't always enough. He'd go looking for the trouble he needed to get himself into and out of to feel alive. Today he looked exhausted, but there were no tell-tale specks of blood on shirt cuffs, no wincing as he leaned forward for another hit of caffeine. Maybe last night was just a particularly energetic young ingénue trying hard to convince him she was enough to give up the others.

'Don't be fooled by the bland recruitment talk. "Tenebris" is Latin for "dark" and this is without a doubt a dark force we're dealing with,' said Hattie. He nodded at Geraint. 'Take us through it, G.'

Geraint tapped a couple of buttons and a screenshot of a website homepage was projected onto the whiteboard. 'The Tenebris Network is a major new threat to the security of not only all our assets and informants but all Security Service agents both here in the UK and abroad. It's an app that's a cross between Tinder and LinkedIn. On one side there are the profiles of Employees – for example, civil servants, agents, analysts, intelligence officers – while on the other are the Employers – foreign intelligence services, crime syndicates, drug kingpins and all manner of bad people. Tenebris confidentially connects Employers to Employees with a simple right swipe.'

A PowerPoint presentation flicked through example pages of the Tenebris website and finished on their Terms of Business. We were all quiet as we took everything in.

Geraint continued, 'Let's use our friend Black as an example. The international drug cartel he had infiltrated posted an ad on the Tenebris Network saying they wanted to know if there were any ongoing investigations into them. The Employees who replied to the ad would've included details on their position, security level clearance and their fee for finding out. The drug cartel would go through the Employee bids and swipe right on the one they wanted. Click. A match is made. The Employee supplies the info. The Employer gives them cash. All done through Tenebris and completely untraceable. I've spent some time on it and both the app and website appear to be impenetrable. They must have exceptional people on staff.' Geraint bowed his head. Admitting defeat was new for him.

'Black was working on a joint operation with Six. How do we know the Snake isn't a Rat? We're relying on the new protocols to presume we're all clean?' asked Jake. Since Sandy's betrayal, additional security protocols had been actioned. They added extra man-hours to all our admin as everything needed cross-unit approval, but we figured it was worth it if it meant limiting the chances of another unit leader going on a traitorous rampage.

'The drug cartel was matched with King666,' said Hattie. 'That username has, to date, bid on four different jobs – all to do with intel related to Six. All four of those operations ended in failure for Six with dead agents and dead informants. It's why we're convinced that the Snake is a Pigeon.'

In Eight we called those from Five and Six 'Pigeons', as they were dotted all a round London and, in our opinion, would shit over everything. Whenever our paths crossed they seemed to add complications rather than solutions.

Pixie frowned. 'How did you get the information on King666 if the website is so unhackable?'

'A few days ago Tenebris approached a Six agent asking if he wanted to sign up as an Employee. He accepted but brought it to his superior. Tenebris gave him a working login for their website. Six was then able to use it to hack into the hidden doors and download information. It was twenty-four hours until Tenebris discovered the breach and disabled the agent's username. The information Six gained from the hack is how we were able to get to Black in time. It is, however, now back to being completely impenetrable. And Tenebris now know that we're onto them.'

I thought about everything Hattie was saying. 'So it's a head-hunting service for traitors. A recruitment agency for the international criminal underworld.'

Hattie nodded. 'Tenebris is very much the facilitator in this whole operation. We've learned they act as guarantor and bank and take a forty per cent commission fee on every match. Once the deal is agreed they give the Employer and Employee a contact email address to set up a meet on and then bow out. It's a very clever business plan. The Employee doesn't dare rip off the Employer as they know Tenebris has all their personal information: name, home address, family members. If they don't deliver, Tenebris passes it on to the Employer and they're dead. Their family is dead.' Hattie rubbed his beard as he spoke. 'The Employer will always pay as before Tenebris take them on as a client, they are scrupulously vetted and have to hand over their bank details and statements to verify what level of funds they have access to. Tenebris will not put them in touch with the Employee until Tenebris have been paid the full amount. Tenebris then take their commission and pass the rest on to the Employee once the job is completed. Considering the type of information that is being sold on here and the vast database of Employers on there, Tenebris is without a doubt a multi-million-, if not billion-pound company.'

Hattie gripped the back of the chair in front of him. 'And they're going to do whatever it takes to protect it. They know we're looking for them. We need to get to them before they come for us.'

'Eight are all on leave until the lockdown is over – that means no Surveillance? No R & D?' asked Jake.

'And no one manning the canteen so no fry-ups?' Robin looked more upset at that thought than the actual threat of Tenebris.

Hattie's mouth was set in a fine line. 'Correct. We're on our own on this. Until the Snake has been located and eliminated and the Tenebris Network is out of operation, the Committee are taking no risks.

'I've been speaking to our international counterparts. Tenebris operates across the world. All intelligence agencies are affected. Everyone is concerned. With King666 we have the strongest lead and we have confirmed proof Tenebris is a British-owned outfit. America have been able to offer up some assistance. One of their East Coast operatives is in London at present.'

America had its own branch of underground assassins.

On the East Coast they worked out of Track 101 in Grand Central Terminal in New York. They were a much larger operation than us and as such utilising disused tracks and tunnels under the largest train station in the world was a fitting home for them. We had worked alongside them before and 'Trackers', as they called themselves, were frighteningly efficient. We were the small, independent shop compared to their large micro-managed corporation.

'She will be here any minute.'

She?

Great.

There was only one East Coast 'she' Tracker at present.

She hated me.

But then she hated everyone.

Cameron Clarke had followed a similar career path to me. Recruited out of university and assigned straight into Track 101. The last time we had met it was crushing an international sex-trafficking ring. We had gone in undercover together and wreaked carnage on our would-be captors.

Despite spending a month together in some pretty grue-some circumstances, I still couldn't work out if she was over-compensating for being a woman by being extra ruthless and sadistic or if she was just like that naturally. I had started the mission naively hopeful that working alongside another female assassin meant we would become besties and spend downtime bonding over frappuccinos and how tough it was fitting a gun in our waistband when having a fat day.

'Why the hell do you guys work in such a dump?' asked the tall woman with cropped peroxided blonde hair who'd just stepped into the meeting room.

But she just wasn't a very nice person.

Hattie uncurled himself from his plastic chair and got to his feet. 'Everyone, please meet Cameron.'

Cameron was wearing a black polo neck, leather trousers and was vigorously chewing gum. 'Take it in turns to stand and state your name and job,' she barked.

Robin, Geraint and Pixie obliged. Jake and I remained seated.

Jake waved. 'Jake. Rat. Hello.'

'Lex. Rat. We've met.'

Cameron stared at me. 'You're still here then.' She had a nasal New York accent that grated. Or maybe it was just that I disliked her and everything about her grated. Cameron looked around the meeting room. 'I had no idea it was such a shithole down here. Track 101 just had another full renovation. Upgrades with under-floor heating, Sonos speakers in the canteen, the full works.'

'You let builders down there?' One of the many reasons why Platform Eight functioned on the bare essentials was that every-thing that needed doing to it we had to do ourselves. No outside contractors.

'We killed them all,' she deadpanned. 'Just joking.' Not a muscle moved in her face.

I made a mental note to check if there were any reported stories of an American contracting firm losing a vast percentage of their workforce.

Cameron looked at me again and cocked her head. 'You look different.'

'She's a mama now!' called out Robin. 'You must be seeing the glow of motherhood.'

'If by "glow" you mean older, more tired, and more badly dressed, then yes. She's sooo glowing.'

'Thanks, Cameron. You're too kind.' I tried to recall if there was anything in Cameron's background that helped explain her being so awful. Something to give her a little humanity. But from what I remembered she'd had a nice upbringing and loving parents. I remembered her file included a photo of a teenage her on a pony. Maybe that's what it was. She was a testament to how bad it was to spoil your kids.

'What do you reckon?' murmured Jake in my ear. 'We pop her and call it a training accident.'

'Well, Cameron, you've just met all of Whistle. Please take a seat.' Hattie motioned to the chair next to him.

'Why do you Brits have to be so twee?' asked Cameron as she sat down. 'Whistle? How the hell is that inspiring? Why not have names like ours – Independence, Liberty, Patriot – you know, names that mean something.'

Robin cleared his throat. 'All our unit names mean something. "Megatron" is because their unit leader Dave is a big Transformers fan. Then there's "Grinch", which is another obvious one . . . Well, it would be if you met their unit leader, misery-guts Gavin.

"Jagger" is because Dennis has the "moves like Jagger".' Robin paused to chuckle to himself. 'Whereas "Watermelon" is because Joe thought to do this job you needed balls as big as—'

'That's ridiculous. And sexist.' She looked at me as she popped her gum.

'Cameron, I think the only thing offensive about boys wanting to name something after their ball-size is having to work with people with such a lame sense of humour.'

Cameron turned to Hattie. 'So is this really it?' She gestured towards us all. 'This is all the personnel you have working on this?'

'Yes, Cameron, this is our team. And there are two others at Six. You all know Dugdale, I gather? As Department Head he was the one who the Six agent approached with information on Tenebris.'

Harry Dugdale. Duggers. If you had told me back in Oxford that the rugby-playing chin downing yards of ale on the other side of the college bar would end up being one of the only people who knew what my job really entailed, I wouldn't have believed it.

'Dugdale and the agent have been running their own off-the-books investigation but have now come to us to help them finish. They'll be in for a meeting tomorrow. We need to get this resolved fast. The Tenebris Network threatens the very existence of Eight. Of all our Security Services. Tenebris is a terrifyingly efficient way of not only organising but recruiting Snakes. We're going to be severely incapacitated if we start having to put additional security protocols in place to try and protect our intel from our own employees.'

Tenebris's Terms of Business were still up on the whiteboard. From a business perspective it was impressive. Tenebris had seen a gap in the market and gone for it. Those working in the

Security Services who wanted to sell information could hardly offer it up on eBay or post an ad. Tenebris legitimised it. Snakes being able to absent-mindedly flick through an unhackable secure app deciding who to sell what to, at what price, took away the severity of what they were doing. There was no hovering in dark alleyways exchanging USB sticks and briefcases of cash. They didn't have to seek out criminals and dangle the carrot of information in front of them. These Snakes didn't even have to deal with the risk of associating with ruthless employers who could choose to kill them rather than pay them. Tenebris's Inappropriate Behaviour clause meant that if the Employee came to undue harm after the information exchange, Tenebris would be paid their share and the Employer would be struck off for future job postings. The Snakes were protected. Christ, they were one step away from having their own union.

Chapter Two

'WELCOME, EVERYONE.' Yvonne clasped her hands together. 'We are so delighted that you were able to make it here tonight to get a chance to meet each other and see some of the wonderful work your children have been doing.' She gestured behind her to a wall covered in multicoloured paint splodges and an array of colourful card with pieces of pasta glued onto them in haphazard shapes. 'Please do mingle and help yourself to refreshments.'

Next to Yvonne was a small table bearing plastic cups of tepid white wine and some wilted sandwiches.

An evening of attempting to make friends with Gigi's new friends' parents was the last thing I needed after a stressful day at work trying to come up with a plan to take down a business that was getting colleagues killed and threatening the way all our Security Services operated.

Long ago I had determined to avoid any event that required me to wear a name badge. No fun was ever had anywhere you needed to announce your name to anyone casting a glance at your left breast. Yet here I was, 'Alexis Tyler, Gigi's Proud Mummy!' stuck on the lapel of my leather jacket. I looked around the room wishing Will hadn't got stuck at work. I needed an ally.

I walked over to the table and picked up a plastic cup of warm white wine, took a sip and winced. Right. Now to 'mingle'. Why did that sound about as appealing as 'torture'? The other parents seemed already deep in conversation with one another. I recognised one mother from the morning drop-offs; we had yet to break through the weather small-talk barrier.

I walked around the classroom, cup in hand. At the wall at the back there was a display titled 'My Family', so I looked for Gigi's. There we were. Somewhat creepily, mine, Will and Gigi's heads had been cut out of the family photo I had dutifully supplied one morning and stuck on stick figures made out of penne pasta pieces that were all holding hands.

'Jesus, this is terrifying. Why have we all been impaled by angry pasta?' A man in a suit had joined me and was staring at the wall, grimacing.

I smiled. 'Which happy family are you?'

'Here we are.' The man pointed to the one next to Gigi's. His wife was blonde, and with those jutting cheekbones I doubted her body was much more filled out than the pasta stick figure on which her photo was currently stuck. Her pasta body was holding hands with a round baby head of indeterminate sex and a frowning white-blonde-haired girl I recognised from drop-offs.

'Oh right, so you're Florence's dad. Gigi talks about her a lot.' I remembered the anonymous bite victim and made a silent prayer that I wasn't about to be on the receiving end of a lecture on violent pre-schoolers.

'Yes, that's me. Florence's dad. Although my name outside of this Portakabin is Frederick.' He held out a hand. It felt strangely formal considering the setting. I shook it. Was it my imagination or did he hold it just a moment too long?

'Alexis.' I motioned to my name badge. 'But everyone calls me Lex. Nice to meet you.' I nodded my head towards their family portrait. 'She has your eyes.' I really thought it was just something people always said when they didn't know what to say when admiring a baby or child. But in this case Florence really did have Frederick's eyes. Piercing blue with a fleck of green. She didn't share the rest of his features – strong jawline, coiffed dirty-blond hair. And thankfully the delicate little two-year-old did not have his build. He was broad shouldered, and his white shirt seemed to be straining to fit what looked like a very defined torso.

'The photo doesn't really look anything like me but I do look just like that under my clothes.' He motioned towards the penne.

I laughed. 'Now that's something I'd like to see.'

'I . . . Well . . .' He looked surprised, then smirked.

Shit.

'I mean . . . that would be funny, if you really were made of pasta. How could you be? I mean, where would the food go? I'd better check where my husband is. Yes, my husband. Right. Bye.'

Abort. Abort. Mission abandoned.

I headed for the door, nodding a few hellos along the way, downed the wine and dropped my plastic cup in the bin on the way out. What the hell was wrong with me? Could I not make it through a standard social evening without imploding? One encounter with a Hot Dad and I was simpering about wanting to see him naked. I was acting like a highly-sexed desperado. It's not like I was deprived. Or was I? I tried to think of the last time Will and I had sex. It couldn't have been that long ago. There was that time last week. Or was it last month? I had a vague rec-ollection of Will murmuring a post-coital 'I think we've got time

30

for one more' and the relief when I realised he meant another episode of *Game of Thrones*.

I just needed some perspective. Yes, I had embarrassed myself in front of a fellow parent at Gigi's nursery by implying I wanted to see him naked. But chances were I wouldn't see him again.

Apart from potentially every drop-off and pick-up.

And then just at any school event.

I thought back to the detailed school calendar we had been sent. There was an upcoming harvest festival, a Halloween party, fireworks night, nativity play, Easter bonnet parade, spring bake sale, summer concert, sports day.

How did a two-year-old have such a packed social schedule? And why couldn't I at least wait until the end of the school year to make a tit of myself?

Why did parenting never get easier?

Will and I had celebrated when we survived the first year: the constant waking in the night, teething, explosive nappies. And just when I felt like I was finally finding my way, a new set of challenges were catapulted at me: fussy eating, tantrumming, potty-training. Now it seemed biting was part of the repertoire too. And if all that wasn't enough, always in the background was the fear that I was screwing this up. Screwing her up.

Will always did what came naturally to him. Didn't over-think things. She worshipped him; whether it was being chased squealing round the house by the Tickle Monster, to weekday afternoons spent in the park, just the two of them, hunting conkers and holding hands. He'd sneak away early from the office, citing a meeting, and I'd come home to find them out there, kicking leaves and eating ice cream, no matter the weather. I'd ask 'Aren't you worried you'll get in trouble?' and he'd shrug and say, 'Fuck 'em. I missed her.' He adored her and knowing that he was her father, that he therefore knew what was best for her, gave him all the confidence he needed.

But I felt the crushing responsibility of raising a daughter. I found myself poring over parenting articles. Reading the latest studies. Listening attentively when more knowledgeable mothers waxed lyrical about what was expected. I now overthought everything to a terrifying degree. I feared an offhand comment here, a simple observation there, would have the butterfly effect of determining the type of person she was going to become.

It meant any given everyday situation was suddenly a cause for concern.

At playgroup:

'Here you go, sweetheart.' I handed Gigi a doll. *There I was, gender stereotyping again.* 'You can have this too.' I quickly gave her a truck. 'Play with what you want. You can do anything you want.'

'I want doll.'

'OK, that's great. But remember you can have the truck too.'

A visit to my mother:

'Now go and give Granny a kiss.' *There I was, forcing her to be physical with someone against her will.*

A playground altercation:

'He doesn't mean it when he pulls your hair. He's doing it because he likes you.' *Now I was teaching her that it didn't matter if men hurt you as that was how they showed affection.*

A new dress:

'You look so pretty.' *Oh God, I mustn't focus on her looks.* 'I mean, you look so clever.' *I need to show her that intelligence* and personality are more important. But how can I celebrate her brains when she's only two and a half and can only scribble and count to seven? Maybe I big up every little achievement. A big HURRAH for zipping up her coat. But then won't that give her an inflated sense of self-worth? Will I be giving her a big ego and she will expect praise every time she wipes her own bum? Actually, I really would give her praise for that – when does that start?

Doing up her Velcro trainers:

'Let me do that.' *I was teaching her not to be self-reliant.* 'I mean, keep on trying, you're doing a great job.' *She needs to learn how to solve her own problems. That perseverance is eventually rewarded with success. Even if it does take her twenty minutes to fasten up a Velcro strip . . . Even if it takes all day . . . Oh fuck it, we're late.* 'Come on, I've done it, let's go.'

Going to have her hair cut:

'No, darling, we aren't going to keep the fringe – Daddy doesn't like it.' *A man's opinion on your appearance is more important than your own.* 'I mean, Mummy and Daddy don't like it.' *We are in charge and we determine how you will look.* 'I mean, you don't like it.' *I am telling you your own opinion.* 'You know what? Keep the fringe if you like it.' *You're the boss and I have no control over you.*

This nagging internal monologue could take over any interaction.

Even telling her I loved her:

'I love you, Gigi.' She carried on playing with her doll. I nudged her. 'I said I love you.'

'Love you, Mama.' *I was forcing her to declare love. Teaching her that to be loved you have to love. There was no unconditional love.*

It was an absolute minefield. The demands, the worry, the all-encompassing need to keep her safe, the endless pressure to raise her right. To do the best job to give her the best start. The weight of expectation was exhausting. No wonder there were days when Rat felt more natural to me than Mother.

It was less pressure when the only life on the line was yours.

Chapter Three

I PUNCHED THE EASTER BUNNY.

That was why I was back here at Platform Eight.

After everything that had happened a couple of years ago I had questioned returning to Eight. If it was too much to handle. Rat and Mother. People trying to kill me, bosses betraying me; who needed all that shit when I had teething and tantrums and potty-training to deal with?

But then walking back from Sainsbury's with Gigi one afternoon I had taken a shortcut down a quiet street. I'd heard loud footsteps approaching us from behind, and a large hand seemingly reach out to grab Gigi. Pulling her towards me, I'd swung round and punched the incoming threat with two hard jabs to the stomach. As I watched the Easter Bunny go toppling backwards and hit the ground hard, his basket of brightly coloured foil eggs spilling round him, I realised I may have made a mistake.

When apologising to the winded eighteen-year-old underneath the bunny head, I blamed the war on sugar for my spirited response to his attempt to give my daughter a free promotional chocolate egg.

The truth was it felt good.

Not so much the assaulting an unarmed teenager, but the buzz of using my specialist skills. The buzz of being in control, of fighting back. Of remembering the power I had.

Holding Gigi's hand as we watched the bunny stagger away clutching his basket, I had rung the Platform and finally confirmed my return.

It was best for everyone.

I was a coiled spring. Just one gentle nudge and my talents as a Rat would be unleashed.

Who knew how it would next manifest itself?

Would I challenge Gigi's judo teacher to a fight? Break into our neighbours' house to check they really hadn't stolen our missing recycling bin? Hack the nursery's reading reports to verify a smug mother's claims of 'Arabella is only two and already blending sounds together'?

What was the point of specialist training if you couldn't use it?

Platform Eight was where I belonged.

Home needed to be a place I felt happy to retreat to, not desperate to break free from. To keep the good life there, I needed a bad one here. To roar round my underground world, wreaking terror, stopping terror, calling the shots, firing the shots.

Fly high here and lay low at home.

I entered the meeting room and joined the rest of my unit awaiting Dugdale and the Six agent. I glanced around. This was the first time Platform Eight itself was under threat.

And we were the ones tasked with and trusted to save us all.

It was good to remember that when my instructions to behave were being ignored by a two-year-old pelting me with breadsticks.

Robin leaned over to Jake and me. 'So when it all ends happily with us saving the Security Services, will you two finally sign off on me getting my own unit?'

Jake and I looked at each other. 'We need to talk about it,' said Jake.

Hattie had been running Whistle for over a year now but had stated he would defer to mine and Jake's judgement about whether Robin was ready. Jake had reservations but I knew we needed to let Robin go. We had to remember that, just like us, he'd been through the Farm. Spent months being tested, prodded, pushed to the limit to wean out who was worthy of being a Rat. Eight's elite training facility was situated in a remote part of West Scotland. 'The Farm' nickname was down to our on-site sleeping quarters in neat rows being tiny cage-like rooms, that lined the enormous warehouse and made us feel like battery hens. Graduating from the Farm into a trainee Rat position was always meant to be a short-term placement, and I knew the best end to his education would be not to have us to rely on.

Harry Dugdale strode into the room. He had been promoted since we worked together last. A feat I'm sure would've put a spring in his step if he wasn't now having to battle the biggest threat the Security Services had ever faced.

Somehow, I wasn't surprised by the fact I recognised the agent he was with. Somehow, I got up as he approached the table and calmly put out my hand.

He shook it.

And held it just a moment too long.

'Hello, Lex.'

'Hello, Frederick.'

We stood there staring at each other.

Hot Dad.

Just brilliant.

Hattie looked over at us and frowned.

'You two know each other? Your records don't mention your paths ever crossing before.'

'They haven't at work.' I tilted my head.

Dugdale cleared his throat. 'We have a little confession to make. When I discovered Frederick lived not that far from Lex, I saw an opportunity. We need a safe exchange point. Frederick is likely to be under surveillance from Tenebris. So I encouraged him to switch his daughter to the same nursery as yours, Lex.'

Frederick looked at me. 'Sorry. I was about to introduce myself properly to you last night but you . . .' he smiled, 'well, you made a very fast exit.'

Dugdale looked between us. 'Due to Tenebris's sophisticated online capabilities we cannot risk any online correspondence. Everything has to be done in person, or at a push by coded text message. Due to this nursery link you can have legitimate daily meetings on the school run.'

It was a clever move from Duggers. And at least with it just being information exchanges there should be no undue risk to Gigi or Florence. Frederick and I could be seen together without it leading to a flurry of suspicions from whoever had him under surveillance. Thankfully I'd had nearly two and a half years now to practise my 'harmless mum' cover story.

'You were lucky to get a place at Yvonne's. It's meant to be the best nursery school in the area.'

Frederick frowned. 'Actually, the place I had her down for, Little Lambs, is the best.'

'Really? You didn't think behind the perky schoolma'am façade Miss Sophie was one art attack away from a full-blown mental breakdown?'

Frederick shook his head. 'Her medical records flagged nothing troubling.'

'That's because she's held it together so far – but no one that enthusiastic about the alphabet is on the right side of normal.' I remembered her manic grin as she enunciated each letter with unbridled joy. 'What did you think of the other schools?'

'Well, I ruled out the Forest School because if I wanted her to be outside all day playing with mud I'd just stick her in the garden.'

'What about Miss Mary's?' I asked.

'Miss Mary was a bitch—'

'Who didn't believe in playtime,' I finished for him.

'Bright Bambinos?' he asked.

'One of the teachers didn't pass the security checks.'

'Are you talking about the one with the drug-dealing boyfriend?'

'No, the one using a fake name with an arrest warrant outstanding for fraud. What about Snowdrops?'

Frederick laughed. 'Don't be ridiculous. Ofsted rated it Poor. Pretty sure they use the kids to garden to save on bills. It's a kiddie sweatshop.'

'So why did you choose Yvonne's Young Ones then?'

'It's Montessori.' He shrugged. 'I still don't understand what that means.'

'Yeah . . . well, me neither. But it's meant to be good.'

'It'd better be for the amount I'm paying for Florence to finger-paint.'

'I'm so glad we've all learned so much about West London nurseries, but can we finally get back to the bloody mission?' drawled Jake.

'Amen to that,' said Cameron. There was another crack as she popped her gum. Hattie winced a little. It was comforting to know even the unflappable Hattie found her grating.

Hattie nodded at Dugdale and Frederick as they sat down. 'Take us through everything.'

Frederick started. 'After four different operations blew apart and agents and informants were killed, my boss Thatcher knew there had to be a Snake within Six. We'd all heard rumours of some sort of dark web recruitment site and he was sure this was what the Snake was linked to. Thatcher came to me with his concerns and we devised a plan to draw them out. We emptied my bank account, killed my credit rating, drafted letters from the bank saying they were going to foreclose on our house. I started asking around Six if anyone knew of any private work going, implied I was going to make a break for it. Within two months I was contacted by Tenebris.' He shook his head. 'It was far worse than we could possibly have imagined.'

'How did they make contact?' asked Geraint.

'They took control of my laptop. Opened a new email and started writing. Said they knew I was in financial trouble and they had a way out. Gave me a weblink and a login and password. There was an introduction video that explained the Tenebris Network and how it worked, and then I was invited to create a profile, listing what security clearances I had as well as what other access. I was assured only potential Employers would see it.'

'Were you able to see the other Employees?' That was the key data we needed.

'I couldn't navigate the site in full. Under my login I was only ever able to flick through the Employers who'd posted ads. Thatcher and I approached a top-level hacker off the books and with his help we were able to get into a few of the Employee profiles – that's how we found out about King666 and got to see his bidding history. Clearly, though, we didn't take enough precautions. Within twenty-four hours my login was frozen, the hacker was missing and Thatcher was dead.'

'I'm sorry about Thatcher,' said Hattie softly. 'He was one of the good ones.'

'What happened?' asked Jake.

'Shot in the head on his way home from work.' Frederick's jaw clenched. 'The day before he died I was sent abroad on an assignment. Last contact I had from him was a text before I left saying he was testing a theory and would be in touch once he had something concrete.'

I was betting Frederick was former military. His boss had just been murdered, he was on the radar of a ruthless corporation and he was holding it together with not a hair out of place. He had to have some kind of combat experience to be able to process everything that had happened in the last few days and remain professionally detached enough to continue.

Dugdale nodded his head at Frederick. 'The two of us have attended far too many funerals these last few months. I don't want to have to hold hands with another crying widow and tell her how sorry I am and what a good man her husband was. I want my black tie to go back to languishing at the back of my wardrobe. We need to shut these bastards down.'

'Are there any leads on Thatcher's shooter? An ID could lead us to Tenebris.' We needed some kind of real-world lead on how to get to a group of people who seemed to operate only remotely.

'No leads. No CCTV. Nothing,' said Duggers. 'Considering it's a multi-million-pound business, they can afford a professional hit squad. Probably even their own army of Ghosts.'

It made sense they would have muscle-for-hire under their employ who didn't officially exist. Ghosts had no higher purpose other than to hurt, maim and kill for money. They didn't care who or why. They just cared about getting paid. They were people who didn't officially exist. They lived off the grid, making sure they had no verifiable identity. They did what they were told and then they'd disappear, and they were never told anything more than what to do and who to do it to. They never knew who they were working for. They were low-level, low-skilled and totally expendable help.

'Are you not worried they'll come for you?' I had some concerns about doing the school run with someone who had an army of heavily armed Ghosts after him.

Frederick shook his head. 'Whatever got Thatcher killed was what he found out when I was away. Tenebris must know that he never managed to get the info to me or they would've put a hit out on me too. They clearly didn't want to kill me as a precaution as the death of two agents from the same division within a week would raise more attention than they could handle.'

'And you have no idea what Thatcher had found?'

'None. His computer was wiped clean. His mobile is missing. There are no clues as to what he discovered. I approached Dugdale as he was the only other person within Six I knew I could completely trust with this.'

'And we have a further problem,' said Duggers. 'Tomorrow afternoon China's Minister of Commerce, Siew-Yong Peng, and a high-level Chinese delegation will be arriving into London. Peng is the President's closest ally. She's also the highest-ranking woman to ever hold office in China.'

I remembered reading about Peng. She had started out as a junior clerk in the People's Congress and worked her way up, shouting down her more vocal critics and being the subject of scathing editorials every step of the way. Peng was undoubtedly impressive and a hopeful step forward for a country that had previously seemed to regard women as second-class citizens incapable of high office.

'She's over here representing the President and warming up UK-China relations with a potential new trade deal. From the twenty-four hours of access we had to the Tenebris Network, we learned that an Employer, most likely the powerful right-wing fringe group, the Chinese People's Alliance, was advertising for information on Peng's UK itinerary. It's clear to us from the intel we have that they're planning to have Peng assassinated during her stay here.'

'Because it's easier to get to her abroad than on home turf when she has full security,' I surmised.

Duggers nodded. 'Exactly. As soon as the Employer posted this request for information on Peng they were immediately matched with King666. He's still active and a major threat. If Peng dies here, on our watch, due to a security leak from one of our people, we're facing a major diplomatic disaster that would start by destroying the tentative exchange deal we have in place.'

China was currently arranging for the transfer back to the UK of the forty-six British Security Services operatives they had never officially acknowledged having, just as we had never officially acknowledged sending them. In exchange, we were opening up several lucrative trade contracts to China. Looking complicit in the death of one of their most high-level ministers would place us on China's shit list for the foreseeable future and the forty-six would either be left not officially existing in a high-security, impossible-to-find Chinese prison, or would be executed.

Dugdale looked round at us all. 'We have to face the possibility that there could be more than one Snake within the Security Services right now. We won't know for sure until we tear Tenebris apart. Right now the only Snake we need to focus on finding is King666. He's the only one that is a current active threat.'

Hattie cut in. 'This Snake will be selling information on all our security protocols and the best opportunities for Peng's assassination. To do this they must have up-to-date intel on the delegation's movements, maybe even have a source inside the delegation. Peng will be having numerous meetings that aren't on her official schedule as she tries to broker other deals off the books. Our intel suggests the Chinese People's Alliance have hired a Coyote. A lone gun. The Snake will be in direct contact with the Coyote – giving them the intel they need to make the hit.'

Geraint looked up. 'Tenebris know the authorities are circling so they've no doubt specified an IRL directive for any information transfer.'

'In Real Life,' Pixie said in response to Hattie's frown.

'Right. Exactly,' said Hattie. 'If they're having to communicate in person, if we find the Snake they'll lead us to the Coyote.'

'Dugdale and I have narrowed down the Snake's identity to three analysts at Six.' Frederick handed a USB stick to Geraint.

'The Snake will be hoarding hidden cash – we estimate they would've earned a tidy five to eight million for the information they've sold so far. These analysts all had access to the intel that tanked the last few missions and they all have links to China from previous postings, meaning there's a chance they could have someone inside the delegation.'

'Why don't we just kill them all? Wouldn't that be the safest way?' asked Cameron.

All heads round the table swivelled to her.

'Cameron,' I sighed, 'these people are our colleagues. Two out of three of them are completely innocent.'

She rolled her eyes. 'We're talking about the greater good. Your Security Services being compromised. *All* our Security Services being compromised. If this was happening back home they'd all be dead by now. And we'd be on to the next mission.'

'We aren't as trigger-happy as you Americans. We also prioritise getting information out of them first.'

Hattie stared at Cameron. 'The Committee has authorised that when it comes to our own people only the Snake gets popped, and that's only once we have confirmed proof of their guilt, and after we've interrogated them for all usable intel on Tenebris. If you're "assisting" us, Cameron, you'd better abide by our rules.'

Cameron gave Hattie a small salute. She took out her gum and stuck it under the table. 'What?' she said to Hattie's grimace. But she unpeeled the gum and dropped it in an abandoned mug of coffee on the table.

Geraint plugged in the USB stick, clicked a few buttons and up on the whiteboard flashed a photo of a portly man in his fifties with greying hair and round glasses.

Frederick motioned towards the photo. 'This is Ronald Bowcott. He's been at Six for the last fifteen years. Generally considered a steady pair of hands. No major grievances in his record, no commendations either. Next is Suzannah Sheldon.'

Her photo flashed up next to Ronald's. It was a surveillance photo from outside a house. She was wearing a trouser suit and speaking into her mobile. Blonde hair pulled back into a high ponytail.

'Suzannah has been working alongside Ronald for the last five years – since she joined Six. Generally considered a bit of a know-it-all. Can rub colleagues up the wrong way.

'Finally we have Neil Hicks.' A photo of a well-built man in full military uniform joined Ronald and Suzannah on the whiteboard. 'Hicks was in the army for twelve years before making the move to Six two years ago. He's a quiet man, keeps to himself, but has been impressing superiors with his natural aptitude for the job.'

Hattie motioned towards the line-up of photos. 'Code names. Lex, can you do the honours?'

I stared at the photos.

Ronald Bowcott. Man with a tummy and glasses. Looked a bit of a buffoon. It seemed strikingly obvious to me.

'OK, Ronald is Daddy Pig.'

Suzannah Sheldon. A know-it-all and a bit annoying. 'Suzannah can be Peppa Pig.'

Neil Hicks. Quiet man. 'Well, as we're on a theme now, Neil is George Pig.'

'How exactly is naming the targets after a family of pigs not going to draw attention to yourselves?' Jake asked

I ignored him and turned to Frederick.

'What do you think of Daddy Pig?'

'He gets a hard time. He's just trying to do what's best for his family and he's mocked and maligned for his weight, for his lack of DIY ability. I think it's impressive he remains so upbeat when he's got a tiresome daughter, a near mute son and a wife who likes to flaunt her superiority over him. It's just not—'

'Peppa Pig is an incredibly popular children's cartoon,' I cut Frederick off mid-flow. 'Every parent has been forced to watch at least one episode, if not five hundred. No one with kids would think anything of hearing their names mentioned.'

'She's right.' Dugdale nodded, himself a father of two.

Hattie motioned to the board. 'Daddy Pig, Peppa and George. One of these three little piggies has been getting our people killed. We need to know everything about them.' He looked round at us all. 'We're looking for large amounts of extra unaccounted for income and covert meetings or communications with the Coyote. We need to run through their lives and analyse every online and in-person interaction. We find out which one is the Snake and we stop the Coyote.

'Peng arrives into London tomorrow and she's here for six days. This is our one chance to end the Tenebris Network. Once Peng is assassinated or leaves the country, the trail for both the Snake and the Coyote will go cold. With no active mission they both disappear back into hibernation. Right now, they're the only lead we have to Tenebris. And we need that website offline. By any means necessary.'

I sensed the Committee had authorised multiple bloodshed. This was a website that had the power to completely shut down Platform Eight and severely incapacitate Five and Six. And that was before you added into the mix a dead high-level Chinese minister on our turf.

'I've actioned a Six initiative that was still in the development stage,' said Dugdale. 'Lex, you will be the primary contact on the "We are Family" programme.'

I frowned. 'The what?'

'"We are Family" is designed to make the families of everyone at Six feel that they are all in this together. One big happy community. A series of meet-ups where they all get to bond over how tough it is having a partner who can't talk to them about their work. A safe space where everyone understands the downsides as they are living it too.'

'So that's the fluffy HR version – what's the truth?'

'That you will be using it as cover to get to grips with the three Pigs' home life. If there's extra money coming from somewhere then their other halves are going to know. The Snake has been very good at covering their tracks at work, but with any luck they will be less careful at home. Frederick will continue to monitor them in the office. The two of you can use the nursery pick-ups to swap intel.'

Hattie leaned forward as he looked at Frederick and Dugdale. 'Joint missions with Pigeons never tend to work out well. I will not have egos and tantrums about who's in charge. Let me state it once and once only: this is now Eight's mission. You've brought it to us and we now take over. You abide by our rules. Our protocols. Frederick, I've seen your record. It's impressive. But if you're going to work with us you need to understand Lex is in charge. You report to her. You follow her orders. Is that clear?'

'Completely.' Frederick shrugged. 'We're in your hands.' Frederick turned to me. 'I have an informant inside the Chinese Embassy. Codename "Y". I've been using him for the last two years. He's a mid-level Embassy employee. I trust him. It's best you take over as his handler. I can't risk being seen with him. I'll set up a meet for after the nursery's Natural History Museum trip.'

I remembered something in the diary about Gigi's class going to a puppet show at the museum this afternoon. I had felt bad about missing her first trip to see the dinosaurs.

'You mean . . . We need to go?'

'Very much so. I set the whole visit up.'

Duggers checked his watch. 'You'd better leave now, Lex. The "We are Family" introductory meet and greet starts at ten a.m. at the Warehouse. You will be the Family Liaison for a group that will contain the three Pigs' other halves. I'll email you the info.'

I stood up.

Geraint pointed to my mobile phone. 'Click on the latest email from me and your phone will download a WhatsApp group chat invite with a worm hidden inside. You just need to put in the targets' numbers, get them to accept the invite and the worm will get to work. It will take twenty minutes or so to download everything off their phones and all future messages will automatically download to our server.'

'Remember, Lex,' said Hattie, 'the quicker we find the Snake, the better the chance we have of Peng flying out of here in the comfort of her first-class cabin bed and not in a box in the hold.'

From what Frederick had said it was clear Tenebris were actively recruiting from our Security Services. Stalking potential targets, getting to know their weaknesses, understanding who they could bully or tempt into turning over sensitive information. Frederick can't have been the first they approached – he was just the first who was working to bring them down. How many Snakes could be within the services right now, turning our own people against us and attacking us from within?

Tenebris were a formidable enemy. By incapacitating our Security Services they were putting the whole country at risk. We were vulnerable to not just terrorist attacks but information hacking, data mining and interference in our elections, our very government. Outside hostile forces could swoop down on our country, knowing we were running on a shell, that our Security Services were compromised, and they could wreak havoc not just with our safety but our everyday life. Tenebris had to be stopped. With so much at stake we couldn't afford to fail.

Part Two

Play

play, *n.*
1. Activity engaged in for enjoyment and recreation, especially by children.
2. The state of being active, operative, or effective.

Chapter Four

THE WAREHOUSE WAS A LARGE three-storey space in Vauxhall, situated close to the train lines. It used to be a sweet factory and was now officially a 'storage facility' for the Security Services. Unofficially it was an off-the-radar location for informants we wanted to hide, hostiles we wanted to interrogate or training events we wanted to hold. On the ground floor what used to be the factory floor was now just a vast empty room. It had hosted mental health initiatives like: 'Fire then feel fine: How to cope with killing for your country' and 'Who are you? How to remember you when playing them', as well as workshops such as: 'Creative control: Killing using everyday objects'.

Access to the Warehouse was usually in through one of the several back doors under the cover of darkness. As this was the first time non-Security Services personnel would be attending, an effort had been made to tidy up the front entrance. There were two drooping pot plants either side of the front door, where a suited Six employee I didn't recognise ticked me off a list and handed me my 'Alexis Tyler, Liaison Officer' badge. I looked up at the sign announcing 'We are Family!'– with the arrow pointing towards the factory floor, or the 'conference room' as we were now calling it.

I opened the conference room's double doors and took in the room packed with Sheep. A hundred or so innocent members of the public, mostly women. Apart from the three Pigs, Duggers had chosen certain other Six analysts and their partners to take part in the 'We are Family' initiative. He had clearly pulled out all the stops to get everything up and running, with enlarged posters of stock photos of happy families and a banqueting table set up with biscuits and tea and coffee cups laid out. A nice, no-frills conference where, according to the Liaison Officer 'We are Family' crib sheet, we should lead discussions with points such as: 'They don't tell you everything but they are giving you everything' and 'Their mouths may be sealed but their hearts are open'.

I looked around the room and spotted a few familiar faces from Six. Junior analysts that had been drafted in to act as Liaison Officers. I clocked my name on the table plan and my assigned table number. Eight. Good to see Duggers still had a semblance of a sense of humour.

'Hello, everyone, and welcome!' came a loud, booming voice over the PA system. I glanced over my shoulder to see an elderly woman at the front of the large room holding a hand-held microphone.

'I am Mrs Moulage,' the woman announced.

I swivelled round to look at her.

Mrs Moulage was an Eight legend and, as the first female Rat to ever walk the hallowed halls of Platform Eight, a hero I had always wanted to meet.

'I'm delighted to welcome you to this' – she peered at her clipboard – '"We are Family" initiative. This is the first time we've opened up our charming training location to non-Security Service personnel. Welcome to our world.'

As Mrs Moulage launched into a description of the initiative I watched her talk. None of the people listening as she trotted out buzz words like 'caring communication', 'social cohesion' and 'circle of trust' would have any idea as to just how impressive this woman was. The only nod to the fact she wasn't exactly your normal pensioner was her outfit. An emerald green silk trouser suit. Beautifully cut. And undoubtedly Christian Dior.

The Dior Dame.

Deadly, driven and always dressed in Dior. She may have been given this nickname by a scathing Cold War-era pack of Russians but she loved it. She took to scrawling DD in red lipstick across the foreheads of kills she wanted to lay claim to.

Mrs Moulage was not her real name. Rumour had it she grew up in Birmingham – there was talk of abusive foster families, a difficult time on the streets and a trail of dead men who all had it coming, but no one really knew. Somewhere along the way she came to Eight's attention and became Mrs Moulage, an elegant, well-dressed assassin who spoke with no discernible accent and had no discernible problem with even the most violent of undertakings. No one ever knew if there was, or ever had been, a Mr Moulage – or whether the name just fitted the persona she adopted.

Supposedly semi-retired, she now ran a crematorium in South London called Requiem. As well as being a legitimate business, which apparently ran a tidy profit, Requiem was also where all the bodies Eight needed disposing of would end up. There was also talk that even now Mrs Moulage was sometimes activated for certain missions. I wasn't surprised. Finding her next to a dead body, no one would even think to suspect the delicate, grey-haired old lady of being anything other than a traumatised witness.

The Dior Dame was someone everyone had an opinion on. Vicious, violent, uncontrollable, dangerous.

I thought she was fucking fabulous.

We were instructed to go to our designated tables. I wondered if Mrs Moulage knew who I was. The Rat among the Sheep. Was there something about me that shone? That would make it clear that we shared a secret? That I was just like her?

I was the first to Table Eight. I took a seat and waited for my assigned charges to arrive. I had scanned over Dugdale's email on the WAF initiative on the way. All our mobiles and laptops were set up so that Platform Eight encrypted emails looked like junk mail. What looked like a HORNY_AS_F$*K!!! announcement from a busty underwear-clad teenager could actually be decrypted by entering our unique authorisation code. We had five minutes to read it before it reverted to an image of someone promising all manner of things in exchange for a credit card number.

Three potential Snakes. Three partners I needed to get to know in order to find out exactly who was hiding what. Gossiping that was really intelligence-gathering.

I looked up as three women approached me, all holding cups of tea.

The first to reach me was wearing a purple shirt, black trousers and a warm, open smile. She had a round face and long, curly hair.

'Hiya! I'm Naomi Bowcott. We all actually found each other at the table plan.' Naomi motioned to the two women beside her. 'This is Kate Hicks and Dionne Patterson.'

Kate had her long, brown hair down, long limbs encased in a black jumpsuit. Dionne was a blonder, younger, scruffier version, her hair up in a messy half-bun and wearing paint-stained dungarees.

'Lovely to meet you all,' I said as they all sat down at the table. 'I'm Alexis. I work for the Government Communication and Data Specialisation Branch.' I smiled at the three women in front of me. I was confident my job sounded dull enough they wouldn't ask any questions.

'I'm here as your "We are Family" liaison to help guide you through the process. Now, it'd be great if we could start by you saying a little about yourselves?'

Naomi cleared her throat. 'Well, I've been married to Ronald for nearly twenty years now. Two girls aged eight and thirteen . . . yes, teens are as terrible as everyone tells you!' She gave a little laugh and quickly took a sip of her tea. I knew from their file that Naomi had met Daddy Pig when they worked together at an insurance company, and he had left to join Six a few years after they got married.

'Right, so I'm Dionne,' said the blonde, denim-dungareed woman next to her. She had an Australian – or was it New Zealand? – accent. She looked to be in her mid-twenties. I glanced down at my notes, trying to place her. 'I work as a nanny for Suze Sheldon. Suze is a single mother, so yep, I guess I'm her significant other.' She grinned round at us all. 'Suze has a two-year-old called Bella. She's at nursery right now so thought I might as well come and meet the gang.' She reached for a biscuit. Peppa's right-hand woman.

'Great. Nice to meet you, Dionne.' I kept my fingers crossed that Dionne was going to be one of those nannies that loved gossiping about their boss.

The brunette in the jumpsuit next to her flicked her hair. 'I'm Kate. I'm an actress. But you probably already know that.' She swished back her long hair and graced us with a dazzling smile.

Her dimples gave her a girlish sweetness that made me think she'd never age. George Pig and Kate had been childhood sweet-hearts who'd grown up on the same street. She liked to giggle 'I'm the girl next door who married the boy next door' in all her interviews.

'Yeah, I thought I recognised you,' said Dionne, staring up at her. '*EastEnders*?'

'No.' Kate winced.

'Are you sure? You're not messing with us?'

Kate gave her a withering look and continued, 'My husband Neil has been with MI6 for two years now. Before that he was in the army. I may play at saving the world but he really does.' She held a hand to her chest.

The military hero husband was clearly a line she liked to spin in press junkets.

I had scanned Duggers' summary of Kate's acting career on the way over. A couple of leading roles in ITV dramas, one sup-porting role in a Hollywood movie, where she'd fought some kind of alien in a tank top and hot pants. She'd made big money from some lucrative advertising contracts.

Kate continued, 'We've got three boys. Twins who are nearly two and a seven-year-old.'

A tall, blonde woman approached our table.

'So sorry I'm late. I'm Camilla.'

'Welcome, Camilla.' I smiled.

She sat down next to Dionne, her several silver charm brace-lets jangling. She was wearing high-waisted tweed trousers with a white shirt. She looked familiar. Where had I seen her before? Why was she here? All the three Pigs' other halves were here. I looked down at my notes, trying to place who she was. Naomi,

Kate and Dionne introduced themselves to her. Camilla nodded at each of them with a faint smile. Her long, dainty fingers kept tapping against her knees as if playing an imaginary keyboard. I remembered what Dugdale's email had said about having to make it groups of four. Camilla was a nobody. A buffer.

'My husband Frederick Easton has been at MI6 for six years,' she announced softly.

Well, not quite a nobody.

Frederick's wife.

Of course.

The blonde head stuck on a pasta body.

It made sense that if Dugdale had to allocate groups of four he would put in Frederick's wife. If things went wrong, if more cover was needed, we had another ally in the group. Or at least someone easily manipulated

I looked up at her again. She was beautiful. Of course she was. And so well put together. She was a perfect match to Frederick's chiselled features and immaculately tailored suits. I bet their wedding photo looked like it came with the frame. I fingered the frayed hem of my shirt.

'Alexis?' said Naomi.

'I . . . yes?' I noticed everyone was staring at me. 'Sorry, I missed that.'

'I was just asking how come we meet so often this week and then nothing?'

'Oh right. We're calling this the Initiation Stage. For the programme to work we really need to spend a lot of intense time together in this first week. I will be here guiding the sessions and once the week is over it will all be up to you to arrange the meet-ups and keep in touch.' I smiled round at everyone. 'Now, if you could just whip out your phones and accept the Whats App invite I sent you all it will make planning things so much easier.' I took out my mobile and they all followed suit. I clicked onto WhatsApp and watched as each one of them joined the group. 'Wonderful. Here we all are. Linked together.' I checked the settings and noted each of their numbers now had a download icon next to it. The worm was doing its work.

Ten minutes of getting-to-know-you chat and I was already flagging. I nodded as I tried to pay attention as Naomi droned on about the difficulty she was having with school choices.

And then I heard it.

The alarm.

It was faint. It was coming from the corridor outside. Whoever had done up this room had the foresight to silence it in here. But they hadn't disabled the light that was hidden behind one of the family posters. A grinning mum's white shirt was flashing red.

There was an intruder.

It had to be Tenebris. What were they after?

I looked round the busy room. Or who were they after?

Mrs Moulage had clearly heard it too. She had already stood up and was heading towards the double-doored exit.

I got up. 'Please excuse me a moment. I just need to check on something with a colleague. Do carry on.'

Walking towards the exit I slipped my earpiece in. Jake crackled in on Eight's secure channel. *'We're on our way. We got the alarm notification. There in seven.'*

'Copy that. I'm checking it out now.'

Mrs Moulage had already gone out through the doors. I caught up with her in the long corridor.

'Mrs Moulage?'

She stopped and turned around, smile in place.

'Oh, hello there, dear. If you're wondering about the noise, it's nothing to worry about. They're just testing the alarm system.'

'I'm Lex. I'm the Rat.'

The fake smile dropped.

'The unauthorised entry is at Door Three. How far away is back-up?'

'Seven minutes.'

'Do we know what they're after?'

'No idea. No one here is considered a target.'

Mrs Moulage opened the green silk clutch she was carrying and pulled out a pistol. She tucked it into the waistband of her trousers. The peplum top neatly covered the bulk of the gun. Fashion and function.

Jake crackled into my earpiece, '*G confirms that four minutes ago two hostiles entered through Door Three.*' The Warehouse only had cameras outside the front and back entrances. There were none inside as we never wanted anything here recorded.

I turned to Mrs Moulage. 'Two hostiles in the building.'

I opened my tote bag. R & D had inserted a false bottom into it that could only be opened with my thumbprint. Toddlers could get everywhere and empty everything. I pulled out my gun and secured it into the customised hole. The barrel now peeped out of what looked like a buckle on the side. Innocent-looking to a stray WAF delegate, deadly to an invading Ghost.

'This is meant to be a secure location.' Mrs Moulage glowered at the security violation.

'The Snake must have sent them straight to us.'

I tried to think of the last time I'd fought alongside an armed pensioner.

I was drawing a blank.

'We need to make sure no one gets inside this room.' It was down to us to protect the lives of the Sheep inside. The 'We are Family' initiative was meant to help us identify the Snake; we never considered that we could be putting innocent lives at risk. Whatever these women knew, it was clearly enough to rattle the Snake.

Mrs Moulage looked over my shoulder and her hands flew to her mouth. 'Please don't hurt us!'

I turned to see a short bald-headed man in a dark jacket walking towards us, gun raised.

'Oh my God, what do you want?' I put a quiver in my voice I was particularly proud of.

'Keep quiet and I don't hurt you.'

Mrs Moulage started going through the motions of hyperventilating. I rubbed her back and looked up at the Ghost with the gun. 'Just please, please don't point that thing at my mother. She has a heart condition.'

Mrs Moulage now started to make strange high-pitched sounds as she continued with the heavy, exaggerated breathing noises.

'Just hold on, it's going to be fine.' I kept my left arm round her, my right hand clasped firmly at the gun inside my handbag. Ideally we needed to disarm him without firing a shot. Gunfire would cause panic among the hundred people on the other side of the double doors.

'Fuck's sake.' The Ghost spoke into his earpiece. 'I've got two women here. One of them's about ninety. She looks like she's about to cark it.'

He turned his head slightly as he listened to what his colleague was saying. That was all we needed. The briefest of seconds to transform from terrified women to women in charge.

He looked back to see two guns raised at him.

'What the—'

'Drop it.' I motioned towards his gun.

'Now, fuckwit,' said Mrs Moulage. She took a step towards him.

He did as instructed and his gun clattered to the floor.

'We've got one,' I announced to Jake.

'We're pulling up outside now.'

'What's your mission?' asked Mrs Moulage. 'What are you here to do?'

The Ghost kept his mouth closed in a firm line.

Mrs Moulage cocked the safety off her gun and raised it to his face. 'You do realise I'm looking for any reason at all to justify shooting dead the man who dared to call me ninety.'

The Ghost muttered a series of expletives. 'I'll tell you. But not here. Let's get outside this building and I'll sing like a bird.'

'Sing here and sing now,' Mrs Moulage told him, pressing her gun firmly into his forehead.

'Listen lady, get the hint – we need to get outside.' He was pleading now. 'We were given a black box and our orders were to install it in the first-floor office with the glass window overlooking the big room. My associate is doing it now.'

That did not sound good.

He was describing the factory manager's office. An incendiary device placed in there would cause maximum damage to the factory floor below. The Snake surely can't have been so threatened by today's gathering that the solution was to blow the whole place up?

'I was just meant to make sure no one went upstairs.' The Ghost glanced back over his shoulder. 'He's probably about to finish, so come on, we have to get out of here.' He was fidgeting now. Sweat was beginning to drip down his bald head. A glistening cue ball.

'Why the rush? It's not like you two idiots are going to activate the device while you're still here?' asked Mrs Moulage.

The Ghost shook his head. 'We were told not to touch it. To install it and get out. They said someone inside the big room was going to activate it. So please. Let's just go, OK?'

'Entering the Warehouse now.'

I took a step back from Mrs Moulage and the Ghost to talk to Jake. 'Go straight to the manager's office. A Ghost is installing an unidentified electrical device in there. We have the second Ghost.'

'Copy that.'

Mrs Moulage looked across at me. 'I'll take him outside. You'd better get back in there.'

She was right. Until the device was found I needed to be in there keeping watch in case whoever they had inside the room triggered it. Rigging the Warehouse to blow up a room full of MI6 operatives' husbands and wives seemed a little extreme. What were they trying to achieve?

The Ghosts were irrelevant, they'd never lead us to anyone, but whoever was inside that room, and about to activate a questionable device, was on the inside. And we needed to unmask them. They couldn't know that we'd intercepted the Ghosts, that Jake and Robin would be working fast to deactivate the device. We needed them to think everything was still in place so that when they tried to trigger it we would know who they were.

I needed to return to that room, keep cover, drink tea, continue to talk about what school options there were for intellectually advanced but socially immature eight-year-olds. And ignore the fact the room could blow up.

I took several deep breaths as I opened the double doors to the conference room. I took in the people still happily talking and pouring tea and munching biscuits. No one stood out. No one had the look of someone itching to activate a countdown switch.

I arrived back at my table. 'Sorry about that, everyone. Mrs Moulage just needed a little help with something.' I sat down and dropped my handbag on the floor between my feet. 'What have you been discussing?'

'Husbands hiding things from us,' said Camilla as she put her teacup down. It was hard to read her face but considering what Frederick had been through in the last week she was clearly going to have noticed something serious was happening.

'That sounds an understandable problem.'

'*In pursuit of the Ghost,*' an out-of-breath Jake crackled into my earpiece. I kept my face impassive as I took a sip of luke-warm tea.

'I think they all take advantage of it.' Naomi looked round at everyone. 'I mean, using work as a cover for when they just can't be bothered to actually get home in time to do some parenting?'

'*Argh . . . For fuck's sake . . . You little . . .*'

I tried not to wince at the sound of what sounded like a head hitting a wall.

Naomi sighed. 'I want to believe him when he says he has to be away for certain dates. But how come it seems the Security Services can't do without him every time a school social is planned? Or when my mother is staying with us?'

'*Robin! Get to the device!*'

'It sounds like you've been getting right to the heart of exactly what the "We are Family" initiative is all about.'

'I'm at the device now.' Robin spoke fast. *'It's a black square box about thirty centimetres wide and plugged into the phone socket below the large window. There are five small lights on the top right corner, all green. Three switches on the side. I have no idea what the hell it is.'*

'It's so good to be able to share how tough it can be being married to people who hold back such a big part of their lives,' said Naomi. 'How sometimes it's too much and you just think—'

'Should we evacuate?'

'We won't make it,' I said. If I started an evacuation, whoever the Snake had inside this room could still activate the device as everyone was leaving.

'That's it exactly.' Naomi touched my hand across the table. 'Sometimes I feel like that. But—'

'We must carry on,' I cut her off.

Naomi nodded. 'Yes, exactly, we carry on despite everything. Despite the never knowing exactly what they're doing or where they are.'

'And what really helps is talking to someone else,' I said slowly. 'Someone who knows a lot about these issues.'

'Copy that, Lex. I'll video chat G.'

Kate nodded. 'I wish my husband understood that, although he's on some top-secret mission, he can still share things with me.'

'The Ghost is secure.' Now it was Jake's turn.

'What's he saying?'

Kate sighed. 'Not much. Normally he comes home late and, if I'm still awake, he just wants, well . . .' she giggled, 'you know.'

'Not much. He's unconscious. Our interaction was . . . heated.'

I gritted my teeth. 'Why do men always feel the need to bypass conversation for action?'

'I know, it's just ridiculous, isn't it?' said Kate. 'Don't they understand, like a beautiful flower, we need to be nurtured in order to grow?'

'All right, Lex, give me a break, I hit the sod a little harder than I meant to.'

'Any sign of anyone else?'

Kate laughed. 'Oh no, I doubt that. I mean, he just wouldn't find the time, let alone the energy. Do you know how exhausting three young children are? I can't remember the last time we slept past 5.45 a.m.'

'No one. The first floor is secure.'

I laughed along with the other women.

'I think what's important is to make sure everything is OK. That nothing else troubling is hidden.'

'Copy that. Searching the top floor now.' Up there were several soundproofed rooms used for low-level interrogations.

'You're totally right. Communication is everything,' said Naomi.

I looked up as the double doors opened and in walked Mrs Moulage. Head held high.

She came up to me and said softly, 'That friend of ours is safely in the car.'

'Thank you, Mrs Moulage. I'm just waiting to hear if things will end on time as planned today.'

She nodded and patted me on the shoulder as she headed back towards her table.

'Top floor is clear. Robin, what did G say? Come in, Robin?'

I chewed my lip and nodded encouragingly at Dionne sharing her frustrations at Peppa never wanting to eat the healthy vegan meals she made for them, citing trauma at work dictating the need for cheese, carbs and wine.

Why was Robin taking so long to reply?

'I'm here.'

I braced myself.

'We're all clear. It is not a bomb. Repeat, it is not a bomb.'

'Wonderful, that's just brilliant, totally brilliant.'

The women looked a little taken aback at my enthusiasm for the John Lewis sale that was currently on.

'We're taking the device and the two Ghosts back to the Platform,' said Jake.

I turned round to catch Mrs Moulage's eye. I gave her a small nod. Her shoulders slumped.

I tried to concentrate on the original mission. Bonding with the three Pigs' significant others.

I clocked back in to what they were now discussing. The women had moved on to their frustrations of living with people who often read the newspapers with guffaws and a refusal to explain what they found so amusing. All three of the Pigs had high enough security clearance to know about Wolves.

Rats were not the only under-the-radar branch of the Security Services. A division named Demon Communications would run agents we regarded as Wolves in Sheep's clothing to unduly influence public opinion.

Wolves could grab the headlines we wanted and bring down those we considered enemies without the bloodshed us Rats specialised in: the business mogul who was getting too much power crushed by a four-page interview with a prostitute he gave insider stock market tips to. The Conservative who was undone by the drug dealer he had been buying cocaine from. Little people bringing down the big ones. With just a little guidance. A little manipulation. All for the good of the country. As the Committee deemed fit.

I checked my watch. The WAF session was due to finish in a few minutes. Was there really someone working with the Snake inside this room now?

'Don't you think, Alexis?' I looked up to see the four women staring at me.

'Sorry?'

'I was just saying it seems very unfair they try and make us feel guilty for wanting to be normal. It doesn't matter how important their job is; why don't they understand keeping us happy is important too?' asked Kate.

'Yes, the way Ronald made me feel for complaining when he got called away to Birmingham on Tuesday, it was as if he'd forgotten all about the times I've just accepted the last-minute nights away without comment,' added Naomi.

They really were taking this initiative to heart. And I was meant to provide the answers.

'Well . . . You all make good points. I think, speaking from the inside, our work is so all-consuming it can be difficult to remember to give home life the respect it deserves.'

It was advice I could myself follow.

'Right, well, we're actually out of time now. And this has been just great. I'm looking forward to us all catching up again the day after tomorrow,' I looked down at my notes, 'at Kate's house. Thank you for offering, Kate.'

'My pleasure. It's so refreshing being around normal peo-ple who aren't intimidated by my fame. It's hard to find other women who don't resent me for looking like this. Especially after three children.' She paused. We all remained silent. 'Espe-cially as two of them are twins and still so young.'

'Oh, right. Yes, of course you do look amazing.' Naomi loy-ally trotted out what she needed to hear.

I looked over at Camilla. She was running a finger around the rim of her teacup. She had been the quietest. Did this mean they were blissfully happy? Maybe. Or was it that she just didn't share personal information with strangers? Perhaps. Were these musings mission-relevant? Definitely not.

We all got up and after a flurry of goodbyes I was left at Table Eight alone.

If the device was not a bomb, what was it? Who in this room was the one tasked with activating it – and why hadn't they?

Mrs Moulage came up beside me.

'Do we know anything yet?'

I shook my head. 'Our tech support will run tests on the device back at the Platform.'

A blonde woman in a fur gilet passed us and gave a start as she saw me.

'Lex. I didn't realise you'd be here. How nice.' She said this unsmiling.

Annabel. Duggers' wife. We had known each other at uni-versity. Known each other, but not been friends.

'Yes, well, I'm here doing my bit. I'm a Liaison for one of the groups.'

'That's great. I thought you were too high up to be dealing with initiatives like this, but I guess not.'

'It's something Duggers really believes in, so happy to help.'

'No one calls him that anymore. Well, no one serious.' Annabel gave a little giggle and walked off.

'What have you ever done to her?' asked Mrs Moulage as we watched Annabel's furry back departing.

'I slept with her husband.'

Mrs Moulage nodded. 'That'll do it.'

'Back at university, before they got together,' I added.

Mrs Moulage smiled. 'It probably meant more to him than to you.' She opened up her clutch and took out a long, thin cigar and a silver lighter. 'What a morning. Nothing like worrying you're going to get blown up while some balding recruitment consultant from Kent tries to explain what something called BitCoin is.' She lit her cigar. 'This was not what I signed up for.' She let out a long drag of smoke. 'Goodbye, Lex. It was good to meet you.'

'Goodbye, Mrs Moulage. And thank you.'

'What for?' She cocked her head.

'I wouldn't be here if you hadn't paved the way first.'

'Oh sweetie, you would've found a way.' She gave a throaty laugh. 'This isn't a job, it's a calling.' She stalked out the double doors, a shimmer of green silk and cigar smoke.

Chapter Five

'WE KNOW WHAT THE GHOSTS' device was for.'

I walked into the meeting room to find Hattie in front of the whiteboard; a black screen with an 'Error' message was projected onto it. Pixie and Geraint were at the table, fingers flying across their laptops. Next to them was a large plastic box of what looked like toys. Robin was in front of it holding a Thomas the Tank Engine.

'All the files that the WhatsApp worm downloaded off the women's phones have been corrupted.'

The Ghosts, despite their ineptitude, had succeeded in their mission after all.

Geraint handed me an iPad with a report on the device loaded onto it. I scanned it.

It turned out I was the one inside the room who activated the device.

By sending the women the WhatsApp invite.

As soon as the device was plugged in it wirelessly logged onto the network and corrupted all file transfers occurring in a thirty-foot radius.

'The Snake must have known that one of the women had something on their phone that would incriminate them. But how did they know we were even going for their phones?' I asked.

Pixie looked up at me. 'The Snake would know our protocols. Initial contact with targets usually involves some kinda worm or bug to get to grips with their hardware. It wouldn't be a stretch to work out we would start with downloading their phone records and that the WAF meeting was the likeliest time.'

'Jake and Cameron are interrogating the two Ghosts now. Doesn't look like they know anything but they seemed keen to try,' said Hattie.

There was a clunk as Thomas the Tank Engine fell out of Robin's hands and back into the box of toys. We all turned to look at him.

'Sorry,' Robin offered. He picked up a fluffy bunny rabbit and started squeezing its stomach.

'How quickly can we get another go at their phones?' I asked.

Pixie frowned. 'The worm needs around twenty minutes to download everything off the phone. Our best chance is to install an update to their home wireless network.'

'Get the tech ready,' said Hattie. 'Robin can install it while he's at their houses.'

'I'm just checking all the kit.' Robin motioned towards the box in front of him. I glanced over at the assortment of Lego pieces, Barbie dolls, small cars, fluffy bunnies and a few elves. 'I'm breaking into the Pigs' houses and leaving toys there. I'm Father Christmas.' He grinned.

Using children's toys as Trojan horses masking listening devices was inspired by the mess of my own home. No one with kids would notice if something they thought was in one room was now in another. I thought of the time I'd found a legless Barbie stuck in my underwear drawer. Just this morning there had been a tin teacup and two marbles inside my right shoe. And as Hattie had pointed out, Security Service operatives would be on the lookout for devices in the more usual places like the landline or the smoke detectors. Not the very toys that they were permanently tripping themselves up with.

'By the end of today we should have the Pigs' online histories, their phone records, and be able to listen in on all their conversations. Having their whole lives in our hands will fast-track any intel that rings alarms bells.'

'I'm betting whatever they didn't want us to find on the phones would've been deleted by now. They wouldn't risk us making another grab for the intel without making sure it was wiped.' I knew this as it's exactly what we would do.

Hattie nodded. 'And that's why you need to stay on the women. Be their friend. Find out what you can. They will know something but they probably don't even realise its significance. They're our best chance.'

Jake and Cameron walked into the meeting room, each holding a large chocolate bar.

'Thank God the vending machine still works,' was all Jake said as he slumped down into a chair.

'That was a total waste of time. Those Ghosts know nothing,' Cameron said as she tore off the wrapping with her teeth and took a bite. I remembered that she was one of those people who ate whatever she wanted and 'just couldn't put on weight'. Her annoyingly fast metabolism was yet another reason I couldn't wait for her to disappear back to America.

Hattie eased into the seat at the head of the table. 'Each of you will have individual operational objectives outlining exactly what you need to. Please familiarise yourselves with everything expected of you.'

Hattie observed us as we all pulled out our phones and clicked onto a '$$$HornyHotMums' email.

'I don't need to remind you that we only have each other. We're running on a shell on the biggest mission we've ever had. But the Committee were clear. Until the Tenebris Network is shut down no one else can be trusted. Dugdale and Frederick will not come back to the Platform again – it's too risky. Any intel we want exchanged between Six and Eight happens through Lex and Frederick at the nursery.'

We all scanned through our email orders.

'We need to be incredibly efficient,' said Hattie. 'Unmasking the key players is how we destroy them. I will focus on identifying the Coyote. Lex and Frederick on identifying the Snake. Jake and Cameron will be working through a list of hackers that we believe have the necessary expertise to fortify and manage the Tenebris website. We just need one of us to succeed. Exposing one of them will help topple the others. We need to get Tenebris offline and keep Peng alive.'

Cameron looked back to her phone and read out, 'Authorised force level – light. Maimed or critically injured computer programmers could warrant unwanted attention.' Cameron sighed. 'You Brits are so boring.' She finished her chocolate bar, scrunched up the wrapper and dropped it on the floor.

Robin waved his phone at Hattie. 'So I'm just providing support to everyone.'

'Yes. G and Pixie will be supporting us on the tech side and you will be actioned in the field as and when it's needed.'

'There are no small parts, only small agents.' Robin grinned. 'Don't worry, boss, I won't let you down. We can call this my graduation mission, right? The one where I prove I deserve my own unit?' He looked round at Jake and me. We averted our eyes and tried not to notice his face fall. It was like kicking a puppy. I would talk to Jake later. Things were complicated enough without me having mum guilt over our treatment of Robin.

'You all have your orders. Now get out there.' Hattie spread his hands. 'We need your best work. The quicker we solve this, the quicker we get Eight back up and running. I expect regular encrypted updates.'

We all stood up. Robin with his box of toys was the first out the door. Off to a running start to make a good impression.

Jake came up to me. 'What do you think of Frederick?'

'Fine. He seems fine.' I avoided meeting his gaze.

'I don't like him.' This was no surprise. Jake didn't like most people. 'Having some pretty-boy Pigeon along for the ride is only going to make things more complicated.'

'We wouldn't even know about Tenebris if it wasn't for him. And we can't do this without him. We need someone inside Six monitoring the Pigs day to day.'

'He'd better be up to the job.'

'I'll make sure of it. You're the one who's going to have it tough.' I motioned towards Cameron, who was already by the door scowling at us.

'I can't wait for this mission to be over,' sighed Jake as he went to join her.

Pixie bounded up to me, pineapple earrings jangling. 'Sweetness, I need to see what's in your handbag.'

'What? Why?'

'We need inspiration on what options we have for hidin' kit in. We've just finished the items you'll need for the Natural History Museum.'

I opened my large tote bag. Inside were five conkers, a half-drunk smoothie, a Tupperware box of biscuits, a pack of babywipes, a small pair of purple woollen tights, a pair of Tinkerbell pants and a naked doll. At the bottom was a piece of chocolate cake still wrapped up in a *Paw Patrol* paper napkin and remnants of crushed Pom-Bear crisps. I tried to remember when the last birthday party was and whether that cake would still be edible.

Pixie wrinkled her nose. 'Are those pants clean?'

'Of course,' I said with a confidence I didn't really feel.

As I was getting on the tube to South Kensington my phone buzzed. I looked down. Several messages had arrived into my personal WhatsApp group: 'Group Therapy'. Although at first glance seeing messages such as: 'There's just so much blood. An unstoppable flow that soaks through everything' might seem more related to work, it was actually a discussion on the pros and cons of the copper coil. The members of the group were my real-life friends Tamara, Shona and Frankie, and the Group Therapy moniker created by Frankie was a nod to how it was a safe place to discuss parenting fails and generally feel better about ourselves. It made me think how the 'We are Family' initiative, despite its dishonourable intentions, had its heart in the right place.

We all needed a support system. Considering one of the 'We are Family' spouses or employer was a traitorous Snake unlikely to live past the week, it was good they would have friends that they could lean on when the inevitable happened.

Chapter Six

'I'D LIKE TO START by thanking our parent volunteers.' Ms Yvonne was standing on the steps of the Natural History Museum, addressing our rabble of teachers and parents. The adults all sported name badges with smiley faces, the children bright yellow safety vests.

'Trips like this are only possible with your help. And a particularly special thank you goes to Frederick Easton for organising today's visit to see the Prehistoric Pete Puppet Show.'

Although sucking up to his daughter's headteacher was an added benefit for Frederick, this nursery visit was a cover.

Frederick had learned from his informant, Y at the Embassy, that Peng would always have with her a security card with an inbuilt GPS tracker. It was a security protocol for whenever a minister was abroad. Tomorrow evening the Natural History Museum was presenting Peng with an ancient Chinese scroll to return with her to China. This exclusive event would be happening in the library and Robin would be doing security at the door – his handheld scanning wand would pick up the tracking device signature and relay it back to a control box. The perfect location for this box would be the Marine Invertebrates room, directly opposite the library, and the location of the Prehistoric Pete Puppet Show.

Our objective this afternoon was to securely position the control box into the Marine Invertebrates room and test that the radio range would have no interference.

A class-load of overexcited two-year-olds aside, it should be a straightforward mission.

The other parents, mostly mothers, were talking among themselves. Thirty-six kids, covered by nearly as many adults. I wondered whether it was the health and safety dictating ratios or if many of the parents had taken the afternoon off specially to accompany their little ones on the big museum day out. I stood beside Frederick as Florence and Gigi whispered and giggled to each other in front of us. Gigi was wearing a red mackintosh and floral-embroidered jeans. Her brown hair was tied back in pigtails. One was already half coming out. She was so excited for this trip. Every time she looked at me her dimples shone as she grinned the biggest grin. I was so glad to be here.

With Yvonne leading the way, holding a yellow flag on a stick high above her head, we all headed inside the museum.

I leaned towards Frederick. 'Last Tuesday Daddy Pig apparently went to a conference in Birmingham.'

'Tuesday . . .' Frederick was a quiet for a moment. 'No, there was nothing on the schedule. He was still in the office when I left around seven p.m.'

'It could've been a meeting with the headhunters. I'll get G and Pixie to check his credit card and the CCTV records. We might be able to pick him up leaving the building.'

'Has Hattie rethought giving the Pigs trackers? I can easily fit them.'

I shook my head. 'He thinks it's too big a risk. If any of them discover a tracker they'll know we're closing in and that they're under suspicion. Tenebris may know we're hovering but they mustn't know how close.'

I looked down at Gigi and Florence still giggling together. I wondered if I could get Eight to set up a trip to the Aquarium next. Much better going during the week and missing all the weekend crowds.

'Hello, there.' A young blonde teacher with a clipboard came up to us. 'Now, are you Florence's parents? Or Gigi's?'

'I'm Florence's father.'

'And I'm Gigi's mother.'

'Oh, right, sorry. I just presumed . . . Apologies!' she trilled.

'We work together,' I offered.

'How lovely. Great. So you have your two covered. And I'm going to allocate you Milo and Jack as well.' She made a couple of ticks on her clipboard and motioned towards two boys who were chasing each other up and down the corridor. 'Milo! Jack! Come here, please.' She beckoned them over to us. 'This is,' she peered at our name labels, 'Alexis and Frederick, and they'll be looking after you on this trip so make sure you do exactly as they say.'

The boys barely looked at us before they tore off again. The blonde teacher went after them with a sing-song 'no running, boys!' plea that was totally ignored.

'Hello, Alexis.' A mother with her dark hair held back in a tight ponytail came up to us. I recognised her from the school gates; she seemed to know everyone. Or make it her business to know everyone. She tilted her head at Frederick. 'Aren't you going to introduce me?' She looked at me expectantly.

'Ah yes, Frederick, this is . . .' I looked down at her lapel. Dammit, her name label was covered by her pink scarf. '. . . Raquel.'

She grimaced at me. 'Rochelle. It's Rochelle. I know Will, remember? We used to work together?'

Looking at her I did now remember her irritatingly over-familiar fawning over my husband. *'Oh, you're married to the wonderful Will. We go way, way back. He is such a poppet. Can't believe we live so close now. I must give him a ring and organise drinks . . . I mean for all four of us, of course.'*

'Rochelle. Of course. Sorry. Haven't had enough caffeine this morning.'

She ignored me and gazed at Frederick.

'Nice to meet you. So great to see dads being hands-on and showing an interest.'

'Why wouldn't I? She's my daughter too.'

Rochelle's mouth opened and shut a few times before she muttered, 'Yes. Quite,' and looking over Frederick's shoulder waved at someone else and dashed off to them.

The blonde teacher reappeared with the two boys we had been charged with. 'Here they are!' she announced and quickly disappeared off. We ushered them along with Florence and Gigi towards the security guards that were at the entrance to the main part of the museum.

Geraint had warned us that security would be tighter than usual due to the high-profile event the next day.

Frederick was motioned straight through while the security guard stopped me to rifle through my tote bag. There were two dolls, several packets of snacks, a Tupperware box of biscuits, a Peppa Pig toy phone and an Etch A Sketch. He handed me back the bag with a grunt.

As we entered the main part of the museum, Yvonne, still tightly clasping the flag above her, addressed us all. 'Everyone, please make your way to the Marine Invertebrates room. It's just round the corner. We'll go at a very slow pace so everyone can keep up.'

She was not kidding. It was a painfully slow pace.

I spoke softly to Frederick. 'I'll go ahead and fit the box. You OK with the kids?'

He looked down at our motley crew of two-year-olds shuffling in front of us. Gigi and Florence were holding hands. The tallest boy was picking his nose. The other had his hands down his trousers.

'Last time I was out on an op in charge of four subordinates it was under heavy gunfire in Afghanistan and we had to make it across twenty miles of desert.' He shrugged. 'I think I'll be OK. If Ms Yvonne continues with this speed I'll see you there in ten.'

I bent down to Gigi. 'Mummy's going on ahead. You stay with Florence and her daddy.'

'Bye, Mama. Bye bye.' Gigi kept swinging Florence's hand as they walked.

I swiftly overtook the rest of the nursery group and Yvonne and her flag.

There was nothing like being relieved of your two-year-old to realise how free you feel being able to walk at a good speed. I headed straight to the Marine Invertebrates room. Another group of school children were already in position on the floor waiting for Prehistoric Pete's arrival. I looked around. The display cabinet at the back of the room was the one closest to the library door opposite. We already had its exact dimensions from Duggers and Frederick's previous reconnaissance visit. As long as the measurements were correct the Etch A Sketch should fit snugly into the gap between the floor and the curve of the cabinet.

I put my tote bag on the floor and rummaged inside. I pulled the Etch A Sketch out and, using my handbag to mask what I was doing, slid it under the display cabinet. If it was discovered, a lost toy from a careless child wouldn't raise any red flags with security. They wouldn't bother dissecting it to find the receiver carefully hidden inside.

I patrolled round the room, stopping for a token admiring glance at the exhibits in each display case. At the back of the room was another door that led out into a large corridor. The library was opposite it. There was already a 'No Entry' sign on the door and a rope cordoning it off. Slumped in a chair on the right of the library door was a uniformed security guard. He may have just been blankly staring at his phone but his presence was a sign they really weren't taking any chances with the security for tomorrow's event.

Yvonne and her flag finally entered. I watched as kids and parents filed in after her. Where was Frederick? More importantly where was Gigi? I kept scanning the faces of every child in the room.

It looked as though everyone was here except Frederick and his four charges. I checked my watch. I'd left them over fifteen minutes ago to walk thirty feet. Could someone have intercepted them? My heart rate sped up. Where the hell were they? I headed out the door and was making my way back down the corridor when I saw them.

Frederick had Florence in his arms and was holding hands with Gigi as the two boys ran behind them, stopping every few seconds to give each other a shove. 'Milo! Jack! I said, NOW!' Frederick hissed at them.

'Mama!' Gigi let go of Frederick's hand and came running to me. She clung to my leg as Frederick looked at me, shaking his head. His hair was dishevelled. His eyes wild.

'What took you so long?'

'They all needed a wee. All of them. Have you ever tried taking four two-year-olds to the loo? It was a fucking disaster zone. The loos are blocked. I just . . . And then I nearly lost one. He ran off and I couldn't remember what the little shit looked like. Do you know how many kids here are wearing Spiderman T-shirts? I grabbed the wrong bloody one, which led to screaming and an awkward conversation with his mother.'

'It's OK, Frederick, calm down. You made it. The puppet show's about to begin.'

He took a few deep breaths. 'I'm fine. I'm going to be fine.' He smoothed a hand over his hair.

Frederick put Florence down on the floor and we ushered the four of them into the room.

'Go sit with your friends,' I said to Gigi and pointed towards Yvonne and the rest of her class. They were all sitting cross-legged in a line in front of the makeshift cave stage.

Prehistoric Pete announced his arrival with a wolf howl. We all turned to see a hairy, rotund man in a shaggy black wig, wearing an indeterminable furry animal skin and brandishing a club, come lunging into the room. 'Helllloooooooo, children,' he said in a deep voice. 'Me Pete. Me like puppets. You want show?'

The children remained quiet, not quite sure what to make of him.

'Yes!' called out a couple of teachers and parents; they were clearly feeling charitable to the grown man being left hanging by a bunch of toddlers.

Frederick leaned towards me. 'Did you manage to fit the box?'

I nodded. 'Once the puppet show is over we need to test the range.'

As Pete busied himself climbing into his cave with more howls and pulling out his mammoth and saber-toothed tiger hand puppets, I talked Frederick through the status of the library.

Frederick shook his head. 'It's not a good sign for how tight security will be tomorrow night.'

Pete went into a brief stilted monologue about the mammoth and tiger's eating habits. The children conveyed their lack of interest the only way they knew how, with fidgeting and loud stage whispers of 'want snackkkk'.

'Arghhhh, you no hurt me, we friends!' shouted Prehistoric Pete as the mammoth and tiger puppets went for his neck. He kept hitting himself with them and his cries of pain were rewarded with the magical sound of toddler laughter.

Pete seemed to have found his stride and every time he attacked himself, Frederick and I continued our conversation, debating security issues for tomorrow evening, masked by the noise of giggles, squeals and shouts.

The puppet show ended to a round of applause. Pete and his puppets gave a majestic bow. Pete's forehead was now covered in sweat from exerting himself so enthusiastically while sporting a heavy animal fur and a synthetic wig. He was now being affectionately shoved by an array of toddlers shouting, 'Silly man! Silly man!' Would he consider their enthusiasm a win? Or just another hellish day in the life of a children's entertainer?

Gigi and Florence came up to us. 'He funny!' they said, laughing. I realised that his supposedly prehistoric way of talking was actually toddler talk.

'Look what Mummy's got for you.' I pulled a doll out of my bag and gave it a shake at her. 'Florence, I've got one for you too.' I pulled out another identical one.

Gigi grabbed one of the dolls and held it tight. Frederick pushed Florence towards me. 'Go on, darling. Take it.' She took the remaining doll a little more hesitantly.

'Why don't you girls go and have a little run around with your new dollies?' I motioned towards the library door with the guard seated outside. 'Why don't you race Florence up to that door and back? If you do it three times you get a biscuit.'

'Yayyyy, biscuit!' they cheered.

The two of them went skipping off, grasping their new dolls.

We watched them go.

Frederick asked with a smile, 'How are you feeling about using your daughter to trial the radio range of a scanner needed in a top-secret mission?'

'Pretty good. She's getting a free doll out of it. The microchip inside can be removed later. You?'

'Same.' We watched them leaving the room ahead of us. 'Chances of them doing what we say?'

'I'm quietly confident. Gigi would do pretty much anything for a chocolate biscuit.'

They were running now along the corridor.

I looked down at the Peppa Pig toy phone. The light was green – but the girls were still nowhere near the library door. We just needed confirmation that the security wand scanner would be in range of the console box.

Halfway across the corridor the girls stopped. They were brandishing their dolls at each other and chatting animatedly. It was sweet, wondering what they talked about. Their own little people. They were now swapping the dolls between them and comparing them next to each other. I gave myself a pat on the back for going for two identical ones to prevent any chance of a row over who had which.

'MINE,' said Gigi, reaching for the doll Florence was holding.

Oh great.

'No, MINE.'

Gigi threw the doll she was holding onto the floor.

'Well, that's not good,' said Frederick.

I needed to get them back on mission. I rushed up to the girls. 'What's going on? Don't forget the running race. And the biscuits.'

'I want that one.' Gigi pointed at Florence's doll.

'Gigi, they are exactly the same. What does it matter?'

'Because it's mine.' She snatched the doll from Florence and stared up at me, her mouth in a firm line, chin jutting out.

Florence burst into tears and tried to grab it back. 'No, MINE.'

The two of them sobbed and tussled, both holding onto the doll.

Frederick joined us. 'What's the problem?'

'Our daughters are fighting over an identical doll.'

'We don't want to attract any undue attention.'

As if they could understand what he was saying the crying from each girl went up another decibel.

Frederick squatted down next to Florence. 'Now come on, Florence. This is not on.'

The girl ignored him and continued the tussle over the doll.

We needed to take action. I had found the right-on parenting favourite of 'use your words' worked as well on a sobbing toddler as it did on a psychopath brandishing a gun. Bribery was the only solution.

'Gigi, let Florence have the doll and you can have a biscuit.' I rummaged through my bag and grabbed the Tupperware box. There was a pause in her tears and she dropped the doll as she observed me. Florence quickly grabbed it and held it tight in her arms. I opened the lid.

Bloody hell.

'What is it?' asked Frederick

'They haven't travelled well.' I showed him the inside of the box and broken biscuit bits.

'What does it matter?'

'You'll see.' I sighed. I put on the perkiest voice I could muster. 'Here you go, Gigi, two yummy biscuits.' I pulled two halves of a biscuit out.

She looked at them and then at me as her face crumpled.

'B-B-But IT'S BROKEN,' she howled.

'Gigi, we've been over this a hundred times before. It tastes just the same. It's actually better. You get TWO.'

'I WANT WHOLE ONE.' The sobbing continued.

I looked up at Frederick. 'Go find some chocolate. Or a lollipop. Or a fudging cake. Anything that's full of E-numbers or bad fat. Go now. We're meant to be leaving to go see the dinosaurs in a few minutes.' I looked over at the teacher rallying the parents and children into a line outside the Marine Invertebrates room. He shot off.

Gigi continued to sob with the word 'biscuit' and 'doll' being screamed in amid the snot and tears. Florence was now sitting quietly, holding the doll tight in her arms.

'Florence, how about you take the dolly and go stand by that door? You know the big one over there where that man is sitting?' Florence wouldn't even make eye contact with me, let alone acknowledge what I was saying. She continued to sit clasping the doll.

I clearly didn't have a way with other people's kids. I should at least fare better with my own. I picked up the discarded doll on the floor.

'Come on, Gigi, this one is much better.' I handed it to her. 'Remember the fun race to the door? Stop crying. Please, Gigi. For Mama? Frederick is getting you an amazing treat. And I'll carry you?' She continued to howl. 'And you can have my phone? I promise?'

'NO.' She flung the doll across the room. It slid against the polished floor and hit the library door. I looked into my tote bag – the Peppa Pig mobile light was still a steady green.

The security wand at the library door would be in range. Mission accomplished.

Frederick came racing round the corner holding a bag.

'Gigi! We do not throw, remember?' I gave the thumbs up to Frederick.

'Thank God,' he muttered as he pulled Florence to her feet.

I stood up and turned round. The guard walked towards me holding the doll. 'Here you go.'

'Thank you. Sorry about that.'

He laughed. 'Don't worry, I've got two of my own. No pleasing them sometimes.'

Gigi looked up at me as I handed her back the doll. She looked down at it for a moment and then took it and tucked it under her arm.

'I stop cry. Where yummy treat?'

'Frederick?'

He handed over the bag. Inside it was a lollipop the size of my hand. I gave him a look.

'It was all they had.'

I pulled it out, took off the wrapping and handed it to her. She started licking it. 'Now Mama carry. And Mama phone. YOU PROMISHED.'

I did.

I'd promised. I sighed and handed the phone over.

I looked over at the line of nursery mothers watching us, their well-behaved children standing quietly in front of them.

'Mama, can I have one?' a boy in a tartan shirt pointed at the lollipop clasped in Gigi's hand.

'No, Sebastian, you know we never have treats before dinner,' his mother replied in a loud voice.

Rochelle made a noise that sounded like she had something stuck in her teeth. Either that or she was tut-tutting me. She couldn't really be. Could she?

Gigi's tantrum had nearly derailed a mission and now I was being judged for being a lazy, spoiling parent who had no control over her child. I tried to hold my head up high as I walked past them carrying my two-year-old as she licked the enormous lollipop and stared at the Peppa Pig YouTube video playing on my phone.

They might be thinking 'crap mother' but I'd been acting for the good of our country.

Gigi and I stood together, hand in hand, staring up at the magnificent skeleton of a diplodocus. 'Isn't this amazing, Gigi? We're seeing an actual dinosaur.' I'd always been fascinated by these enormous magnificent animals that had roamed the Earth long before our existence. And now I got to share the wonder of them with my daughter.

'Juss bones,' said Gigi as she continued to lick her lollipop. 'Gimme phone.'

The magic of parenthood.

I continued to drag her round each display. I felt marginally better for the fact I hadn't actually specially taken time off for this non-magical bonding experience.

Yvonne eventually blew a little whistle and waved her yellow flag. 'Time to go, everyone! We will now depart for the school, where we can do some nice drawings of our favourite dinosaurs.'

Frederick came up alongside me and spoke low into my ear. 'You have to meet Y at five p.m. Exit four of the Marble Arch pedestrian subway.' I felt his breath on my cheek. 'Wait for him at the bottom of the ramp.' He showed me Y's photo on his phone. He had thin eyebrows and a large mole on his right cheek.

I nodded.

'That was fun, wasn't it, Gigi? Mummy has to go back to work now. But you're going back to school to do some drawings and Ganma will pick you up from there. OK?' Ganma was Gigi's name for my mother-in-law; her first attempt at Grandma was to us so sweet we had kept it going. I held my breath as Gigi computed what I was saying. There was always the fear she would let rip with a round of quickfire words that stung: 'Why, Mama? Why you leave me? Don't go, Mama. I just want you. Only you.'

It had been so much easier when they couldn't talk. When they were just a bundle you could give a kiss and a wave to and skip out the door to your other life. Now there was the fear there would be tears and recriminations. Guilt dragging you down. Making you feel a terrible mother for daring to leave them.

But not today. Thankfully she just nodded. 'OK, Mama, bye bye.' And walked off holding Florence's hand.

Chapter Seven

THE MARBLE ARCH UNDERPASS was surprisingly quiet for rush hour.

'Looking good, beautiful.'

A man stood in the middle of the underpass staring at me. He was skinny with pockmarked skin, peroxided hair and wearing a long dark coat. I dismissed him as a random sleaze.

'Come on, give me a smile.'

I gave him the finger over my shoulder as I carried on walking.

'I'll be seeing you, Alexis Tyler.'

I stopped, spun around and rammed him up against the wall, my right hand clutching his throat.

'Who are you? Who sent you? How do you know my name?'

He shakily pointed down to my jacket lapel.

'You're . . . you're . . . wearing a name label.'

'Right.' I released him. 'Stop fucking catcalling women. We don't like it. And some of us will enjoy showing you just how much.' I made a jolt towards him. He ran.

I looked down at my lapel and tore off the label.

First and last time being harassed had actually been useful. The creep had at least stopped me from attending a covert meeting with a Chinese Embassy informant with my real name pinned to my breast.

Bloody name badges.

A hazard of my dual life.

Y was late. I walked up and down the underpass. I could see why it was a good meeting place. No one would be able to get close to us without making themselves known.

I leaned back against the wall and watched each person that walked past. In the distance I saw a Chinese man coming towards me. Was it Y? I waited until he got closer. Thin eyebrows. Mole on his right cheek. Identity confirmed. I waited for him to catch my eye. He was walking slowly, staring at the ground. He was in a suit with a navy duffle coat on top, a battered satchel slung over his shoulder. He was nearly next to me when he finally looked up. I gave him a small nod and started walking alongside him.

'I talk. You listen,' he said quietly. He looked straight ahead.

'The Ambassador will meet Minister Peng at Heathrow VIP arrival suite. There they discuss the itinerary for her trip and any other upcoming business. You need to listen in. That is important meeting. Very important,' he repeated. 'No more contact with me again. Too dangerous now.'

'But we need—'

'Peng's PA, Ling Ling. She records all meetings with her Dictaphone so can type up later. Dictaphone always in her bag. You get the Dictaphone you always know what's been happening.' We approached the beginning of the ramp leading back up onto the street. 'That's it. No more contact. No more.' He kept walking as I stopped and turned round.

I needed to get back to the Platform. We had less than twenty-four hours until Peng and the delegation arrived into Heathrow, and we needed to find a way to bug their arrival suite.

'Time for an update briefing,' said Hattie as I walked into the meeting room. Hattie was in his position at the head of the dining table. Both Robin and Cameron were missing, presumably still out on their ops. 'Jake, let's start with you.'

'Cameron is unhinged,' said Jake. 'She punched four hackers in the face this afternoon. One of them made the mistake of asking if she was on her period so he got punched twice.'

I didn't often agree with Cameron but I thought that was fair enough.

'They'd all heard of the Tenebris Network. They knew it was a headhunting website on the dark web and that it was causing a bit of a stir. A few thought they were hunting actual heads. Which in fairness is more fitting in terms of the sick shit you find online.'

'Do any of them know anyone who actually took a job there?'

Jake shook his head. 'What they did say seems to match Frederick's intel that Tenebris's technological set-up points to a London-based operation.'

'Where's Cameron now?'

'Quite a few of the names on the master list of hackers are Americans supposedly living in London – she's over at the American Embassy making sure we have the most up-to-date information on all of them.' Jake shook his head. 'I can't believe I'm working with someone that makes me the calm, restrained one.' Despite the darkness in him, Jake worked hard to be a consummate professional. He carefully planned and executed his duties and rarely lost control. If he ever teetered on the edge that was when I reined him in.

'Keep an eye on her. We don't want her going rogue.' Hattie bridged his hands together on the table. 'My update on the Coyote is that no known aliases – of any of the assassins we have records on – have entered the country in the last week. It was naïve to hope they would be an easy spot. I'm continuing to speak to my sources to see if we can get any clue as to who or where we should be looking.' Hattie looked down at his iPad on the table. 'Now let's talk about the Pigs.'

'Robin has successfully installed the listening devices and phone worm at Daddy Pig's house,' said Geraint. 'We've started an initial download of their phone and internet history, and the audio is transmitting clearly. He's just finished Peppa Pig's house and is on his way to George's now.'

'Frederick told me Daddy Pig never went to Birmingham. We need to look into his movements last Tuesday.'

Pixie looked up from her laptop. 'I'll go through his mobile phone history. That'll show us where he really was.'

Hattie turned to me. 'Tell us about your meeting with Y.'

'Y stated that we should try and tap Peng's PA's Dictaphone as she uses it in all important meetings. He also confirmed that Peng and the delegation will be met in the Heathrow VIP Arrivals Suite by the Chinese Ambassador, who will go over their itinerary for the week and no doubt confirm any extra meetings not on the official schedule. We find out her plans for the whole stay and we have a better chance of working out when the Coyote will be likely to strike. We need to get ears into that room.'

'G, what are Peng's flight details?'

There was a pause as Geraint tapped a few buttons on his laptop. 'Peng's plane lands at Heathrow Terminal Three tomorrow at 12.35.'

Jake shook his head. 'It doesn't leave us much time to do the usual maintenance route and sort out getting in as an approved supplier.'

I had an idea. 'Peng and the delegation will be put in Suite One, won't they? The one reserved for heads of state and A-listers?'

Geraint's fingers flew across his laptop as he scanned the screen. 'I've hacked the bookings spreadsheet for Suite One and Peng is the only one listed for that day.'

'We have to use a Golden Wolf to get in there,' I said. 'One of us can join them as part of their entourage and we fix the room with listening devices. G-Force, scan the list of anyone we have currently abroad that we can get on a flight landing back into Heathrow tomorrow morning.'

Metal Wolves were celebrities. They did the same job as Wolves just with an added sprinkling of star status. Ranked according to their level of fame: Gold, Silver and Bronze. Metal Wolves were sometimes recruited but often made. In exchange for a deal with the devil they were given the career of their dreams – with just a small sideline in serving their country as and when requested.

'There's only one Golden Wolf with status high enough they'd definitely be guaranteed Suite One. He's currently in Dubai and there's a flight we can get him on landing into Heathrow at 9.05 a.m.'

'Who is it?' asked Hattie.

Geraint cleared his throat and looked at me. 'Johnnie Mac.'

Brilliant.

I needed to think fast. 'Can't we get Cameron to talk to Track 101 and send us a Kardashian? That would work?'

Hattie shook his head. 'We only turn to Track 101 for emergency favours. We can do this with Johnnie Mac.'

Jake laughed. 'So the success of this operation relies on Johnnie and Lex working together. Boss, you do realise these two can't manage to be in the same room together without there being sex, shouting, screaming and swearing. Sometimes all at the same time.'

'Don't be ridiculous, Jake. What do you—'

'I was in the next-door hotel room on that tour in 2012. Remember?'

Hattie observed us quietly. 'I note there is history there, Lex.'

'Yes, boss.'

'We want no drama. You just need to greet him off the flight, accompany him to Suite One, get the audio transmitting devices and the receiver installed, and then get out of there. I'll talk to Demon and make sure he's been briefed too. We don't want any undue attention.'

'Does it have to be me? Maybe it'd be better if Jake did it?'

Jake shook his head. 'Johnnie's a platinum-album-selling rockstar – he always travels with an entourage, which at last count was a team of about six people. To ditch them all and head to Suite One alone would be pretty strange unless it was you greeting him off the plane and requesting a private catch-up.'

I saw his point.

I sighed. Nothing like adding spending time with an ex who hated me to an already stressful week.

*

Standing outside my front door I could hear my daughter laughing. The best sound in the world. I let myself in and followed the squeals and giggles to the sitting room.

Will was in an old pair of jeans and a T-shirt, lying on his back with his legs in the air, holding hands with Gigi, who was balanced on her stomach on his feet.

'Hello, Mama. Me flying!' She grinned. Her hair was in a lopsided ponytail, her favourite *Frozen* pyjamas on.

'Wow. Look at you go.' I walked up and kissed her cheek.

'Uh oh, turbulence,' shouted Will as he shook his legs up and down. Gigi kept giggling as she wobbled about.

'Have you been back a while?'

'Meeting finished early so got back in time for her dinner.'

'We had pizza and choccy milkshake,' said Gigi proudly.

'Two more take-off and landings and then bed, little miss.'

'No, Dada. No. You do twenty-five one hundred more.'

I listened as the two of them negotiated and tidied up the toy explosion round the living room.

By the time Gigi was splashing in the bath, Will had already opened a bottle of red wine. We were each clasping a large glass of it on the floor outside the bathroom, watching Gigi sing songs and dunk her mermaid.

'What's happening at work? Are you about to disappear again?' asked Will.

'The next week or so will be very busy but then things will calm down. Might actually be getting a lot of time off soon.'

It was a sign of how serious a threat Tenebris were if I thought it was worth mentioning to Will work could be about to get very, very quiet.

'I'm not going to get my hopes up. It's not like your job has ever been particularly reliable when it comes to working hours.'

Will still hadn't forgiven me for having to cancel our summer holiday. What would've been the three of us spending ten days in Tenerife in the sunshine was replaced with four days staying with my parents in Berkshire. And it rained. Every single day. An urgent operation had come in and I'd had no choice but to go. The only proper time off I could get was a long weekend. When my parents found out we weren't actually going to be abroad for Mum's sixty-third birthday we were told that the long overdue visit we'd kept promising needed to happen during the family celebration she had planned. Will looking over and hissing: 'Mojitos on the beach' as my great-aunt regaled him in graphic detail about the effect the menopause was having on her sex-drive was a particular low point.

As I'd kept repeating to his stony face, if it had been his work stopping us going, I would've understood. My vague explanation of it being something to do with Brexit had not gone down well. In fairness, I had overused that excuse but it was such an easy go-to as it had just the right combination of utter fucked-up mess but being so boring no one wanted to talk about it.

'I know things have been busy this year. But it's all about to get better and I'm going to have a long period of time off for Christmas.'

I knew I'd been working too much the last few months and with any luck the blower I'd applied for would be approved so I could have most of December off. Blowers were Platform-approved extended periods of time off. They were so called as, considering the intense high-pressure nature of our work, it was mandated we needed weeks away from the Platform to blow off steam. And to stop us blowing off our own heads.

'Lex, it's got to get better. You're hardly present. Last month my mother spent more time with Gigi in this house than you.'

That stung.

Will's mother Gillian now lived nearby and was a huge help with Gigi. She didn't keep track of the hours she helped with nursery pick-ups and bedtime when we were working late. But it seemed Will did.

'I do the best I can. Yes, I work full-time, just like you, but I come home every night . . . Nearly every night.' There were times work had taken me out of the country. Just like it had for Will. The double standard was becoming clearer and clearer. I was expected to be here. He wasn't.

'Wheels bus round roundy round,' Gigi sang on flatly from the bathroom.

It was a great soundtrack to a tense marital stand-off.

'You're never really here. Even when you make it home you're tired and rundown and just want to cuddle Gigi. You barely want to talk.'

Will never got to see me at work. He never got to see me at my best. Those moments where I felt like the world was mine for the taking. The confidence of being armed, dangerous and able to take down anyone who got in my way. The immediate post-mission adrenaline high of feeling invincible.

He just got the aftermath. The crash. The exhaustion, the aching body, the not having the energy to speak and just wanting to hold or be held.

'I understand that your work is hard. My work is hard too. But when I'm home I'm fully here. That's all I want from you.

Your full attention. I've never felt more distant to you and it's because we don't spend any proper time together. Things need to change. We can't carry on like this.'

He was saying we were in trouble.

And I hadn't even noticed.

I remembered a Russian couple we had once known. We'd come home from a sparkling dinner party at their palatial Notting Hill mansion and Will had commented on how they weren't even playing on the same side. To be fair he'd been right. They weren't – to the point where she was conspiring with the Platform to have him killed. But I had felt smug. Will and I were together. A team. Us against the world. Our marriage was strong. We were a winning combination.

But it didn't feel like that now. If felt more like we were on opposing sides. Battling each other, not alongside each other.

I loved him. Of course I did. He was the one, the only one, who'd been able to make me give up the stumble-home single life. He was the one who'd shown me that being in a couple didn't have to mean the death of fun. It could be more fun. It had been a long time since we had one of those nights where we'd get drunk over dinner, then charge into an irritatingly cool club and dance about with the carefree abandon of people who were getting laid no matter how much of a tit they made of themselves on the dance floor. Will was right. We needed to reclaim some time for us.

It was just that right now, it was near impossible to be thinking of anything outside work.

This was not the time to have a marriage breakdown.

But if I cared enough surely I would drop everything?

I imagined announcing to Hattie and my team: *'Sorry, guys, I just need to take a little couple-time, disappear off on a mini-break. Good luck and all.'*

'Other people would be considering another baby about now,' said Will.

'I . . .'

'I can tell by the look on your face you clearly haven't.'

'I . . . no . . . Well . . . Of course I've thought about it. Just not quite yet.'

It hadn't even occurred to me.

I was finally fit again. I was enjoying my work. Getting more sleep. I couldn't imagine going back to the new baby stage. The childbirth-ravaged body, the sleepless nights, the non-stop feeding. And then starting again. Trying to reclaim normalcy. I was exhausted even thinking about it.

But then that's what most couples did. They went on to have more kids.

I was an only child. Having one child was my normal. Besides, I was stretched as it was now. Between work and Gigi and clearly Will. How could I fit in another person to love? Another person to keep safe? I didn't know if I had it in me.

'Mummy on the bus say, shhhh shhh shhhhhh!' Gigi continued to sing on.

'I'm not just another problem to deal with. I'm your husband. If things are bad at work, tell me about it. If things are stressing you out, tell me about it. I want to help you. I want to be there for you. We're meant to be a team.'

'Out now, out now!' shouted Gigi. She stood up in the bath.

Will went to her, plucking her out and onto the bathmat. 'Rub a dub dub, three men in a tub,' he said as he wrapped her in a towel, tickling her as she squealed.

I took another sip of wine. Peng was due to leave London in a week. With any luck she'd still be alive and Tenebris shut down. Or if we failed I'd pretty much not have a job anyway. And then with all that downtime I could really focus on my marriage.

I woke with a jolt. I could feel someone there, in the darkness. Silently watching us. I tensed and braced myself.

A soft whisper of, 'Mamaaaaa,' then again, a little more insistently, 'Mammmaaaaa.'

I wondered if I kept feigning sleep she might just wander back to her own room.

There was a pause and then, 'PSSSST. MAMA,' she shouted.

'What? Huh? Hello?' Will sat up with a start.

'Bad dweam. Very, very, very bad dweam,' said Gigi, already climbing into our bed.

'What was it about, Gigi?' I asked.

'Can't 'member.' She got in between us and pulled the covers over her.

Ping.

The faint sound of a text message alert came in. Will grappled at his bedside table and picked up his phone.

I looked over Gigi's head as I saw him stare at the screen, switch it to silent and put it back down.

'Gigi, you know this is naughty.' I nudged her. 'You're a big girl. You need to sleep in your bed.'

'I just want to be with you,' was the plaintive response.

Parenting books had taught me that boundaries were important. I may be desperate to get back to sleep but a tense twenty-minute negotiation now was worth it for the future nights of unbroken sleep and a bed to ourselves. It was going to be tough but it was going to be worth it.

Will rolled over and gave her a kiss on the forehead. 'It's OK, we're here, Gigi. No bad dreams in this bed. You sleep tight, little girl.'

Or there was that tactic.

Surrender.

I couldn't be the bad guy now. I listened as Will seemingly drifted straight back to sleep. Gigi swiftly followed suit.

I stroked her cheek and cuddled up to her. Soft skin and washing-powder scented *Paw Patrol* pyjamas. I felt her warm body beside me and listened to the gentle sound of her breathing and tried to forget about the stresses of work, the dangers that lay ahead, and the fact my husband was receiving text messages in the middle of the night.

From: dodgycompanywants@yourbankdetails.com
To: lex.tyler@platform-eight.co.uk
Subject: $$$ MAKE MONEY FAST $$$
MISSION: #80521
UNIT: WHISTLE
DATE: Tuesday 1st October
ALERT: PENG ARRIVES TODAY

Chapter Eight

I WALKED INTO HEATHROW'S WINDSOR SUITE to find a thin-faced woman with greying hair.

'Good morning . . .' I peered at her name badge, 'Pam. I'm Alexis from Demon Communications. I'm meeting Johnnie Mac off his plane.'

She looked down at the paperwork on her desk.

'Please follow me.' Pam stood up and slipped on a hi-vis vest on top of her trouser suit.

We headed down a corridor before she led me to another room. Inside was a small X-ray scanner belt. 'As you're going airside you'll need to have your bag checked.'

'Of course.'

I placed my bag onto the belt and watched as it moved through the scanner. The screen lit up with the image of an iPad, an iPhone, a small toy robot, an Ella's Kitchen smoothie pouch, a thick pink headband, a *Frozen* camera and three fidget spinners. The security guard's face didn't move from the monitor.

'Thanks,' I said to no acknowledgement as I picked my bag back up. I walked through the security door. Nothing beeped and Pam ushered me out the door leading to a car park.

During the five-minute drive in the chauffeured BMW, Pam gave monotonous one-word answers to my attempts at small talk. She wasn't the chatty type.

We parked up alongside the waiting bus that would be transporting the non-VIPs to the terminal.

Johnnie Mac was the first off the plane. He lolloped down the stairs and walked straight towards us. His trademark long hair was now short. It suited him. A battered canvas holdall was slung over his shoulder. He was wearing a pair of baggy black trousers and a Pink Floyd T-shirt. A black leather jacket and sunglasses completed the off-duty rockstar look.

'Hello, Alexis.'

'Johnnie.' I gave him a nod.

Johnnie spoke over his shoulder to the small group of skinny-jeaned men and women now coming down the stairs behind him. 'Guys, sort out your own car, OK? I just need a little catch-up with Alexis.'

'Sure thing, Johnnie.'

I ignored the smirks as they headed onto the bus.

Johnnie turned to Pam next to me.

'Hi, darling, now how are you doing?'

'Hello, Mr Mac,' Pam simpered. She stared at him with a giddy smile.

'I see you've met my publicist.'

'Yes. We've met.' Her eyes didn't leave Johnnie.

'I'd like a little time in the welcome suite so I can freshen up before we leave – I'm going straight to an interview.'

'Of course, Mr Mac, you take as long as you need. If you just follow me to the car . . .'

Pam did not stop talking the whole journey back to the Windsor Lounge. She had clearly been saving all her friendliness for him. 'It's so amazing that you're going to be honoured with an OBE for all that charitable work you've been doing.'

'It's not confirmed yet,' said Johnnie.

'Oh, but I've been seeing it everywhere online.'

The Wolf Cubs had been working hard campaigning for Johnnie to be recognised in the New Year's honours list, as for some reason Eight needed him at that ceremony. Wolf Cubs were teenagers in our employ whose sole purpose was to help turn the tides of online opinions to our favour. Whatever issue we needed to gain traction on we would brief the Cubs to get things going. Up would spring gifs, memes, hashtags, all fighting the good fight for us. Going to battle against bots, they had the advantage of actual personalities and an idea of what would take off. A few months ago the Committee wanted a certain journalist quashed – leading to the Wolf Cubs creating a meme of him kissing a ruthless dictator's arse. It went viral to the point it was being printed on tea-towels. That campaign was then taken to print by getting numerous Silver and Gold Wolves to allow photo shoots in their homes where the tea-towel just so happened to be in shot in their fancy bespoke kitchens. The image became so associated with the journalist's reputation he was relegated to a daytime television sofa.

Pam unlocked the door to Suite One and flung it open with a flourish. A large vase of white roses was on the centre of a dark wood dining table with matching chairs. Behind it a large flatscreen television was fixed to the wall. Sleek grey sofas encircled it.

Johnnie dropped his holdall to the floor.

'Do not disturb, OK, love? I'll call if I need anything.'

'Of course, Mr Mac, of course.' She was still standing there, smiling as he closed the door.

Johnnie went to one of the sofas and, without looking at me, slumped down onto it before pulling out his phone.

He clearly didn't want to talk. That was fine. I was here to work. I put my earpiece in.

'OK, I'm in.'

I opened my bag and took out the three fidget spinners. I popped the circular piece out of each side of each spinner. Nine little listening devices were now in the palm of my hand.

'G, I am positioning the bugs now.' Using the extra-strong adhesive that was inside the Ella's Kitchen smoothie pouch, I stuck them round the room – behind questionable paintings and underneath every armchair and sofa. The final two were stuck underneath a couple of the chairs round the wooden dining table opposite the door.

Geraint crackled into my ear. 'Looking at the blueprints, the best place to position the receiving device is inside the air vent.'

Each of the listening devices transmitted over Bluetooth back to the receiver, which would then record everything. Jake and Hattie would retrieve the listening devices and the receiver tomorrow, as soon as their maintenance visit was approved.

I looked up. There was one large vent directly above the dining table.

'I see it. I'll get it into position now.'

I emptied my bag onto the dining table. I looped the back of the *Frozen* camera onto the pink headband and put it on my head. I clicked a button and an extra-strength flashlight shone out of the camera lens.

I twisted the robot's head off, exposing the top of an electric screwdriver. I turned to Johnnie. 'This could get noisy.'

Johnnie pressed a few buttons on his phone and turned on the Sonos system.

Gorillaz blasted out the surround speakers.

I climbed up on the dining table and set to work on the vent. There were four different sets of screws. I carefully unscrewed each one, putting them in my pocket. When the last one came loose I lifted the vent cover off. It would've been helpful to be able to hand it down to Johnnie but he was still slumped on the sofa flicking through his iPhone, doing his best to pretend I didn't exist.

If I'd known, all those years ago, how badly sleeping with him would turn out, I would've managed to resist.

I thought back to the tour we'd met on, the two of us in a bar at 3 a.m, the hot, much younger, rockstar staring at me as he took a slow drag of his cigarette.

OK, maybe not.

I thought about the sex. The hours spent in hotel rooms all over the world. The occasional broken bed. And that time he did that thing with the . . .

OK, definitely not.

But I would've thought twice about it.

Things had come to a crashing halt at the end of the tour when it was clear he'd wanted more. I hadn't. And we'd reached a healthy compromise of just sleeping together every time we saw each other. Until the day I'd had to say no. Because of Will. And then all hell had broken loose. He could understand a girl not ever wanting to settle down. But not a girl not wanting to settle down with him.

I carefully brought the vent cover down and dropped it onto the floor. Retrieving the iPad from my bag, I got back up and slotted it in through the open vent.

The iPad contained the digital receiver to which all the listening devices transmitted back.

Now came the tricky part.

I put both hands onto the open vent and hauled myself up. I clicked on the receiver and started it up. 'No signal' flashed up.

'G, it's saying no signal.'

'There could be interference from the other electronic devices there. Try it further down the vent.'

I wasn't sure how stable the vent was going to be or how far down it I could get. I pulled myself up and looked around; the light from my head torch lit up enough to see how the vent narrowed. I pushed the iPad further across. I peered over the top. There was still a red cross.

I reached over and clicked the refresh button. Still nothing. I was going to have to risk going further in. I pulled myself fully up into the vent and crawled along it with the iPad.

I kept refreshing the screen with every inch I moved forward.

It was only when I was six feet from the opening that a green tick appeared. It was finally online. I clicked on the links button and saw nine green lines. All the listening devices were working and linked. We were up and running.

I reverse-shuffled back towards the opening to Suite One. There was a creaking noise and then another.

Fuck.

It clearly wasn't going to hold my weight.

There was no time for a graceful re-entry. I propelled myself backwards through the hole in the ceiling with one big push and landed on the dining table. The thump of my weight cracked it, and sent the vase of flowers flying. It smashed onto the floor.

'Bloody hell!' said Johnnie, leaping up from the sofa.

I lay on top of the broken dining table. A little dazed but otherwise unhurt. I shook myself and slid off the table. Then I reached down to pick the vent cover off the floor, climbed onto a chair and slotted it back into place.

'Hand me the robot.'

Johnnie quickly did as asked and I tightened all the screws back in.

I got down and shoved the robot, my head torch and the Ella's Kitchen smoothie pouch back in my bag, making a mental note to throw it away as soon as I got home – accidentally feeding my daughter super-strength glue would be a traumatising end to the day.

There was a knock at the door.

'Is everything OK in there?' came Pam's voice from outside.

'Just wait a minute!' Johnnie called. He came up to me and rumpled my hair with both his hands and tugged open my shirt. Johnnie went to the door and opened it a crack.

Pam was stood there beaming at him. A security guard was by her side.

'Security were concerned by the noise. Just had to check all was—'

'Could you call for the car, please, love?' Johnnie cut her off as he swung open the door. She took in the broken table, the mess on the floor and the mess of my hair.

'I . . . Well . . .'

'Yeah, sorry about all that.' He leaned towards her. 'Things got a little crazy. If you know what I mean.' He gave her a long stare as colour creeped up her cheeks. He motioned towards me. 'Come on, babe. Time to go.'

The security guard stared at my exposed cleavage. I pulled my coat across and tried to walk out with as much pride as someone supposedly caught having wild sex with a rockstar could muster.

The BMW had been replaced with a limousine, with a handy screen separating the back from the uniformed chauffeur in the front. I gave an address to the driver and then joined Johnnie in the back seat.

'Where are we dropping you?' he asked as he continued to stare straight ahead, sunglasses still firmly on.

'Just off the Hogarth Roundabout.'

He didn't respond.

'Traffic's meant to be a nightmare on the M1,' I offered.

'I'm sure the driver knows.'

'Right.'

I looked down at my phone. Google Maps said the journey was going to take twenty-nine minutes.

Prolonged uncomfortable small talk with an ex who hated me.

The shit I had to do for my country.

We sat in silence for eighteen solid minutes. I kept flicking through my phone. Johnnie didn't even pretend to keep himself busy. He continued to sit staring straight ahead.

I refreshed my email inbox again. Nothing. Where was that urgent life or death email for your immediate attention when you needed it?

'I'm sorry about the song.' He didn't look at me as he spoke.

Last year Johnnie had penned a hit song using me and our troubled history as inspiration. It was a scathing nod to my heart-less nature and called, somewhat unimaginatively, 'Killer'.

'My therapist encourages me to write down my feelings. Sometimes they turn into songs.'

'I've noticed how that seems to happen.' 'Killer' was the second song I'd inspired Johnnie to write. The first, 'Lady', was his very first hit as a solo artist and referenced my older woman allure and the cruel trampling of his delicate heart. It seemed that as much as he complained about our relationship, it had at least proved lucrative for him.

'It's just, it's . . .' He sighed. 'You're difficult to get over, Lex.' He pulled his sunglasses off and for the first time properly looked at me.

'Don't be so dramatic, Johnnie.'

'I mean it. You steamroll into my life, bowl me over with your fun and funniness. And then you're gone. And a life that I was perfectly happy in before feels empty. There's no one stretching in my bed shouting at me to make some bloody toast. No one flinging me up against a wall the minute I walk through the doors. You realise you're impossible, right? You get what you want and don't care how. You're incapable of thinking of anyone but yourself.'

I'd first met Johnnie nearly eight years ago when I was in my late twenties.

I thought back to how I was then.

My life before Will.

He wasn't wrong. Not unlike my now-toddler daughter, I never really saw a world outside of what worked for me. What I wanted. What made me happy.

'But even now, after all these sodding years, there are nights on tour when I put the hotel key card into the lock, watch it go green and open the door wishing I'd find you there waiting. Why the hell did you never give us a chance? I know it wasn't the sex.' He laughed and shook his head. 'Jesus, it can't have been the sex. What was it? What made you not want to stay?'

'I just . . . I . . . I wasn't there yet. I wasn't ready. I was happy having no one. I didn't think I needed anybody.'

'But this guy, this guy you married. What makes him so special? I get that because of what you do you meet some pretty incredible people.' He leaned towards me and lowered his voice. 'Is he some super spy? Can he kill a man with one finger? A high-level scientist who's found the cure for cancer?'

I didn't want to say that Will was a lawyer whose biggest super skill was making a mean gin and tonic, but that I loved him and he made me happy. That together we had fun and that he had changed my life for the better.

It was good to be reminded that I had chosen Will. That he was the only one I ever decided I could have a future with. I thought of the early days when I realised he was different. That we were different. Things might get ropey now and again. And there were days when it was hard to remember that he wasn't just a co-parent, a housemate. That we were more than that. There was us, too, in there. Among all the other stuff. He was in this with me. We were a family before Gigi came along. We chose each other.

Johnnie was staring at me, waiting for a reply.

'It just works, Johnnie. We just work. And that's all I can tell you.'

He pondered this.

'It's OK. I get it. My therapist believes I've had trouble letting you go because I'm so successful and talented and sexually attractive I've never had anyone not do what I want.'

'It sounds like your therapist fancies you.'

116

'Let's be friends. Can you at least give me that? To have someone I can talk to about being a Wolf?' He lowered his voice as he said 'Wolf' and cast a glance at the oblivious driver behind the screen. 'It's tough having to keep a part of what I do secret. I'm getting written off as just a spoiled rockstar. No one knows what I do for my country.' He looked down and shook his head.

Johnnie seemed to have convinced himself he was a patriotic James Bond-type figure. Not just a former boyband singer we'd coerced into a deal to do our bidding with some light low-risk tasks in exchange for making his solo career.

'Friends. Yes. That'd be great.' What else could I say? If we could at least get on it would take the inevitable dread out of having to see him every time our paths crossed at work. But, I mean *friends*? It's not like we'd be meeting up for drinks and discussing life. And I certainly couldn't ever introduce him to Will.

I looked out the window – we'd finally reached the Hogarth Roundabout. The driver pulled off at the Chiswick turn and was making his way down Chiswick Lane.

I leaned over and knocked on the partition at the driver. 'Just drop me here.'

'Is this where you live?' asked Johnnie.

'No but it's close.'

'You don't trust me to know your address?'

'Goodbye, Johnnie.' I got out of the car and headed down the road. I heard the car door slam and felt his arm on mine.

'That's not a proper goodbye. Can't I at least meet him? This man who managed to change your life? Seeing as we're going to be friends and all.'

'Don't be ridiculous. He doesn't even know I know you. Please just get back in the car. This is my neighbourhood. What do you—'

'Alexis? Alexis, is that you?'

I looked up. Fuck. Rochelle was standing on the pavement. Leopard-skin coat and wedge trainers. Shopping bags in her hands. Mouth agape.

Johnnie's arm was still on mine. I shook it off.

'Rochelle. Hi. How are you? I'm just back from a work event.'

She looked up at Johnnie. 'And where exactly do you work again? Hi, Johnnie. Big fan. Alexis and I know each other from nursery. Our daughters are great friends, aren't they, Alexis?'

Johnnie turned to me. 'You ... You have a kid?' His jaw clenched. I guess friends are meant to tell each other stuff like that.

He nodded at Rochelle. 'Nice to meet you. I have to go.' He grabbed me by the shoulders and gave me a hard kiss on the lips. 'Goodbye, Lex.'

Thanks, Johnnie.

He disappeared into his car.

I tried a laugh. 'Oh, those music types. Always so affectionate.'

'How do you know him? You're clearly very close. Did you know him before he was famous? Do you think he'd open the school fair for us?'

'We've known each other years. We, err ...' I pulled my phone out my pocket. 'Oh, I'd better take this,' I said to the blank screen. 'See you, Rochelle.' I put the phone to my ear as I walked off at a fast pace.

I checked my watch. I had just enough time to pick up Gigi and meet with Frederick. With any luck the fact Rochelle was laden with shopping bags meant she was leaving pick-up to her nanny. I couldn't face a further interrogation at the school gates. I looked back over my shoulder. Rochelle was still standing there, watching Johnnie's limousine drive away. She was clearly going to enjoy telling all of Chiswick about my questionable relationship with a world-famous rockstar.

This mission was too close to home in every sense.

It was unnerving knowing the Ghosts were out there, poised to strike. Waiting for the order. How could we protect ourselves when we didn't know how many there were? Or even who they were?

We usually had the whole might of Platform Eight behind us. But now our unit was alone. There would be no one else coming if we needed back-up. We were out here solo. A pack gave us protection. Now we were exposed. And easy to pick off. One by one.

I walked through the park towards the nursery. Three men in T-shirts and paint-splattered jeans were on a bench, drinking cans of beer. Further up ahead two women were pushing prams. A man in a suit. A jogger. A couple of dog walkers.

Just people going about their life.

Or incoming threats.

It was a constant feeling of unease. Never quite knowing when this façade would crack. A seemingly normal tableau would fall apart and all the innocent personas would drop and they would be coming for us.

The only ambush on the school run I wanted to worry about was from a well-meaning mother insisting I come along to a mums' night out.

It was bad enough stressing about whether me working was affecting Gigi emotionally, let alone it being a threat to her actual physical safety. Over-the-top concern about harm coming to your child was one of the staples of parenthood – it was right up there with lack of sleep, unflushed toilets, and having to hide to eat a biscuit.

I was strong. I was capable. I could scan a room and assess the threats. I could work out who could cause me harm. Who I could take in a fight. Who I couldn't. I had confidence as I knew where I stood. I knew what I could do.

But when I looked at Gigi all that confidence fell away. I was vulnerable. She was my walking, talking weak spot.

I took a deep breath. It was just five days I had to get through. Five days of looking over my shoulder and assessing everyone giving me a second glance as a potential threat.

I could do this for five days.

Then I'd take a long overdue blower and spend some proper time with Will.

Keep Peng alive, save the Security Services and get my marriage back on track. As to-do lists went, it was an ambitious one.

Sophia counted to twenty!

Florence rode a bike!

Barnaby wrote his name in cursive script!

Scarlett loves her baby sister and sang a song for her!

Evie didn't wake up Mummy and Daddy and slept the whole night in her bed without Calpol!

A noticeboard was covered with stars listing children's achievements.

I was in the hallway of the nursery Portakabin with Frederick, waiting for the doors to open and our children to be released into the wild.

'What's this?' I motioned towards the board. 'And why doesn't Gigi have one?'

'They're Wow cards. Parents are meant to bring them in whenever they do something you want to make a big deal of.'

'Oh, right.' I racked my brains for something Gigi had done recently that warranted a celebratory public shout-out. She hadn't pooed her pants for a whole week now but I felt that might be an announcement that lowered the tone.

It seemed just to be an avenue for parents to show off about their kids. Well, except for Evie's achievement. That had an air of desperation. And perhaps social services.

The doors opened and the children were dispatched to us one by one.

Florence came first, then Gigi, both brandishing chocolate cupcakes covered in what looked like mini marshmallows.

'Look! Cooking!' shouted Gigi. There was a chocolate smear round her top lip.

'Well done, girls. Come on, let's get home.' We ushered them down the steps and past the other parents waiting to be reunited with their sugar-hyped children.

'Playgound! Playgound!' said Gigi as she ran circles round me.

Florence watched her and added her own quieter, 'Playground. Please?' With any luck Gigi might learn from Florence's exemplary manners, seeing as my attempts hadn't seemed to make much progress.

Frederick checked his watch. 'We can go but only for ten minutes.'

'Thank you, Dada,' said Florence so seriously and quietly I could barely hear her. She stood completely still while Frederick whipped out a handkerchief and rubbed at the tiniest speck of chocolate on her cheek.

The girls ran ahead.

I turned to Frederick. 'We're looking into what Daddy Pig could've been doing when supposedly in Birmingham. Nothing untoward was turned up in any of the Pigs' houses but we now have audio recordings, their mobile phone data and internet histories. With any luck we'll get some leads off that.'

Frederick nodded. 'George Pig took a day off last Thursday. See what you can find out from the wife. He's been distracted this week. He's disappearing off on his mobile a lot.'

My phone pinged. *Royal Mail delivered your item CHINAP-ENG at 12.35 p.m. today.*

'The flight from China has landed. Keeping Peng alive for the next few days is officially now our responsibility.'

Frederick sighed. 'Well, here's to hoping the kids sleep this week.' He ran a hand through his hair and rubbed the back of his neck.

I wondered if it was just his children that were keeping him up at night. Considering he was a Pigeon with no training, he was doing impressively well. He was stepping outside the safety of Six, working alongside us Rats to bring down a Snake. He was putting himself on the line for the greater good. Right now he was one of us.

'Which one usually gets you up?'

'Bloody both. Some nights they tag-team. It's a living hell.'

I would mention this to Will – how this was another reason sticking to one child was a good idea. After a night of being kicked and elbowed by a wriggling Gigi in our bed, this morning I'd woken up to her grinning face right in front of mine. Full of delight at being cosily ensconced between her parents. Chances of her not trying for a repeat tonight were slim.

Frederick looked at me. 'I don't know how you do it. Your work is a lot more high-pressure than mine. I couldn't imagine doing what you do without a full night's sleep. Clearly it makes you even more heroic.' He smiled and gave my shoulder a gentle touch.

Frederick knew what I was capable of. He knew exactly what my job entailed. He knew everything and he liked me more for it. He was impressed by me. By what I could do. I saw myself through his eyes and it felt good.

The girls weaved into the playground.

We took a seat on a bench and watched them. They went straight to the slide. Gigi's thin silver necklace glinted in the sun when she reached the top. It was a St Christopher's medallion. Inside it was a thin GPS tracker that I'd got R & D to carefully insert. I kept reassuring myself it didn't mean I was a crazed helicopter mum. If people could get their dogs microchipped without judgement, surely I should be allowed the reassurance of having my daughter's location constantly updated to a specially modified GigiMap app on my phone?

'Tonight's mission is important.' I looked at Frederick. 'If we don't get the GPS details from Peng's card we have no way of tracking her and it's going to make everything a hell of a lot tougher. You done much work in the field?'

Frederick shook his head. 'Being out in the field for me has meant being in a literal field. Dressed for combat. This undercover sneaking around is new to me.'

Using a Pigeon on a high stakes op like this would usually have been out of the question. But we had no choice. There was no one else left. Jake and Hattie would be out retrieving the iPad receiver from Heathrow airport, while Cameron was busy at the Warehouse with the kind of forceful interrogations Frederick definitely wouldn't have the necessary steel for.

'You'll be fine. Just follow my lead and remember you need to keep a low profile. There could be any number of Tenebris Ghosts at the museum and if you do anything to draw attention to yourself we're all compromised.'

A mother laden down with Sainsbury's bags and two young boys came towards us. 'Sorry, could you?' She motioned to Frederick to move up.

'Of course.' He shuffled up next to me, making space for her and her many bags. We sat, legs touching, as we watched our girls charge around the playground.

It was a sunny day. Gigi was happy. For a moment life felt simple. I could forget about the potential assassination of a foreign dignitary, more dead colleagues and a compromised Platform Eight. And just enjoy the sun on my face, soak up the smiles of my happy child, and the feel of a thigh against mine that wasn't my husband's.

Chapter Nine

THE NATURAL HISTORY MUSEUM was aglow with bright spotlights, the impressive building perfectly lit on a dark night.

By the time I got to the library door my name and invitation had already been checked twice.

Robin was at the entrance in a guard uniform, the security wand in his hand.

'Excuse me, madam, if you don't mind.' He waved it over my black dress with a theatrical flourish. 'Please go in.'

I took a glass of champagne from a hovering waiter and looked around the library.

Six-foot-high red scrolls with beautifully calligraphed black Chinese characters had been hung from the ceiling in each corner of the library.

I was one of the first to arrive. Frederick was already at the back of the room talking to the Foreign Secretary. He was clearly well-connected. I wondered how much was on his own merit or down to the school he'd attended and the privilege he'd been born into.

I shook it off. How was it relevant? I continued to scan the room.

For Robin's modified security wand to read Peng's GPS tracker card, he needed to hold it over it for five seconds. Not an easy task when he couldn't know for sure where exactly it would be. We knew that Minister Peng never carried a handbag, meaning we had to presume it would be in one of her pockets.

There was now a steady trickle of people arriving. I recognised another cabinet minister and two opposition MPs. I spotted at least another five security staff members within the room. The suits, the stance, the not speaking just watching. They were easy to pick out.

Minister Peng walked in. She was thickset with greying hair, wire-rimmed glasses and a ready smile. She was wearing a blue trouser suit and large black pearls. Robin greeted her in Mandarin and continued to talk as he held the security wand over Peng's right jacket pocket. One. Two. Three. Four. Five.

Peng laughed. Maybe Robin was funnier in Mandarin? Peng clapped hands with Robin, shaking them vigorously.

'Bingo! We've got it,' Geraint announced in our earpieces. The wand had successfully cloned the GPS tracker. Geraint was monitoring from our van outside the museum. Now we just needed to retrieve the receiver box from the Etch A Sketch hidden in the Marine Invertebrates room and we were home free.

A waiter came up to Peng with a tray of canapés and she pointed to a spring roll.

'Are there nuts in here?' she asked the waiter brandishing the tray. She spoke clearly with a faint accent. I remembered from her file that she'd lived in England for a year while doing a Masters degree in Buckingham.

'There is a small amount of peanut sauce inside.'

Peng waved the tray away. 'No thank you.'

'G-Force, Peng could have a nut allergy.'

This could be a disaster. If the Coyote was looking for an easy way to kill her, spiking anything and everything with nuts was a simple form of attack. Policing it would be near impossible.

'*Accessing the Foreign Office records on Peng. They must have made a note of it somewhere.*' A few seconds passed and then an: '*It's OK. She does have what's been classed as a mild nut allergy. It's not deadly. Her PA and bodyguard carry EpiPens in case of an attack.*'

I exhaled.

I watched as the room slowly filled up. We needed everyone present before we tried to make a grab for the Etch A Sketch receiver.

Robin crackled into my ear. '*Two security outside library door.*'

I had a simple remit. To cause a disturbance that was big enough to draw waiting security in. But not so big that it would make news or draw attention to anyone monitoring Peng.

I looked up again at the four Chinese scrolls hanging from the ceiling.

I looked across at Frederick. He was now deep in conversation with a white-haired woman who had her hands clasped round his.

'I hate to break things up,' I said into my earpiece. I watched as a small smile formed. 'But you're going to need to let go of your girlfriend and get ready. I'm moving in in three.'

At the back of the library was a narrow spiral staircase leading up to a small mezzanine level. The lack of alcohol and canapés on offer there meant no one had yet ventured up. I quickly ascended, glass of champagne in hand. Party guest going for an explore. At the top of the stairs I could see how each banner was held by a piece of rope in a pulley system that was fastened to each corner of the room. The banners were made of thick parchment with a wooden base. I walked up to the pulley and slipped off my right shoe. With one deft click the heel came off, exposing a thin blade.

My killer heels really were killer.

I used the blade to slice at the rope. I kept going until there were only four strands left. I estimated I had a minute before it snapped.

'*Outside the library. Waiting for your order,*' Frederick crackled in.

I quickly replaced the blade in my shoe and slipped it back on. I descended the stairs and made my way back to the centre of the library where I had a good view of the banner with the sliced rope.

The Foreign Secretary was addressing the room.

'All of us here are very proud to be able to return this ancient scroll to China. Minister Peng, we are honoured that you will be taking it back in person.'

Minister Peng strode over to the Foreign Secretary and the two of them held the scroll together as a cacophony of flashbulbs went off.

It had to happen any second now . . . I saw the banner start to break away and shouted, 'Look out!'

There were panicked cries as people underneath the falling banner rushed out of its way. It landed with a crash on the floor.

I heard Robin in my ear. '*The door is clear.*' The security that had been standing guard outside the library had no doubt come charging in.

'*Go now, Frederick.*'

There were two beats and then, '*I'm in.*'

I watched as security helped the museum staff pick up the banner and move it away. The museum director took to the microphone and was reassuring the crowd with, 'I promise no other works of art will try to kill you.' There were titters but I noticed everyone was moving more to the centre of the room just in case. The two men who had rushed in at the sound of my scream and the crash of the banner hitting the ground talked to their three colleagues. They were all scanning the room.

'*I have the control box,*' said Frederick. The small box concealed within the Etch A Sketch could be swiftly pulled out and discreetly hidden inside a pocket.

I moved towards the door. We needed to make a fast exit.

Through the earpiece I heard, '*Sir, what are you doing in here?*'

Dammit. There must have been extra security we either missed, or they'd been called in for the disturbance.

'I was just making a phone call.'

'You didn't see the "no entry" sign?'

'What? No, sorry, I didn't. Look, I'm going, OK. Excuse me. Please move.'

'We're going to have to search you, sir.'

I walked quickly across the corridor and shoved open the door to the Marine Invertebrates room. It slammed hard against the wall. The three men turned to look at me.

I stared at Frederick. 'There you are! What the hell are you playing at?

'I . . . I . . .'

'Finding a little place to sneak off to call her? Give me your phone right now. If I find you've been talking to that slag again,

I swear to God I'm leaving you and taking you for everything you've got.'

'Now calm down, sweetheart.'

'Don't you dare tell me to calm down. You give me your phone right now.'

'Can we talk about this at home?'

'What? I'm making a scene, am I? Embarrassing you in front of your new friends? Well, you should've thought about that before you started fucking around.'

'Can you both please leave this area?' said the taller of the two men.

I turned to him. 'I'm leaving this area. And I'm leaving him. You hear that? I'm leaving you, you piece of shit.' I turned and stalked out.

Frederick followed behind me. 'Darling, please let's talk about this.'

'Don't you bloody touch me.'

I sped ahead fast.

Frederick was right behind me and headed for the exit. 'We're exiting now. Control box is secure. Confirm no one following.'

We quickly climbed into the back of the waiting van.

Robin crackled in. '*No tails. Security still outside the Marine Invertebrates room shaking their heads. Not a bad performance, new boy.*'

'Just keeping up with the boss.' He smiled as he said this. We locked eyes.

Geraint leaned round. 'I can run you both back.'

'Thanks, G.'

I broke eye contact with Frederick. Jesus, I had to get a grip.

I brought out my phone to busy myself with writing an email update to the rest of Whistle.

No matter how much I tried to ignore it, there was an attraction between us.

Simmering.

Everything about Frederick shouted about how in control he was.

Except the way he looked at me. As if I was something to be devoured. I could read everything in that look. And he knew it. He wanted me to know it.

I see you.

I want you.

What it'd be like to have you.

This was ridiculous.

I was with Will. I was happy.

Wasn't I?

Will thought we were in trouble.

Will was receiving middle-of-the-night text messages.

Why hadn't I just asked him about it? Or checked his phone? Was it better to admit I didn't trust him? Or to trust him and never know?

It had to be nothing.

He wouldn't cheat on me.

Would he?

Will thought we were in trouble.

Will was receiving middle-of-the-night text messages.

And I was making eyes at a colleague.

Goddammit.

We were in trouble.

And Frederick?

He was just a flirtation.

A harmless, passing flirtation.

One of those reminders that were far and few between where I felt like a woman. Fanciable.

Fuckable.

Not just a mother.

It was harmless. Totally harmless.

As long as the only action that happened around him was violent.

Part Three

Cling

cling, *v.*
1. Adhere or stick firmly or closely to; be hard to part or remove from.
2. Remain persistently or stubbornly faithful to.

From: 88888@site-optimisation.com
To: lex.tyler@platform-eight.co.uk
Subject: Increase your Google rankings!!!!!
MISSION: #80521
UNIT: WHISTLE
DATE: Wednesday 2nd October
ALERT: 4 DAYS UNTIL PENG'S DEPARTURE

Chapter Ten

A MAP OF KNIGHTSBRIDGE was projected onto the meeting-room whiteboard. Hattie stood in front of it leading our morning briefing. His large frame blocked most of the image; a blue dot flashing at the Mandarin Oriental hotel on Hyde Park was just visible at his right elbow.

'It's confirmed Peng is in there. Cloning the GPS card reader was a success. And having retrieved the listening devices from Heathrow we now have a rough schedule of exactly what Peng is going to be doing for the whole time she's here.'

I was seated at the dining table between Jake and Cameron, all of us clutching large Pret-a-Manger coffees. The canteen's coffee machine had broken and none of us knew how to fix it. Pixie and Geraint were opposite us, their laptops in front of them, Pixie resplendent in a purple unicorn jumper and a feathered blue and green headband, Geraint rocking a grey T-shirt with what looked like a ketchup stain down the front.

Hattie looked round at us all. 'Good work and well done, everyone. We now have enough intel that we have a decent shot at protecting Peng from the Coyote.'

We all exchanged glances. The sincerity in Hattie's praise was still hard to get used to considering our previous unit leader only got as nice as: 'Well, it seems you don't have total shit for brains.'

'Let's start this update briefing with Peng's movements over the next few days.' Hattie motioned towards the whiteboard where Peng's schedule was now projected. 'Robin translated everything Peng and the delegation discussed on the Heathrow recordings. This is a fully up-to-date schedule.

'While Peng is here in the UK she's going to be heavily protected by Parliamentary and Diplomatic Protection Officers. I've cleared it with the Met Police for us all to have temporary IDs. It means we all now have an official reason to be in the vicinity of Peng at all times. Considering how tight security at both the Foreign Office and the Chinese Embassy is, it's low risk the Coyote will strike at those locations. Robin is with Peng now at the Embassy.'

Jake looked round the room. 'I thought it was surprisingly peaceful in here.'

Geraint cleared his throat. 'Robin checked in a half-hour ago to say Peng's first meeting had started and that none of the Protection Officers' mobile phones work there. They must have some kind of signal blockers. It means if we ever need to make contact with anyone at the Embassy, use the police radio frequency only.'

'This Wycombe shoot that's on the schedule for Saturday' – Jake motioned towards the whiteboard – 'I'm guessing it isn't in London.'

'It's at Cherwell Castle, Lord Wycombe's estate in Oxfordshire. Lord Wycombe runs a hedge fund but the family business, in which he still has a substantial stake, is a plane-building company that is hoping to sign a joint venture with China. This is why he's pulling out all the stops to give Peng the full English aristocratic experience of staying in a castle, shooting pheasant, and being guest of honour at a four-course black-tie dinner for a hundred and fifty people. Peng and the delegation drive back to London on Sunday morning and that afternoon attend an exhibition and auction of Asian contemporary artists at Christie's before heading back to China on a ten p.m. flight.'

I said, 'Peng is attending an event where she's going to be surrounded by people holding loaded shotguns?' Just when we thought the security aspect of this mission couldn't get any more challenging.

Hattie nodded. 'It's going to be impossible to vet everyone at the shoot and the dinner, not to mention the risks involved in an overnight stay in a private residence with multiple entry points.'

'Can I go to this castle?' asked Cameron. 'It sounds like the fairy tale Britain I actually want to see – not this,' she gestured round the room, 'grotty underground reality of—'

I cut her off before she could launch into another attack on the Platform, London, us. 'Can't we just advise her security detail for her to not attend?' Considering we were up against an unknown hostile in an unknown location, our chances of keeping Peng alive were slim.

'It's the main event of Peng's whole trip to the UK. There's not just the potential joint venture with Wycombe's family business at stake but all those attending the dinner are big powerhouses in the aviation business. There is no way they would cancel. Especially as we can't give them information on what the threat exactly is.'

I saw now how it was urgent we found the Snake and Coyote as soon as possible. Having to try and protect Peng at the shoot was going to be a logistical nightmare.

Hattie leaned over to Geraint's laptop and pressed a button. The whiteboard updated to a photo of a pretty Chinese woman in her twenties. The text next to it stated she was 'Ling Ling Chuan, Minister Peng's PA.'

'Next step: we need access to Ling Ling's Dictaphone so we can install a bug. Being able to listen in on every meeting they have will give us a major operational advantage.'

'Any chance of doing it today?' I asked.

'Ling Ling is at the Embassy all day with Peng. I'm going to join Robin there as soon as we've finished here but it's unlikely we'll get an opportunity to get close enough to her to do it.'

As Protection Officers they would be able to keep watch on Peng and intervene if there was any incoming threat, but getting to Ling Ling's Dictaphone without being noticed would not be easy.

'Robin and I will keep an eye on her movements. Wherever Ling Ling goes after the Embassy could present an opportunity for us to get to the Dictaphone.'

Hattie nodded at Geraint and the whiteboard screen updated to three columns, each headed up with photos of Ronald Bowcott, Suzannah Sheldon and Neil Hicks.

'Let's move on to the three Pigs.' Hattie turned to Geraint and Pixie. 'Now you've been through all the data and recordings, anything to note?'

'No obvious red flags,' said Geraint. 'It seems the only conversations the couples have are what to have for dinner, what to watch on TV. And then silence.'

I was tempted to interject with: 'It could be a companionable silence.'

'There are no hushed phone calls and there's no unusual internet activity – apart from George Pig's wife Kate googling herself ten times a day,' added Pixie.

'She's an actress,' I offered.

'Oh. Right. Well, yeah, that explains that then.'

Geraint said, 'The only questionable contact to note is George Pig receiving unusual emails to his private account. We've been working on them for the last few hours and if they're in code we can't crack it.'

'What address are they from?' asked Hattie.

'Just a random Hotmail address that isn't in his contacts,' said Pixie. 'The last couple said, *While I slice the final sandwich, tell me how you won the prize* and, *He will travel further than the end of the world in search of a worthy person.*'

'They sound like junk or a phishing scam,' said Jake.

'We thought that at first too,' said Geraint, 'but they go straight into his inbox. And he reads them. He's been getting them every week for the last month.'

'Frederick told me he had a day off last Thursday. It could be linked to that. Look into his movements that day and see what comes up.'

Geraint tapped into his laptop and '*Coded emails, day off Thursday*' came up under George Pig's photo.

'Peppa's been textin' someone on a pay-as-you-go mobile,' said Pixie. 'They seem to be trying to set up a meet – lots of back and forth with times, dates and locations. Soon as they sort a definite plan we'll let you know.'

'*Texts with Unknown Subject*' was added to Peppa Pig's column.

'Daddy Pig emailed a man called Daniel Wheal, a banker at Goldman Sach, saying he would meet him at the Christie's Asian art exhibition on Sunday for the "handover",' said Geraint. 'We can't find anything on Wheal. He seems legit.'

The fact Daddy Pig had arranged a meet at an event where Peng would be in attendance, combined with his night away, made him my current leading choice for being the Snake.

'How are we doing on where Daddy Pig was when he was meant to be away in Birmingham?'

'There was no sign of Daddy Pig after leaving the office at 7.34 p.m.,' announced Geraint. 'Nothing on his credit cards. His mobile phone remained in the vicinity of Vauxhall the whole night.'

I frowned. 'Sounds like he could've left his phone at the office and gone walkabout. Naomi reported Daddy Pig has another Birmingham trip planned for Friday. Have we learned anything from their online history?'

Geraint looked up. 'There's been a lot of activity on Daddy Pig's home computer. But it looks more like only the wife uses it.'

'How can you be sure?' I asked.

Geraint tilted his laptop screen towards me.

Google: Normal to wee a bit when sneeze?

Google: How to strengthen pelvic floor?

Google: Strong pelvic floor better for sex?

Google: Reasons husband not interested in sex

Google: How many times a year need to have sex so marriage not classed sexless?

Google: Does it matter if marriage sexless?

www.dailymail.co.uk/marriages-need-sex-to-survive

www.dailymail.co.uk/seven-day-diet-cleanse

www.dailymail.co.uk/poldark-hottie-strips-off

www.amazon.co.uk/poldark-boxset

'Right. I see your point.'

'I've double-checked the security of the links. They're all genuine. There aren't any dummy websites leading through to a chatroom.'

'Keep monitoring everything just in case,' said Hattie as Geraint added '*Birmingham trips, Daniel Wheal*' to Daddy Pig's column.

Pixie looked over at me. 'Poppet, did you spot anything out of place in Daddy Pig's emails from the children's schools?'

I shook my head. 'Nothing jumped out as suspicious or coded.' I'd skimmed through the folder Pixie emailed me on the tube this morning and, after reading the tenth letter from the school on subjects ranging from nit infestations to name-taping requirements, I was starting to dread just exactly what lay ahead. There was so much to remember.

'OK, so these,' Hattie motioned to the three Pigs' columns, 'are our working leads. G and Pixie, you focus on chasing these down. And Lex and Frederick can keep working on getting us some more.'

The slide on the whiteboard was now replaced with a list of thirty names. Four of which had a line through.

'Hackers,' Hattie announced. 'How's it going, Jake and Cameron?'

'Slow-going,' said Jake, 'but we're getting there. We're working through the list by area. Trying to save time by focusing our interrogations to a designated postcode.'

'It'd be much quicker if you approved the cattle-prod,' added Cameron.

'It's not happening, Cameron,' Hattie told her. 'Remember, you find just one hacker that works for Tenebris and we can shut them down. Keep at it. Within reason.' He shot a look at Cameron.

The whiteboard changed again, this time to a photo of a clown.

'Not this guy,' groaned Jake. 'I hate the creepy sod.'

'I got confirmation from one of my sources an hour ago that the Clown is in town and meeting with a contact this afternoon about an upcoming hit. There is a strong chance he could be the Coyote the Chinese People's Alliance have hired to assassinate Peng.'

The Clown was a notorious Spanish assassin. The only photos of him on file were in full make-up and costume. No one had any idea of his real name or what he really looked like. In the days leading up to a kill he would never not be in character, hiding out in the open. People may always remember a clown but what did it matter if you couldn't ever find them? Or describe them? And it meant anywhere he went while tracking his target his real face was never seen. If he were here now in London, prepping for a hit, arranging a meet, that would mean he would be in costume. And there were only so many places a clown could hang out during the day without drawing undue attention.

'Are there any circuses currently in town?'

'Checkin' now,' said Pixie. There was a flurry of key tapping and then, 'No circuses. Closest we have is a funfair that's on at Ravenscourt Park.'

'A funfair is a good place for a clown assassin to arrange a meet with someone,' I said. 'He'll be wanting to pick up the intel face to face. The noise, the chaos will mean they don't worry about anyone listening.'

'Lex, you've met him before. Head down there and try and find him. Talk to him peer-to-peer. If it's not him he might know who did book the job.'

'The funfair doesn't open until lunchtime,' said Pixie. 'So an afternoon meet there fits.'

'I can go after I've picked up Gigi from school.'

'Take Frederick with you. If the Clown is the Coyote then Frederick might recognise whoever he's meeting. If the Snake isn't going in person they could send someone in their circle.'

The whiteboard screen now showed a black slide with just a quote in white cursive script on it.

'What you seek is seeking you – Rumi.'

Whereas our previous unit leader would end briefings with vicious swear words and a graphic description of the violence we could be subjected to if we screwed up, Hattie liked to finish on an inspirational quote. Yes, it doubled as a warning, but in a much more tactful way.

'You all know what you need to do. Let's get on with catching ourselves a Snake and a Coyote.'

I checked my watch. It was time to depart for a WAF meeting at George Pig's house. A coffee morning followed by picking up Gigi from nursery and taking her to a funfair.

It was great getting to do normal mum things.

Just with the small ulterior motive of trying to locate a traitor who was compromising the existence of the Security Services.

Chapter Eleven

INTERROGATIONS USUALLY TAKE PLACE in a box-like room. Food and water are withheld. Questions are fired at the target until they relent.

Undercover attempts to garner information were much more pleasant. Here we were in Kate and George Pig's very beautiful, very white home, sipping on soy lattes.

Kate had started to unburden her frustrations at George Pig never getting up in the night:

'He says there's no way he can decide on matters of national security without a full night's sleep and that me doing it is helping keep the country safe.'

Naomi on Daddy Pig coming home drunk:

'He claimed it was part of his cover. He must think I'm stupid.'

Dionne on Peppa not being able to get home at a designated time:

'She says, "I can't tell the President of Brazil's security team we need to cut this meeting short as my nanny has dinner plans."'

Kate on George Pig forgetting a wedding anniversary:

'He missed all my hints about a weekend at Babington House. Ignored the Tiffany's brochure with the earmarked pages. Claimed that it was because the week before he'd been testing an experimental truth serum and a side effect was memory loss.'

Kate bit her lip. 'Yes, jewellery would've been nice but it's more about being reminded that you matter, that you haven't been forgotten about.'

Naomi reached over and patted her hand before reaching for the coffee pot and filling up everyone's mugs. She fussed over us all: tucking in Dionne's jumper label, mopping up a splash of milk off the countertop, handing a tissue to Camilla the second she sneezed.

'I totally get what you're saying, Kate,' said Dionne as she curled a finger around one of her plaited pigtails. 'Sometimes I really feel a hug or a "Hey, wow, Dionne, aren't you doing great?" would make me feel like I was really valued.'

I thought, considering the amount Peppa was paying her, Dionne should get over the lack of hugs and compliments. She was leaving at the end of the month to go back to Australia. I figured losing her nanny was a point against Peppa being the Snake. Surely the stress of finding replacement childcare would rule out having the time to sideline in betraying your country.

I looked over at Camilla. In her tailored black trousers and striped silk shirt she looked the part of efficient businesswoman but she didn't seem able to fully engage with whatever we were talking about. She'd drift off towards the garden while we were in the middle of a conversation. Seated at the table, untouched cup of coffee in front of her, she had only nodded vacantly to my enthused declaration that our daughters were friends and that we lived close to each other. I wondered if Frederick knew this when he married her. That she was a beautiful Barbie doll living in another world. I pictured her in her slick Mayfair gallery. Files piled up on her desk as she stared out the window. Had she always been like this? Had he once found it charming? Why did I care? I shook it off.

By the time the coffee morning was drawing to a close the only mission-relevant information I'd learned was that Daddy Pig had cancelled dinner tonight with Naomi and her mother. A man avoiding spending time with his mother-in-law was normal behaviour opposed to suspicious, but we needed to know exactly what he was doing instead.

'My mother will be so disappointed,' Naomi was continuing to fret.

'I haven't spoken to my mother in two years. She hasn't even met the twins,' said Kate.

'Oh Kate. I'm so sorry.' Naomi's eyes filled with tears.

'No, it's fine. I'm OK with it. She's a total bitch.'

Which kind of drew an end to the conversation.

By the time I got up to leave, the women were swapping Instagram handles. They were officially becoming friends.

'Hello, parents,' Ms Yvonne greeted the crowd of us waiting from the top of the Portakabin steps. 'We've had such fun with our artwork today. We've been learning how to paint like Picasso. Lots to take home for Mummy and Daddy.'

Great. More crap to leave in a pile in the corner of the kitchen for a few weeks before I guiltily dropped it in the bin once Gigi was in bed.

Frederick joined me. 'More art? We're running out of space.' He looked so earnest in this concern I didn't feel I could share with him my storage area for the more questionable pieces.

As we left the nursery courtyard I briefed Frederick on this afternoon's funfair operation.

He pulled out his phone. 'I'll let Camilla know I won't be back until later.'

Gigi and Florence were twenty feet behind us, plodding along slowly, each laden down with their art folders. I went to join them as Frederick spoke to Camilla.

I knew how to get them to speed up. 'Girls, we've got great news for you. We're going to the funfair now.'

'Hurrah hurrah hurrah.' The two of them jumped up and down. Gigi flung herself at me. 'Best mama ever.'

They both thrust their folders into my arms and skipped ahead.

I re-joined Frederick as he was returning his phone to his pocket. 'Do you ever,' he turned to look at me, 'think about how often you need to lie to the person you're married to?'

'We don't lie about the big stuff. That has to count for something.' Frederick was not the person to be opening up to over any marriage insecurities I might be having.

'But there's a big part of your life, a big part of you, that this person you share a home with, share a family with, knows nothing about.' He chewed his lip. 'I often think if Camilla knew how high-pressured the job could be maybe I'd get more support from her.'

'How so?'

'Camilla is . . . Well, she finds a lot of things difficult. I try and help as much as I can. What's important to me is that Arthur and Florence are well looked after. Camilla just needs a little reminding of that now and again.'

Frederick was only confirming my opinion of Camilla. I guessed she'd grown up privileged and didn't need to work for anything. Didn't need to concentrate on mundane day-to-day details as she'd always had someone else to do it for her. She could float around enjoying living in a nice house, going for nice lunches and do some light dabbling in the art world to feel she had something to say for herself at dinner parties. But surely no matter how privileged she was nothing made you stop being selfish more than having children? It wasn't about you anymore but them. That was pretty much the first lesson of parenthood. It was strange that she hadn't shifted her focus.

'Adjusting to motherhood can be tough. I know it didn't come easily to me at first. It's still not easy. There's always a worry you could be doing more. That you could be doing better.'

'Come on, you're killing it. Anyone can see that.'

I glowed a little.

And tried not to think of how Will never congratulated me on what I was doing right. That he just drew attention to what I was doing wrong. Kate was right when she'd been complaining about George Pig. We all needed to feel valued. To feel cared about.

And I wasn't getting that from Will. He wasn't a partner wanting to help me solve problems, he was just being the problem. Calming him down was just another task to tick off an ever-growing to-do list.

He was right when he said we were in trouble.

But until now I hadn't realised how much.

Chapter Twelve

FUNFAIRS WERE CUNNINGLY DESIGNED child-catching traps. Bright flashing lights, bright coloured rides and bright E-numbered snacks. Everything shouted: 'This is where all the fun is had and if your parents don't take you they don't really love you!'

I looked round at the mini rollercoaster, the spinning tea-cups and the lurching plane rides and tried to forget one of the many *Daily Mail* articles my mother-in-law had sent me about funfairs' poor health and safety implementations leading to severe concussions and crippled children.

'Mama mama mama, look look look!' Gigi pointed to a woman pushing a cart advertising Haribo ice cream. 'Please please please?'

I sighed. If we were going to go for the full funfair experience we might as well load them up with sugar and sweets to puke out on one of the rides.

As I went to pay I turned to Florence. 'Do you want one?' She shook her head. Of course she didn't. Her exemplary behaviour even extended to not having a sweet tooth.

I looked around at the funfair and motioned towards the bouncy castle. 'Let's set the kids up there.'

The massive Mickey Mouse-decorated bouncy castle, with several different turrets and a netted centre that contained a giant ball pit, looked the least likely to sever limbs.

'How much?' Frederick asked the surly man in front of the velvet rope cordoning off entrance to the bouncy castle.

'Ten quid – ten minutes.'

'Seriously?'

The man just held out his hand. Gigi and Florence had already ducked under the rope and were tugging off their shoes. Frederick and I each handed over a ten-pound note.

'I don't care if they get bored after two minutes,' I said, 'they're staying on there until he drags them off. Unless . . . do you think we can expense it?'

He laughed. It was a nice sound. 'Are you going to eat that?' He motioned towards Gigi's melting ice cream.

'No, you can have it.' I held it up to him, implying for him to take it. But instead he leaned down and took a bite of it. So yes. There it was. I had just fed him ice cream.

'Thanks,' he said.

We stood there staring at each other.

'I . . . I meant, take the whole thing. Really, it's fine. I don't want any of it.'

'You should have a bite at least.'

There was no way to lick an ice cream in front of someone staring at you without it looking suggestive.

'Lex!'

I spun round to see my friends Shona and Frankie. Shona's five-year-old daughter Willow was next to her, holding her hand and clasping a violin case in the other.

'You're here too! How great.' I thought fast. Everything was fine. Nothing to see here. No homicidal clowns to meet. No Chinese ministers to save. I was just at a funfair with a school-run dad. I looked across at Frederick. Maybe they wouldn't notice his piercing blue eyes, chiselled jaw, broad shoulders and toned torso all packaged together in a perfectly cut suit.

'Shona and Frankie, this is Frederick. Our daughters are at nursery together.'

They both looked at him. 'Hello,' they chorused. Frankie may have smirked.

'Owwwwwwww!' Over on the bouncy castle Florence let out a cry. She was lying stricken on the mat.

Frederick said, 'Apologies, I just need to . . .' and he charged off to Florence.

Shona and Frankie both watched him leave and then turned to look at me.

I took in their raised eyebrows. 'What?'

'What are you doing?' asked Shona.

'I'm just . . . it's a funfair. We were both coming here anyway so thought we might as well come together.'

Frankie was shaking her head the whole time I was talking. 'No, no, no. The ice cream licking, the laughing, the eye' – she looked down at Willow – 'fudging. This is trouble.'

How long had they been watching us?

'Two people of the opposite sex can be friends.'

'You're choosing that guy, Mr Male Model, as a platonic friend?' said Frankie. The two of them fell about laughing.

'You told me I needed to make more effort with the parents at Gigi's nursery, so I am.'

'Have you learned anyone else's name?'

'Of course. I know . . . Rochelle.'

'Isn't she the one that fancies Will?' asked Shona.

'And you hate her,' finished Frankie.

'Yes but I've learned her name.'

Frederick came back up to us. Florence's tears had dried and she was now back bouncing alongside Gigi.

'Crisis averted.'

'Mama, we need to go. The concert starts soon.' Willow was tugging on Shona's hand.

Shona checked her watch. 'OK, OK, we're going. Nice to meet you, Frederick.'

'Yes, very nice to meet you, Frederick,' added Frankie with a smile. 'Lex, we'll talk to you later.'

'Clown,' said Frederick, interrupting my thoughts about how I was going to cope with the WhatsApp assault later.

I looked towards where he was pointing. Over by the carousel was a clown in a bright yellow outfit with enormous red fluffy buttons and a rainbow ruffle around his neck. His full face of white make-up was complete with painted-on black eyebrows, elongated black eyelashes and giant red lips. The look was finished with a spiky red wig and a stuck-on red nose. He was leaning against the side of the carousel with his arms crossed. I looked down at his feet. No comedy big shoes, just combat boots. The rest of his costume may be different but he had been wearing those same boots and the spiky red wig the last time we met.

'Keep an eye on the girls.' I handed him the ice cream.

'Hello. Remember me?'

The Clown observed me as he put a cigarette in his mouth.

'I don't think you should.' I motioned to the many children running around.

The Clown said nothing as he pulled a lighter out of his over-sized pocket and lit it. He took a long drag and blew the smoke in my face.

'How's Hake?' The Clown's thick Spanish accent was suppos-edly the reason he always pronounced Jake like this, although I was sure it was just because he knew it irritated the hell out of him.

'He's good.'

'I keep waiting for him to leave you do-gooders and become one of us.'

'Lucky for you he's staying put. You'd never book a job again with him on the market.'

The Clown shrugged. 'Maybe true. But worthy competition keeps us all at the top of our game.'

'Are you in town for the Peng job? If you are we need to talk.'

'And why would I talk to you?'

'Because you don't want to piss me off. You Coyotes are out there on your own and we're a pack. Remember, this is our town. You upset one of us and you upset all of us.' I took a step closer towards him. 'And you know what they say about Rats. You're never too far away from one.'

The Clown took another few long drags and then stubbed his cigarette out on the side of the carousel. 'I am in town for work. Not this Peng you talk of, though. Getting close to my target will require my particular level of expertise.' He gave a wave across his made-up face. 'I'm here for,' he leaned closer to me, 'Adam Pants.'

'Is that some kind of codename?'

'I thought you would've heard of him. He's a kids' entertainer. Very popular.'

'What the hell has he done to get a hit out on him? Handed out too much sugar? Not made the birthday boy feel special enough?'

The Clown frowned. 'You don't know about the drugs?'

'What drugs?'

'There's a pretty big market for it in the kiddie entertainer world. My employers have it covered but Mr Pants has been trying to muscle in and start his own supply chain.'

'I . . . what? That can't be right?'

'Have you ever seen a children's entertainer perform? You think anyone has that type of energy naturally? That kind of patience? Come on. They're all on uppers, downers, anything that can get them through a gig. They have a faster burn-out rate than professional athletes.'

I thought of Prehistoric Pete and how naïve it was to think they all just ran off shattered showbiz dreams and an enthusiasm to make kids smile.

'Have you heard about the Peng job? It's happening here in London.'

The Clown shook his head. 'No one's approached me about it and I haven't heard anyone else muttering about it. But then you know us Coyotes.' He leaned towards me. 'It's not like we all hang out together swapping stories on who's popping who.'

'You don't know of any other Coyotes currently in town?'

'I haven't heard of any that are and I haven't seen any. I only landed this morning and this is where I'm meeting my contact for the Pants information. In fact, you need to go. You could be scaring them off.'

'You'd better not be lying to me.' I had to bite my lip to stop myself adding, 'Or I'll wipe that smile off your face.' He must get that a lot.

'That's why I've told you the name of my target. When he hits the news you know I'm not lying. I am telling you everything. Playing nicely. So you and your pack can leave me alone. *Comprendez?*'

I nodded. 'We'll be happier once you're out the country.' I walked away from the carousel, back towards the bouncy castle.

Gigi and Florence were now in a pink glittery train carriage and doing royal waves out their windows at Frederick. I came up alongside him.

'The Clown is here on a job. But his target's not Peng. He's here to top Adam Pants.'

'The kids' entertainer? I saw him perform at a third birthday party last week. Very impressive.' Frederick thought for a moment. 'Must be some kind of drugs hit, right?'

'How did you know?'

'If you've got thirty kids trying to honk your nose and pull your pants down and you're still smiling, there must be some of kind of chemical help.'

'He hadn't even heard of the Peng job so couldn't give us any clues on who the Coyote booked for it is.' I blew kisses at Gigi as she went round again.

'I believe him. We should go.'

The train ground to a halt and the girls climbed out their carriages and came bounding over to us.

'Where next, Mama, where next?'

'It's home time, Gigi.' I braced myself for the inevitable tantrum.

'We going back on bus?'

156

'Yes.'

'OK. I love bus.'

'Me too. I love bus,' said Florence. It was good to know that next time they wanted to go to a funfair we could save fifty quid and just stay on the 94.

We took our respective daughters by the hand and headed towards the exit.

I looked back across the noise and colour of the funfair rides. I could still see the Clown leaning against the side of the carousel.

Gigi spotted him too. 'Look, Mummy, a clown! I love clowns.'

'Not that one, darling. Not that one.'

He gave me a slow wave.

All Gigi's books featuring clowns would be going in the bin as soon as we got home.

Chapter Thirteen

Down at the Platform it was eerily quiet without the sounds of the other Rats scurrying around. I left the lift and walked down the corridor. There was no flickering of the lights as an interviewee was interrogated. No intermittent moans escaping from the soundproofed doors. No sounds of cutlery hitting plates from the canteen as the thirty-strong workforce fuelled up with fry-ups and caffeine. No howls from the gym as Rats pounded punchbags, or each other. No clinks from the weight machines as they pushed themselves to keep lifting.

It was too peaceful. Just the rumble of the tubes that passed alongside our network of offices and tunnels.

Only Geraint and Pixie were in our office; the others were all out watching Peng or tormenting hackers. Pixie seemed to be vigorously wiping at the ketchup stain on Geraint's T-shirt as he typed. Geraint stood up as I walked in.

'Babe, I hadn't finished yet,' complained Pixie.

'It's fine,' he huffed. 'Lex, I think we've found where Daddy Pig went when he claimed to be in Birmingham last week. I got this CCTV of him entering this block of flats.'

Geraint pressed a few buttons and grainy CCTV footage was projected up onto the whiteboard. 'He enters at 7.43 p.m. Can't see him exiting but there is an underground car park.'

'Dammit. So he could've met anyone in there and left at any point. Anyone we know live in that building?'

'Waiting to get the building tenancy records. Lots of these flats get sub-let on the cheap so hard to work out who's actually living there.'

'Start rolling the lobby footage of people arriving from six p.m. We might spot someone familiar.'

We all stared at the black and white footage of people walking into the lobby.

'There are so many of them,' complained Geraint, 'it's going to take ages to run them all through the system.'

We kept watching as another flood of people entered.

One woman in a suit was scratching her head as she waited for the lift. Something jogged in my mind.

I tapped the screen. 'Run her through the system.'

Pixie zoomed in on her face and clicked a few buttons. 'How did you know, darlin'? Vicki Forbes works for Six. Executive Assistant on the second floor.'

'Marital status? Children?'

'Single. No kids.'

'She's got nits,' I announced.

All heads swivelled back to the screen. She kept scratching her head.

'Daddy Pig and the whole family have just had nits.' I remembered a circular from the school. *Please be advised there have been several cases of nits reported in your child's class. Please make sure the whole family follow the below instructions for treatment.* Their Amazon history had also showed an order for an industrial-sized bottle of nit lotion and several combs.

'So you think . . .' started Geraint.

'I think Daddy Pig, who has just had nits courtesy of his kids, entering a building where a colleague, who has no children but can't stop scratching her head, happens to live, is too much of a coincidence. Check her credit cards. Look for footage of the two of them going into that building around the same time on other dates.'

If Daddy Pig's lying about his movements was simply down to cheating, at least that was progress. All that was left was the questionable meet he'd arranged at the Christie's auction. We just needed to completely rule him out and we could focus all our efforts on the two remaining Pigs.

'I've got another lead on George Pig,' said Pixie. 'Last week when he took that day off he flew to Zurich. I'm hacking any historic CCTV feeds of that day, focusing on streets with private banks. If he's the Snake it could be where he's hidin' the cash.'

We were getting closer. I could feel it.

Making it back home in time for Gigi's dinner, I had naively thought that hanging out with my daughter would be a welcome break from the high pressure of work. In the stark grey Platform, I always imagined sitting down for a cosy dinner with Gigi while we discussed her day was something I was sad to be missing. But by the time she'd refused to eat the pesto pasta I'd made her as it was too green, by the time she'd thrown the carrots I'd lovingly peeled and chopped on the floor, I was wishing I was back in the sanctuary of the Platform where people were actually scared of me.

'Eat three mouthfuls.'

'No.'

'Two mouthfuls.'

'No mouthfuls.' She clamped her mouth shut. 'Yucky. Horrible. Dis-GUSTING.' She pushed her plate away.

As criticism of my cooking went it was pretty harsh. Especially considering I'd splashed out on the fresh pesto, not the jar kind. I tried to comfort myself with the fact I shouldn't hold too high the culinary opinion of someone whose idea of a perfect dinner was a slice of bread covered in ketchup.

'Come on, Gigi, two mouthfuls and then yummy pudding.'

She shook her head.

'Don't. Want. It.' She cupped her chin with her hands and stared at me. Blue eyes unwavering.

After an hour of this I retreated. I crammed two chocolate biscuits into my mouth while hidden behind a cupboard door, wondering why I could negotiate with terrorists but not my two-year-old. She could clearly sense weakness. The no-television-for-a-week threat was a bluff. We both knew it.

Being a parent grounded you. Children didn't care what you did out there, you existed solely for them. Last month, a day that had started with the adrenaline-high of armed combat and apprehending a target off our most-wanted list had ended with me fishing a poo out of the bath.

For children, parents' only purpose was to make them happy; to provide, to soothe, to hold. The noise of expectation of what we should've achieved, where our lives were going – all of that was quiet with them. You were just a happiness-enabler, a hug-giver, biscuit-provider, bottom-wiper, story-reader. All they wanted was you. To do exactly what they wanted. With such simplicity it should be peaceful.

'Neeeee nawwww neeee nawwww,' Gigi was now shouting as she rolled a police car up and down the kitchen floor.

But kids were fucking noisy.

By the time she was down after eight stories and three different last-minute requests for toys she just couldn't sleep without, I was exhausted. I slumped down at the kitchen table opposite Will. His tie was off and an open beer was in his hand. A large pizza box was on the table.

'Can we talk now about getting away somewhere?'

'Let me speak to work. I'll see what I can do.' I wondered how long I could stall him for.

He took a sip of beer. 'I feel I never really know what's going on with you.'

'Don't say that. I tell you everything,' I lied.

'Most of the time you're in your own little world. You're here but you're not really here. Who knows where your mind is.'

I reached a hand over to his. 'You realise I'm probably just wondering if I've missed the editing cut-off time for the Ocado order?' I wanted to ask, 'And what about you? Who the hell is messaging you in the middle of the night?' But I didn't. When it came to inappropriate contact I didn't really feel I had the moral high ground. A few hours ago I had fed another man ice cream.

'How was your work today?' I wanted to get him off the subject of my job and onto his. As he started telling me about his day, I thought about how maybe he would be better off with someone like Rochelle. An easier life with a wife who wouldn't lie to him nearly daily. A wife who would be interested when he talked about his work and not zone out and start wondering what pizza toppings were inside the delicious-smelling box on the table.

I had no excuse – no matter how packed my brain was with information for the security of this country, no matter how much I needed to try and keep track of childcare arrangements for Gigi and worry she was getting everything she needed, I should be able to spare a thought for Will. And at least listen when he tells me about the large shipping case that he just won against the . . . I want to say pirates but that can't be right. Pirates? Is he tricking me? I focused back on what Will was saying and heard the word 'Sumatra'. Oh, right, that made more sense. Captain Pugwash holding a machine gun seemed a little out there. Wasn't Captain Pugwash another one on the shit list as being an inappropriate character for children to read?

'Right, Lex?'

Shit, I'd zoned out again. Bloody Pugwash.

'Yes, totally.'

'So you really think I should do it?'

'Yes. It's a great opportunity.' See, I could be supportive.

'You think I should leave for sea and become a pirate?'

'Haha. I knew you were joking. Oh, we have fun, don't we?'

He gave me a look. 'You aren't going to tell me about your day?'

He was distracted by my phone ringing.

We both looked over at it.

I could see the 0845 number that was calling. 'I'm sorry. I have to take it.'

I stood up and walked away from the table. I heard the automated voice tell me, 'Have you ever been missold PPI insurance?' I waited for the beep and said, 'Lex Tyler' as the voice recognition listened. I knew what was coming. 'You are required on an urgent operation. Please confirm attendance.' The beep sounded and I spoke. 'Confirmed. ETA twenty.'

I turned back to the table. 'You know I have to go in when we're on high alert. It will probably be a late one.'

He slumped back in his chair and folded his arms. 'Just go.'

'Love you.' I took two slices of pizza out the box, grabbed my motorbike helmet from the hallway and left. I felt bad that I was relieved to be going. Relieved to be walking out of an uncomfortable conversation and into what could be a dangerous operation. Was it a sign of how bad my marriage currently was, or how much I loved my job?

'You need to go to a fashion show,' was how Pixie greeted me as I entered the meeting room. Pixie and Geraint were next to each other at the head of the large dining table, their laptops in front of them.

'This is what I got called in for?'

'Hattie just rang it in, darlin'. Ling Ling went straight from the Embassy to dinner. We don't know where she's eating but we do know she has tickets to a fashion show. The recordings from the Embassy will still be on her, all stored on the Dictaphone. Jake, Hattie and Robin are all on Peng. She's gone to a casino, which is going to be a security nightmare.'

I listened to what she was saying. 'So that means . . .'

'You have Cameron. She's meeting you there. The show starts in an hour and straight after that is the after-party.'

I checked my watch. 'The show starts at nine p.m.? Why so late?'

'Nine p.m. is late?'

'I . . . OK. Well, not that late.' I needed to remember I was a cool secret agent. Not a knackered mother whose plan to be in bed by 10 p.m. was flying out the window along with my street cred. 'Where is it?'

'East London.'

'Great.'

I would be lucky to be in bed by the early hours.

I had forgotten the other world out there. The one where people started partying late and came home as daylight was creeping in. I had been a part of that world once. And now I needed to make a cameo role in it again.

'You need to leave in ten minutes. But we need to do something about your outfit.'

I looked down at what I was wearing. A long-sleeved black top and grey jeans.

'What's wrong with this?' As I motioned downwards I noticed the top had orange dust from Gigi's Organix carrot sticks stained down the front and that the ends of my right sleeve were a little covered in dried snot. For some reason Gigi's streaming nose only ever seemed to happen whenever there was no tissue in the immediate vicinity.

Pixie wrinkled her nostrils. 'You're going to a top designer's latest fashion show. You need to look like you belong there.'

The shops would now be closed and I couldn't waste time going back home. I thought for a minute.

'I've got a red lipstick in the bathroom. Gym kit in the locker room. I could go for a kind of Brit Pop 90s trendy look?'

Pixie shook her head. 'I've got a much better idea.'

Half an hour later I was staring at my reflection.

I was wearing a Platform-issue black catsuit. It was designed to ensure no trace of our DNA could be left behind on break-in jobs. It was not designed to be accessorised with red lipstick, backbrushed hair, my Adidas trainers and Pixie's large mirrored sunglasses. Yet here I was. Pixie came up to me holding a stone-washed denim bumbag. I recognised it as belonging to Norm. A Rat in his fifties who, with his anorak and plastic glasses, was not known for his on-trend fashion sense.

'Inside here is what looks like an iPhone charger. You need to clip it to Ling Ling's Dictaphone and it will download everything on it and install a bug that will link the Dictaphone back to G's IP address.'

'Meaning?'

'That every time she presses record it will upload to his computer.'

She clipped the bumbag round my waist and took a step back.

'Perfick,' said Pixie, admiring her handiwork. 'This is the perfect undercover look.'

'It's grossly attention-seeking and completely ridiculous.'

'Exactly. You're going to fit right in, darlin'. I've got you a pass as a fashion blogger.'

'But what if anyone asks me about fashion? I don't know anything.'

'No one will ask you anything. Just keep taking selfies and pout a lot. Talk in hashtags. And don't take your sunglasses off.'

I'd got halfway to the car park when I realised I'd left my mobile phone on my desk. I went back to get it and, passing the open meeting room door, spotted Geraint and Pixie holding hands. Seated in front of their laptops, headphones in, his right hand and her left clasped together on the dining-room table, their free hands scrolling through what they were reading on the screen. Pixie pointed at something on her screen and they both laughed.

I watched them for another second, out of sight from the side of the door. That new relationship bubble. I remembered what that was like. Where you made an effort with how you looked and what you said. And kissed a lot. Wasn't there lots of kissing? I missed the days when kissing was more of a feature presentation. Not just the adverts you could fast forward.

I walked down the corridor towards the lift. I was happy for them. I wondered if they would last. It would help they had the same job, the same security clearance. I thought of Will's face as I'd left this evening. He wasn't an idiot. He knew I was hiding something from him, he just didn't know how big it was. Everyone had parts of themselves they wanted to keep hidden – but they were usually more along the lines of unhealthy shopping addictions, webbed feet and lingering feelings for an ex. Not killing people.

Chapter Fourteen

I ARRIVED AT THE FASHION SHOW unfashionably on time, 9 p.m. on the dot. A few people were already seated. The designer was an up-and-coming Eastern European with a name that consisted of so many consonants that it seemed wholly unpronounceable. The music was pounding. It was so loud I could barely think. How could anyone talk over this? Was it really necessary? God. That was it. I was officially old.

I scanned the front row until I spotted Ling Ling sitting with two friends. Pixie and Geraint may have got Cameron and me passes for entry but they had failed to secure us front row seats.

I stood by the door watching people enter.

Cameron strutted in. She was wearing a sleek black dress with mesh panels and towering Louboutin heels. Her peroxided blonde hair was slicked back. She looked amazing. She came straight up to me.

'What the fuck, Lex?' She cast a glance over what I was wearing. 'Are those your work clothes? Is that the BlockRelease2000 suit?'

'I was short on time.'

'What is it with women letting themselves go as soon as they pop out a kid?'

I gritted my teeth. Working with Cameron meant keeping a hold of your temper was as challenging as the mission itself.

'Have you located Ling Ling?' she asked.

'She's over there. Front row. No point making a move until the show is over. We won't be able to get close enough.'

It was nearing 10 p.m. by the time the show actually started. I watched a long parade of skinny women strutting down the catwalk in strange outfits. I didn't get fashion. I got stuff that looked nice. But who the hell was ever going to wear a dress stuck together with two thin straps and that opened to show your granny pants? The last time I had worn underwear that high was post C-section.

It went on for twenty minutes. Ling Ling was transfixed. Her phone never left her hand, her bag positioned firmly on her lap. Soon as it finished she clapped enthusiastically, nodding to her friends.

'Now what?' asked Cameron.

Ling Ling and the rest of the front row were being herded straight along the catwalk and through a large set of double doors.

'Let's just try not to lose her.'

The doors opened into a huge room that was already packed. It seemed the people in the know had bypassed the show just for the actual party. I remembered from the blurb that this warehouse used to be a slaughterhouse. The line of giant meat hooks that hung from the ceiling in the centre of the room was an ominous reminder. A headphone-wearing DJ of indeterminate sex, in a tight corset and feathered hat, was dancing in a booth that was fixed halfway up the back wall.

I spotted Ling Ling and her two friends for a moment before they were once again lost in the crowd.

Getting the Dictaphone off Ling Ling in such a crowded place would be easy. If we could actually get close to her. I motioned to Cameron that she take the left side of the room.

Trays of champagne held aloft by waiters in black were circulating. I looked at my watch. It was nearing 11 p.m. and I wanted to be in bed. Or at least in pyjamas on the sofa in front of Netflix. Not at a party in a skintight catsuit surrounded by fashionistas, working out how to rummage through another woman's handbag. The music had now ramped up a further notch. I looked over at Cameron. She was swaying to the beat with a glass of champagne in one hand. She was having fun. I remembered when I thought nights like this were a perk of the job. Just like her I'd roar into a party, in my best dress, my highest heels, and I would drink and I would dance and I would feel the beat of the music, soak up men's stares and feel good. I was strong, powerful and just the right level of drunk.

I could have them or I could kill them. I was invincible.

Working late now held no appeal. I'd rather have an early night with my husband and then feel less exhausted when getting up early with my daughter. I looked again at Cameron. She wasn't that much younger than me. We'd been in this business for nearly the same length of time. My desire to have a family was what changed me. I wanted to be a Rat and I wanted to be a mother. I wanted to do both. That moment might never come for Cameron. She would carry on steamrolling through life just as she was now and be perfectly happy. The real difference between her and me was that I could respect her choice, while she couldn't respect mine.

I finally caught sight of Ling Ling. She was at the stainless-steel bar that ran along the back of the wall underneath the DJ booth, waiting to be served.

I nodded over at Cameron. She elbowed her way across the room to the bar, squeezed in next to Ling Ling's friends and within seconds had the bartender's attention. Ling Ling's bag was on her right shoulder. I jostled past a group of men with handlebar moustaches, until I was just behind her and waited.

Pixie had briefed us that at the end of the last meeting Robin had seen Ling Ling replace the Dictaphone into the middle section of her large Balenciaga tote bag.

Cameron came up to them with a tray of shots, big party-girl grin in place. With a few whoops of encouragement each of them took one. As they downed the shots, amid the bustle of clinking glasses and grimacing faces, I reached into the middle section of Ling Ling's bag. I clasped my hand around what felt like the Dictaphone. I quickly pulled it out, put it straight into my bumbag and turned around. I was officially a bumbag convert. It wasn't a dated 80s accessory, it was a hands-free handbag allowing me to be fully operationally effective. I fitted the iPhone charger to the Dictaphone and turned back to check on Ling Ling and her friends.

Cameron seemed to be trying to persuade them to do something but there were a lot of shaking heads. She glanced over at me as they left the bar and headed back into the throng of people.

I looked down at the iPhone charger. The small light on the back of it was still red. The transfer wasn't complete.

We had to get the Dictaphone back inside that bag. With the remote bug in place, transferring audio files back to Geraint's IP address, we would be able to hear everything at every meeting.

This late night was not going to have been for nothing.

We followed Ling Ling and her friends as they negotiated their way through the crowds. We were halfway across the room when the light finally went green. I disconnected the Dictaphone and handed it to Cameron. She strode ahead and I watched as she danced up to Ling Ling as if they were now old friends. She could be nice when she needed to be. She put an arm round her as she shouted something into her ear and slipped the Dictaphone back into her bag. Cameron then high-fived Ling Ling and her friends and sashayed off, hands in the air. Party Girl and Rat was definitely an easier fit than Mother and Rat.

Our mission had been accomplished. Now back home to bed.

And then I saw a Ghost.

He was broad with clipped hair and wearing straight-leg jeans with a light green fleece. He had a nose that looked like it'd been broken more than once. He was not far behind Ling Ling. Ignoring the music. No phone in hand. That and his unfashionable attire made him stick out. I scanned the room and saw another Ghost not far behind him. He was a thickset man, stood alone, just staring at Ling Ling.

Why the hell were Ghosts following Ling Ling? Were they also wanting the Dictaphone? Were they going to grab her? Was it a trap to draw us out? To see how much we knew?

Ling Ling was still talking to her two friends, mobile clasped in one hand, drink in the other, her Balenciaga bag still slung over her shoulder.

Cameron looked over to me and I gave a nod at the two Ghosts. She turned to look and then reached for another glass of champagne.

We couldn't leave. Ling Ling wasn't going to stand a chance if they came for her.

We needed to watch. To wait and see what they did next. Ling Ling and her friends were now dancing. So much for hoping they were on their way out.

I checked my watch. It was coming up to 1 a.m. Surely she must be wanting to go back to the hotel. I remembered the delegation's schedule. She had an early start. She should really be in bed. All around us people were dancing, heads swaying, hands moving.

The Ghosts kept Ling Ling in their sights. I knew why they hadn't made a move. Too large a throng of people. No fast exit.

I scanned the room again and spotted a third Ghost. This was not good. Assigning this many to her meant they were after something.

Ling Ling and her friends huddled together as one held out a phone and snapped a photo. They walked towards the exit, arms linked.

Cameron looked totally absorbed in the good time she was having but seeing them move she immediately extricated herself from the man she had been gyrating with and followed me towards the door.

The large warehouse opened out into a side street. Ling Ling and her friends came laughing out the door with me directly behind them. There were small groups of people outside smoking and vaping.

The side street had been closed to cars. The three women walked down it, back towards the main road. Cameron arrived at my side. We watched their progress down the street.

One of the Ghosts followed them. He came up on the right of them and overtook them. What was their plan?

I turned to look for the other two Ghosts. One was far over on the left. The third? The third I spotted as he followed directly behind the women.

They were in formation.

They were going to make a move.

The third Ghost would make a grab; if he failed, the first was up ahead to try again. The second Ghost was now peeling off to another side street – he must be retrieving their getaway vehicle.

The minute those women turned off the street out of view of the smokers, the Ghosts would pounce. We had to wait until they did.

Cameron clearly reached the same conclusion. 'I'll get the one going for the wheels.' She set off after the second Ghost. Cutting off their means of escape was a good bet at upsetting whatever they had planned.

Ling Ling and her friends kept stopping to look and laugh at one of their phones. They turned onto the main road. I waited a beat and then followed. I turned the corner in time to see the Ghost pull the bag off Ling Ling's shoulder and push her to the ground. She let out a cry of pain as she hit the ground. Her two friends went to her and shouted at the departing Ghost. I didn't understand Mandarin but it sounded far angrier than anything that could've been said in English.

I chased after him. He had the bag. We had to get it back. What Ling Ling might write off as an unfortunate incident with a random London mugger, we knew must be a tactic to find out Peng's schedule for the next few days.

The Ghost was fast. I was grateful that Pixie had allowed me to wear my trainers. I sped after him at full pelt. He turned back once to see who was after him. Seeing a woman in a catsuit with backbrushed wild hair and sunglasses on her head was probably not what he expected.

There was another warehouse on the corner. I was betting it was where their vehicle was parked. He would have to slow down to turn the corner – that's when I needed to hit.

I kept up my pace, never more grateful for the fact that despite work, despite Gigi, I still made the time to run twice a week. The Ghost slowed slightly as he approached the corner. I pushed myself further; I was nearly there. He turned the corner just as I came flying at him. We both fell to the ground. He landed badly. With me on top of him. He was unconscious, or doing a good job of pretending to be.

A van came screeching down the road towards us and pulled to a halt. Cameron got out the driver's seat.

'So you can still run. Even though you are a bit more . . .' she tilted her head, 'squashy.'

I tried to get my breathing to return to normal. My heart was still racing.

'My Ghost is in the back.' She motioned towards the back of the van. 'Any sign of the third?'

A small Vauxhall Astra came racing down the road and passed us and the van without slowing. It turned left down the main road at full speed. The final Ghost was leaving. No attempt to retrieve fallen colleagues. No honour among thieves, no loyalty among Ghosts.

'I already spoke to G,' said Cameron. 'He's wiping us from any CCTV but we need to move fast. A police car will be here in seven. Ling Ling's friends called them. I'll play the helpful American tourist, return Ling Ling's bag to her and then we get back to the Platform.'

The Ghosts needed to be logged in and interrogated, the Dictaphone recordings safely delivered to Geraint, and Hattie updated. Considering this latest attempted attack, we were going to have to up our protection of Peng. They were getting ready to strike.

I got up. My breathing was slowly returning to normal. I managed an 'OK'.

'How did the Ghosts know she was here?' asked Cameron.

'They must have all of the delegation under surveillance. We've got to be more careful. If they made a play for the Dictaphone, chances are they aren't waiting until Lord Wycombe's shoot to make the hit.'

We bent down and together picked up the unconscious Ghost and dragged him into the back of the van to join his friend. We slammed the doors shut.

'Do you Rats always work like this? This buddying up to do missions?' asked Cameron.

'We always work as a team.'

'It's strange this whole hanging out together. The jokes. The chit chat. We usually just get a secure encrypted email and we go out and do it. Alone. I can go weeks, months even, without going into Track 101.'

'Don't you want to know why the target needs to die? Doesn't it help to understand why what you're doing is for the greater good?'

Cameron frowned. 'I don't need to know. The order's been given. I follow it.'

It didn't excuse Cameron being Cameron, but it did help explain why she was so bloody difficult to work with.

'It sounds lonely.'

Cameron shrugged. 'It's less complicated. You learn to rely only on yourself. No emotional attachments. Track 101 don't have to worry about your mental state if anything happens to anyone on your team. It's a more efficient way to work.'

'It doesn't mean you have to apply the same attitude to your personal life.' It must be my maternal side. Trying to help Cameron be a better person.

'Not everyone wants to end up a monogamous martyr and ruin their body and career prospects by popping out a kid.'

It was a lost cause.

I handed Ling Ling's bag to Cameron. 'Go give it back and we can get out of here.'

We both turned at the sound of a van approaching down the road. It slowed as it came past us. A man popped his head out the passenger window. We both tensed.

'All right, darlings, give us a smile,' he leered as the van passed us by.

We ignored him.

For us the Ghosts were easy to spot. Hired muscle looking like hired muscle.

We were written off as women on a night out. They wouldn't know the power we had. The men who'd fallen at our hand. It was still there. This belief we didn't need to be taken seriously. This idea that we could be overlooked as a threat. More fool them. We were still the unexpected. It's what made us better than them. They never saw us coming.

Daylight was slowly starting to creep in by the time I got on my bike and headed home. I ran over the evening's events. I might be a little more tired. I might be a little more squashy. But I could still do my job just as well as before Gigi.

And now I got to go home to her.

The feeling of watching her sleep. This little person that I made. Pulling her duvet over her. Tucking her in. It felt like another life. One I didn't deserve.

Everything else melted away.

Whatever was going on with Will would get better. It had to.

Marriage was tough. Marriage after kids was tougher. What the hell was that phrase 'band-aid baby'? How could a baby hold a relationship together? 'Baby-bomb' would be more accurate. It could blow you apart. Less sleep, less sex, less fun.

I thought of the three of us in our bed yesterday morning. Her sweet round face, her dimpled cheeks, her rumpled hair. Lying between us as Will stroked her head and I held her hand. As she sang along to the *Peppa Pig* theme tune, we'd caught each other's eye and laughed. Isn't she perfect? Isn't she wonderful? Aren't we lucky? She's ours.

Day to day it was harder. But Will and I were bonded together. Connected for life through the child we made. Our love for her plastering over the cracks.

Band-aid baby.

She helped us want to make 'us' work.

I parked my bike down the road from our house. The streets were empty. I figured I had enough time to creep in, change into whatever clothes I had in the clean laundry basket and pretend I'd fallen asleep on the sofa. Coming home at this hour was not going to help a relationship that was currently blighted by claims I worked too much.

I was nearly at my front door when I heard a 'Lex!' I turned round to see a smiling Rochelle in running gear jog over to my side of the road.

Rochelle seemed to be making a habit of turning up without warning at particularly inopportune moments. She was an early period on a white jeans day.

'Look at you. Very impressive. Do you always run this early?' I tried to start a conversation as if I didn't look as if I was dressed like a prostitute crawling home on a walk of shame.

'Always. I go for an hour, come back, quick shower and a green smoothie, catch up on emails, and then I get the kids up for school.'

'Right.' Of course she did. You didn't get to be Supermum by starting your day whenever your child woke you up and by cramming jam crumpets in your mouth with a litre of caffeine.

'Where on earth have you been?'

'I'm just on my way back from the shops.'

Rochelle looked at her watch. 'It's 5.40 a.m.' She gave me a once-over, taking in my smudged eye make-up, tight black cat-suit and rumpled hair.

'There's that big twenty-four-hour Tesco's.'

'What did you need to get so urgently it couldn't wait?'

'Baking stuff. For that charity coffee morning today.' Take that, Supermum. 'You know how it is. I couldn't sleep and sud-denly remembered I hadn't made any cupcakes. And I couldn't let the school down.'

'Right. So you got up, got dressed in a catsuit . . .'

'It's actually a Weight Loss Onesie. It's made of special imported Italian fabric that burns fat while you sleep.'

She looked at each of my empty hands. 'But you didn't buy anything?'

'All in here.' I tapped the bum bag. 'Vanilla essence and sprinkles.' She couldn't catch me out. I was a trained liar. 'You'd better get running if want to get that full hour in.'

'I can't wait to taste them. Make sure you show me which are yours.' She gave a little wave as she jogged off.

I doubted I had convinced Rochelle. But at least what was reassuring was that she would just presume I was cheating opposed to fighting.

It wasn't easy leading a double life. If a nosey school mum could spot the cracks, my husband could too.

I had to be more careful.

From: noonewants@genitalwarts.com
To: lex.tyler@platform-eight.co.uk
Subject: TOP SECRET Natural Herpes Remedy!
MISSION: #80521
UNIT: WHISTLE
DATE: Thursday 3rd October
ALERT: 3 DAYS UNTIL PENG'S DEPARTURE

Chapter Fifteen

'THEY'RE SO AMAZING, MAMA.'

Gigi was staring at my lopsided emergency-baked cupcakes, covered in pink icing and rainbow sprinkles.

'They best cupcakes ever, Mama.' It was moments like this that made it worth having children. Blind adoration. I was already dreading the day she grew up and knew better.

'I didn't hear you come in.' Will came up behind me.

'Passed out on the sofa down here.'

'And already been baking?'

'A mother's work is never done.' I looked over at Will pouring himself a coffee. 'Did you know Rochelle lives round here? Her son is at Gigi's nursery.'

Will took a sip of coffee. 'I did know that, yes.' He went to sit down at the table with Gigi. I watched him continue to drink his coffee as he stared at his phone.

I wondered if Rochelle was the one texting in the middle of the night.

If he was going to betray our marriage vows and cheat on me, it had better be with someone worth it. One of those human rights lawyers he sometimes came across at work. An intense, worthy sort, who he fell deeply in love with because she was saving children in Syria.

That I could take. And kind of understand. But Rochelle? A simpering busybody in wedge trainers? Fuck no. He didn't get to screw up our life for someone like that.

It was useful to know that there were different levels of how angry I could get if he was cheating, dependent upon how good a woman his mistress was.

I watched him continue to scroll.

Had things got so bad I would be setting Special Projects on him as soon as Platform Eight were off lockdown? Instruct them to do a deep dive through all his emails, texts, WhatsApp messages? I had always resisted the temptation to use the many avenues available to me as a government operative. If I didn't trust him, what was the point?

Will's phone pinged as a text message came in. He smiled as he read it and then slipped his phone into his pocket.

The point was I would know for sure.

And knowledge was power.

If I was fighting for my marriage I needed to know what I was up against.

After a coffee morning where I heard the words 'are these gluten-free?' as often as 'they look amazing but I won't, thank you', I came home and slept for two hours. Enough to reset and feel vaguely ready for what would be another long day.

I woke to an urgent email with the title: 'HOT CHICKS AVAILABLE NOW$$!!'. I tapped in my authorisation code and the X-rated content merged into a request from Hattie that I go to a church in Putney where Dionne had taken Peppa's daughter Bella. My mission was to retrieve a bag that was currently in the base of the pram.

On Robin's morning round of collecting the audio from the receivers at the three Pigs' houses, he'd seen Peppa and her daughter rush into a café down the road from her house and then reappear five minutes later, clutching a very small bag bearing a green logo. She had put it in the base of the pram and, despite meeting Dionne on the corner and saying goodbye to her daughter in her buggy, she did not take the bag with her. Considering we had nearly ruled out Daddy Pig, the Snake was now either Peppa or George. Hattie considered this a big enough lead that whatever was in there could be anything from a security pass to a USB stick of intel for the Coyote.

I arrived in time to see Dionne enter the church hall with Peppa's daughter, Bella. Robin came up beside me.

He nodded towards the stream of mothers, nannies and toddlers going into the church. 'There's a buggy parking area round the side but it's overlooked by the whole hall.'

'OK, I'll go look. What kind of buggy is it?'

Robin frowned. 'Black? With wheels?'

I realised that although I may be able to recognise and list buggy brand names as easily as if they were cars, this talent may not extend to childless colleagues.

He stretched and yawned. 'Sorry, late night.' I noticed he was in the same clothes as yesterday.

'Stuck with Peng?'

'Stuck in Shawna.' He reached out for a high five. I left him hanging. 'We got talking on the Northern line one night and just had our third date.' He sighed. 'She's so beautiful she makes my balls ache.'

'Robin, we talked about this.'

'You said girls liked compliments? I want to marry her.'

I looked at him smiling to himself. Robin had been a trainee Rat for coming up to three years now – nearly double the time it took most Rats, including Jake and me. Despite this Robin had never really complained – the odd jibe about it being time to move on was as far as he got. Finding someone so upbeat and nice in this industry was rare. He never had dark moments or silent moods you had to tiptoe around. I realised a lot of why I was stalling on Robin graduating from Whistle was because, as much as I complained about him and his crap jokes, I would miss having him around. And that wasn't fair.

'I'm going to talk to Jake about you getting your own unit.'

'Really? You mean it?' He grinned. 'Thanks, Mum.' And held out his arms for a hug.

I waved him off. 'Just get back to the Platform. I've got this.'

He blew me a kiss as he walked away, whistling to himself.

Everyone was always in a better mood when getting some. Maybe that's what Will and I needed to do. Have more sex. Maybe then we'd argue less. Although when to fit it in? I thought of our plans for the week. Scheduling sex. Sexy.

There was a 'Buggy Park' sign with an arrow pointing round the side of the church. I turned the corner to be confronted with around thirty buggies.

I checked each one. A plastic bag with a green logo. That's all I was looking for.

It was on buggy number twenty that I finally found it. I opened it.

Poo.

Poo in a small pair of Princess pants.

Bella was clearly not doing so well at the potty-training.

If Peppa was using her daughter's crap to smuggle information to Tenebris, all power to her. But I was pretty sure the suspicious behaviour and suspect package could be explained away as a rush to prevent an accident and a clearing up of the aftermath.

Either way I wasn't going to rummage through it to check. I handled enough at home.

I was on my motorbike back to the Platform when my phone rang. I looked down at the screen as I approached a red light. It was Gigi's nursery. I clicked answer and a voice crackled through my Bluetooth.

'You need to come immediately.' The line broke off slightly and I just heard 'unacceptable'.

'Ms Yvonne? I can't hear you? Is everything OK?'

'I ... really ... Gigi nearly killed someone.' That last line came in very clear. I screeched to a halt and turned the bike around.

As I sped across London, going through nearly every red light, all I could think was: nature v nurture. Clearly it's in her genes. How could the violence of my working life already have filtered through to my two-year-old daughter? The biting was the start. And now ... Now what? What the hell could she have done? Water-boarded Felix at the water-play table? Tried to suffocate Sophia in the sandpit? Stabbed little Lulu with the safety-scissors? My mind burst with toddler *Hunger Games* scenarios.

A solitary peanut was placed in the middle of the table.

'Do you not think . . .' I cleared my throat. 'Do you not think this is a slight over-reaction?'

Yvonne observed me silently. 'This is a nut-free environment. It is on all our literature. It is proudly written underneath our sign in the entrance hall.'

'Is there any child here, right now, who has a nut allergy?'

'That is not the point. We have rules for a reason.'

'I understand that. And, Ms Yvonne, I totally respect that. But just hear me out. If currently no one at this nursery has a nut allergy, Gigi accidentally bringing in a nut, which must have been in one of her pockets, could not be classed as having "nearly killed someone".'

'There could be children who have nut allergies that have not yet manifested. We are not going to have children put in danger. Not on my watch.' She straightened her back and puffed out her chest.

I had come across people like Yvonne before. There was no point arguing with her. Health and safety was her religion. And she worshipped at the altar of form-filling and box-ticking. I just needed to pay my dues and get back to work.

'I'm very sorry. This will never happen again. We will become a nut-free household – just in case any of us are perhaps allergic and it has not yet manifested.' I tried to smile.

I saw Frederick at the head of the queue for picking up on the way out. 'Everything OK?'

He looked confused that I had already been inside and that the doors were now once again closed. Ms Yvonne was a stickler for timekeeping and there were officially still three minutes until pick-up.

'Nuts are a problem.' I rolled my eyes.

He frowned.

'Don't worry, I've got it sorted. Anything on the Pigs?'

'Nothing to report.'

'There's a WAF play date at your house after lunch. Hopefully I might learn something from the wives.'

'I'll make sure I'm out of the way. I need to get back to Peppa and George anyway.'

'Oh God, those pigs,' a Scottish mother behind Frederick in the pick-up line cut in. 'I swear I go to sleep humming that theme tune.'

A conversation among the waiting parents was then launched as to just how many millions the creators must have made, followed by a debate as to why their town had both a doctor and a vet when they were all animals, and then there were more specific questions between a few mothers at the back:

'Is it just me or is Danny Dog hot?'

'Marianne, he's a dog.'

'And a child.'

'And a cartoon.'

The doors opened and Ms Yvonne waved the other children out.

'Don't forget, everyone, it's our Roald Dahl celebration tomorrow. We can't wait to see some beautiful costumes!'

The demands from this nursery never seemed to end.

Chapter Sixteen

I RANG THE DOORBELL of Camilla and Frederick's house and waited. There was always a murmur of excitement at getting to nose around someone's house. I was going to enjoy this.

I looked down at Gigi in her princess dress and sparkly shoes. My daughter was a princess, day in, day out. She loved pink. And she hated getting dirty. I loved her. She was my everything. But dammit, I couldn't help but wish she was a little less conventional. I had tried my best. Given her trucks to play with. Told her she could do anything she wanted. That 'like a girl' meant being strong. Fearless. But this was her. This was my Gigi. And if this was how she was, I would love and accept her. As a pink-loving princess.

The door finally opened. 'Alexis, Gigi. How lovely.' Camilla smiled at us. 'Come on through.'

We followed her into a beautiful kitchen. Dark blue cabinets with a marble countertop. As befitting an art gallery owner, what looked like expensive, but not necessarily nice, art was dotted all over the walls. Crittall-style doors led out to a garden with fake grass. Kate and Dionne were already there. Kate's twins were chasing each other round and round as Peppa's daughter Bella and Florence sat colouring at a mini table and chairs. Gigi immediately ran to join them.

I looked round the large open-plan space. Everything was immaculate. The only nod to the hectic family life was a large noticeboard brimming with reminders from the nursery and an abundance of Florence's artistic masterpieces.

Camilla noticed me staring at their noticeboard. 'Frederick insists we keep everything. He's surprisingly sentimental.'

'Is he very hands-on?' asked Kate as she and Dionne joined us from the garden.

'Oh yes. He's the one that gets Florence up in the morning. Well, more likely she gets him up. She has never slept well. Sometimes they're already in the playground by seven a.m.'

'Don't think my husband has ever got up with any of ours,' said Kate, shaking her head.

'Frederick's an early riser anyway. Doesn't seem to mind. He takes a coffee, catches up on emails, has some fresh air before being stuck in an office.'

It was strange to think of how other couples did things. Like in any partnership you slipped naturally into what became your responsibilities and what became theirs. I was always the one on early shift. I'd never really thought about it but it would be nice if Will occasionally stepped up and did it instead.

Why was I comparing them?

'Frederick has even been picking her up from nursery every day this week.' Good to know our latest mission was getting him credit with Camilla. 'I guess he just likes doing his bit. It's just the way he is. He likes to get involved in everything. He even helps me with the gallery, accounts, invoices.' She gave a little laugh. 'The stuff I'm no good at.'

From what I knew of them it seemed more like he had to help her with everything as she couldn't cope. I watched her yet again getting distracted and looking off into the distance. She was a fragile flower. She needed looking after so he took charge. She played the little woman so he could be the big man. Every relationship needed a certain dynamic to work and maybe that was theirs.

I wondered why I felt I had a more accurate insight into Frederick and Camilla's relationship than I did the others', whose conversations and online correspondence I had been monitoring for the past few days.

I looked at Kate. Hers and George Pig's relationship seemed mostly about surviving the chaos of their children. Kate took hours getting the boys to bed and they seemed to visit them intermittently throughout the night. I didn't know how Kate managed to hold it together so well. I was sure we would come across a prescription for amphetamines or Prozac at some point, but so far nothing. She seemed to run solely on caffeine and high-energy protein shakes. Solid food didn't seem to be a feature in her life. She was staring with a slightly terrifying intensity at the untouched Victoria sponge on the table.

The doorbell rang and Camilla went to get it.

I turned to Kate. 'How about Neil, does he do his bit?' I needed to somehow get the subject onto George Pig.

'With tearaway twins and a seven-year-old, he has to. But I get that it's tough. Work is busy at the moment and seems to be taking its toll.'

'Poor him. How?'

'He's made me cancel the weekend in Cornwall we had planned next week. Said he can't leave London.'

Camilla re-entered the kitchen with Naomi and, after the obligatory air-kisses and laying out of teacups, we all sat down.

'And how about you, Naomi, how are things with you?' I looked at her red-rimmed eyes. 'Are you OK?'

Naomi burst into tears.

'Sorry . . . I . . . You think you're fine and then, well . . .' Naomi wrung her hands and looked up at us. 'My husband's having an affair.'

There was silence as we all took this in.

So she knew.

Naomi let out another sob.

'Naomi, I'm so sorry. What a shit. What a total shit,' Kate said as she flung an arm round Naomi. Camilla got up from the table and went to get a box of tissues.

'That utter bastard.' Dionne said it loudly enough the children in the garden outside turned around. 'How do you know for sure?'

'I've found enough proof. He isn't being very discreet.' Camilla handed her a tissue and she dabbed her eyes with it and blew her nose.

'Have you confronted him?' I asked.

'No. I'm scared. I'm worried about losing the house. I'm worried about losing Bertie.'

'You don't need to worry, Naomi, the mother always gets custody,' Kate told her.

'Oh.' Naomi looked up. 'I'm not worried about the kids. I know I'll get them . . . Bertie is our dog. Ronald loves that dog. But I *really* love that dog. What if they give him Bertie as a kind of consolation prize? He's the one that keeps me company all day when the kids are at school. I can't imagine sitting down in a chair without him curling up on my lap. I can live without my husband. But . . . but not my dog.' She smiled and shrugged her shoulders. 'Twenty years of marriage. The bastard not only had an affair but didn't even have the respect to try and hide it better. He works for MI6, for God's sake.'

'Have things been bad between you for a while?' asked Kate.

'It happened slowly. But then doesn't everything when you've been married as long as us? One day it's fine. You work. Things are ticking along. You've got into your routine. You know your roles. Some days you might notice you're not really having sex. Some days you might notice you're not really talking. Exchanging information, yes, but not really talking. But you decide it doesn't matter. No marriage is perfect. No husband is perfect. You're just getting on with life. And you're both pretending that this is all fine. That you're happy because you aren't miserable. You'd know if you were miserable, right? And you have children. You're their parents and they need you to be together. And you wouldn't want to upset them when you aren't really miserable. Yes, this is never what you imagined. But then what's the alternative? You aren't going to find anyone else. Your children are happy, they're settled, this is the life they know. And isn't seeing them happy enough? It should be enough. It should be.' She stopped to draw breath and took a sip of tea. We were all quiet, waiting for more. She was calm now. Her tears had stopped.

'You want to say things. Of course you do. Can't you speak a little nicer to me? Why don't we laugh anymore? And even though you aren't happy, even though you haven't been happy for a long time, you don't do anything because you don't want to rock the boat.' Naomi looked down at her hands. 'And then you realise the boat's already sunk. You find out he's sleeping with someone else. And it makes you sad. So sad. Until you realise you're not sad that he's cheated, that he's lied, that he's broken your wedding vows. You're sad that he didn't do it earlier.' She shook her head. 'That years have been wasted in this limbo. This living through your children and forgetting the rest of your life.' She let out a long breath.

We all sat there in silence. Kate broke it first. 'You're right, Naomi. You're completely right. And you're so brave to take the first step. You don't need him.' She reached her hand across the table and clasped Naomi's.

Camilla was stirring her tea, staring off into the distance. Naomi's marriage problems were either boring her or she didn't know how to cope with such an unbecoming display of emotion.

'Just remember we're here for you, Naomi,' continued Kate.

'Yes, yes, of course we are. Anything you need,' I added.

'Look, darl, I can get the name of Suze's lawyer,' Dionne told her. 'The guy was a total shark. Got her everything. She kept the house and had enough left over to buy herself a ski chalet. And they can't even bloody ski!'

I turned to Dionne. No mention in any of Peppa's records showed anything about a ski chalet.

'That's amazing. Whereabouts is it?'

Dionne grabbed another slice of cake. 'Dunno. French Alps somewhere. They haven't been in ages.'

A property abroad was a good way to hide money you didn't want being found.

'How long has she had—'

'So, Naomi, are you going to talk to the lawyer?' Kate gave me a glare. She was right. It was a little insensitive to be asking about ski chalets just when Naomi had dropped the cheating husband bombshell.

'I guess so.' She sniffed and took a deep breath. 'It will be a relief, actually. To take the next step. What is it they say about raising children? It takes a village. Well, I had my village. I just realised my husband didn't live in it.'

After we all said our goodbyes, I watched Kate insist on Naomi coming back to her house for a bottle of wine.

Good women bonding over a bad man. A fast-tracking of a friendship. It was nice to see a bit of light amid the darkness.

Part Four

Mess

mess, *n.*
1. A dirty or untidy state of things or of a place.
2. A situation that is confused and full of problems.

Chapter Seventeen

'WE NEED TO DO BETTER.' Hattie stood at the head of the meeting room, hands clasped together in front of him. We were all in our usual seats round the table. Only Jake was missing as he was watching Peng. 'We aren't making fast enough progress. Forget striking a blow against Tenebris; we haven't even made a tiny ripple. I still have no promising leads on the Coyote.' He turned to Cameron. 'How are you and Jake doing with the hackers?'

Cameron popped her gum. 'So far we've confirmed no one is with Tenebris and there are only a few left to talk to. One in Surbiton, one in Hackney and one based in Watford. I'll need Robin for that interrogation. He's Chinese and subjects always revert to their mother tongue when in intense pain.'

'Me? With you?' Robin glanced across at Cameron.

'Correct,' Cameron answered without looking at him.

'OK.' And that was all he said. No wisecracks. No jokes. He was clearly intimidated by Cameron – he was refreshingly quiet around her.

Hattie looked at Geraint. 'How are we looking with the Dictaphone?'

'The link is up and running. Every time she clicks the red button we get a direct line to whatever it is recording.'

Hattie nodded. 'Good. Lex, what's the update on Daddy Pig?'

'Daddy Pig's wife knows about the affair – my gut says if he couldn't hide infidelity from her, chances are he wouldn't be capable of hiding high-level espionage from all of us.'

'And he got another email from Daniel Wheal – the man he arranged to meet at the Christie's auction,' said Pixie. It was hard not to stare at her lime green jumper – it was adorned with the face of a large black pug with its tongue out. 'The handover is a set of keys for Wheal's weekend place in Oxford. He's clearly just planning a weekend away with his mistress. He ain't a Snake, just a dirty pig.'

'That's it then,' said Hattie. 'We officially rule Daddy Pig out.' Hattie walked up to the whiteboard and drew a red cross over Daddy Pig's details. He looked back at me. 'What's the latest on Peppa?'

'Peppa has a ski chalet we didn't know about and a property abroad is a good place to hide money.'

'Let's look into that, but I think George Pig should be the main focus of our attention.'

I nodded. 'I agree the Switzerland link is the best indication he's guilty.'

'With the trail on the Coyote totally cold we need to identify the Snake fast. We've got three days until Peng flies out of here. Once she leaves, the Snake goes quiet until their next mission and we lose any chance of locating them and shutting down Tenebris. The Committee will not reinstate Eight until Tenebris is taken down. Remember, it's not just Peng's life you're working for, but your jobs and the future of the Security Services as we know it. Tenebris threatens everything.'

*

The storage locker key Robin had found during a search of George Pig's house was now considered an important enough lead to follow up. Earlier this evening Geraint had tracked down which storage company he had an account with. Jake was driving down the M4 to it now in the hope he would unlock it and find a few million hidden in suitcases and then we could tie this all up nicely. Hattie was watching Peng as she attended an event at the Embassy.

Cameron and Robin had gone out to Watford to undertake the interrogation of the Chinese hacker. He was the last one on their list of suspects. If he failed to be working for the Tenebris Network, that line of investigation was officially dead.

Geraint and Pixie continued to trawl through George Pig's online history while I focused on Peppa Pig.

The ski chalet looked like it was owned by Peppa and her brother, who was in property development. Considering how little they'd bought it for I wasn't holding out much hope it would turn out to be anything more than a small investment to help her sibling out.

Apart from the odd email from this unknown character trying to arrange a meet-up, nothing else in Peppa's life was raising any red flags. She worked, she came home, sometimes in time to put her daughter to bed. And nights were spent alone online as she watched Netflix or surfed the internet for anything from 'what developmental milestones a three-year-old should be reaching' to 'ways to get rid of mum tum'. There was the odd terse email exchange with her ex. But other than that life seemed quiet.

I wondered if she was happy or lonely.

At 10 p.m. I sent Geraint and Pixie home. Will was away for the night at some legal conference in Bristol and my mother-in-law was staying the night. I tried to convince myself my dedication to working late was down to the critically important mission we were on, as opposed to not wanting to have to make small talk with Gillian.

I went to the canteen and checked my emails as I ate a sandwich stuffed with pretty much everything I could find in the fridge. The nursery was requesting we bring in any unwanted bottles of wine for the school charity tombola they were holding in a few weeks. Unwanted wine? We were parents. All wine was wanted.

I left the canteen and, turning the corner, found myself face to face with a bald man in black, holding a gun. A not unusual sight down here.

Apart from the fact I had never seen him before.

My heart was hammering, but I kept my voice level.

'Hi, you must be Greg. The computer is just this—' I kicked him in the stomach as I was talking. He went down hard. He was back to his knees before I ran and jumped at him, knocking him backwards. His head made a deep clunking sound as it hit the concrete flooring. I picked up his gun and ran to the keypad on the wall ahead. I typed in a six-digit code triggering a silent alarm.

We were compromised.

For the first time in Platform Eight's history we'd been infiltrated.

And it was on my watch.

I patted down the unconscious man. Nothing. No ID, no phone. Another Ghost. Activating the alarm meant all active

200

Rats would be notified by emergency text. On a normal day that would mean within a few minutes I could expect anything from one to thirty colleagues blasting round the corner with an arsenal of weapons. But right now we were working as a shell and that meant only my unit was registered as active. Three Rats apart from me in operation. Only those three would get the emergency call to arms.

I had no idea how far away help was.

And I had no idea how many Ghosts were down here.

I needed more hands on deck.

I pulled out my phone and text Frederick. *Nightmare! Gigi been dreaming she's home alone and ghosts invading.*

He pinged back in seconds. *What a nightmare! I'm about fifteen minutes from home. What's that password for the phonics website?*

I texted back the code for the lift emergency authorisation code number and code word. We didn't rely on fingerprint recognition for entry. We had found if people really wanted to get in somewhere that needed it they'd just cut off fingers. For the same reason we didn't use iris recognition. Or facial recognition. While the entry code followed by 'open-sesame' would activate the lift and take you to our lower level of offices. Entering the code and 'sesameseeds' would mean the lift would take you down to a level below the main offices where a wall of alerted, heavily armed Rats would be waiting. If we were compromised and forced to give up the entry code, we had the chance of giving one that would save everyone inside. We were dead anyway but a final act of rebellion, a massive fuck you from the grave to our murderers, was a nice consolation.

Whatever the Ghosts were here for it had to do with the Dictaphone. The Ghosts at the fashion show last night had failed to secure it. Tenebris must have realised that Platform Eight had it and were prepared to risk an all-out invasion to get whatever intel we had stolen off it. Why was it so important to them? I'd scanned a copy of Robin's translation of the meeting notes and had seen nothing of interest.

Yet Tenebris making a strike to get it just showed how valuable the audio files must be.

And made me all the more determined to keep them safe.

I opened the chamber of the Ghost's gun. A full six rounds. I clicked it back. I heard the sound of desk drawers slamming from down the corridor as his companions searched the offices. How many were there?

The Dictaphone recordings were saved on a hard drive, which was right now in our office inside Robin's desk drawer. I'd seen him putting it there just before he left. As we were on lockdown nothing was getting saved onto the server in case the Snake could access it. All the information we had to do with the ongoing mission was saved to our individual laptops and to hard drives or USB sticks. The Ghosts wouldn't know what we'd saved the audio onto so would have no idea what they were looking for. They would take everything just to be safe. If they left with all our hardware we were fucked. Not just the Dictaphone intel but all our intel would be gone.

I needed to stop them.

With just six bullets.

The artillery room was at the end of a long corridor next to the car park. A room filled with weapons of every size and shape, and a pick and mix of bullets. But who knew how many Ghosts were between me and that room? The locker room was opposite me. I picked up the feet of the unconscious ghost and dragged him in. At least he was out of sight if anyone came looking. I got to my locker and pulled out my bag. I opened it and rummaged round inside – I needed to make do with what I had in here. The irony of being thirty feet away from an arsenal of weapons yet having to go into battle with a borrowed gun and the contents of my tote bag was not lost on me.

As I came out of the locker room I was face to face with another Ghost. His gun wasn't raised. Mine was. I fired. The bullet hit his stomach. The shock made him drop his gun. But he was still standing. And there was no blood. Bulletproof vest. He charged at me, slamming me up against the locker room mirror. The force shattered it. Splintered glass cut into me as I fell to the floor. He pulled me to my feet and clamped an arm across my chest and dragged me down the corridor towards the sound of his colleagues searching the offices. I knew what came next. A little heated questioning about where to find what they were looking for.

That wasn't going to happen.

I opened wide and bit down on his arm with everything I could muster.

Like daughter, like mother.

He yelped, 'Bitch!' and loosened his grip just for a second, but it was enough. I stamped down on his foot and a sharp elbow to the stomach before spinning round and slamming him in the balls with my knee. He screamed out and keeled over.

It was funny how many men wore bulletproof vests. Sometimes helmets. Yet never thought to wear anything to protect the part of the body that could so easily incapacitate them. I jumped on his back and held him in a sleeper hold until he went limp. I dragged him back to the locker room next to his resting friend. Two down.

I felt a sharp pain in my left side and looked down. A mirror shard had sliced into me. It was a deep cut and bleeding heavily. Rummaging through my locker I pulled out a scarf and tied it tightly round my waist, hoping it would stem the flow.

I needed to get to our office before they found the hard drive.

At least I now had two guns. I tucked one into the side pocket of my bag and held the other. I flung the bag over my shoulder and pulled the locker-room door shut, typing a code into the door's keypad that locked it from both the inside and outside.

Things had gone quiet down the corridor.

Had the mirror man's shout alerted them? Were they waiting for me? I reached into my bag and pulled out Gigi's beloved Elsa doll. I leaned round the corner and flung it down the corridor. I heard the sound of her plastic head hitting the floor as she burst into: 'Let it go, let it goo—' *Bang bang bang.* Her high-pitched plea was cut off by the sound of gunfire.

There were definitely two guns. Maybe even three.

Thanks, Elsa, you did not die in vain.

I made a mental note to Amazon one-click a replacement. If I survived tonight I was going to need to make sure I didn't have to deal with an incandescent toddler missing her favourite doll tomorrow.

Now what?

Two to three Ghosts. Armed. And those were only the ones I heard. There could be more.

I didn't want to get shot again.

I didn't need another scar to have to hide for the summer.

Another story to create for a concerned husband.

I had to use everything I had to my advantage. And the fact I knew the battleground was a major one.

The Platform's fusebox was fixed to the wall next to the locker room. It was a frequented area. Due to the intense nature of our interrogation techniques, the lights often flickered and fused. The two Ghosts I had locked into the locker room didn't have night-vision goggles so it was a fair guess their colleagues wouldn't either.

I opened the fusebox and flicked every switch. All the lights went out.

Shouts on my right from the corridor and offices and from back past the canteen. Jesus. How many of them were there?

While I was at the back of the canteen, chomping through my sandwich, worrying about what to donate to the school tombola, they must have walked straight past without seeing me.

Inside my bag was a small dinosaur torch of Gigi's. I couldn't risk turning it on in the corridor. I felt my way from the fuse box towards our office. I needed to get the hard drive from Robin's desk and break protocol by copying its contents, and everything else we had on the mission, onto our server. Right now the risk of exposing the info to our network was lower than the risk of losing the intel altogether.

I got to our office door, reached inside my bag and pulled out two packets of Pom-Bears. I sprinkled them all around the hallway and the entrance to our office. Inside the office I turned on Gigi's torch – a T-Rex projected onto the floor. Checking around the room showed that each of the desks had a laptop on it. I left Robin's but picked up the rest and took them to the safe on the back wall, gently placing them inside and securing the door. I went to Robin's desk and got the hard drive out of his drawer and connected it to his laptop. With the press of a few buttons the laptop was logged onto our server. I started copying over both the hard drive and the desktop folder labelled with Peng's mission number. 'Nine minutes remaining' said the screen.

Nine minutes to hold them off. I watched the screen as it copied. At least if they got all our hardware we would have a copy of everything relevant to the mission saved on our server. At six minutes to go I heard the unmistakable crunch-crunch of heavy boots on crisps. I gently lowered the laptop screen and crawled under the desk. Six minutes until the intel was safe.

With any luck reinforcements would've arrived by then.

I heard more crunches as the footsteps entered the office. There was a pause. I could nearly feel him staring round the dark room, straining his eyes.

There were more crunches as another Ghost entered.

The first spoke in a low voice: 'No sign of anyone.'

'There are clearly people here. We don't even know where the fuck all the others are. I saw three torches fixed to the wall just past that canteen. Get them. We don't leave until we've searched every office.'

I listened as their footsteps went back down the corridor, away from the offices and towards the canteen. Dammit, they'd seen Eight's emergency torches. It would only take a few minutes for them to get there. I needed to act fast. Soon as they had those torches they could potentially find the fuse box and get the lights back on.

With the dinosaur torch in one hand and a gun in the other, I left our office, my bag still slung over my shoulder, and headed down towards their colleagues along the corridor. I limbered up and stomped my feet and waved the torch light around.

Come on, boys.

Come and play.

There was a shot.

Great. I fired two rounds into the darkness. I doubt I hit anyone but that wasn't the plan. I turned and ran, my feet thudding against the floor. Shouts and I heard them chasing. I held the torchlight behind me, a jostling light leading the way. I ran to the corner and fired another shot.

I ran towards the canteen. No torch lights shone back at me. I still had time before they got to them.

Now for the hard part. Timing was everything.

I rolled my torch down the corridor towards the canteen and fired a shot to my left and to my right before diving through the door to the interrogation room behind me.

Next was an array of gunfire as the Ghosts fired at each other.

I stayed inside the interrogation room, up against the wall.

I hoped I'd be at least a few Ghosts down by the time they realised they were killing each other.

A shout. Followed by another shout. The gunfire stopped.

The penny had dropped. But how many men had?

I heard three different voices.

'What the fuck, Jerry?'

'Someone was here, they were shooting at us.'

'This place was meant to be empty. There's who knows how many people down here fucking with us.'

'Is this everyone left?'

'Fucking hell.'

'Come on, we've found some torches.'

I heard footsteps going down the corridor as they headed away. I waited a minute and then quietly opened the door and slipped out.

A hand grabbed me by the throat and pinned me against the wall. Fuck. One had been waiting. These guys weren't total amateurs.

He pulled the gun out of my hand and tucked it into his waistband. Least it was the one whose chamber I had already emptied of bullets.

'Pass me the bag.' He spoke in a low tone, clearly worried as to where my colleagues were.

I took it off my shoulder, slipping my hand inside it for the briefest of moments, and handed it over to him.

He threw it to the floor.

'You're going to turn the damn lights back on. And no more tricks. What other weapons do you have down here?'

'You know what this place is, right? We have every sort of weapon imaginable. My favourite is totally unnoticeable ... Until you're breathing it.' I opened my hand in front of his face and blew onto my palm. The man screamed and rubbed at his eyes as he was showered in an impossible to escape substance.

I charged at him, pushing him backwards into the interrogation room, and pulled shut the door and bolted it.

I headed down the corridor, brushing my hands together.

Glitter.

It really did get fucking everywhere.

Chapter Eighteen

B Y MY COUNT THERE were only two or three Ghosts now left. I looked down at my watch. The files should've all copied. I needed to get back to our office and secure the box.

I took a deep breath. I pulled the one remaining gun out my bag. I turned the corner and heard a familiar sound. Lift doors opening. I flattened myself against the wall and held my breath. Reinforcements. Mine or theirs?

Frederick stepped out. Gun raised. Thank fuck.

'Frederick, I'm here,' I whispered. I put a hand on his arm.

He swivelled towards me. 'Lex, you OK?'

'I'm fine. We need to get down there.' I motioned back towards my office. 'They're after all our intel. They can't leave here with anything. By my count two or three Ghosts are left in play.' I winced as I felt my side; blood had soaked through the scarf. 'Follow my lead.'

Frederick would be as blind as the Ghosts having only been down here once before. With his hand on my shoulder we made slow progress down the corridor. We got to the corner before the offices; the flash of torchlights lit up Watermelon's office at the end of the corridor.

'My office is the one nearest to us. You need to cover me when I get in there. How much ammo have you got?'

'Just what's in the chamber. Six shots.'

'Well, I hope it hasn't been too long since you fired. Just stand at the door. If they look like they're coming in, start firing.'

I felt my way through our office, I felt past my desk, then Jake's and finally got to Robin's. I opened the laptop. The screen announced: 'Transfer complete'. I unplugged the hard drive and slipped it into my jeans pocket. I moved Robin's laptop to the safe on the back wall and shut the door.

'Lex!' I heard Frederick shout and then two shots fired.

I stumbled back through the dark office.

Frederick was still by the doorway. He was lit up by the torch on the floor next to the body at his feet.

'I saw the torchlight coming this way and just fired.' He didn't take his eyes off the corridor ahead. He was right not to. Another Ghost could be coming.

'Good call.' I winced and held my side as I reached down to the body and pulled the gun out his hand and the torch off the floor.

I thought about what I'd do if I was one of the last remaining Ghosts. In an unknown territory. With an unknown number of hostiles. I heard a clatter from the office down the hallway. One was running. The torchlight was flashing down the corridor.

'Come on. We can't let him get out.'

We ran after him, Frederick a little ahead, the searing pain in my side slowing me down. I saw the swing of the torch light as the Ghost half-turned back towards us. Getting ready to fire.

Frederick hesitated.

I didn't.

I fired and the Ghost went down. There was a cry and a series of '*Fuuuuucckkk*'s.

We approached him slowly, guns still raised, torch shining right on him. He held his hands up against the light.

It was just a leg wound. I kicked his gun away from him.

'Stay with him. I'll get the lights back on. Keep your gun on him; if he makes a move, shoot him.'

I was halfway down the corridor when all the lights came on. I blinked three times, adjusting. Hattie and Jake were walking towards me. Both of them held a gun in each hand. I went towards them holding my side.

'Lex, you're bleeding.' Jake came straight to me.

'I'm OK.'

'How many are there?'

'There are two in the locker room and if you go back towards the canteen there are probably two or three down there. All of them are either dead or near dead. There's a live sparkly one locked in Interrogation Room Three. There's a dead one outside our office and an injured one outside Jagger. Frederick arrived five minutes ago.' I winced as Jake peeled back the scarf to look at the cut. 'He's watching the one by Jagger.'

'You're going to need stitches.'

'Figured as much. I'll do a quick patch-up now and drop in to the Kensington Wing later.'

The exclusive, private Kensington Wing of Chelsea and Westminster Hospital was where all injured Rats ended up. We all had comprehensive health insurance, which covered our frequent stays there, where we were cared for by a fleet of security-cleared doctors and nurses who knew not to ask any questions and write reports to fit in with designated cover stories.

'Get to the canteen and use the first aid kit there. We'll go relieve Frederick and round up the Ghosts.'

As I was easing myself into a chair in the canteen I heard Jake opening the interrogation room door, followed by laughter and 'Do you always wear glitter when on a break-in?'

I used the special glue inside the first aid kit as best I could. I just needed to stop the bleeding. I was bandaging myself up as Frederick walked in.

'I didn't realise you were injured.' He came up to me and helped me fasten the bandage.

'It's just a scratch. I'll be fine. Are you all right? You look a little pale.'

I felt bad. This wasn't what he was used to. But he'd got my call for help and he'd come. One gun and little experience, blazing to try and do what he could.

'I'm OK. I just . . . well, what will happen now?'

I shrugged. 'The usual – interrogation for the live, the Clean Team for the dead.'

The Clean Team were incredibly efficient at eliminating any trace of a crime having been committed or a body being left behind. They worked for Mrs Moulage at Requiem, Eight's crematorium business. The only way to drive around London without worrying about having a body in the boot is by having a business where you were expected to have a body in the boot.

I walked over to the cabinet at the back of the canteen and took out a bottle of whisky. I opened it and poured him a large shot.

I didn't want to probe, didn't want to ask, but that Ghost may have been his first kill. Having scanned his service record, eight years as an officer speeding through the ranks in the army didn't mean close combat. It didn't mean having to cut down a man coming at you.

I poured myself one and downed it. It burned the back of my throat.

Frederick downed his and I poured him another.

'I used the Clean Team once,' he said.

'Really? I didn't think they let you get that down and dirty at Six.'

Frederick smiled. The whisky was doing its job. A bit of colour was returning to his cheeks.

'My brother and his family were staying. We all got NoroVirus. Pretty much every imaginable surface of our kitchen and living room was sprayed with puke.' He shook his head. 'The smell just wouldn't go.'

'So you called in a favour.'

'Well, there have to be some perks to the job, right? It was amazing. They got stains out of the wooden floor that had been ingrained in there since we bought the house four years earlier.'

'You got any other tips?'

'Yes.' He took another gulp of whisky. 'Get one of those battlefield-grade, military-issue iPad covers. Perfect for when on tour in Afghanistan or at home with two kids under three.'

Jake and Hattie came back into the canteen.

'Seven in total. Three still alive. I've run them all through the system. No IDs, no facial recognition. As expected they're all Ghosts,' said Hattie.

'I've had a brief chat with them.' Jake's eyes flashed. 'All they know is they were hired for a break-in and their objective was to steal all our hardware – laptops, USB sticks, hard drives, anything they could find.'

It made sense. Tenebris had a sophisticated IT team who would undoubtedly have little trouble hacking any of the hardware the Ghosts brought them.

'They're pretty pissed about the site being occupied and it not being the easy job that was advertised. I said they should take it up with HR. Although they should be pretty embarrassed that the seven of them got defeated by one Rat with a doll, a handful of glitter and some fucking crisps.' Jake looked at me and laughed. 'I'm impressed, Tyler.' He went to the back of the canteen and got another couple of glasses.

'How did they get in?' I asked Hattie.

'Through one of the service tunnels. They used some sophisticated device to hack the system and a faked security card. These goons would've had to get the information from a Snake. To manage to get in, even with some clever technology, they would have to be familiar with our protocols.'

Jake took the whisky bottle and filled up all the glasses.

'The fact Tenebris would risk an operation like this tells us that we're close. It's a good sign. An even better one is the fact they got away with nothing.' Hattie downed his drink. 'We're a covert branch – people aren't meant to know where we live. Enemies aren't meant to be able to come knocking. The Snake is not just threatening upcoming missions. They're threatening Platform Eight's very existence. And anyone wanting to do this country harm will be circling, knowing we're vulnerable. What we need to do next—'

I cut Hattie off. 'Ten minutes.' They all looked at me. 'I would've heard them coming in from the office and I was in the canteen for about ten minutes before I bumped into the first one. They could've . . .' I put a finger to my mouth.

'Goddammit,' sighed Hattie, 'we need to shut down the whole network and do a thorough sweep. It will take a day. If not two. I'll call Demon. Get them onto the Unions.'

Hattie motioned to Frederick and me. 'You two get out of here. We'll finish up.'

We both downed our drinks and left the room.

Standing in the corridor, talking to a couple of men in black overalls, was Mrs Moulage. She was wearing a fur coat and Mary-Jane shoes. She click-clacked up to me with a smile.

'I hear you've prepared some Ghosts for me.' Her face was perfectly made-up. 'The boys don't need me.' She motioned to the two men behind her. 'But I couldn't resist a look around my old stomping ground.'

'Has much changed?'

'Everything and nothing,' she said simply. 'Get yourself home, my girl. You've had a busy night.' She cupped my chin and then click-clacked down the corridor. The men in overalls followed.

Frederick and I were both silent in the Uber all the way back to Chiswick. It pulled up outside my house first. I opened the car door and turned to Frederick. 'Thank you for getting there so fast. It might have ended differently without your help.'

'I doubt that. Looked like you had it pretty well covered.' He shook his head. 'I don't know how you do it.' We stared at each other for a long moment. And then another.

'Hello, miss? Miss?' The driver turned round to look at me. 'You getting out, miss? Two-minute drop-off rule. Going to affect your star rating if you make me wait.'

'Well, that really would be a shitty end to a bad evening.' I smiled at Frederick as I got out and closed the door behind me. I could still see Frederick looking at me as the car drove away.

A Sky News alert flashed up on my phone as I opened our front door.

*TUBE STRIKE TOMORROW. LONDON WILL GRIND TO
A HALT. UNIONS IN EMERGENCY TALKS.*

In case Tenebris hadn't done enough to hurt our country, they had now inconvenienced all of London with their invasion of Platform Eight. I winced as I dropped my keys on the hallway table. I should really have gone straight to the Kensington Wing to get stitched up but I was exhausted. And after an evening of close calls I'd just wanted to get home, stare at Gigi and be grateful for still getting back to her. I walked into her room and checked on her. She was fast asleep. I got into her bed and lay beside her, stroking her hair.

My mind was whirring with everything that was going on. What the hell had tonight been about? This mission was always going to be tough, but being attacked on our home turf?

I stared at Gigi's soft round cheeks and her long eyelashes, and listened to the sound of her deep breathing. I tried to think only of her and not work. My little biter. Was this new habit something else I should be feeling guilty about? Was she lashing out as I wasn't around enough?

Could I be a better mother if I wasn't a Rat?

Would I be menu-planning for the week, checking her developmental chart, ticking off milestones, pushing her forward to the next one? Slicing and dicing for homemade casseroles? Was I doing enough to make Gigi the best she could possibly be? Did I see her enough? Did I do enough with her? Was she watching too much television?

Could I be a better Rat if I wasn't a mother?

Would I be taking those extra weekend training courses? Brushing up on my special skills. Slicing and dicing in a different way. Was I doing enough? Or just doing enough to get by?

Was I pushing myself like I used to? Or just waiting to clock out and get home to my family?

Questioning myself never ended.

I shook it off.

Tonight could've ended badly but it didn't. I was here, pretty much intact, ready to fight another day. And Gigi was here. She was safe. She was happy. I was doing this.

I gently rolled out of Gigi's bed and left her bedroom. I got carefully into my bed and popped a couple of high-strength paracetamol. I was glad Will wasn't here. Faking being normal would've been more effort than I could manage right now. I'd go straight to the Kensington Wing as soon as I'd dropped Gigi at nursery.

Tenebris were spooked. We were close. The invasion proved that. Tomorrow could be a big step forward in shutting them down.

I thought of Frederick. The way he had looked at me as I'd left. I wondered what he was feeling. If the shock had worn off yet. If he was going to be getting any sleep tonight. I picked up my phone and clicked on my text messages to Frederick. Dots. He was typing something to me. I waited. The dots went. Another beat and they came back. I stared at my phone. I was back to being thirteen. Waiting for the postman to arrive. The dots disappeared and didn't come back. Whatever he wanted to say he couldn't find the words.

Or it was an iPhone fuck-up and I'd spent ten minutes transfixed by a software error.

I couldn't work out which was more tragic.

What was wrong with me?

I was a mother of one having indecent thoughts about a work colleague. This was tried, tested and clichéd ground. I was hoping, as a trained assassin, if I was going to have issues in my marriage it would be something a little more original. It would turn out Will was actually a secret agent for a foreign intelligence but turned by his intense love for me he'd confess all and allow me to bring him in, leading to a happy, genuine marriage and a massive promotion for me. Or that I was forced to forget my wedding vows to seduce someone incredibly attractive, not because he was incredibly attractive but because the safety of the UK's population decreed it for reasons I hadn't quite determined – maybe some kind of nuclear threat. It wouldn't count as cheating as it was for work. For saving my country.

But feeling like this, about a colleague, a school-run dad – it was all so depressingly normal.

Frederick was in my head when he shouldn't be. He knew what I did, he knew what I was – and it didn't stop the way he looked at me. It didn't stop him wanting me. That's what it all came down to. I'd known Frederick only days and it was already a more honest relationship than the one I had with my husband.

I knew I couldn't ever tell Will about exactly what my job entailed.

Because above all was the fear that if he found out the truth he would leave me. And I would realise he never really loved me, because he never really knew me.

From: insatiable@ride-me-cowboy.org
To: lex.tyler@platform-eight.co.uk
Subject: HotHornyMums WAITING HERE!
MISSION: #80521
UNIT: WHISTLE
DATE: Friday 4th October
ALERT: 2 DAYS UNTIL PENG'S DEPARTURE

Chapter Nineteen

'PRINCESS.'

'Darling, there aren't any princesses in Roald Dahl.'

'Be PRINCESS.'

Today was the Roald Dahl celebration at Gigi's nursery and we were having creative differences in our opinion of what she should wear. I looked at my daughter, standing in a bright pink glitter-covered tiara and an extravagantly sequined princess dress, her arms folded and mouth clamped in a firm frown.

Part of my training as a Rat was understanding when a subject was never going to crumble. There was no defeating this two-year-old. At least not without offering up a whole lot of bribery and I didn't think filling her up on Haribo before nursery was something Ms Yvonne would commend me for. Besides, my Matilda costume offering of a blue dress and three books was lame and we both knew it.

'Fine. Wear that.' I admitted defeat. My side was starting to ache. I reached down to touch it and felt blood. 'Mama's just going to finish getting ready. You can watch *Peppa* until I'm back.'

'Hurrah, Peppa!' Gigi plonked herself down on the sofa as I switched on the TV.

'I'll just be upstairs.' Gigi didn't even look at me, her eyes already transfixed on the bright screen.

I got to our bathroom and pulled off my top. I looked at the bandage. Red blood was streaking through it. Dammit, my quick fix last night hadn't held. I gingerly took off the bandage and rummaged around the bathroom cupboard looking for another. I found one and pulled it out.

'Mummy bleeding.' Gigi was in the doorway. She frowned. 'Mummy hurt.'

'Oh no, sweetheart. Mummy's fine. Just a little ouchie.' I quickly wrapped the bandage round me and pulled my top back on. 'Why aren't you watching *Peppa*?'

'It finished.'

Of course it did. What the hell was the point of episodes that lasted less than five minutes?

'One Ghost got away.'

Hattie was waiting for me as the lift doors opened into the Platform and a flurry of activity. Numerous technicians were in every corridor.

'The meeting room has been cleared. It's safe to talk in there.' He led me through.

My detour to the Kensington Wing to get stitched up and max-up on painkillers had taken longer than expected. Geraint, Pixie and Robin were already there.

I took my seat at the dining table as Hattie moved to his position in front of the whiteboard.

'We checked the CCTV from the tunnels and one of the Ghosts made a run for it when Lex got them all firing at each other. He slipped out the side tunnel door they came in. We have a pretty good visual of him.'

Geraint projected a close-up of the Ghost's face onto the whiteboard. He had short dark hair and thick eyebrows.

'We need to find him,' said Hattie. 'We've done a full inventory and nothing seems to be missing but we need to be sure. He could've managed to download intel off a laptop and take it with him.'

Pixie cut in. 'I'm searching all the different databases to try and get an ID. I've put an alert out for him – at airports, train stations and even ferry ports. He'll be going underground. He's got to be at least semi-professional and know what he needs to do to stay off the grid.'

I had an idea.

'G-Force, log on to one of the analysts' Facebook's accounts and upload a photo of him. I will add the text to go with it.'

Geraint logged in and passed me the laptop.

I created a post and typed:

WARNING PARENTS – CHILD KIDNAPPER
Everyone be vigilant – this man has been caught trying to abduct children from playgrounds. He's been spotted in three different schools in three different areas (W12, N3, SW12). He could be trying every school he comes across. If you see him DO NOT APPROACH. Call the police with ref 88842. They will come immediately.

'Now post it onto every school Facebook group you can find. Get some Bronze Wolves onto this too. We need it to go viral.'

'OK,' said Geraint. 'Doing it now.'

'Cameron has emailed in an update on the Ghosts in interrogation.' Hattie looked down at his mobile. 'As expected, no
useful intel. Their orders were to take all the laptops and electronic equipment they could find. They had a pay-as-you-go
number to call once they left here to arrange collection of the
items and payment.'

Hattie looked at Robin. 'Is there anything on the Dictaphone
audio files that explains why they'd risk breaking in?'

'I've listened to the files multiple times. All that's on there
is a meeting with the Chinese Ambassador. They discuss nothing outside a potential trade deal with France.' Robin flicked
the screen on his iPad. 'There was a warning that they shouldn't
make public the fact the UK were going to award them a new
aircraft contract. A talk of Lord Wycombe's shoot and dinner that they're both going to in a couple of days' time. Some
other chit chat with the Ambassador about how his children are.
Plans for Peng to go to the theatre as a guest of another business
associate of the Ambassador.'

'Maybe they weren't after what's already been recorded,'
I said, 'but wanted to make sure we couldn't listen in on a meeting Peng is going to have today?'

Robin shrugged. 'It's possible, but all that's on the schedule
for today are more business meetings in the City or back at the
Embassy.'

Hattie had been listening intently. 'What I don't understand
is how they would've known we had bugged the Dictaphone?'

I thought about it.

'Y. The Embassy informant. They must've got to him. He's
the one who told me about how we needed a bug on it.'

'Is there any way of getting in touch with Y?' asked Hattie.

'Frederick.' I pulled out my phone. *Really want to go to that Chinese you recommended. Can you get a booking for me?*

He pinged back immediately. *No. It's closed down permanently. Have you not seen the news?*

'G-Force, pull up *Sky News*. Looking for a story to do with the Chinese Embassy.' Geraint scanned through the *Sky News* headlines.

'Nothing about the Embassy mentioned. There is ... hang on ...' He flashed a photo up onto to the whiteboard. A Chinese man with thin eyebrows and a mole on his left cheek.

'That's him. That's Y.'

Geraint read from his laptop, '*Yesterday morning the body of Peter Yan was discovered in the Brixton area. Yan had been shot in the head in an apparent mugging gone wrong. Police are investigating. Peter Yan worked as a waiter at the Phoenix Palace restaurant in Mayfair.*'

Hattie frowned. 'Shot in the head. Just like with Frederick's boss Thatcher. It's almost certainly Tenebris.'

'The Chinese won't even admit he worked at the Embassy.' Robin rolled his eyes. 'They could've come up with a better cover story than Chinese restaurant waiter.'

'Eliminating him shows they're getting desperate,' said Hattie. 'We've made them nervous enough that they couldn't risk leaving him alive. We have two days until Peng flies out of here and the Snake goes back underground.'

The Chinese hacker in Watford that Cameron and Robin had interrogated the night before had turned out to be a woman and a big fan of Peng. It became clear that even if she had been working for Tenebris she would've turned on them instantly to keep her hero safe. The hacker line of enquiry was officially dead – Cameron and Jake had now ruled out every suspect on the list. We were now pinning everything on unmasking the Snake.

Hattie picked up his iPad. 'Where are we at with tracing George's movements out in Switzerland?'

The Switzerland link was still our best lead. If George was hiding the trip from Kate it was not too much of a jump to think he was out there depositing money in an untraceable bank account.

'I've got the hotel receipt for where he stayed,' said Pixie, her eyes not moving from her laptop. 'I've been combing through Zurich CCTV records to try and track his movements. So far we've got him in the vicinity of the Lienhardt and Co. bank. Facial recognition confirmed him on the street corner. We're making a start on hacking the bank's records. He flew back to London that evening. He received one call on his mobile from a Swiss hotel number the next morning. Whatever was said on that call obviously was of great importance as he left work early that day. Cited a family emergency. Although he did not make it home and he made no calls to Kate.'

'That's good,' said Hattie, nodding. 'From that we can surmise he met with someone in Switzerland who rang him the next day, potentially arranging a meet in London.'

'And the meet could've been with the Coyote,' cut in Geraint. He pressed a few buttons. A map of London projected onto the whiteboard. 'The sightings and mobile phone tower records we have of George Pig that afternoon are all around here.' He circled New Cavendish Street and Harley Street. 'This is an interesting area for George Pig to be visiting as, as you will see here –' he motioned towards a red dot – 'this is Asia House. Who, according to a visa application form, sponsored a Patrick Ng's arrival into the UK on a flight from Switzerland that morning.'

'And you think Patrick Ng is the Coyote?' asked Robin.

'We have no way of knowing,' replied Geraint. 'Professor Patrick Ng is from Beijing University with a specialisation in pan-Asian – European economics. That's if it was the real Patrick Ng who entered the country.'

'Lex, you need to make sure Frederick keeps a close eye on George Pig at work,' said Hattie. 'If the Coyote is now in London he's going to meet with him again. There must be a safe house in the area.'

Geraint motioned towards the map on the whiteboard. 'We've had no hits for George Pig on the street CCTV, despite his mobile phone logging him there – he's probably arriving by car to a building with an underground car park.'

Hattie looked round at us all. 'We catch George meeting with the Coyote and we've cracked it. We're on our way to closing down the Tenebris Network.'

Chapter Twenty

A MOTHER IN A CANADA GOOSE jacket bounced up to me.

'You're Gigi's mother, yah?'

'Yes, that's me.'

'Did you know that Miss Jenna is not Montessori-trained?'

'I . . . I did not.' I struggled to place who Miss Jenna was. I figured she must be either the middle-aged dark-haired one or the new young blonde one.

'Well, don't you think it's outrageous that they are marketing themselves as a Montessori nursery yet one of the key members of staff has no Montessori qualification?'

'Yes. Absolutely.' I read the situation and figured agreeing was the only option.

'I'm going to—' Canada Goose mum was cut off by Frederick's arrival at my side.

'Afternoon, ladies.'

'You're Florence's dad, correct?'

'Yes. I have no name of my own.'

The mum ignored him and repeated what she had just told me.

'Good God, but what are we are paying those hugely inflated fees for then?' he replied monotonously.

'Yes. Quite. I'm going to petition the owners. I . . .'

She abandoned the conversation upon seeing the nursery doors open and jostled past the other parents to get to the front of the queue. The rest of us obediently lined up.

'How was the WAF play date yesterday?'

'It was great. You have a beautiful home.'

'Thank you. It was a lot of work and a lot of meetings but I'm very happy with how it all turned out.' Again, it didn't surprise me that Frederick had taken the lead in the house renovation. He really was gunning for Superhusband of the year – early morning shifts with the kids, writing out Wow cards, helping his wife with her work, managing the house build, and all that with a full-time job that was more demanding than most.

'What have we got here?' Frederick reached down to the ground and picked up a Cinderella Barbie with a missing head. He waved it at me. 'Don't you find there's nothing more ominous than a doll with a missing body part?' He ran a finger over the neck stump. 'An innocent subject. Butchered.' He propped the headless doll up on the steps. She did look a little terrifying, a victim of a brutal crime, still perfectly dressed in her grand blue ball gown.

'You could start up the West London Mafia and that could be your calling card to your enemies. Forget horses' heads at the end of the bed, you can do decapitated Disney princesses.'

He laughed. 'You'd be my first hire. I don't think I'd do too well as a sinister mob boss without you by my side.'

We smiled at each other.

It was nice he found me funny.

When did I last make Will laugh?

When did I last try to?

Florence and Gigi came out together and stomped down each step of the Portakabin. They were each brandishing yet another folder of splodged artwork.

'Hello, poo poo head,' said Gigi to me.

'Hello, poo poo head,' copied Florence to Frederick.

The girls erupted into giggles.

'Now, Florence. We don't talk like that, do we?' said Frederick with a straight face.

Florence stopped laughing and her head dropped. I marvelled at how obedient she was, while Gigi carried on dancing around still shouting, 'Poo poo head, poo poo head!'

'Gigi, stop that. It is not a nice way to talk.' The annoying American mother who liked to spam us all with health studies into the effects of processed sugar on children's development was staring at us unsmiling. Her pale son stood quietly in front of her watching. The poor sod had had a cake made of cacao and sweet potato for his birthday party.

I leaned down and whispered into Gigi's ear, 'Stop saying "poo" or no chocolate when we get home.'

Gigi stopped. I straightened up. Appearance was everything and right now it looked as though I had some control over my daughter.

'Good, no more silly words. You're a big girl now. We talk nicely.' I held my head up high as we walked past the line of mothers waiting to pick up.

'Yes, Mama. Talk nicely get chocolate,' Gigi said.

Goddammit. My smile fixed in place, I ushered her after Florence and Frederick. I was sure I heard the American mother mutter 'cycle of addiction' as we left the courtyard.

The girls ran ahead together as Frederick and I walked across the green.

'One Ghost got away.'

'Did they get anything?'

'Doesn't look like it but we're tracking him down to be sure.' I looked across at him. 'How are you doing?'

'I'm fine. Slept well, actually. Surprising, all things considered.'

I didn't want to pry further.

'How are the Pigs?'

'Peppa implied she was going to be out of London for the weekend.'

'I've heard from Dionne that Peppa is bringing her daughter to the WAF pottery café morning tomorrow. But I guess she could still head out of town afterwards. We'll look into it.'

'George Pig is leaving the office in an hour. Requested leaving early for vague "family reasons".'

'Kate said he was slammed at work and they've had to cancel a Cornwall trip next week. So there's no way he'll be going home.' I thought for a moment how it was going to be pretty depressing if he was having an affair too.

'You need to make sure he's followed. I'll keep watching Peppa at the office.'

I pulled out my phone and emailed Whistle the update for Robin to get in position to follow George as soon as he left the office.

I turned to Frederick. 'I still think the Coyote will strike at the Wycombe shoot tomorrow. Hattie has got me inside Cherwell Castle as a Protection Officer but he's struggling on getting anyone else in.'

'I was at school with Lord Wycombe. He's actually already invited me to the shoot and the dinner. So you don't need to worry. I'll be there to back you up. To hold your bag for you when you go get the bad guy.' He smiled.

'Don't put yourself down. You handled yourself just fine last night.'

We watched as the girls skipped ahead across the green, exclaiming at the daisies dotted across the grass. I envied them. Who really wanted to grow up and have to deal with all the other crap life threw at you. Like mortgages, and problems at work, and people trying to kill you . . .

I dropped Gigi at home to a waiting Ganma and hopped on my bike to the Platform. I screeched into the underground car park just as Jake was climbing into a black BMW with a siren on top.

'We've got the missing Ghost. Just had a 999 call from someone saying that that paedo off Facebook had been secured and that it was getting pretty heated.'

We went full pelt to Clapham, siren blaring.

I checked my watch. The Facebook post had found the Ghost fast. I looked at how many hundreds of thousands of times the post had been shared. The parent network was alive and well and out for blood for anyone who was a threat to their children.

Jake spoke to me over the blare of the siren. 'You need to talk to Will.'

'What about?'

'Next weekend. He wants to surprise you. He asked me to make sure you aren't working those days. I didn't know how to tell him I couldn't control whether or not a Chinese minister was going to be assassinated and how that might affect you being granted time off for a mini-break to the Cotswolds.'

I frowned. 'You ruined the surprise now – I didn't know he was planning the Cotswolds.'

'Seriously?'

'OK, OK, just say what I told him, which is: we're all on standby for a big information leak from America.'

'Too late – I already said we're on standby for a Russian informant coming in. Is that going to be a problem?'

'No, it's fine. I'll adjust my story to yours when I see him.'

Will was seemingly ignoring my directive to not plan anything until work had calmed down. I didn't know whether to be touched at his dedication to us getting away together or annoyed that he wasn't listening to me.

As we approached the location the 999 caller had given, there was a bustle of around thirty people, nearly all women, on the street corner. We pulled to a halt next to them. There was a lot of shouting and jostling.

'I've done nothing! I've done nothing!' came the lone male voice shouting from inside the circle. We got out of the car.

'Police! Coming through,' I yelled above the din.

'Lock him up and throw away the key!'

'Fucking paedo!'

'Here. This is his.' A couple of women handed me a battered brown wallet. 'It fell. His name is John Thompson.'

'Thank God you're here.' John himself said this.

We got to him and Jake grabbed him under his right arm while I took his left.

I tried to address the crowd over the yells of abuse. 'Thank you, everyone. We've got him now.'

We headed back towards the car, with people parting to let us through.

We pushed John into the car.

'Hey, why am I in the back? Shouldn't you be arresting them all for assault? What have I done wrong?'

'How about breaking and entering a covert underground government agency?'

'I . . . I . . . I want a lawyer.'

Jake laughed and started the engine.

'Do you really think this is how it's going to work? Where we're taking you, you're going to wish to be back with that baying mob.

'Save us some time, and yourself a lot of pain, and tell us what you took with you.'

The man shook his head vigorously.

'I took nothing. Everyone around me started dying and I figured we weren't paid enough for that so I should get out while I still could. It was meant to be fucking empty. No one said that there'd be a fleet of assassins down there.'

Jake smirked. 'There wasn't a whole fleet. Just one. That one.' He nodded at me.

I grinned and gave John a little wave.

'Fuck me. A girl? You're shitting me?'

'How about we drop John back off with that other bunch of girls he was having such trouble with?'

'OK, OK, I'm sorry. I just . . . Look, I took nothing, OK? I know nothing.'

Jake took John on to the Warehouse to join the rest of his colleagues in a continued interrogation with Cameron. If he had taken anything they would find out. I doubted he had. Having met him I was inclined to believe he was more of the cowardly running-for-his-life ilk and not efficient-operative-making-fast-getaway-with-the-goods.

I returned to the Platform to help with the Snake hunt.

'Robin is in position,' said Hattie, 'waiting for George to exit Six.'

233

'Frederick seemed to think Peppa might be leaving London after the WAF pottery café morning tomorrow.'

'We should get a tracker on her,' suggested Geraint.

'I don't like it.' Hattie shook his head. 'She finds a tracker and it's game over. Both Peppa and Tenebris know we're onto them.'

'How else we goin' to keep eyes on them?' asked Pixie. 'She's trained. We can't risk losing sight of her location.'

'Wherever she's going she's bringing her daughter, Bella. Dionne the nanny is away for the weekend and mentioned that Peppa had various things planned with her.' I was flicking through our surveillance photos of Peppa, Dionne and Bella. I looked at the dolly clasped in Bella's hands. I'd never seen her without it. It was in every surveillance photo.

'Dolly,' I announced.

'What?'

'Bella's dolly. She takes her everywhere with her. We find a replacement and stick a tracker inside it.'

Hattie nodded. 'Do it.'

I looked at Geraint and Pixie. 'We need to source an identical doll by this afternoon so it's ready in time for tomorrow morning's WAF meeting.'

Pixie's fingers were flying across her laptop.

'DollyWorld stopped making this type of doll last year. But there's one on eBay from a seller in Hoxton. I can get a courier to pick it up within the hour.'

Pixie pressed a few buttons and the Hoxton dolly image was projected onto the whiteboard alongside the real dolly.

I assessed the two photos.

'Bella's dolly has clearly been through the washing machine countless times. And look here – the hem of her dress has come undone. There's a small hole in the hood. And there's one patch here that seems to be the most faded of all – that must be where she rubs it. It has to be perfect. Gigi can spot a fake Monkey a mile off. There's no way of knowing this little girl won't be the same. Soon as it arrives you need to get to work on it.'

A ping came in to all of our phones. An Uber alert. George Pig had requested an Uber and Robin had accepted the job.

One of Eight's preferred method of securing targets for interrogation was through waiting for them to book an Uber and then sweeping them back to Platform Eight in a modified car with unlockable passenger doors and soundproofed tinted windows. Or in this case taking them to whichever destination they inputted, safe in the knowledge there was no greater way to know where your target was going than by being the person driving them there.

'The destination is the corner of New Cavendish and Harley Street,' read out Hattie.

'Asia House is on New Cavendish Street,' said Geraint.

'He's either going there or they have a designated meeting spot or safe house close by. Lex, get to Asia House. If he goes in there we can presume he's the Snake. G, Pixie, start checking CCTV of New Cavendish Street in the last twenty-four hours. We need to know if anyone else we recognise has been there.'

I parked my bike just off New Cavendish Street and took out my phone, checking the Platform Uber app. Robin was just about to turn the corner. I looked up and saw him. He gave me a nod as he pulled to a halt next to where my bike was parked. I stared down at my phone as George Pig got out the car.

I watched as he set off in the direction of Asia House.

It was looking promising.

I followed behind. '*We're watching through the CCTV,*' Geraint came in through my earpiece.

I kept a good twenty feet behind him. Not so close he would notice me. We were four doors down from the entrance to Asia House.

In my ear I heard Geraint. '*Asia House are hosting an event called Asian Development Outlook. That can be your cover.*'

I kept my eyes on George. He walked straight past Asia House and into the café two doors down. The meet must be happening there. The café was busy but I spotted him in the corner by the door as I entered. He was standing by a table. He looked over at me as I walked in. I stared straight ahead and went up to the counter. I spent a couple of seconds admiring their pastries before risking a look around.

George Pig was nowhere to be seen.

Dammit, could he have recognised me from somewhere? Had I spooked him?

I rushed out the door and looked up and down the street. He can't have gone far. Could he have slipped into Asia House already?

I was about to call Robin for back-up but then I spotted him.

He was walking away from me just up ahead. How had I missed him? I walked fast; the distance between us closed. He was a street ahead when I noticed something was off. He was walking slowly. Why? I crossed the road. I was now ten feet behind him. Was he . . . was he pushing something?

He suddenly stopped and turned towards a building entrance. I caught sight of what he was pushing, and the building he was going into.

Everything became clear.

We had got it so wrong.

A few phone calls when I got back to the Platform confirmed that I had reached the correct conclusion.

Zurich doesn't just have private banks.

It also has Dignitas. A place where those with terminal illnesses could go to die. And Asia House was on the street next to the Harley Street Clinic.

There was no traitor visiting private Swiss banks and having covert meetings with assassins.

Just a man trying to reconcile his wife with her mother before she died.

I had taken one look at the occupant of the wheelchair George was pushing and I had known. Even with a scarf delicately tied round her head, I could see the family resemblance.

'I don't get it.' Robin shook his head. 'The woman in the wheelchair could be a plant? He could still have been meeting the Coyote inside the clinic?'

'It's his mother-in-law. She's got terminal cancer. He found out she'd booked herself into Dignitas. He flew out there to talk her down and bring her home.'

'How come the wife didn't talk about it?' asked Hattie.

'She didn't know. They're estranged. He's done it all on the quiet. Booked her into a private clinic for more treatment and no doubt a chance to make things right with Kate before she dies.'

What George was doing was admirable. He knew, despite Kate's apparent ambivalence to having her mother in her life, that she would be heartbroken if she left this world without making things right. For all Kate's worrying and complaining that she wasn't appreciated, that she wasn't valued, I hoped she would see the love in what George was doing and how next to that, all the little stuff paled in comparison.

'Being a good husband shouldn't rule out the fact he could still be the Snake,' said Hattie. 'We continue surveillance on him, but Peppa has now become our priority.'

'We've found a link between Peppa and the Chinese Embassy,' said Geraint. 'Peppa's local dry cleaners is owned by a Karen Lim. Her sister Alice works at the Chinese Embassy. We've red-flagged this connection, as in the last couple of weeks Peppa has visited the dry cleaners on five different occasions.'

'And this is a deviation from her usual pattern?'

Pixie squinted at her screen as she scrolled down. 'In the last year, her usage of this dry cleaners was more like once every two to three months.'

'What do we have on Alice Lim?'

'Limited information. She's been at the Embassy for nearly eight years. Implies she's pretty high up. We haven't been able to locate her yet. If she's funnelling confidential information about Peng and the delegation to Peppa using the dry cleaners, it's a very safe way of doing it. No in-person interaction.'

Hattie nodded. 'It makes sense. If Alice and Peppa are working together then the Coyote will have all the information they need to make the hit. How are we doing with the doll?' He motioned towards Hoxton dolly on the meeting room table.

'The tracker is inside the doll's stomach,' said Geraint. 'We used our thinnest, most lightweight model. It means the range isn't as good but anything bigger would've made her look noticeably pregnant.'

I held up Hoxton dolly against the enlarged photo of the real dolly on the whiteboard. They looked identical. 'I think it will be OK. The only problem is the smell.' I picked up Hoxton dolly and gave it a sniff. 'There's just no way of knowing if they smell alike. She could reject it outright.'

'I checked the brand of washing powder Peppa uses and used the same one,' offered Pixie.

'So our whole plan for success rests upon whether a three-year-old can spot a fake doll?' Hattie sighed and looked round at us all. 'We're in trouble. Real trouble. We haven't confirmed the identities of the Snake or the Coyote. They are both still in operation and out there circling Peng. Tomorrow she will be at Lord Wycombe's shoot surrounded by guns and well over a hundred of people we haven't cleared.'

'What are you suggesting we do, boss?' asked Robin.

'We need to get her to understand the risk and to cancel.'

'Admitting to Peng and her people that we have a security leak and that's why she could end up dead is something the Committee would never approve,' I said. 'It's giving China the heads-up they can place all the blame at our door should anything happen.'

'We could try and get her to back out without explaining why it's so high-risk?' suggested Robin.

'Peng is not going to listen to the British Security Services. She has no reason to trust any of us, especially if we can't explain the situation in full.' Hattie pinched the bridge of his nose as he leaned back in his chair. 'If any of us had a relationship with her we'd have a shot, but it's not like we're going to be welcomed into her suite for a cosy off-the-record chat.'

I remembered something from a file I had read a long time ago. About a Rat and a certain mission in China. Could it be? I looked it up on our server as everyone continued to debate the situation. A few clicks and it was confirmed.

'I have an idea,' I announced. 'I just need to make a call.'

Chapter Twenty-One

I KNOCKED ON THE DOOR of Peng's suite at the Mandarin Oriental. Her assistant Ling Ling opened the door.

'Hello, Miss Alexis, Minister Peng is expecting you.'

Ling Ling showed no sign of recognising me as the catsuited woman chasing her would-be mugger, but then she would've only had a brief glimpse of me streaking past her as she lay winded on the street.

Ling Ling led me through an opulent entrance hall and into the suite's large sitting room where the floor-to-ceiling windows framed an impressive view of Hyde Park. I took in the lavish silk wall coverings, marble fireplace and deep sofas. A large platter of breakfast pastries had been placed in the centre of the marble coffee table, alongside a vast china teapot and three matching dainty teacups and saucers.

The largest sofa next to the coffee table had an ornate wooden frame and plumped-up pale-blue cushions.

And upon it sat Minister Peng and Mrs Moulage.

They both stood up.

Ling Ling nodded at Peng and left the room, closing the panelled door behind her.

'Hello, Agent Tyler.' Peng strode forward and clasped my hand in hers. 'It is good to meet you. Doris has filled me in on everything. Please come sit.' She motioned towards the armchair next to them.

Doris? Did I finally know Mrs Moulage's real name?

'Thank you for meeting me, Minister Peng. I understand this is unorthodox but when I saw from our files that you had crossed paths with Mrs Moulage, I hoped you might be open to an off-the-record conversation.'

'We've known each other for over forty years.' Peng turned to Mrs Moulage. 'I owe everything to this woman, yet requesting that I meet with you is the first time she's ever asked me for anything.'

'The files mention your first meeting, how it was at the People's Congress during the aftermath of a high-profile delegate's assassination. Did you help with her mission?'

Peng and Mrs Moulage exchanged a look.

'The files won't tell you the full story of what happened that night.' Peng reached over to the teapot and filled up each of the teacups. 'I was working late. I was ambitious even then, as a junior clerk. One of my superiors came across me alone in one of the offices and decided to take advantage of the situation.'

She poured a tiny splash of milk into Mrs Moulage's teacup and handed it to her.

'Milk? Sugar?' she asked me.

'Just milk, please.'

I watched as her hand shook a little as she poured it in and handed it to me.

'I made quite a bit of noise.' She took a sip of her tea. 'Thankfully, Doris was passing by that office at that moment and heard the commotion. She didn't have to get involved. It could've risked her whole mission. But she walked in on us, shot him dead and told me to run.' Peng looked over at Mrs Moulage. 'She saved me.'

'And then you saved me back.' Mrs Moulage smiled.

'Doris was caught by police just outside Congress; one of them thought he had recognised her from earlier, behaving suspiciously. She was trying the lost tourist act and they weren't believing her.'

'Until you came up to me saying, "Audrey, there you are. Audrey, let's go for dinner now."'

The two women laughed.

'I thought she looked like Audrey Hepburn and it was the only foreigner name I could think of. We were able to walk away from the police and were eating Beijing's best *jiaozi* dumplings before they found even one of the two dead men in Congress that night.'

'The details of how Siew-Yong and I met are not in the files because what I did went against all our protocols. Especially the part where I let her walk away because I trusted her to never tell anyone what she knew. But sometimes you have to rely on your instincts and do what you think is right.'

'Well, Doris, you have good instincts. All these decades later and this is first time I've spoken about it.' Peng reached over and patted Mrs Moulage on the knee.

'I'm glad you rang me, Lex,' said Mrs Moulage. 'After the warehouse I did worry your mission had something to do with Siew-Yong and I no longer have the required clearance to get into Eight's system. You need to explain to her what you told me.'

'Minister Peng, we are coming to you, unofficially, to warn of an imminent threat to your life. The Chinese People's Alliance have hired an assassin to kill you while you're here in the UK.'

'I know,' said Peng. She topped her cup up with more tea. 'They're always trying to kill me. They and various other terrorist organisations. I seem to make a lot of people very angry. Most of my dresses have to be tailored round a bulletproof vest.'

'That's sacrilege, Siew-Yong, utter sacrilege.' Mrs Moulage, resplendent in a beautifully cut dark pink midi-dress, shook her head.

'Minister Peng, I understand you're used to living with the threat but this time it's different. It's much more dangerous. Right now our Security Services are compromised. There is a leak. We don't know if we can trust even our own people.'

'And you worry they are feeding information to my enemies.'

I nodded. 'The Wycombe shoot that you're attending tomorrow. It is most likely they will strike there and we won't be able to protect you. There are too many variables. Too many points of entry. Too many guns.'

'I understand the risks. But you must understand I have to go.' Peng put her cup down on the table. 'There are things I prefer to not go into but getting this contract with Lord Wycombe's company signed relies on certain conversations I need to have with certain people who'll be attending. Returning to China without this contract will be considered a massive failing on my part. I will struggle to maintain control and respect. The factions that seek to undo me will try that bit harder, and have that much more support.'

'Is it worth dying over, Siew-Yong?' asked Mrs Moulage.

Peng sighed. 'I know that both of you will understand how to get to this position I have had to fight every step of the way. In China our most influential philosopher, a man called Confucius, believed "women are to be led, and to follow others". He died nearly two and a half thousand years ago and his influence is still ingrained in most of the government's way of thinking. That is what I am up against.'

Peng put her teacup back on the table.

'Over my years in office I've seen average men thrive without any real effort. And I've seen brilliant women sidelined and ignored. Ling Ling and the rest of my staff, the ones who really know me, they call me *biàn sè lóng*. The chameleon. Because that is what I have had to be. I don't get the privilege to be myself. I don't get to just turn up. Each meeting I have I prepare for, I have to research everything I can about who will be sitting across the table from me. I find out what kind of "me" they will respond to. Respectful, grateful, pleading, strong, fearsome. If I need to charm, if I need to threaten, what I need to do to win them over.

'I'm sixty-four now. I've worked my whole life to get to this ministerial position. And this will be as far as I ever get. But at least right now there will be girls growing up getting to see me here. In a position of power. And that is all I want. To be seen here, to be seen doing my job well, and bowing out still with my head held high.'

Peng's voice never wavered as she spoke. I knew I wouldn't be able to convince her to do what was best for her own safety. She couldn't show weakness, she couldn't fail, she couldn't stop. She was fighting for her legacy.

'I understand, Minister.'

'I'm glad we met, Lex. I feel in good hands with you.'

'I will do my best,' I said. I meant it. Meeting Peng, being impressed by her, made me all the more determined to keep her alive.

We all got to our feet. Mrs Moulage shrugged on her fur coat and picked up her snakeskin handbag.

Peng and Mrs Moulage embraced. 'Stay safe, Siew-Yong.'

'And you, Doris.'

*

245

Mrs Moulage and I got into the waiting lift together. I pressed the ground-floor button and the doors closed.

'Doris Moffett,' Mrs Moulage announced into the silence. 'That was the name I was born with. Little Doris Moffett had no control over her life. She didn't get to say where she lived, what people did to her or who she really was. So one day Doris Moffett became Mrs Moulage. And everything changed.' She turned to me and smiled.

'Is there a Mr Moulage?'

'There's never been a Mr Moulage. I changed my name for me. I used the Mrs as I was operating in an era where I needed it. Men bothered me less, women liked me more.'

The lift doors opened and we walked to the Mandarin Oriental main entrance. Mrs Moulage turned to the cheery-looking uniformed doorman. 'Taxi, please.'

'Certainly, madam.' He headed out into the cold.

'You'll need to keep your wits about you at the shoot. The Coyote is unlikely to attack without a fleet of Ghosts behind him.'

'I know. It's not going to be easy.'

The doorman opened the door with a flourish. 'One's here, madam.' He led the way with his arm.

We walked out together and stood at the top of the steps.

'If they come for her' – Mrs Moulage touched a hand to my face – 'you knock 'em dead, sweetie.' She walked down the steps and got into the back of the waiting black cab. 'You knock 'em dead,' she repeated as she pulled shut the door.

'Nothing like a pep talk from your mum, is there?' said the doorman as we watched the taxi drive away.

Chapter Twenty-Two

'WHO'S FREDERICK?' Will was in the kitchen waving my phone at me. He must have arrived back from the office while I was upstairs changing.

'I work with him, and funnily enough his daughter is at nursery with Gigi. You know Florence? The sweet, quiet one?' I walked over to Will and took the phone out of his hand. 'Why? What's he saying?'

'I just saw something about a password for a phonics website.'

That message was sent a day ago during the Platform Eight invasion.

'You've been going through my messages?'

I thought with a start how lucky it was I'd deleted the many post-funfair WhatsApp messages from Shona and Frankie grilling me on Frederick.

Will shrugged. 'I was bored waiting for the kettle to boil. You seem to get a lot of junk mail.'

'Sorry my phone doesn't have more interesting information for you.' Whereas I thought going through Will's phone would be an admission that I didn't trust him, he clearly had no such qualms.

'Come on, finish that coffee, we need to go.'

Will gulped it down and followed me out the kitchen. 'So where are you taking me?'

Anita, our neighbour's nineteen-year-old daughter, was already slumped on the sofa in the sitting room with *Geordie Shore* playing loudly on the television.

'The hottest ticket in town.' I handed him a leaflet.

He looked down at it: *Ms Yvonne's Introduction to the Early Learning Syllabus.*

'Are you kidding me? This is what we've booked a babysitter for? Why do I have to come?'

'Because we're both her parents. Because anything that's deemed important enough for a letter from her headteacher we should go to. Especially considering since BiteGate we have some making up to do.'

'She hasn't chomped on anyone else, has she?' Will couldn't keep the laugh out of his voice. He didn't seem to take Gigi's violent lashing out as seriously as me.

'Thankfully not.'

'Will Rochelle be there?'

I turned round to look at him. 'Why? Do you want her to be?'

'You jealous?'

'Please. I'd like to think you'd have better taste than a fawning lapdog.'

'Because of course men hate it when women tell them how brilliant they are and make them feel good about themselves by being transfixed by everything they say.'

'Right.'

'Yes, what we really love is being mostly ignored, never getting a straight answer and being left alone for long evenings while they're out doing who knows what with who knows whom.' He pulled on his coat and headed out the door.

It seemed we continued to be in a bad place. And Will now thought it was OK to go through my phone looking for answers to questions he hadn't asked me yet.

Upon arrival at Gigi's nursery we were immediately accosted by Ms Yvonne telling us that we were not to leave without Gigi's runner bean plant. 'These plants teach the children important lessons about nurturing and growth.'

I took in the plastic cup with a wilted bit of greenery stuck in some soil and kitchen roll and resisted the urge to add, 'And the inevitability of death.'

We headed through to take our seats. I noted how Rochelle was, of course, seated right at the front. She cut off her conversation with the woman next to her to give an enthusiastic wave to Will, and a less enamoured one to me once I walked in front of him. I looked round the pokey Portakabin packed full of parents crouched into small children-sized chairs and spotted Camilla in the row behind Rochelle. No Frederick. I was relieved. I tried not to think too much into why I didn't want Will and Frederick to meet.

The only empty chairs left were a few over from Rochelle in the front row. So now not only did we have to sit through the talk but we were right in front of Ms Yvonne and couldn't get away with checking our emails in the boring bits.

After an excruciating hour, where I mostly learned I had no idea how to pronounce the alphabet phonetically, the Early Learning talk was finally finishing. We were all getting up to make a break for the door when Weather Mum put up her hand.

'As we're all here, Ms Yvonne, we were wondering if we could make a request for the children to be read more of the classic fairy tales they all love at home.' Weather Mum smiled round the room.

Yvonne's face remained impassive. 'We do not believe in reading children horror stories.'

Weather Mum looked startled. 'That's not what I ... Ms Yvonne, we are talking about fairy tales. You know, all the favourite classics like *Cinderella* or—'

'*Cinderella*?' Yvonne cut her off. 'I cannot support a political story re-imposing beliefs of "us" and "them".'

Weather Mum frowned. 'What do you mean?'

'*Cinderella* is an allegorical depiction of how we treat immigrants. She's the invisible help maligned and living in rags and doing all the work no one else wants to. The Prince symbolises benefits and the help that our great country can offer. Yet in order to receive it the needy are forced to dance around numerous bureaucratic applications and only if the glass slipper fits, if they tick all the boxes, can they be fully assimilated into the United Kingdom.'

'Right,' said Weather Mum.

'But what about *Sleeping Beauty*?' asked Felix's mum. 'My son loves that one, even though it's about a princess.'

Yvonne shook her head. '*Sleeping Beauty* is a tragic story. I mean, the whole pricking of a finger on a spinning wheel, we all know what that really means.'

'We do?' I asked.

'She was raped,' Yvonne announced.

I looked round the room at parents struggling to hold it together. Will actually looked up from his phone.

'What the fuck?' is all he breathed into my ear.

Yvonne sighed. 'The poor girl spiralled into a towering depression from which only medication – symbolised by a kiss – could rescue her from. It's a terrible story where even if you don't understand the deeper message it perpetuates some pretty disturbing ideas about consent.'

Rochelle raised her hand. 'I guess you feel the same about *Snow White*? I do agree that fairy tales really shouldn't romanticise the idea that it is acceptable for men to kiss unconscious women.'

Weather Mum shot her a filthy look.

Yvonne nodded at Rochelle. 'I'm afraid it goes so much deeper than that with *Snow White*. It's really a commentary on how the patriarchy represses women.'

Will chuckled. 'I thought it was all just nice songs and little people.'

Yvonne ignored him. 'The talking mirror is male – the evil queen's actions are in response to toxic masculinity ranking women by their looks and pitting them against each other.'

We were all silent as we digested this.

'So ... so ... the evil queen is not a baddie?' asked Rochelle, pen poised over her notebook.

'The man behind the mirror twisted and turned the evil queen's insecurity on looks and age into a weapon. Young and old, Madonna and whore – society wants us women to fit neatly into boxes. Snow White is a symbol of the male ideal of purity, youth and beauty that the evil queen cannot measure up to and so she tries to destroy her. With an apple. Just like Eve.'

The fact a nursery teacher had just said 'whore' in a nursery was the least surprising takeaway from that speech.

'And why does the evil queen fail to kill Snow White? Because another man sexually dominates her incapacitated form, egged on by seven small men who are clearly a personalisation of the seven deadly sins.'

'I just . . . I . . . what?' Will looked around the room. 'What's going on?' I gave him a sharp jab with my elbow. He swivelled to me. 'She's nuts, right? We let this woman look after our child and she's totally nuts.'

Yvonne continued, 'So, you see, women can try and take control of the narrative, take charge of their own image, yet the overwhelming power of the patriarchy means they will fail. The man in the mirror belittles the evil queen and turns her against the sisterhood, yet when she tries to destroy this male concept of female perfection she cannot succeed because a woman is no match for a man's virulent sexuality. The evil queen is ruined twice over by two different men.'

We all sat in silence for a minute. A respectful quiet to mourn the loss of fairy tales' innocence.

'On reflection,' said Weather Mum weakly, 'the books you read are fine. Totally fine.'

The coup was crushed.

'Please do feel free to stay for a drink,' trilled Yvonne as we all got up to charge for the exit. We passed by her, heads down, muttering about needing to get back for the babysitter.

Halfway back home I realised in the rush to exit I'd left Gigi's runner bean plant under my chair. I relayed this disaster to Will and we analysed just how much not having the plant she'd been talking about all week would screw up our morning.

Will sighed. 'You go on. I'll get it.'

'You're my hero,' I said to his departing back.

By the time Will walked in, wilted plant in hand, the kitchen table was unpacked with Chinese takeaway.

'Ta-daa. Look, honey, I ordered.' Deliverooing on the walk home was a mark of genius on my part.

Will dropped the plant on the kitchen counter, went to the fridge and took out a beer.

'Rochelle was still there when I got back to the school.'

Shit.

'She couldn't stop talking about how funny it was seeing you and Johnnie Mac being dropped off in a chauffeur-driven limousine.'

'He's actually an old friend.'

Will stared at me. 'You know that his music is on every bloody playlist I have. And you've never thought to mention you're actually mates with him?'

'It's a bit awkward.' I walked past him to the drawer for the bottle-opener. 'We had a bit of a thing. It was years back.'

'You. And Johnnie Mac.'

'Yes. Well, kind of.' I took the beer out his hand, opened it and handed it back. 'It wasn't anything serious.'

'Jesus. That song. "Lady." It's about you, isn't it?'

'I . . . Well . . . Not necessarily.'

'*The three freckles were a pathway to heaven. A heaven that'd torment me to hell.*' He quoted one of the lines of the song. 'You really think there are others out there with three freckles underneath their hip bone leading down to—'

I cut him off. 'He's a rockstar. He's probably slept with hundreds of women. Odds are, when talking about such vast numbers, there could be one or two, maybe even three with freckles round there.'

'Who are you kidding? God, to think I used to chuckle when I heard that song and thought about my own little pathway to heaven. And now I find out it's a fucking well-trodden road as this guy has slept with my wife.'

'Look, it's not that big a deal.'

'I just don't understand why you wouldn't mention it. I mean, it's pretty amazing. Even in an anecdotal kind of way. How was it that at no point when we were in our getting-to-know-you stage, that lying in bed discussing exes, you felt any desire to say, "'Hey, funny story – I screwed around with a rockstar and it messed him up so much he wrote a song about it?'"

'I just found it a bit embarrassing. You know I don't care about celebrities and all that showbiz stuff.'

'How did you even meet?'

'It was through work. He was assisting us on an intelligence matter. Look, you know I can't say more. National security.'

'How. Convenient.'

'Come on, Will, it's not that big a deal.'

'And what the hell were you doing with him a few days ago? Being driven back from a bloody lunchtime quickie?'

'Don't be ridiculous. We were at the same work meeting. You don't have anything to be jealous of.'

'Don't try and make me out to be some crazy, jealous husband. Look at Jake – I've never said a word about whatever history there clearly is between you two. I like the guy, I even let you make him godfather to our child. It's a little different when it's some rockstar who, up until today, I thought the closest we both got to was drunk dancing to his music. What the hell else don't I know about you?'

He stormed out of the kitchen holding his beer. I sat down at the table and looked at all the food laid out. I was positive he'd come back and I'd hand him a plate of his favourite noodles and his anger face would drop and we'd have a little giggle about how his hunger had ruined his big exit.

But he didn't come back.

Part Five

Tantrum

tantrum, *n.*
1. An uncontrolled outburst of anger and frustration, typically in a young child.
2. A fit of rage.

From: euromillionslottery@goldenticket.org
To: lex.tyler@platform-eight.co.uk
Subject: You are a WINNER$$$$$
MISSION: #80521
UNIT: WHISTLE
DATE: Saturday 5th October
ALERT: PENG DEPARTS TOMORROW EVENING

Chapter Twenty-Three

HATTIE WAS HOLDING COURT at the front of the meeting room. 'Today Lord Wycombe and his family will be hosting Peng and the delegation in their modest little forty-bedroom castle in Oxfordshire, where they'll be treating them to the full aristocratic experience. Peng gets there for lunch and then will partake in a pheasant shoot followed by a spot of duck hunting, rounded off with a champagne reception and a four-course black-tie dinner.'

I'd got to work this morning with a renewed vigour for succeeding in this mission. Sitting at breakfast, Gigi had sung-shouted 'Twinkle Twinkle, Little Star' to us as she spoon-fed porridge to her dolly, and I had apologised to Will again. Holding his hand, we'd reached another temporary truce as I'd promised quality time away together next week. Now we really needed to wrap this mission up so I could deliver. Peng, alive, and out the country. Frederick, back at Six, and out of my life. And me, focusing on my family.

'We all know this is the prime time for the Coyote to strike,' Hattie continued. 'It's a security nightmare and I've only been able to get Lex inside the castle. They would only grant permission for one Diplomatic Protection Officer as it's a private event and they're claiming they have more than enough security present to keep Peng safe.'

'Frederick will be there too,' I said. 'He told me he was at school with Lord Wycombe so has already got himself an invite.'

Jake snorted. ''Course he has. Why am I not surprised they're chums?'

'Jake – we'll be on-site monitoring the perimeter. With Lex and Frederick within the main party, at least we'll have eyes in the midst of any potential action.'

'Peng's spending the afternoon surrounded by people holding shotguns. I'm not sure just Frederick and me are going to be enough protection.'

'Let's just bear in mind the Coyote is going to need an exit plan,' said Hattie. 'A gun for hire is for profit. No point in succeeding in the mission if he's taken out or caught in the process. He needs to walk away from this and that is our best hope of catching him.

'Remember, things are looking up. Tenebris are running scared. They're making mistakes. And we're very close to unmasking the Snake. Peppa is now the prime suspect. Daddy Pig's marriage is imploding – there's a flurry of activity online and the audio is all about divorce lawyers and shouting matches. Even if he was the Snake he wouldn't have time to be covertly passing on information. George Pig has now told Kate about her mother and he's got his hands full with her grief and guilt and all the rest. I still don't like those suspicious emails but it's looking unlikely he's the Snake.'

'What are we waiting for then?' asked Cameron. She took a bite of the large bacon sandwich she had just unwrapped.

'We pick up Peppa now and we end this,' she said through her mouthful.

'We have no direct evidence that Peppa is the Snake,' said Hattie. 'The Committee have clearly stated we cannot act until we have something, anything, confirming our suspicions. Peppa will shortly be attending the WAF pottery café morning and we've intercepted a text message from an unknown number – it's registered to a pay-as-you-go – saying they must meet today.'

'No confirmation on where or when?' I asked.

'None. They must've arranged it in person or using some form of communication we haven't managed to monitor. It's why we can't let her out of our sight today. Getting that dolly with the tracker into play is vital so that Cameron and Robin can monitor her while we're all away at the shoot.'

'I'm heading to the WAF meet now. I'll let you know when the switch has been made.'

I stood up and picked up my bag. Jake came up to me.

'I hear Will found out about Johnnie.'

'What did you tell him?'

'Just that he needn't worry. He was just a twat in tight trousers. That you never gave a shit about him and that—'

'I meant, what did you tell him about how we met?'

'I said he was an informant. What did you say?'

'Something similar, thankfully.'

Jake looked at me. 'Are you OK?'

'What do you mean?'

'You're stressed. You're not normally this stressed.' He took my hand and held up my left thumb and ran a finger over the bitten-down nail. 'You haven't given this little guy such a battering since that time we were trapped out in the middle of the Sahara.'

I looked at my thumb. I had no idea I did that.

'Lex. Come on. Talk to me if you need to. I'm family, remember?'

'It's just Will stuff. Keeping things hidden is hard. This mission is hard. Not getting enough sleep is hard.' I shrugged. 'Everything is hard. But don't worry, I'll get through it. And it helps knowing you're here if I need you.'

'Always,' said Jake softly.

I looked around the meeting room. 'Where's Robin?'

'He's late. When he gets here I'll give him a lecture about the responsibilities of timekeeping when he's got his own unit.' It seemed Jake was also coming around to the idea of us finally granting Robin his freedom from our watch.

I walked into the Fulham branch of Potty for Pottery holding Gigi's hand. At one end of the expansive café was a large soft play area, complete with ball pit, slides and mini trampoline. The cacophony of cries, screams and laughs were interspersed with the crinkle and thud of little bottoms hitting plastic matting. I looked around at the children flinging themselves down the slides. Alternating mothers shouting, 'Archie/Matilda/Otto, do you need a wee?'

I already missed the quiet solitude of the Platform.

Gigi had torn off into the ball pit.

I looked around. No one else from our WAF group was here yet. I surveyed the room. Whoever Peppa was meeting could be here now.

There were a group of seven or so mothers at a large table by the café counter. All had prams parked next to them. Half had babies clamped to their breasts. They were the perfect advert for the sign that hung on the wall behind them: *Potty for Pottery WELCOMES breastfeeding AND bottle-feeding mothers. AND fathers.* The sign was doing its best to be as politically correct as possible.

It was busy, with most of the larger tables taken by groups of parents catching up for a Saturday brunch as their offspring catapulted themselves round the soft play.

I walked between tables and heard snippets of conversation between the mothers.

'Marnie is a wonderful sleeper. We are very blessed.'

'Araminta doesn't sleep at all. But it's because her mind is so active she finds it hard to shut down. It's one of the real downsides to her being so intellectually gifted.'

Competitive parenting didn't take time off, even on weekends.

A line of women stood alongside the soft play area, a few chatting to each other, most shouting instructions at children who were being threatened with time-outs, the thinking step, the naughty corner and a clip round the bleeding ear – the mum who kept shouting that threat was being stared at more than the misbehaving toddlers.

'She clearly wasn't hugged enough when she was a child,' sighed the tall, willowy mother who had arrived next to me. Her disapproval radiated out every perfectly manicured pore. She had a shaggy brunette cut with a fringe and was wearing a block-print jumpsuit with Isabel Marant trainers.

'Her son does look a terror.' I motioned towards the curly-haired boy running around, pushing over anyone who came near him.

'Frieda, sweetheart. Go to the slide!' the tall mum shouted to a little girl in grey harem pants and a chequered hoodie. She motioned towards a slide on the opposite side of the soft play to the pusher.

'Great outfit she's wearing.'

Tall Mum smiled. 'I only buy gender-neutral clothing.'

'I completely agree. It's so important that girls don't feel stereotyped.'

Tall Mum nodded approvingly. It was good to meet a kindred spirit. Someone else who understands that the lines between what was for girls and what was for boys could benefit from being more blurred.

'Mamaaa, I want snack.' Gigi came bounding up to us. She was wearing a bright pink flowered dress with a puffball skirt, teamed with rainbow socks and pink sparkly trainers.

Did I need to explain that I let her choose what she wanted to wear this morning? That the dress was bought by a doting grandmother? Or that the awful trainers were a result of a hungover shoe shop trip where I didn't have the energy to fight the 'But I love them!!!!!' tantrum. Tall Mum's nose may have wrinkled at my daughter, the pink explosion.

My street cred dented, I needed to make a retreat.

'Come on, Gigi. This way.'

I took her back towards the table that had a 'Reserved for Alexis' sign.

'Let's sit and wait for everyone.'

I pulled a couple of rice cakes out my bag and handed them to Gigi while I scanned the room again. A man at the table next to us stood out. He was wearing sunglasses and had a baseball cap pulled down low. I stared at him again. He definitely didn't look famous. And that was surely the only excuse to be so questionably attired in a soft play centre on a cloudy October day. Unless of course he was just trying to be cool. But he didn't seem to be a poser. He wasn't lounging back in his chair, guffawing with equally ridiculously dressed friends. He was alone, staring down at a cup of coffee. I hadn't even seen him with a child. One to watch.

Peppa walked in with Bella. Her blonde hair swung in a high ponytail. She was wearing jeans and a striped shirt. It was the first time I'd seen her in person. Although having learned so much about her from her online correspondence and internet history, I felt we were old friends. There was so much I could say to her. *'That guy on Match.com with the nice blue eyes who "works in the Midlands half the week" is clearly married.' 'No, you're not stupid, I didn't understand the ending of* Lost *either.'* And, *'Ignore that cow you were at school with; choosing not to have Botox and to still eat carbs is not a sign you've given up on life.'*

'Hello, Bella,' shouted Gigi as she tore off back to the soft play, with Bella following.

'Hi, Suzannah, I'm Alexis. Lovely to meet you.'

'Call me Suze.' She shook my hand.

Camilla arrived with Florence. 'Hello, Alexis. Hello.' She nodded at Suze just as her phone rang. She looked at the screen. 'Sorry, I need to . . .' She peeled off, motioning for Florence to go join Gigi and Bella, who were now jumping into the ball pit.

'I'll just check they're OK,' said Peppa, nodding towards the girls.

Naomi walked in with Kate's twins. 'Hi, Alexis. Kate sends her apologies. She's having a bit of a family emergency. She might make it, she might not.'

'Of course. Totally understand.'

Naomi busied herself undoing the twins' coats and hats. It was nice that their bonding over Naomi's bastard husband had clearly cemented their friendship. I watched Peppa standing by the ball pit. She wasn't making any sign of looking at anyone other than her daughter, who was gingerly navigating a plastic beam.

I looked over at the man in the cap. He and Peppa had yet to acknowledge each other. A waitress arrived at his table with a heavily laden plate of fried breakfast. He took his sunglasses off, displaying bloodshot, bleary eyes.

Just then a wailing little girl in a tutu came running up to him.

'Dadaaaaaaa, Algie hit me with a ball.'

The cap man winced.

'Christ, Mia, do you *have* to cry so high-pitched?' He handed her a piece of fried bread. 'Now take this and be quiet. Daddy has a headache.'

He went back to cramming a ketchup-laden sausage in his mouth.

So much for enemy threat – he was simply a hungover dad.

I cursed myself for not factoring this into my analysis.

Who else here could Peppa be meeting with? I looked over at her again. Bella was now navigating her way down a slide. Peppa gave her a wave as she headed back to our table with not so much as a glance at any of the caffeine-inhaling adults around her.

Naomi came back to the table with a tray of unpainted tea-pots and teacups for the children and a large pot of coffee for us. She sat down and laid them all out, calling over to the twins.

All the children came charging back to the table. We fussed over them, encasing them in overalls, and let them loose on the array of paints and brushes laid out on the tables.

Naomi looked over at Peppa. 'Hello, I'm Naomi. You work with my husband Ronald, don't you?'

'Yes, I do. Our paths haven't crossed much but he seems well liked by everyone.'

'Oh, that's so nice to hear. Are you the one he's f-u-c-k-i-n-g?' Naomi reached across the table and filled Peppa's cup up with coffee.

Peppa glanced round at the children painting teapots.

Camilla actually let in a fast intake of air.

'I . . . I . . . No, Naomi, I'm not,' Peppa finally said.

We all stared down at the table. I felt the need to break the now painfully loaded tension.

'Naomi has just found out he's having s-e-x with someone at work. It's a difficult time.'

'I'm leaving him.' Naomi, took a bite of biscuit. 'I told him last night.'

On the way over I had scanned the transcript of their conversation. It had been horrible. Daddy Pig stated that he intended to withhold child maintenance and swore to make life as difficult as possible for his 'ungrateful bitch' of a wife. He'd been so cold as Naomi sobbed, I had wished he *was* the Snake so we could pop him and she could be free of him, without the costly lawyer bills that 'a dumb cow who hadn't worked in over ten years couldn't afford'.

She was going through hell but she'd got up this morning, given her children breakfast, fussed over their homework, searched round the house for missing ballet kit and told Daddy Pig he would be spending the day looking after the girls as it was clearly 'so bloody easy'. Now here she was helping out her friend Kate who was going through her own family trauma. I watched Naomi humming to herself as she helped one of the twins with their paintbrush.

Peppa cleared her throat. 'If you want any tips on being a single mum you can come to me.'

'What are they?'

'First of all, get used to people asking if you're having s-e-x with their husbands.'

The two women eyeballed each other and then laughed.

'That's lovely, darling. Really lovely.' Camilla adjusted Florence's large bow hairclip as she admired the painted teapot on the table.

Gigi turned to me. 'Mama – see?' She pointed to the teapot in front of her.

'Yes, Gigi, yours is really lovely too.'

Squiggles of green and blue and orange and red all mingled together to make an undesirable sludge brown. In fairness, what did anyone expect with undeveloped pincer grips and cheap paints? At least it meant I had a Christmas present sorted for Gillian, the world's most doting grandmother. Gigi's last finger painting, which Will and I both agreed looked like a wanking giraffe, had brought tears of joy to her eyes.

I looked down at Gigi. She was staring at her teapot again and smiling. I kissed the top of her head.

'You are amazing.' No lie here. She was perfection and I marvelled at her every single day.

I looked over at Bella. 'So what are you doing today, Bella?'

'Claudia! Sleepover!' shouted Bella.

Peppa laughed. 'We're staying with some friends tonight. Their daughter is Bella's age.'

'Sorry I'm late.' Kate appeared at the table. Her eyes were bloodshot and for the first time since I'd met her she wasn't wearing make-up.

'Hello, Mama!' Her twins waved at her with paint-covered hands.

'Hello, boys.' She dropped down in between them and gave them each a kiss. 'Thanks so much, Naomi, for taking them.'

'Anytime.' Naomi beamed. 'Nice to have them, and nice to hand them back.'

'Hi, Kate, we've met before. I'm Suze.'

Kate looked over at her and nodded. 'Nice to see you.'

'You OK, Kate?' I asked.

'I just . . . I've had some bad news. My mother is not doing so well.'

Looking at her there was no doubting that she was genuine. Having seen some of her work I knew she wasn't a good enough actress to fake that kind of raw emotion. She looked terrible.

She fingered her sleeve. 'I just thought we'd have more time. I mean, we've never got on that well. But she's my mum, you know?'

She was interrupted by her mobile going. She answered it and spoke a few monotonous yes and nos, and then, 'OK, got it. And don't forget. It was a special surprise to find four puppies there.'

I looked up at her. That was the sentence contained in the last suspicious email to George.

'Wow, you're getting four puppies?'

'It's a stupid dictation for my eldest son's spelling test. Utter pain in the arse. I leave it to my husband to drill him on them.'

I didn't know how I was going to break it to Geraint and Pixie that their efforts to crack the email code were wasted as it was simply a bloody spelling test.

I looked at Kate as she spoke quietly to her twins and dabbed the side of their teapots. George Pig was fully in the clear. I was glad. The last thing she needed adding to her trauma was us popping her husband.

With George and Daddy Pig ruled out, there was only Peppa left. It had to be her. She was the only one who had the intel on all the missions the Snake had ruined. She was the only one with a potential inside link to the Chinese delegation. We needed confirmation. Time was running out and we still had no idea how or when the Coyote would strike.

Naomi and Peppa were now speaking softly about lawyers and what lay ahead. Camilla and Kate were talking about her mother.

I looked over at Bella. Her dolly was on her lap as she continued to slop paint on her teapot. I just needed to get it away from her so I could make the swap.

Great. This was my life now. Trying to work out how to steal a three-year-old's doll.

I went up to the café counter and ordered a selection of chocolate cupcakes. I placed them at the other end of the table to Peppa and Bella.

'Kids, who wants a cupcake?'

Gigi and the twins leaned over and made a grab for them. Bella shot up from her chair, her doll falling to the floor under the table.

I walked back to my seat, leaning down to put my wallet back into my handbag on the floor. I scooped up Bella's doll and switched it with Hoxton dolly from my bag.

Well done me. Maybe my next assignment could be taking candy from a baby.

Bella came skipping back to her chair, the chocolate cupcake she was holding already half-eaten.

She sat back down, chocolate smeared across her face.

'I think this is yours?' I looked at her, smiling as I waved Hoxton dolly at her.

Peppa looked up. 'Ahh, yes, that's hers. Thank you.' Peppa reached across the table and took Hoxton dolly out my hand. 'Bella, you mustn't forget Dodo, you'd be so upset.'

The girl grabbed it from her and tucked it under her arm. She smelled its hood. She held it back and stared at it.

Here we were, the moment of reckoning.

'Not Dodo.'

'What? Don't be silly,' laughed Peppa. 'That's your Dodo. You just dropped her on the floor.' I watched Bella feel for the worn patch and give it a little rub. She stared again at the doll.

'Want more cake.'

We were OK.

Hoxton dolly had been accepted.

As mornings went it had been productive. Kate had confirmed our belief that all George was hiding was a wish for her to reconcile with her dying mother, I'd switched a girl's beloved dolly with a fake, reinforced my deep loathing of soft play, and Gigi had created a teapot masterpiece for her doting grandmother.

With a flurry of goodbyes Kate and the twins were the first to leave. I looked up and saw George Pig was waiting for them outside with their eldest son. She went straight into George's arms and he kissed the top of her head. They walked down the street together holding hands, the boys running circles round them. She might be going through hell but she had him, he was there to hold her up and do what he could to make things better. It was what having a partner was for. No matter what life threw at you, you had someone alongside you, fighting through it with you.

That's when what you were fighting wasn't each other.

I checked my watch. I needed to drop Gigi with my mother-in-law and get to the Platform. I said my own goodbyes and dragged a reluctant Gigi out of the café.

As I left I saw Cameron outside, map in hand, doing her best American tourist abroad look. I couldn't be sure but it looked as though her nose wrinkled slightly at the sight of Gigi. She must've been assigned Peppa duty.

Chapter Twenty-Four

I CAME OUT OF THE TUBE with Gigi. Straight in front of us were a group of mothers from nursery. I was planning on slipping by with my head down when Gigi stopped and said, 'HELLO!'

The mothers all turned to look at us. 'Oh, hello, Gigi, hello, Alexis.'

'Hi, how are you all?' I knew one was called Louise, one was Mimi's mum and the third was Weather Mum. I wondered if she had recovered since losing the fairy-tale coup.

'Great! We were just talking about the mums' night out. It's going to be such fun,' said Weather Mum.

'Louise is going to hire the back room of that new Italian place – lots of prosecco and prosciutto and high jinks,' giggled Mimi's mum. She gave me a nudge. 'Rather handsome waiters there, if you must know.'

'And as it's a private room we can really let our hair down,' beamed Weather Mum.

'It's going to be a riot,' said Louise.

'Oh yes. The mums' night out. I'm so gutted to miss it. Such a shame.'

Louise stared at me. 'I haven't sent the date out yet.'

The three of them looked at me, unsmiling.

Fuck.

'I . . . I . . . Can you believe that Miss Jenna is not Montessori-trained?'

'What?' said Mimi's mum.

'That can't be right,' frowned Weather Mum.

'But she's Sienna's key worker.' Louise looked aghast.

'Felix's mum called the Montessori board. She's not been registered. I mean, really, what we are paying this premium for if we aren't getting an actual Montessori-trained teacher?'

'That is ridiculous. I'm going to have to talk to the head,' said Louise.

I dragged Gigi away as they started chattering among themselves, my mums' night out faux-pas momentarily forgotten.

Geraint was crying. So was Pixie. They were sat in the meeting room holding hands on the table, tears rolling down their cheeks.

'Come on, you two. Lovers' tiff?' I was trying to be upbeat.

But I could feel it in the air.

Something bad.

Jake was pacing alongside the table on his phone.

'I understand. I get it.' He hung up and looked at me. 'It's Robin.'

I looked again at Pixie and Geraint, and at Jake staring at me. 'No . . .' I gripped the back of the plastic chair in front of me.

'They took him.'

'I . . . Are we sure?'

'He didn't come in this morning and he wasn't answering his phone. I went round to his place. His bed was unslept in. G used CCTV to track his route home from here. Four Ghosts grabbed him ten minutes down the road and bundled him into a van.' Jake threw his phone down on the table. 'He didn't have a chance.'

'Do we know if . . .' I couldn't finish. My head was spinning. This couldn't be right.

Jake walked up to me and put his hand on my shoulders. 'We have to be realistic. They got him. And they have no reason to keep him alive. We need to presume he's gone.'

I stared down at the floor. I knew whatever I was feeling now, Jake would be too. We'd worked with Robin for three years. We'd trained him together.

Just not well enough.

We should've seen this coming.

Why didn't we see this coming?

Tenebris's raid on Eight had failed. They couldn't get our hardware so they got one of us. They must've sent more Ghosts to watch the Platform's exits. Robin was the only one who always left out the street-level door. He lived within walking distance from the Platform. It was harder to spot who we were when we merged with the many weary commuters all heading home on the underground.

Tenebris didn't need our laptops and our hard drives if they got to someone who knew what was on them.

And made them talk.

I shuddered.

'Pixie and G have been doing a search for the van's number plate. We got two hits on the CCTV. One at a garage in Vauxhall last night and one by the M3 in the early hours.'

'I'm coming with you.'

'No, Lex. The mission comes first. It's a long shot that we can track this van down.' He leaned towards me and spoke softly. 'They've had him for sixteen hours. You know the drill.'

I did.

They'd taken him to find out what we knew. And when they got it, or even if they didn't, they would dispose of him. They couldn't have loose trails. They had no reason to keep him alive. I bit my lip.

'This is no rescue mission,' said Jake. 'I just want to find the people who did this.'

I looked down and his fists were clenched so tightly his arms were shaking. He was struggling to hold it together. To contain the rage he was feeling. Those Ghosts, Tenebris, the Snake, the Coyote – Jake would wreak terror on them all. The caged animal inside him, the one he worked so hard to keep contained, was coming out, and he wouldn't be able to stop it.

Hattie walked in, his mouth set in a thin line. 'I've spoken to the police. Nothing yet.'

We were all silent as we took this in. No body had yet been found. It didn't mean anything. Certainly not hope. It was only a matter of time. I thought of Thatcher. And of Y. Tenebris had yet to show mercy to anyone who was a threat to their business.

Pixie let out a sob. 'We . . . we shoulda laughed at his jokes more. Would've made him happy. Thinking he was funny. The silly sod.' Geraint put an arm round her and she cried more into his chest.

This all felt like a shitty bad dream. Robin would walk in and make a crack about why all the long faces, it's not like someone died. And we would tell him he was an idiot and then we'd all laugh and everything would feel right again.

We'd lost colleagues before. More than I could count. Their names were engraved underneath the wooden dining table in this room. But this was the first time we'd ever lost someone in our unit. One of the family.

'I know we're all devastated.' Hattie looked round at us all. 'But if we let this derail us, they've won. We can't forget what's at stake here. We keep Peng alive. We find the Snake. We end Tenebris. That is how we avenge Robin.'

Pixie wiped her tears and disentangled herself from Geraint. We were all silent. I was never more grateful for Hattie's strong, quiet leadership. We needed his calm. His soft tones. I couldn't think right now. I just wanted to be told what to do. I just wanted to be told how we were going to try and make this better.

'We have just over twenty-four hours until Peng leaves the UK.' Hattie checked his watch. 'Right about now she's getting ready to leave the Embassy for Lord Wycombe's shoot. Tomorrow it's the Christie's Asian art exhibition and auction, and straight after that we see her safely onto an Air China flight back to Beijing. We're nearly there.'

He turned to Jake. 'You chase down this van lead but if it goes nowhere, you have to let it go. Do you understand?'

Jake gave a curt nod.

'It doesn't pan out and you focus again on any leads we get on Peppa. We need to get to the people behind Tenebris. You want revenge? You find them and you can do what you want. I won't stop you.'

Hattie looked at Geraint. 'Has Cameron checked in again?'

Geraint shook his head. 'Last we heard from her was fifteen minutes ago. She said –' he leaned over his laptop to read out her message – '"Watching Peppa and kid in Gap. Trying on beige clothes. Target made no contact with anyone. Bored."'

'With any luck, whoever Peppa is meeting today will lead us back to Tenebris.'

Knowing how close we were to confirming her as the Snake, knowing how close we now were to the end couldn't rouse us. Everything felt numb. I looked at the dining table. Robin's coffee mug was still placed in front of his usual chair. I wondered how long it would stay there for. I wondered who would be the first to dare move it. The instant life could simply be over never ceased to amaze and terrify me.

'After all this is over we will remember Robin properly. We'll make sure he's found.' Hattie bowed his head. 'We'll carve his name under here.' He patted the solid table. 'We will mourn him. But now, now is not the time. We get to work and show them we won't be stopped. Pixie and G, remember you don't go anywhere alone until this is over. It's not safe.' He turned to Jake and me. 'You two be careful out there. We're not losing anymore Rats to those bastards.'

'I'm leaving now,' said Jake. 'I'll keep you updated.'

I watched him leave. If something happened to him too I didn't know what I'd do. As if he could hear my thoughts he stopped halfway to the door, came back and wrapped his arms round me.

'Don't worry,' he said quietly, 'I'll be fine. And we'll find the fuckers who did this and make them pay.'

He let go of me and walked out. I took a deep breath and turned to Hattie.

'OK, I'm ready. What's the plan?'

Chapter Twenty-Five

THE GRAVEL CRUNCHED as we made our way down the drive. After rounding the tree-lined bend, a seventeenth-century castle came into view. A fleet of Range Rovers had driven Peng and the delegation safely from the doors of the Embassy right up to Cherwell Castle's entrance. Hattie had driven us down in a Platform-issue van, me beside him at the front, Geraint and Pixie in the back working on the van's inbuilt computers. Tracking Peppa was now solely down to Cameron. We'd yet to hear from Jake. It crossed my mind we might never hear from him. And bodies would just start appearing. Jake unhinged and unrestrained was a dark, dark force.

Hattie parked the van round the back of the castle: the servants' entrance. I got out and walked round to the front. I looked up at Cherwell Castle. It was lucky that Lord Wycombe ran a hedge fund. That kind of income would help pay the heating bills of a forty-room pad like this.

Hattie was going to undertake a full check of the fenced perimeter while Geraint and Pixie tried to hack into Cherwell Castle's outdoor security feeds. Lord Wycombe had several old masters and his insurance company had insisted upon stringent security measures. The party tonight had also led to the hiring of extra security guards at the entrance. No vehicle was allowed in without its occupants being on a pre-approved list with photo ID confirmation. Wycombe's castle was clearly pretty well fortified. Just not enough to keep a Coyote out.

Geraint and Pixie were running background searches on the hundred and fifty names on the list and inputting their photos into our system. The Coyote could have commandeered any one of the guests' identity and be getting ready to walk across the drawbridge this evening in black tie. Geraint had also hacked the catering company's records to get the full list of staff assigned to the event in case the Coyote was going to make a more subtle approach through the service entrance.

I was escorted into the castle's drawing room. I had never been in a room with so much tweed. The Chinese had embraced the British shooting dress code with a passion. All of the delegation were suitably tweedily attired, while Minister Peng cut a particularly elegant figure in her tweed suit that was nipped in at the waist. I felt a little underdressed in black jeans, Hunter boots and Will's old Barbour. Peng caught my eye and gave me a nod.

I scanned the room. There were no more than around forty people in attendance. This was the inner circle. The Foreign Secretary was here as well as a few MPs I recognised. All Conservative. All balding. Numerous uniformed staff flitted around proffering red wine. A couple of the men already looked quite flushed. Nothing like filling them up with alcohol and letting them loose with a shotgun.

I watched Frederick deep in conversation with Lord Wycombe and his wife. She was a round-faced blonde in a polo neck and tweed skirt. This was clearly Frederick's set. He looked at ease here in his plus fours, hand daintily clasping a bone china teacup.

He spotted me. 'Lex, come over here and meet Charles.'

I walked over to them, hand out, and received a vigorous shake from Lord Wycombe and a limp one from his wife.

'Hi there.'

'So you work with this reprobate, do you?' Lord Wycombe had thinning hair and a protruding stomach. Looking between him and Frederick it was hard to believe they'd been in the same year at school.

'I do indeed.'

'We'll make sure a place is set for you at dinner. No standing around with the rest of the heavies. And do you shoot?'

Out the corner of my eye I saw Frederick smirk.

'Yes. Yes I do.'

'Well, how about you share a peg with Frederick. You can get a few goes in.'

'I'd love to. Thank you.' I gestured round the grand room. 'You have a beautiful home.'

He bowed his head slightly. 'It may be our home for the moment but we are mere custodians for the next generation of Wycombes. It's been in our family since the seventeenth century. If you look at the ceiling, you will see original engravings. We've just spent a fortune having them restored to their former glory. Something the National Trust wouldn't be able to do with their dwindling budgets. No, the only way these grand houses can retain their glory is if the family who rightfully belongs in them remains in charge.' He drew me to one side and motioned towards the tapestry on the wall. 'This was woven by fifty local women a few hundred years ago. It portrays a battle that was held just twenty miles from here. This was the last standing port.'

I stared at the ugly tapestry in what I hoped was an appreciative manner.

'When I think about the history of these many walls, I realise how truly privileged we are to be a part of its story. Blood, sweat, tears and . . .' he clasped his chest, 'love. I couldn't give everything to this place if I didn't love it as much as the child I hope to one day have.'

I made a note to never, ever compliment an Englishman on his castle again.

After a hearty lunch of game pie and mashed potato, I felt grateful that clean eating and no carbs had yet to reach the upper classes of Oxfordshire.

The air was crisp. The sky blue. I walked across green grass in picture-perfect Cotswold countryside, feeling the sun on my face, and took a deep breath in.

It was a beautiful day.

And Robin was gone.

We'd never see him again.

People walked alongside you. Until one day they didn't.

It never got easier to accept.

I always thought I would die young. A fair enough presumption considering my line of work. It never really bothered me. But now it did. I didn't want to leave Gigi. I wanted to see the person she was going to be, meet the person she might make a life with, hold the baby she may one day have. Everything that sounded so unappealing – the wrinkling, the ageing, the aches and pain – was irrelevant.

Accepting old age took bravery. That knowledge you were in your twilight years. That it wouldn't be long until it was all over. Your time was about to be up and there was nothing you could do. Except wait. Wait and wait and go full circle. Ending life just as you started it: needing to be fed, unable to walk, a vulnerable bundle reliant on those who loved you. Before Gigi the thought of ageing depressed me because I couldn't see the bigger picture. I couldn't see what it meant. Now I would wear every grey hair, every wrinkle as a badge of pride. I was still alive. I was getting older. I was still here with my daughter.

Not like Robin.

Not like our poor Robin.

A fast blast of a life before he was taken out too soon. Before he really lived. I thought of the Northern line girl Robin had been seeing. He was all full of hope for what lay ahead. And now it was over. I couldn't remember her name. I was dreading having to go through his messages, reading classic Robin lines where he was attempting to be flirty, to be funny. Invading his privacy. The final indignity. But I needed to track her down. I didn't want her to think he was ghosting her. I'd do the right thing. Tell her and his parents a story about a heroic death and grieve with them.

The shooting party were making their way across one of Lord Wycombe's fields to reach their respective pegs. The first drive was about to begin.

I scanned the land around us. There was a forest across the way where the beaters would be trundling through, raising the pheasants. If anyone came towards the shooting party we'd see them well in advance. Peng was laughing along with Lord Wycombe as they approached their neighbouring pegs. Peng's bodyguard was with her. He looked as uneasy about the situation as we were.

Frederick arrived at our peg. 'Gamekeeper has lent us a couple of shotguns.' He passed me a gun and a bag of ammo.

'Tenebris got Robin.'

I loaded the gun.

His eyes widened. 'Are you sure?'

I nodded. I didn't trust myself to speak. Saying it out loud in the open air, not just down in the dark of the Platform, made it all seem so much more real.

'I'm sorry. I'm very, very sorry.'

'Hello there, girlie.' An old man all in tweed arrived to stand at the peg next to us. 'You here for good luck? Come to load, have you?'

A flurry of pheasants flew over of us.

I aimed the gun and fired. *Bang bang. Thud. Thud.* I reloaded fast. *Bang bang.* Another couple of satisfying thuds as pheasants dropped from the sky.

The old duffer's jaw dropped. He nodded at Frederick. 'Your wife knows how to shoot!'

'Better than me,' said Frederick with a smile.

'You taught her well.'

'Actually, I'm not his wife. I'm his boss. And he didn't teach me shit.'

The old man frowned and his mouth opened and shut, opened and shut. A fish out of water. An old man in a new world.

On the second drive, just after a few shots rang out, I heard it. The unmistakable female cries of, 'No no no!'

I looked at Peng. Both she and her bodyguard had turned towards the sound but were unharmed.

I scanned the field. What was going on? Was this a diversion? Was an attack beginning?

'Frederick, stay with Peng. I'll go.' I raced towards the sound, shotgun in hand, and reported in to my earpiece, 'Potential hostile disturbance. Investigating now.'

The noise had come from the edge of the forest. I rounded the corner to see Lady Wycombe, clasping her pearls, staring down at the ground at a dead bird.

What the hell?

Was the lady of the house a secret vegan?

'Is everything OK?'

'No. Things are not. The gamekeeper clearly told everyone that guinea fowl were out of bounds on today's shoot. But someone ... someone has shot George.' She motioned towards the headless bird.

'You name your birds?'

'Guinea fowl are on our family crest. We keep several on the estate that we have raised from birth for good luck.'

I walked away from a mourning Lady Wycombe.

'False alarm,' I said into my earpiece. 'It's a dead bird.'

'But isn't that—' started Hattie.

I cut him off. 'Don't ask.'

We got through another two drives in two different locations with the only casualties feathered. I kept scanning the rest of the shooting party. It was a small group just made up of politicians and business associates. I couldn't see any of them being the Coyote. They were too deep in their element to be anything other than the identities they claimed. If the Coyote was going to strike, it would have to be as an intruder or as a guest tonight.

We got back to the castle to see rows of dead pheasants laid out in lines outside the impressive entrance. A macabre presentation of the afternoon's bloodshed. In case the castle and the dead birds weren't quintessentially English enough, we were all then hustled inside for Earl Grey tea with jam and scones.

Ensconced in a window seat, I observed them all. The crackle of the drawing room's large fire and the clink of fine china. The low murmur and chuckles of the guests in conversation. The thought of a wild Coyote intruding upon this quiet afternoon scene seemed too unlikely.

Frederick joined me. 'What do you think?' – he motioned towards the Foreign Secretary – 'under the buffoon-like appearance he could be a dab hand with a weapon. A Coyote in disguise.'

'With a speciality in boring people to death.'

We watched him gesticulating with a scone, a large dollop of cream at the corner of his mouth.

'The Coyote will strike at the dinner tonight,' I said. 'Everything's pointing to it. The botched invasion at Eight. Taking Robin. They were nervous we were getting close to what they were planning. Clearing the way for tonight.' I looked round the room again. 'I just can't work out who or how.'

'Have you managed to do a check on all the staff Charles has coming in for the dinner?'

'G and Pixie are working on that now. If there are any red flags they'll let us know. We need to check Peng's room. She's staying in the Mountford Suite.'

'I've stayed here a few times before. I can go check it out now.'

I nodded. 'They're about to leave for the duck hunt. I'll stick with Peng and see you out there.'

Dusk was coming in. As I walked towards the duck hunt I looked back towards Cherwell Castle; towering turrets and old stone basked in the orange light from outdoor spotlights.

Wycombe's gamekeeper led me to my allocated hide: a rough and ready wooden bench sunk behind some reeds with a camouflage netting overhead. I dropped down, shotgun in hand, and waited. A stakeout. For ducks. And a Coyote.

Peng was in the next door hide with a couple of grey-haired men. I knew one was an MP and that the other was the CEO of Wycombe's family aircraft manufacturing company. Peng's bodyguard stood smoking outside it. This was no doubt one of the several meetings Peng referenced as being essential to have.

Frederick appeared from the surrounding trees. 'Room seems clear. Peng's is right next door to her bodyguard's.'

He sat down next to me, laid his gun at his feet and blew onto his hands, then rubbed them together.

I looked over at Peng's hide. The red glow of the bodyguard's cigarette lit up the dark. 'This is not a good set-up. The Coyote could be out there with a long-range rifle and we'd have no idea. Hattie, do you copy?'

Hattie crackled into my ear. '*I'm here, Lex. We're into the security camera feeds. No hostiles in sight. Staff are arriving at the castle to prepare for the dinner but no one in the area surrounding the lake.*'

'We get through this part and at least we don't have to worry about everyone being armed at the champagne reception.' Frederick picked up his gun. He looked over at me.

'I'm sorry about Robin. I know from my army days what it's like to lose a colleague. You never really get over it.'

'He was a good guy. The annoying little brother I never had.'

Frederick reached over and squeezed my hand. And didn't let go. His hand was cold.

I shook my head. 'He didn't deserve to go like that. Ambushed by a group of chickenshit Ghosts.'

I hoped it was fast. It was a painful waste of a good man.

'He would've been a great Rat. He *was* a great Rat. Jake and I were idiots trying to hold him back, trying to keep him safe. Now look what's happened. We lost him on our watch.'

'You can't blame yourselves. Robin knew what the job entailed. The risk he was putting himself in.'

There were a loud couple of shots from Peng's hide. We dropped hands and leaned forward, guns raised. I heard laughter and Peng shouting, 'Missed!' A few ducks flew straight past us. Neither of us fired.

We stayed in position. But everything was quiet.

No ducks. No Coyote.

Just us with guns poised.

More waiting.

More loaded silence.

Frederick turned to me. 'How's your injury from the other night?'

'It's fine.' He didn't need to know about the steady flow of painkillers I was on to keep the aching at bay.

'How do you hide things like that from your husband?'

I shrugged. 'It's easier than you think. He reckons I'm pretty dangerous on a bike as I seem to fall off a lot. When I was last shot we covered it up as a hit and run.' I felt for the scar at the base of my neck. 'Blamed the wound on me landing on a jagged piece of cracked windscreen.'

'You've never been tempted to tell him the truth?' Frederick paused. 'Well, not the full truth.' He understood exactly what Eight's security protocols entailed. 'But at least an indication of what your job really entails?'

I shook my head. 'It's too risky.'

'It could be a good thing. Knowing what you do might make him love you even more. Make him in awe of your bravery. Of just how incredible you are to do what you do'.

I bit my lip. 'I don't think he'd see it that way.' I didn't want to add, 'But it's good that you do.'

Three shots were fired in the distance. A few shouts followed by murmurs and laughter.

A loud horn sounded, signalling the end of this round of shooting for entertainment. The ducks had fared better than the pheasants.

Peng and her two companions set off back towards the house. The bodyguard followed. I motioned to Frederick and we fanned out either side of them. It was a change being able to guard a subject with a gun in my hands rather than hidden in a holster.

Hattie met us outside the castle as everyone else traipsed into the boot room to de-Barbour. 'Jake tracked down the Ghosts' van. Burned and abandoned.' I braced myself. 'No body inside. But the parkland where it was found is expansive. I've got police combing the area.' Hattie put a hand to my shoulder. 'If Robin's there we'll find him.'

I chewed my lip.

'Cameron followed Peppa all afternoon. She met with a woman in a playground at four p.m.'

'Tell me it was Alice Lim from the Embassy?' A confirmed sighting of the two of them together would be the proof we needed that Lim had been covertly funnelling intel on Peng to Peppa through the dry cleaners.

Hattie shook his head. 'Sadly not. The woman was blonde, mid to late twenties. We've run her image through all our databases and haven't got a hit. Cameron couldn't get close enough to hear anything. She said the sounds of screaming children were unbearable.'

'Did the woman have any kids with her?' I asked.

'No, none. They spent fifteen minutes talking and then left.'

Meeting a friend without kids in a playground didn't make sense.

'This woman could be an intermediary. If Lim and Peppa have been using the dry cleaners to exchange information all this time, they aren't going to risk being seen together in person.'

'Cameron is now following the mystery woman. Jake is on Peppa. We find one solid link to the Tenebris Network on either of them and we'll bring them in.'

By the time I reached the second floor of the expansive castle it was hard to get my bearings. I was following Frederick towards the bedrooms.

'Peng's bedroom is down that corridor on the right. Her bodyguard is in the room next door. He's outside Peng's door keeping guard.' Everyone had gone straight from the boot room to dress for the evening ahead. 'I'm in here.' He motioned to the door next to us. 'And you're just one along.'

'Right.' I looked from his door to mine. 'Great.'

Frederick checked his watch. 'We've got less than an hour before drinks start. See you down there.'

I nodded.

I opened the door to my bedroom. Antique furnishings and a small four-poster bed greeted me. Here I was again. On a mini-break away from my daughter. With a man who wasn't my husband.

I unpacked the small bag that had been taken to my room by a helpful butler. Pulling out my long black dress, I gave it a shake to try and lessen the crinkles. Reaching up to hang it in the wardrobe made me wince. My stitches were starting to throb again. Considering Peng was in her bedroom with her body-guard outside the door, I reckoned I could risk taking a little downtime before resuming protection duties. I took a couple of painkillers, eased myself up onto the bed and lay back on the pillows.

I thought of the lurking Coyote.

If Peng was my target, how would I do it?

I stared up at the ornate four-poster's red velvet canopy as I ran through everything. All the information we had. All the locations she had gone to. What would *I* do? How would *I* kill her?

By the time the painkillers had kicked in and the ache in my side had dulled, I knew exactly what I would do. And I couldn't believe we had missed it from the start. I sat up and radioed Geraint, asking for a small item to be delivered to my room.

I got up off the bed and changed into my black dress. I might be lacking the glittering diamonds and designer labels the other women would undoubtedly be sporting, but my accessories were a little more special. I slipped on my favourite black stilettos with heels that dislodged to reveal three-inch blades. Then a gaudy necklace with a large green stone that with one click unfastened and upon being thrown to the ground set off a smoke bomb. Large rings on each hand with gems that slid back to reveal a needle with a fast-acting sedative.

There was a knock on my door. It was Geraint with the item I'd requested. He quickly handed it to me and disappeared back down the corridor. I placed it in my clutch bag alongside my Glock. Just in case I was right. Just in case this assassin thought exactly like I did.

I walked to my bedroom window and admired the formal gardens below. Gigi would be impressed. Here I was. A princess in a castle. Heavily armed and prepared to take down an evil king to save my underground kingdom. Making my own happy ending.

Chapter Twenty-Six

TONIGHT'S DINNER WAS for a hundred and fifty people. All the great and the good of the aviation industry would be in attendance, along with a healthy sprinkling of politicians and a few titled locals. Peng was guest of honour. Everyone wanted to curry favour with China.

The Coyote could strike at any moment.

Champagne was being served in the drawing room. I looked around the grand room with its high ceilings and old Masters on the walls.

Frederick stood with a circle of people. Black tie suited him, but then I had yet to see a man it didn't. Frederick stopped talking mid-sentence and raised his glass at me.

I swished around the room as I sipped vintage champagne. I scanned the faces of everyone there. They all looked like they belonged. But wasn't that the point? If the Coyote was here they would've made sure they fit in.

An immaculately laid U-shaped banqueting table filled Cherwell Castle's grand dining hall, where gilt-framed portraits of Wycombe's ancestors stared down at us from panelled walls. Peng was in the position of honour at the centre of the top table.

She had Lord Wycombe on her left and on her right a chinless, balding man who was apparently the MP for the area.

I was a few seats down from the corner of the top table, giving me a good vantage point of Peng. I looked round for Frederick and spotted him further down on the opposite side of the room, seated next to Ling Ling.

A scallop and pancetta starter was produced with a flourish.

I sat listening to the man on my right wax lyrical about how everyone should move out of London, the air was so much fresher, the children so much happier and 'we even grow our own vegetables'.

The man on my left was thankfully over-involved in trying to sleep with the bored woman in diamonds on his other side.

I scanned the room. Nothing but people dressed grandly, small-talking their way through a starter.

The main course was brought out. Pheasant. It was good that having spent the afternoon massacring them at least we were being made to eat them. I took a bite. Or maybe not.

The talk from the countryside lover had moved on to fixed-rate mortgages. There were many hazards in my job, I just never expected being bored to death would be one of them.

I pushed the bits of dry pheasant and new potatoes round my plate. I had thought the build-up to an assassination attempt might be a little bit more dramatic. I looked round the room at the exits. I caught Frederick's eye as he did the same.

The MP next to Peng had disappeared off on his mobile so I had a clear visual of Peng. She was looking flushed. Alcohol or something else? And then I saw it. Her eyes widened slightly and she grasped at her throat. Wycombe next to her had not yet noticed. The bodyguard up against the wall directly behind her remained oblivious.

I had to be the first there.

I got up and raced towards Peng, plunging the item in my hand into her thigh.

Her bodyguard was on me within seconds and pulled me roughly away from Peng. When I showed him what was in my hand he let me go and we both turned to stare at Peng.

She was blinking fast. Her breathing settled. Ling Ling was already at her side, talking without drawing breath. She turned Peng's head from left to right and peered into her eyes. She looked at me, gave me a small nod and continued to speak fast to Peng.

'What's going on? Is Minister Peng all right?' Frederick appeared next to me.

'She had an allergic reaction. There must've been nuts in her food.' I added, 'We need an ambulance.' For a listening Geraint's benefit.

Ling Ling approached me. 'Minister Peng is very grateful you English are so good with your health and safety.'

'It's what we're here for. Always prepared.'

Wycombe was fussing next to Peng, horrified that the caterers had apparently poisoned the guest of honour. There was a lot of gesticulating in between holding Peng's hand.

The MP arrived back at the table and looked a little confused that so many people were now crowding round his seat. He hovered next to us, clearly contemplating whether he could reach over and get his wine glass.

Ling Ling continued, 'We want to get her back to a London hospital.'

'Of course. An ambulance is already on its way.'

Geraint crackled in. *'The ambulance we had on standby will be there in three minutes. Hattie says to meet him outside now.'*

I motioned to Frederick to watch Peng and walked out.

Hattie was waiting for me at the castle entrance, his mouth set in a thin line.

'How did you know it was going to happen? Geraint told me you asked him for an EpiPen from the van's medical kit.'

'I had a hunch and it just paid off.'

'What are you talking about?'

'If I was the Coyote I would've used her nut allergy.'

Hattie frowned. 'But her nut allergy isn't severe enough to kill her. You saw the medical records.'

'Yes but it's bad enough it has to be treated with an EpiPen—'

'And an EpiPen is easily tampered with,' Hattie finished.

'Peng's bodyguard and Ling Ling both carry an EpiPen in case she has an attack. We need to get hold of them and get them tested.'

'I talked to the caterers out by the service entrance and they were fully aware of Peng's nut allergy. They said they even took care with cross-contamination by preparing her food in a separate area.'

'So someone would've had to spike it. Don't suppose there are any cameras inside the kitchen?'

Hattie shook his head. 'There are no internal cameras in the whole castle. It could've been anyone.' We both turned to the sound of the ambulance arriving down the drive.

I retrieved my bag from my room and was heading back outside just as Peng was carried out by stretcher. She grabbed my arm as she passed.

'Thank you,' she mouthed. I patted her hand.

Wycombe came rushing to her side. He looked fraught. 'I am so sorry, Minister Peng. This is just terrible.' He continued to offer plaintive apologies all the way to the ambulance. Ling Ling and Peng's bodyguard got into the back with her.

Hattie came up to me. 'I'm going to ride back with them and stay with Peng at the hospital. If the Coyote just tried to strike he could have a back-up plan in place.' He patted my shoulder. 'You did good work tonight. Get some sleep. Tomorrow is going to be busy.'

I watched as he ducked down to curl into the passenger seat of the ambulance.

'Everyone heading back to London?' Frederick joined me on the castle steps as we watched the ambulance leave, the blue and red flashing lights lighting up the ancient stone.

'Yes. If the Coyote strikes again we'll be ready.'

'I see now why they call you Rats the best of the best. Nothing gets past you. I'm impressed.'

Wycombe joined us. 'You two are welcome to stay on. Might as well keep on drinking, despite the bloody incompetent staff ruining any hope of getting this contract signed.' He mopped his brow with a spotted handkerchief. 'Your rooms are all made up.'

'I'd better get back.' I motioned towards our waiting van; Pixie and Geraint were already in the back. 'Thank you, though, Charles.'

'I'll stay for a nightcap and then I'll head back too,' said Frederick.

'Rightio then. Goodbye, Alexis.' Charles gave me a couple of quick air kisses and walked back inside. 'I'll get the whisky out, old boy.'

'Goodbye, Lex.' Frederick leaned down and gave me a kiss on the cheek and rested his forehead against mine for the briefest of moments. He then pulled back sharply and looked at me over his shoulder as he walked up into the castle.

Not having to stay the night here was a relief.

No good would've come of it.

Clambering into the driver's seat of the white van I felt like Cinderella. I'd had my night at the ball. Now I was rushing home in my pumpkin.

I got back by midnight. I opened our bedroom door quietly, hoping to creep in, but Will was still awake, sitting up reading with the bedside light on.

'So you're back.'

'I'm back.'

He closed his book and put it on his bedside table. 'Did you have another accident yesterday?'

I thought fast. Had I left bloodied bandages somewhere? I'd changed quickly this morning – he can't have noticed?

'What are you talking about?'

'On the walk to school this morning Gigi was telling me all about you bleeding, how there was so much blood and how brave you were.'

'Oh, that. No. She, well . . . She came to the loo with me.'

He looked at me blankly.

'I had my period.'

'Oh.' He grimaced. 'Right.'

'Yeah, it's hard explaining to a two-year-old that bleeding out there doesn't hurt.'

'Got you. Say no more.' He yawned again. 'Before I forget, Mum's car has broken down. She's stuck at her friend Julie's house and won't be able to get back to London in time to pick up Gigi from that harvest festival at the church tomorrow. Can you do it? She'll be back here around midday.'

Will was flying to America in the morning and would be away for two days schmoozing some big new clients.

Yvonne's Young Ones had requested that tomorrow all children join the harvest festival celebrations at the church adjoining the nursery. When I'd said yes to this request at the start of term I'd imagined that Gigi's big role as a piece of corn would give Will and me a blessed relaxed morning reading the Sunday papers. I hadn't figured we'd both be working. I now needed to work out the logistics of dropping her off and picking her up. I wasn't sure how I was going to broach this with Hattie.

'Yep. Sure.' I stared at the ceiling. I'd just lost a colleague, I'd just potentially foiled an assassination attempt on a Chinese minister, another strike was likely to happen any minute and I now had a childcare issue.

He reached to turn his light off but stopped.

'You OK?'

'Bad day at work. I'm just really tired.' I rolled over. I closed my eyes but I knew sleep would take a long time to come, if it all.

Peng was still alive.

But Robin was gone.

It felt wrong. To be lying next to Will feeling so utterly bereft and not be able to talk to him about it. There was no spin I could put on this that would make sense. It wasn't right that I could sit in a duck hide with Frederick and talk about everything I was feeling, yet I couldn't with my own husband in our bedroom. I saw what Frederick had meant: by having a job we couldn't talk about we were keeping a part of ourselves back. Will was oblivious to how I was feeling. It wasn't his fault, it was mine. I couldn't blame him for not understanding, for not being there for me, when I couldn't tell him why I was upset. I couldn't expect to keep everything inside and for him to magically know. How could he ever really be there for me when he could never know what I was really going through?

From: boobsboobs@welovedoubleDs.com
To: lex.tyler@platform-eight.co.uk
Subject: LIVE WEBCAM (.)(.)
MISSION: #80521
UNIT: WHISTLE
DATE: Sunday 6th October
ALERT: PENG'S DEPARTURE DAY

Chapter Twenty-Seven

ROBIN. PENG. THE SNAKE. The Coyote. They all raced around my mind. There was too much going on. Too much to let sleep take over.

As daylight started to creep in I checked my phone.

An update from Hattie had come in during the night. Peng was alive and well. No after-effects from the mild allergic reaction she had had at last night's dinner. She was spending the morning at the Embassy and going to the Christie's auction this afternoon before catching her flight back to China tonight as planned. At the hospital Hattie had successfully replaced the two EpiPens held by Ling Ling and the bodyguard with brand new ones. The two they had held were currently being tested. We'd get the results back in a few hours. Jake was still watching Peppa, and Cameron had followed the mystery woman from the playground back to a house that seemed to belong to her boyfriend. She was waiting for her to come out. If we could confirm Peppa as the Snake we had a chance of getting Tenebris shut down by the end of the day. We had no other leads. No other trail back to them.

It was only 6.15 a.m. I had time for a run before Gigi woke up and before Will left for the airport. Maybe I'd bump into Rochelle, wave a smug hello as I sped past her. I changed into my running gear, closed the bedroom door on a gently snoring Will and left the house.

I set off at a slow jog. I knew I would be right. Those EpiPens were going to be positive for poison. It couldn't be a coincidence. How did they manage to switch them over? The Coyote must have someone in the delegation.

I upped the volume on my iPod and kept a fast pace through the quiet streets of Chiswick.

I was meant to be thinking of work. But Will kept creeping in. As long as I was at Eight the lies and secrets would never end. How could I stop them hurting us? How could we be a team when he didn't know the game?

I shook it off. We had no choice. I wasn't quitting my job. I wasn't quitting my marriage. I had to find a way to make it work.

Work. That's what I needed to think of. Would the Coyote dare to strike again? What if Peppa wasn't the Snake? Peng was flying out tonight. If the Coyote and Snake went quiet we lost our only link to Tenebris. They'd carry on posting jobs. They'd carry on recruiting more Snakes. And the Security Services would be permanently compromised. Platform Eight would be on permanent shutdown.

I ran along the river before circling back and heading towards home.

I got to the start of Fisher's Lane and saw Frederick on a bench in the playground up ahead.

Frederick.

I needed a whole other run to work through whatever was going on there.

He was drinking a cup of coffee and looking at his phone. I slowed to a walk. He really wasn't joking when he said Florence was an early riser. I checked my phone: 6.45 a.m. and she was already at the top of the climbing frame. I wiped the sweat off my forehead and headed towards them.

Florence was shouting, 'Daddy!' at Frederick and he was doing a good job of pretending he couldn't hear her. She got up higher and used both her arms to wave.

And then she fell.

I jolted as if I could get there in time, as if I could catch her, even though she was twenty feet away. I held my breath; she landed awkwardly. There was a pause and then a loud wail. Jesus, poor Florence, that was a nasty fall. I sped up my pace, wanting to get there to see if I could do anything to help. And then I stopped. Frederick wasn't moving. He was still on the bench. Phone in hand, coffee in the other.

What the hell? Did he have headphones in? I squinted. Nothing. But even if he did he couldn't miss the fact that his daughter was lying on the ground, screaming in pain, just a few feet in front of him.

I stopped and stared as my mind raced.

One thought came clearest.

He must not see me.

I hid behind a tree. I needed to think.

There had to be a reason. A reason why a father wouldn't go and comfort their child in agony. I looked at Florence. She was lying on the ground just whimpering now. I wanted to go and comfort her. To pick her up and tell her it would be OK.

And she wasn't even my child.

I looked again at Frederick continuing to scroll through his phone.

Maybe she wasn't his child?

But even if she wasn't she was still an innocent child in distress. I watched him take another sip of coffee.

Was she a plant?

Or was he playing a part?

Put in position with a fake daughter?

I thought of Florence's eyes. The blue-green streak. No, she was his. I thought of the way Camilla stroked her hair and whispered to her. She was definitely his and Camilla's. So if the marriage wasn't a sham and the children were theirs . . . What kind of father could ignore the cries of their badly injured daughter?

A sociopath.

That was the answer.

That was the only answer.

You had to be completely devoid of emotional response to not comfort a child. Any child. Let alone your own.

Frederick finally looked up from his phone and glanced around him. I flattened myself behind the tree. He was clearly checking to see there was no one around. No one he needed to pretend he cared in front of. I peered round the tree. He had now gone to Florence. He leaned down and pulled her roughly up by the front of her coat. The little girl stood there next to him. The whimpering stopped. He leaned down to talk to her. I couldn't make out the words but I made out the sharp tone, and the tears continuing to roll down her face. He walked off. She followed behind, holding her hurt arm.

I leaned back against the tree and closed my eyes.

Frederick.

A sociopath.

Devoid of feeling.

Playing the part expected of him.

What did this mean?

Sociopaths had no feelings. No empathy. No loyalty.

Could he be the Snake?

But how?

Why?

It didn't make sense.

We wouldn't even know about the Tenebris Network if he hadn't brought it to Dugdale.

We wouldn't even know there was a Snake.

Why risk drawing attention to the fact there was a traitor? Why not just carry on raking in the money?

I needed to get to the Platform.

Right after I dropped Gigi, dressed as a piece of corn, off at the harvest festival.

I looked around the church. Frederick and Florence weren't here yet. How bad was her arm? Maybe she'd had to go to hospital? I looked at the motley crew of toddlers dressed as root vegetables and tried to shake off the thought they were using our children as props to decorate a very sparse-looking church. It wasn't like any of these two-year-olds would be capable of joining in the rousing rendition of 'We Plough the Fields and Scatter' they had planned. I shook it off. Considering this was free childcare on a Sunday morning, I shouldn't question it.

With Gigi safely planted with the rest of the crop, I waited by the church doors for them to arrive.

My heart skipped a beat as I saw Frederick open the church gate, a pale Florence dressed in a carrot costume alongside him.

Frederick smiled at me as he walked down the pathway. He was wearing chinos and a light blue shirt, the sleeves rolled up. He looked so normal. So handsome. A good apple. With a rotten core.

I smiled back.

'How's Peng?' he asked as he ushered Florence through the church doors and towards a waiting Yvonne. I watched her walk slowly down the aisle. That poor girl. 'Lex?'

'I . . . She's fine.' I needed to remember everything was normal. I needed to brief him and get to the Platform to investigate him. 'Hattie is with her. We're not letting her out of our sight now. I'm just waiting for an update on Peppa. Jake and Cameron have been following her and that woman she met with in the playground.'

'What do you think happened last night? Who spiked the nuts?'

'The Coyote could've been one of the catering staff. We're running deeper checks on all the IDs now.'

'What should I do?'

'Just be on standby. Unless you hear from me, meet us all at Christie's this afternoon for the auction. We should know more by then.'

'We've nearly made it.' He put a hand on my shoulder and stared down at me. I looked up at him and it took everything to not flinch. To not shrug his hand off and slam him up against the door by his throat and ask him what the fuck was wrong with him. What kind of person could ignore their child in pain?

'We have.' I tried another smile. 'All the more reason to be on the alert.'

'Excuse me.'

We both turned to see Miss Jenna.

'Gigi's corn head has fallen off and she says you have a special way to fix it?'

I looked over Miss Jenna's shoulder to see Gigi waving at me to come over.

'Right. Yes. I know exactly what to do.' I followed Miss Jenna down the aisle. I turned back to Frederick. 'I'll see you later.'

He held up a hand and turned and left the church.

My special way to fix the corn head onto Gigi involved a series of bulldog clips and an elastic band.

'There you go. Now don't move or speak or laugh too much and it will be fine.'

I looked round the church. It was slowly filling up with the congregation. A series of parents were all frantically adjusting their little darlings' costumes. Rochelle's son was the sun. He was wearing a bright yellow ray headdress that was around three-feet wide and made from cardboard, industrial glue and a steely determination for one-upmanship.

'I know I could just Amazon one-click a costume but it just doesn't give me the same joy and satisfaction,' she was telling another mother.

The vicar addressed everyone as I headed towards the exit. 'The service will begin in ten minutes. Please try and use this time for quiet contemplation.' A peaceful hush descended on the church.

A quiet that was shattered by the sound of my phone ringing. I looked down. It was Jake. 'Sorry,' I mouthed round to everyone looking at me and answered it as I walked quickly out the side door next to the altar.

'You need to meet us at Bill's Restaurant in Fulham. Come now.'

Chapter Twenty-Eight

JAKE AND CAMERON were waiting for me outside Bill's.

'What's the update?'

Jake motioned inside the restaurant. 'Peppa and the play-ground woman are right at the back. We can't get close to them without being noticed. We still have no ID on the woman. Time's running out. I suggest you just walk in and talk.'

Jake was right. Peng was leaving this afternoon. Risking blowing my cover was worth it if it could fast-track us answers.

I walked into Bill's. It was still early and, apart from Peppa's table at the very back, there were only two other occupied tables at the front. Peppa and the woman were deep in conversation. I walked straight towards them.

'Suze? Suze! Is that you?' Peppa jolted at the sound of her name and turned towards me, her face frozen. All her body language was shouting that she'd been caught. Caught doing something she shouldn't.

But then her face relaxed at the sight of me.

'Alexis! Hello.' She stood up. 'What are you doing here?'

'Just meeting a friend for breakfast. How about you?' I leaned towards the woman with her, holding out my hand. 'Hi there, I'm Alexis.'

The woman took it – 'Sasha. Nice to meet you.' – and she shook it. She had an Australian accent.

'How come you're all the way back here? It's such a nice morning.'

Peppa smiled. 'We're hiding.'

'Hiding? From who?'

'Other mothers from nursery.' Peppa cast a glance over my shoulder. 'I'm trying to steal Sasha off one of them and they're all almighty gossips.'

Sasha giggled. 'It's all rather funny, isn't it? This trying to avoid being seen.'

I looked from one to the other. 'So, Sasha, you're a nanny who works for another mum at the nursery?'

She nodded.

Peppa spoke quickly. 'I know there's an etiquette and all but Dionne is leaving and Sasha is great and, well, I'm happy to pay more to show her how valued she'd be if she moved over to us.'

For. Fuck's. Sake.

No stealing secrets. Just stealing a nanny.

A few hacks of the nursery and their parent contact list and Geraint could easily verify all this, but looking between the two of them I knew it was the truth.

I needed to get into the Platform and start proving I was right about Frederick. He was the Snake. There were no Pigs left and no other explanation.

'Is Peng safe?' Hattie and Geraint were seated in the meeting room when Jake, Cameron and I arrived.

Hattie answered. 'She's at the Embassy all morning with back-to-back meetings, followed by a lunch there, before they leave for Christie's. Pixie is in a van outside. If she leaves unexpectedly she'll call it in. But we can presume as long as she's there she's safe.'

Everyone was silent as I announced my theory about Frederick. 'He's the Snake. He has to be.'

'He couldn't just be a shit dad?' asked Cameron.

'A sociopath is the most likely person to be a traitor. All about the money. No feelings of loyalty. No remorse at getting colleagues killed.'

I thought of him sitting there coldly as his own daughter writhed in pain at his feet.

Hattie's phone rang. He looked down at it. 'It's the lab.' He answered. 'What have you found?' He nodded silently. 'Thanks.' He hung up and looked round at us. 'Lex was right. Both the EpiPens contained a lethal dose of arsenic.'

Jake whistled slowly. 'Good save, Lex.'

'It was the clearest move – the Coyote wouldn't even need to be in the room when Peng died. It would be the perfect cover. He just needed to spike the food with nuts and once Peng suffered an adverse reaction, one of her own team would unwittingly kill her with a spiked EpiPen. They would be the ones under suspicion. It would be chaos. Impossible to pull apart.'

'How the hell did the Snake – Frederick, or whoever – get to all the EpiPens?' said Jake. 'They must have someone inside the delegation.'

I thought it through.

'We did this.'

Everyone turned to look at me.

'We got Frederick access and a reason to be near the delegation – he was one of us. I was updating him on what we'd learned, on the delegation's movements. Everything. He could've swapped the EpiPens over at the Natural History Museum event or Cherwell Castle.' I paused. 'If I'm right, it explains why he came to us with

Tenebris. He needed us to have direct access to Peng. The Snake never had a contact within the delegation. He didn't need one. We did all the dirty work, giving him all the information he needed to make the hit.'

Hattie leaned back in his chair; his fingers formed a bridge.

'It sounds like we've been used.'

Jake shrugged. 'How do we know Peppa isn't also a Snake? That they've been working together? This nanny thing might be true but there's still the dry-cleaning link to the Embassy.'

Geraint shook his head. 'That's looking like a dead end now. Peppa has booked a Rentokil visit for next week. Her house has a moth infestation, apparently. It explains the sudden increase in dry-cleaning visits. Only way to kill the sods and save your cashmere.'

'And I finally tracked down the dry cleaner's sister,' added Pixie. 'The reason we've been having trouble locating her is because she's on maternity leave. She hasn't set foot in the Embassy in the last two months.'

I took this in. 'I think Frederick is the Coyote and the Snake. He was the one selling information that sabotaged those previous Six missions. And he just tried to assassinate Peng.'

'He might still succeed,' said Jake. 'Peng doesn't fly out until tonight. We still have the auction at Christie's to get through.'

'We need absolute confirmation. And if Frederick is involved we need to know to what degree. He might have got close enough to Tenebris to know who the people behind it are. We need names.' Hattie turned to Geraint. 'Do a full search into Frederick's finances, background, everything you can get your hands on. If he has the resources to run, we need to cut them off. We need to take him alive and find out everything he knows.'

I remembered something Camilla had said. 'His wife's art gallery. One of us should pay it a visit. Frederick helped with their accounts. That could be an easy place to hide money.'

Hattie looked at me. 'If Frederick is the Snake he knows that we're going to put this together. He knows that once we get the EpiPen results confirming poison, we'll work out that someone in or close to the delegation had to be involved. You need to throw him off. Make him believe we're onto someone else.'

Hattie was right. Frederick couldn't know we suspected him.

I got out my phone and texted: *We think Peppa is doing so well she has a PA working for her. Meet at Christie's at 5 p.m.*

Frederick pinged back straightaway: *OK. See you there.*

'I'm going to try and meet with Dugdale face to face,' said Hattie.

'You don't think Dugdale is in on it?' I'd known Duggers the longest and couldn't believe he would have any role in tearing apart the Security Services he held so dear.

Hattie shook his head. 'Highly unlikely. But if I lay everything out for him, he can at least shed some light on exactly how the hell this could be happening.'

I thought back over the last few days. How different everything looked if Frederick wasn't one of us but one of them.

Goddammit.

'The invasion at Platform Eight. Outside Gigi's nursery I said something about nuts. Frederick must've thought I was talking in code. That I was talking about work. He thought we'd cottoned on to the EpiPens. That's why they took the risk of breaking in. They thought we were about to unravel their whole plan.'

All that drama.

All those dead Ghosts.

Robin.

Gone.

Just because my daughter went to nursery with a peanut in her pocket.

Jake nodded. 'And when Frederick realised we didn't have a clue about the EpiPens, they went ahead with the plan.'

A throwaway comment I'd made to someone I thought was a colleague, a friend, had set off a chain of events that led to so much bloodshed.

How had I been such a shitty judge of character?

His deadpan sense of humour. He wasn't fucking deadpanning, he just didn't *have* a sense of humour. He wasn't dry. He was deranged. And that meant ... he didn't actually find my jokes funny. And he didn't have respect for women – all his refreshing lack of issue with reporting to a woman was just another part of his condition. I couldn't believe ... I couldn't believe I let my mind go places it shouldn't have. How could I have been so blind? How could I have missed the signs? Was the flirting another manipulation? To confuse me with this pretence of attraction? God, how could I be so easily played? It was all an act. All of it.

Jake put a hand on my shoulder. 'Don't even think of blaming yourself. This is all on him. And we're going to make him pay. *I'm* going to make him pay.' From the minute Jake had found out about Robin, he had been on the edge of losing it. He just didn't know where to direct the rage, the pain. But now he did. Now he had a target. Someone to blame. And no one was going to hold him back.

Hattie heard the steel in Jake's voice and looked up sharply. He addressed the room. 'Remember the greater good here is ending the Tenebris Network. If Frederick is the Snake he's the best link we have. He will have a working access login to the website. He will have received payment from them. They would've set up a way of exchanging information. These are all trails we can follow. He's our only chance of finding the people running Tenebris and getting it permanently shut down and have Eight back up and running.

'G – you and Pixie need to go through all the intel we have on Frederick. We re-look at everything we've learned over the last few days. The wife's art gallery – we need accounts, all painting records. Everything. The Committee wants proof. We find the money, we have the confirmation we need to take Frederick down.'

Hattie turned to Jake and me. 'Go search his house. It's unlikely there'll be anything there but it's worth a try.'

Would it be empty now? I checked my watch. Shit. I was meant to be picking Gigi up. I'd never make it on time.

'Jake, let's go. I need to get Gigi on the way and drop her with my mother-in-law. We can then search Frederick's house.'

I rang the nursery as we approached the Platform's car park. 'I'm so sorry, I've been stuck at work. I'll be there fifteen minutes late.' Yvonne was silent. 'It won't happen again.' She still remained silent. 'Listen, I was going to volunteer to host the next parent coffee morning.'

'That would be wonderful. Thank you. I am leaving the church shortly but I will ensure my staff know you'll be late. Pick-up will be at the nursery.' She clicked off.

I must remember to try that silent technique in my next interrogation.

Chapter Twenty-Nine

JAKE DROPPED ME outside Gigi's nursery and screeched on to Frederick's house. He was going to scope out if anyone was home. If Frederick was there I was going to ring him with a made-up lead he needed to chase down on the other side of London. At least if it was just Camilla there with the kids I could tempt her out to the playground with Gigi while Jake searched the house. Talking to her could also provide much needed intel. I thought of how quiet and withdrawn she'd been at all the WAF meetings. Did she know she had things to hide?

We had fewer than ten hours until Peng flew out of here. We needed to know what was going on. We needed confirmation Frederick was the Snake. That he was the Coyote. We needed answers. That no one else was after Peng and that we could get the Tenebris Network shut down for good.

At least seeing Gigi would make me momentarily forget everything. A blast of brightness on this dark day.

I skipped up the steps to the Portakabin and banged on the door. Miss Jenna opened it. She frowned when she saw me.

'Hi there, I'm here for Gigi.'

'Oh, did Mr Easton not get hold of you?'

My heart skipped a beat.

'I . . . no . . .'

'He picked up Gigi twenty minutes ago. With Florence.' She took in my face. 'We know you two work together and you always usually pick up the girls together. He said he'd be fine to take her as he knew you'd be a while.'

'Right.' I tried to think. Miss Jenna was still staring at me. 'Right. Yes. He must've left a message on my phone. Thank you.'

I heard myself say, 'Thank you.' How British was that. Thanking the woman who had handed my beloved only daughter over to a fucking homicidal sociopath.

I stumbled down the steps of the Portakabin. Hands shaking, I clicked on my GigiMap app. A blue dot was on Frederick's road.

I rang Jake. 'Frederick has Gigi. It could be a test.'

'I've just arrived outside their house.'

'GPS says she's in there. Make sure he can't see you. I'll leave the line open so you can hear.'

I ran. I was at the end of his road in three minutes. I stopped. I had to think. I had to calm down. I took deep breaths.

It could be nothing.

He could've just been doing me a favour.

Or he knows and he's fucking with me.

I waited another beat. Until my breathing was normal. I was normal. And this was going to be the performance of my life.

Frederick couldn't know I was scared. He couldn't know I suspected him.

My heart was still racing. I checked my phone. It was still connected to Jake. I slipped it into my pocket and rang the doorbell.

Frederick opened the door.

'You found us.'

'I did indeed. Thanks for picking her up. I didn't realise I was going to be late.' Where was Gigi? The house sounded silent. 'Yvonne is not someone you want to be on the bad side of. I had to bloody volunteer to host a coffee morning. So could I just grab Gigi now? Her grandmother is coming over so we need to get back.'

'I can't let you do that,' he deadpanned.

'Right. And why's that?'

He threw his arms open. 'Because they're having a wonderful little tea party; we can't possibly make them stop. Come in and see.'

I tapped my watch. 'I'd love to but really, we should be going. Got a lot to do before Christie's this afternoon. If you just—'

Frederick had already disappeared back into the house.

'Come along!' he shouted as he walked down the hallway.

I walked into the kitchen. Gigi, Florence and Frederick were all seated around a small child's table.

'Mama!' Gigi shouted brightly. She grinned at me. 'Look, we're doing tea. You have some?'

I took in her round little face. Lopsided hairclip fixed to messy hair. My eyes. Her father's nose. I loved her more than anything. I was fighting every impulse I had to pull her into my arms and run.

Frederick put an arm round her. 'Gigi, shall we ask Mummy to take a seat?' The two of them looked up at me, smiling. Florence had her head down. She was making small lines on a piece of paper in front of her. On her right arm I could see a bandage poking out the bottom of her long-sleeved orange top.

'Sorry, Gigi, we—'

'YES! Come sit, Mama. Come!' She patted the little chair next to her and I did as she asked. Frederick and I were now sitting opposite each other. Gigi poured me imaginary tea. I picked up the teacup.

'How was the office?' asked Frederick. He locked eyes with me.

'We've been on Ling Ling, the PA, all day. We have evidence she met with Peppa yesterday, meaning she must be her inside link. We still haven't been able to ID the woman Peppa met with in the playground – she could be the Coyote.'

'You all ready for the auction this afternoon?'

'Everyone's stressed. We have no idea what the Coyote has planned next. Makes preparing for another attempt impossible.' I stretched and yawned. 'And now I have to deal with my mother-in-law when I get home.' I rolled my eyes. Keep up the chit chat. Everything is fine. 'So where are Camilla and Arthur?'

'Out shopping.'

'I'm hungry, Mama.'

'OK, Gigi. Shall we go home for lunch and see Ganma?'

'Ganma!'

I got up, holding Gigi's hand. Frederick's arm shot out and held my arm. I looked down at it and then up at him. We observed each other. I had to hope I was managing the staring flirt we'd been so well practised at. That he wouldn't see the terror.

'Stay for lunch here.'

'Tempting. But I think fish fingers with Ganma is calling.'

He stared at me for another second. Then dropped his arm.

'Bye, Florence.' I touched the girl on her shoulder.

'Bye bye.' She didn't look up.

'Right, Gigi, now let's get everything together. Shoes. Coat.' I hoped he wasn't looking at my hands. They shook as I did the Velcro up on Gigi's pink sparkly trainers.

'Now say "thank you" to Florence's daddy.'

'Fank you.'

'I'll see you at Christie's.'

'Goodbye, Lex.'

I smiled and turned towards the kitchen steps. Having my back to an enemy went against everything I'd been trained for. But I had to do it. Gigi skipped ahead, humming. It was ten steps to the hallway. I took each one, listening for a charge, bracing myself for a knock to the back of the head. If he was responsible for everything we suspected, he would have no qualms about attacking me in front of our children.

I made it to the kitchen door, stopped, held up a hand and gave him another look. Felt the bile rise in my throat. I shuffled Gigi along the hallway and out into the fresh air. The front door slammed behind us.

'Meet me outside my house,' I announced to my pocket and a listening Jake.

I picked up Gigi and held her close. 'Mummy is going to carry you the whole way home.' She snuggled into my neck and I clasped my arms round her. My baby. My Gigi. She was safe. We walked slowly home.

Jake was waiting outside our door.

'Look who's here, Gigi!'

'Uncky Jake!' She wrangled herself out my arms and ran into his.

He picked her up and hugged her close.

'Good to see you, little miss.'

I let us in the house. I looked at the photo of me, Will and Gigi in the frame on the table. Had I just come so close to losing her? She had been in harm's way and I hadn't been there to protect her.

'Jake, can you just . . . take her to the kitchen.' I stumbled past him to the bathroom. I just made it to the loo and threw up.

I collapsed to the floor.

Never again.

Never again could I let Gigi get caught up in my work.

I walked into the kitchen and Jake handed me a glass of water. I drank it in one and put it back on the table. My hands were still shaking.

'Frederick knows something's up. But he's not sure what. If he was I wouldn't have walked out of there.' I went to the fridge and pulled out a loaf of bread and some cheese and made Gigi a sandwich.

She was playing in the corner with her toy kitchen.

'Lunch, sweetheart.' I put it down on the table in front of me and she came over and sat on my lap.

'Sangwitch. Yum.'

I held her close as she ate.

'We need to move on him now. Just because he didn't' – Jake looked down at Gigi – 'k-i-l-l you, it doesn't mean he's not going to run.'

'You're right. Taking her was a test. I may have held it together enough to get us out of there but he knows something is wrong.'

'I'll call Hattie.' Jake walked into the hallway.

'Is that good, darling?'

She nodded. I stroked her hair and kissed her head. She was safe. That was all that mattered.

Jake came back into the kitchen. 'Hattie's meeting me at Frederick's house. We're going to bring him in. Time's running out. If he is the Snake we need to use him to get to whoever is running Tenebris. Interrogating him will get us the answers we need. You stay here and I'll call you with an update.'

I nodded. 'Be careful – his daughter is with him. He said that his wife and son were out but I can't be sure. Remember he's a fudging sociopath who's capable of fudging anything and as much I want him fudging ended we need to know what he knows.'

'Understood.'

My front door slammed and we both froze.

'Don't worry, I'm here!' called Gillian from the hallway.

'We're in here, Gillian.'

I pulled out my phone to text a friend who now worked in the private sector. Gillian might be here to look after Gigi but an ex-Special Forces commando would be looking after both of them.

She bustled through into the kitchen holding a Sainsbury's bag. 'Hello, Jake. Found yourself a nice girl yet?'

'Sadly not. Just lots of very, very naughty ones.'

'Oh stop. You're terrible.' Gillian laughed and unpacked her lunch onto the table. 'Alexis, did Will tell you about the carbon monoxide alarm? The other day I woke up in the middle of the night panicking that you didn't have one here. I could only go back to sleep once I texted him telling him how important it was. He said you had one but do you know you need to keep checking the batteries?'

A text. In the middle of the night.

Of course it would be from Gillian. A woman who worried so much about the hidden everyday dangers in the home she wouldn't drink tap water as she'd read it had oestrogen in and she didn't want it upsetting her carefully regulated hormone levels.

'It's OK, Gillian, it beeps when it needs new ones.'

'What a relief.'

'I'm just heading out.' Jake nodded at us both and left.

'Bye, Uncky Jake.'

I listened to Gillian's chatter about the broken-down car and the nice man at the AA and how he taught her a clever trick about the oil gauge and how you can always tell the ones who respect their elders.

My phone beeped, confirming my commando friend would arrive for Gillian and Gigi protection within the hour. I wasn't going anywhere until he was here.

'I'll be off soon, Gillian. I have a bit of time to kill before my next meeting.'

'Not to worry, love, you do what you need to.'

Gigi finished her sandwich and insisted Ganma sit with her on the sofa and read her the same three books she'd got me to read her at breakfast.

I made myself a sandwich and ate, listening to Gillian reading. '. . . and then Little Red Riding Hood said, "Grandma, what big eyes you have . . ."'

Life was so simple in the fairy tales. We knew who the baddies were and good always won over evil. Unless you thought like Yvonne. She'd probably say the maligning of the Big Bad Wolf was transgender prejudice.

I went upstairs to my bathroom. I removed a panel from the cupboard under the sink. A lockbox was inside. I entered Gigi's birthday and it opened. I took out my gun and a set of bullets and loaded it. This lockbox was always here just in case I ever had to go straight from home and out to an op.

I went back into the bedroom and took my modified black Marc Jacobs bag out of my wardrobe. I put the gun inside the false bottom and closed it. I slung the bag's heavy gold chain over my shoulder and headed downstairs. I was on the landing when the doorbell rang. I tensed and reached inside my bag.

'It's me,' Jake's voice came through the letterbox.

Why was he back here already? I went and opened the door.

Jake was holding Florence's hand. She looked like she'd been crying. I bent down to talk to her.

'Hello, Florence. Gigi is just in the kitchen. She'll be happy you're here to play.' I ushered her through. Gillian and Gigi looked up from the book. 'Gigi's friend's come to join.'

Gillian patted the space on the sofa next to her. 'Come on then, love, don't be shy, come listen to the story.'

Florence went to sit down with them.

I shut the kitchen door and went back to Jake in the hallway. I hung my bag up on a hook.

'Frederick's gone. We found Florence alone in the house. He must've walked out straight after you.'

'He just left her? How was she?'

'She was hysterical. Completely distraught about Daddy leaving. We calmed her down with a biscuit and I said I'd bring her here. You need to call Camilla. She knows you. There's a better chance she won't freak out as much on hearing from you that her husband's a psycho traitor who just abandoned their two-year-old home alone to go on the run.'

I thought of Camilla and her fragile nature. I started thinking a lot about Camilla and how everything I knew about her was most probably wrong.

'I'd better get back. Hattie managed to speak to Dugdale. He says he was shocked but believes Frederick being the Snake makes sense. Frederick did bring him the actual Tenebris web address and the login card, but only after the rumours about Tenebris had begun circulating. It was just a matter of time before the Security Services would be tasked with shutting it down.'

I nodded. The pieces seemed to fit. If Frederick knew that Tenebris's time was limited, exposing them was worth it. Especially as doing so gave him a way in to Eight, a way to get close to Peng and secure one final big payday.

'I'll get Camilla here and find out what she knows.'

I pulled out my phone as Jake let himself out.

Camilla answered on the second ring.

'Hi, Camilla, it's Alexis. Frederick had to go out so Florence is with me. She's absolutely fine but you need to come to my house now. I'll text you the address.'

'I . . . I'm coming. I've just got out at Turnham Green tube. I'll be there as soon as I can.'

Chapter Thirty

CAMILLA WAS THERE within five minutes. She must've run the whole way here. She pushed the buggy with Arthur strapped in into our hallway. I called Florence out from the kitchen. She ran to Camilla and she scooped her into her arms.

'Daddy left me, Mummy. He left me all alone.'

Camilla looked from her daughter to me.

I nodded. Her jaw clenched.

'It's because he knows how brave you are, Florence. Isn't that right? I bet you hardly even cried.'

She nodded. 'I got biscuit for being so brave.'

'How about you go back and keep playing with Gigi, and when Mummy's finished talking to Alexis we'll go get ice cream?'

Florence's eyes widened. 'Ice cream!' She ran back to the kitchen.

Camilla leaned down and unclipped Arthur from the buggy and picked him up. I led Camilla through to the TV room and closed the door.

'She wouldn't have been alone for more than ten minutes. My colleagues got there very soon after he must've left.'

'But why—'

I held up a hand. 'Frederick is in trouble. It looks as though he may be working with some very bad people. We think that's why he ran, why he left Florence alone.'

Camilla placed Arthur on the floor and handed him a toy mobile phone out of her bag. She slumped onto the sofa. Her hands were shaking. 'That bastard. Poor Florence. How could he leave her? How could he?'

I sat down on the armchair opposite her.

'Camilla, you know . . . you know Frederick is not right, don't you? That he isn't normal.'

She looked up at me and smiled. And then she let out a sob. She clasped a hand to her mouth. 'I've waited so long to hear someone say that.' She stared at me, eyes glistening. 'He made me feel that I was not normal. That I made him get angry. That I made him not care. That if I did better, if I was more like he wanted me to be, then he would be happy. Then *we* would be happy.'

Camilla stared at Arthur smashing the buttons on his phone. A tinny 'Twinkle, Twinkle, Little Star' started playing. Her whole body was shaking.

'Has he . . . has he always been like this?' I needed to keep her talking. She looked as though she was on the brink of losing it and I needed to learn as much as I could about Frederick.

'When we first met it was a few years after university. At a dinner party. He was handsome, charming, very bright – all the girls were fawning over him. When he asked for my number I felt so lucky. That he had chosen me. And when he proposed I couldn't believe it. I was over the moon.' She looked down at her rings and twirled them round and round. 'I did wonder how well I really knew him. He never seemed to drop his guard. He was . . . too perfect. He always said the right thing.'

'And after you got married?'

'Then I could never say the right thing. Everything upset him. It got to the point where I just . . . I was scared to talk.

When I got pregnant with Florence I thought he'd be happy. That we'd be a family. But it changed nothing. He only showed interest in her when other people were around. Perfect husband. Perfect father. He'd perform when he needed to and the minute we were alone . . .' Her voice broke and she went quiet.

'Did your friends not notice what was going on?'

Arthur tired of his toy phone and crawled round the sitting room, looking for something new to play with.

'Frederick encouraged me to lose touch with my friends. One by one he took issue with something they had said. Anger that one of their husbands had made a joke about his new haircut. Disgust that one of my school friends put on a lot of weight. There was always something. By the time Arthur was six months old everyone had given up on me. People thought it was what happened when you have kids. You just disappear for a while. Frederick wouldn't even let me have my phone when he was with me. He'd take it off me the minute he got home from work and hand it back to me in the morning as he left.'

She watched Arthur as he pulled DVDs off the shelf under the television.

'Did Frederick use your phone when he had it?'

Camilla nodded. 'Sometimes there'd be what looked like encrypted text messages on it. And there was some app he downloaded. Password protected so I could never get into it. I just presumed it was some kind of spyware – so he could see what I was doing on my phone when he was at work.'

I thought of the Ghosts raiding the warehouse at the first WAF coffee morning to wipe the women's phones. The WhatsApp worm I sent to our group would've downloaded Camilla's phone too. Frederick must have been using it to communicate with

Tenebris. It didn't matter if he'd deleted anything incriminating, the worm and Geraint would've eventually found them.

'I'm so sorry, Camilla. It's been horrible for you. You must be so lonely.'

She shook her head. 'Having no friends to see made it easier. I could pretend our strange little life was normal and focus instead on the children. I didn't have to hear how happy everyone else was. How their biggest problem was builders overrunning on their extension. Or finding a good holiday destination with a kids' club. What could I say? What could I share about my life? Yesterday Frederick screamed at Florence – for playing with Play-Doh she found in his office – to such a terrifying degree she wouldn't say a word for hours. She was shaking as he went on and on about how she shouldn't ever go through his things.' She looked up at me. 'Or I could tell them about that time our ten-month-old nearly cut his finger off because Frederick left him alone with the bread knife and, rather than comfort him, rather than try and bandage it or make it better, he locked him in the bathroom so he couldn't bleed on any carpet while he carried on working on his laptop.'

I didn't doubt what Camilla was saying for a second.

'I nearly left him that day. By the time I came back home Arthur had screamed so much he could barely breathe. I even booked an appointment with a lawyer. But I couldn't go through with it. Who would believe me? I'd had a breakdown after Arthur was born. My mental health was what would be considered questionable. I had no evidence of any wrongdoing on his part.' She shrugged. 'I had nothing on him. He was a paper-perfect model citizen and government employee. Even if I had the courage to leave him, he'd still be allowed weekends with them. He'd still be allowed to be alone with them. I couldn't let that happen. He took Florence out early this morning when I was asleep with Arthur in his room. She came back howling with a hurt arm. I don't even—'

'I was there. I was out running. He didn't see me but I was right there. She fell from the top of the climbing frame. He didn't react – didn't look up from his phone.' I thought back to Frederick's look of disinterest. How he'd held her at arm's-length. 'That's when I knew.'

Camilla closed her eyes.

'My poor baby. My poor babies. This is all my fault. All my fault.' She dropped her head into her hands and began to cry.

'Camilla, stop.' I came across the room and grasped her hands. 'None of this is your fault. Frederick is a sociopath. He's fucked in the head. You're a hero for surviving with him as long as you have. We're going to take him down. He's been selling information at work that's getting our agents killed. I promise you he's going to be out of your life very soon. But until we have him, until he's safely locked up, you need to get away. Somewhere he can't find you.'

'Why?' She looked up at me.

'Because . . . because he might try and hurt you. He might try and take the kids.'

Camilla shook her head slowly. 'No, Lex. He won't. He wanted a wife, he wanted a family, because it's what people did. Now you all know what he is, he doesn't need to hide anymore. He doesn't need us as part of his cover.' She smiled through the tears. 'We're finally free.'

Camilla didn't seem fazed when I told her my colleagues were currently searching her home. 'Tell them to take as long as they need. We won't be back for hours.' She walked out pushing the pram and holding Florence's hand, telling her about all the fun they were going to having eating mint choc chip and then looking for a new house to live in. Planning their new start seemed to have invigorated her.

Jake was ringing me. I answered it.

'We've torn apart the house and found nothing. No clue as to where he's gone. Nothing suspicious. And no hidden cash.'

I thought of something in his kitchen that was different. Something had changed since my last visit. I was too focused on trying to get Gigi safely out to notice it at the time but something was definitely missing. The room had seemed more minimalist. Even tidier.

What was it?

Florence's pictures. The ones stuck all over the pinboard. The ones that had made me feel so guilty for binning Gigi's. They were all gone. Why would he have taken them down?

'Have you checked the bins?'

'Yes, we've been through them all. Even the recycling.'

'Any children's drawings or paintings?'

'Yes, there were about twenty of them. Utter shite.'

'Take them apart. They were stuck up all over the kitchen three days ago at the WAF coffee morning. He must've only recently binned them.'

Jake rang back a minute later.

'Do two-year-olds paint by numbers?'

'No, Jake. That's a little advanced.'

'OK then – we've found a code. Under each bit of stuck-on tissue or twirly pasta or glitter are number sequences. I'm bringing everything in to the Platform. See what G and Pixie can make of it.'

'Someone at the nursery. They must be working for Tenebris. Frederick has been communicating with them through the pictures.' I thought of each of the teachers.

Miss Jenna. The one who had just started. The one who was outraging everyone with her lack of Montessori training. The one who had let Frederick take Gigi.

'I know who it must be. We need to pick her up. If she's been the go-between for Frederick and Tenebris then she must know how to get hold of them. Even who they are.'

'Send everything you have on her to G. He'll track down an address and Cameron can go get her.'

'Frederick is definitely the Snake,' announced Geraint as I walked into the meeting room. Jake and Hattie had beaten me back there as I'd had to wait until Kenny the commando had arrived and been briefed on everything he needed to know about keeping Gigi and my mother-in-law safe.

'I've gone through the gallery accounts and things don't add up. The gallery took receipt of seven different works of art by Salvador Dali, Henry Moore, to name but a few, and immediately sold them to seven different buyers. None of whom I can find any record of on any international database. They are genuine people but all with different addresses and nationalities.'

Hattie nodded. 'All his Tenebris earnings were transferred to art. It's easy to hide and easily transportable. And he can sell on as and when he needs the money.'

'Do we know where these works of arts are now?' If Frederick managed to evade us, if we at least knew where he was headed we could be waiting.

'The British Virgin Islands. I've been going through courier records from the gallery and Frederick arranged shipment of seven paintings to an address there. The paperwork may say they are inconsequential ones worth a few grand but I'm betting you they're hiding what's really underneath.'

'Do we think Peng is still at risk?' asked Jake. 'Surely Frederick's not going to make a play for her now he knows that we know who he is? He won't be able to get within a few feet of her without us taking him down.'

I thought about it. 'Frederick knows Peng is going to be at the Christie's exhibition this afternoon and there's no way of knowing he hasn't already got a plan in place for killing her. Look at the banquet – Peng could've died there without him even being in the room. It pains me to say it, but he's good at this.'

'He might not even be working alone,' added Hattie. 'You all go to Christie's. I'm going to head to Heathrow. With Frederick's high-level MI6 credentials, he would've had no trouble gaining access to the airport and potentially tampering with the plane.'

Geraint frowned. 'Surely he wouldn't take down a plane just to get one woman?'

'If Frederick has a questionable moral compass and is gearing up for one final payday, I'd rule out nothing.' Hattie looked round at us. 'The Committee state the priority is making sure Peng gets clear of the UK alive. As soon as that happens we switch to tracking down Frederick. We will get him. He will be held responsible for everything he's done.'

We were all silent. Frederick's greed and treachery may have been responsible for the deaths of several colleagues, but it was Robin we were all thinking of.

Chapter Thirty-One

CHRISTIE'S AUCTIONEERS WAS HOUSED inside an impressively large and beautiful building in Mayfair. This afternoon's auction was of Asian contemporary art. Peng and the delegation would be there for the auction and to meet the artists whose work was being showcased.

People were starting to arrive; the main auction room was filling up fast. I stood by the door, assessing who was entering.

Daddy Pig walked in. I remembered from his email correspondence how his attendance at this auction had been long planned. He was picking up the keys to a friend's country pad for a night away with his mistress. I thought of Naomi and her stoic tears. And his cold determination to make her fight him for every penny.

I stopped Daddy Pig with my arm and leaned in. 'We know you're having an affair.'

His head whipped towards me. 'Who the hell are you? What are you talking about?'

'Just like you, Ronald, I work for a number.'

He frowned. 'What the hell kind of business do Five or Six have with my private life?'

'Not Five. Not Six.' I stared him in the eye. 'Eight.'

He paled.

'I . . . I'm not doing anything wrong. I . . .'

'Your wife might disagree. You treat her right or we might feel the need to intervene.'

'Come on . . . You can't be serious.'

'Do you think anyone in Eight ever jokes about anything? Do you think we'd waste time talking to you unless we had a point to make?'

'No.' He shook his head vigorously.

'Let her divorce you and give her everything she asks for. Remember: we will be watching you. We will be following you. We will know everything. So choose your next move very carefully.'

'Understood.' He swallowed. He walked off fast.

'Oh, and Ronald?' He turned back to me. 'She gets to keep the dog.'

The horror on his face made me smile.

Jake came up to me.

'We got to Miss Jenna. I just spoke to Cameron. She tracked her down to Luton and had a little chat with her.'

I could only imagine exactly what that entailed.

'The Tenebris Network is financed by two fund managers.'

'This great criminal enterprise, capable of crippling our Security Services, is run by a couple of city boys? How the hell is that even possible?'

'Frederick. He brought it to them. Tenebris was all his idea. The three of them have equal shares in it.'

Not just the Snake.

Not just the Coyote.

But the creator of the whole of the Tenebris Network.

Tenebris. Latin for 'dark'. That should've been the first clue. Frederick and his chums showing off their public school education. A smug in-joke. But I hadn't seen it. I hadn't seen anything. Distracted by gooey eyes and the feeling he found me attractive. I was angry. So angry at myself for being fooled. And at him for being a calculating shit with a seemingly natural flair for treachery and deception.

'Is Cameron sure the intel is solid?'

'Miss Jenna's not a professional so it was easy to get her talking.'

I wasn't surprised. The patience to cope with a room full of two-year-olds is not something most of us who had chosen this industry could ever manage to fake.

'She worked as a classroom assistant for a couple years, moved up to London for a teacher training degree but dropped out and got in with a bad crowd. Met one of the hedge fund boys on a night out, name of Mark Somersby. She's been sleeping with him. He pushed her into this, threatened to blackmail her with some compromising photos he'd taken. He'd text her what messages she needed to get to Frederick through the kid's drawings.'

I found it comforting that Gigi had been in daily close proximity to someone who at least had some kind of teaching background.

'How would Frederick report back to them?'

'If Frederick wanted to get a message to them he'd write in code on the back of those Wow cards you have to hand in.'

Hah. I knew it. No way could Florence have been doing all those things the Wow cards said she was. Riding a bike without stabilisers, counting to ten in Mandarin. I should've seen a red flag then.

'G and Pixie are now trying to track down this Mark Somersby. There's an alert out on the car registered to him, so we should be able to locate him soon. We use him to get the name of his partner, and the Tenebris Network will be shut down by the end of the day and those greedy tosspots will be at the Box.'

Up by the Farm was a large square concrete building, with numerous soundproofed rooms that was used for high-level interrogations. Its nickname was down to not only the building's box-like appearance but what a great deal of interviewees would leave in.

'There's just Frederick left.'

'I'm betting he's already en route to the British Virgin Islands.'

I wasn't so sure. 'He knows this is his last chance for a final payday. He succeeds in killing Peng and he gets paid whatever ridiculous seven-figure amount the Chinese People's Alliance have promised him. And then he has enough funds to stay invisible for the rest of his life.'

We looked round. The auction room was rapidly filling up.

'You know him best,' said Jake. 'What do you think his move would be?'

I scanned the crowds of people. He wouldn't risk coming up here. Not when he knew we were looking for him.

Peng walked into the room with the rest of the delegation trailing behind her. She started a slow tour around the room, admiring each piece of art fixed to the walls.

How would *I* get her?

In a room I couldn't be seen in?

If I didn't care who or how many had to die.

There was one way.

But would he have gone for it?

'Yesterday he screamed at Florence for playing with Play-Doh she found in his office.'

Was it really Play-Doh?

'He went on and on about how she shouldn't ever go through his things.'

Or was it C-4?

I looked round the bustling room. There must be three hundred people here.

It had to be C-4.

A bomb. He'd planted a bomb.

If he couldn't get close to Peng without getting caught, it was the only way.

I turned to Jake. 'We need to search whatever is directly underneath this room.'

He took a beat to process what I was saying.

'You're right. It makes sense.'

Geraint and Pixie were in a van parked outside. 'G-Force, pull up the floor plans of Christie's. We need to know where Frederick would most likely plant a bomb.'

'A bomb . . . right.'

'There's a door at the far corner – where does it lead?'

'Down to the vaults. That's the best bet for where it would be. The auction room would be directly above the blast radius. There's another set of stairs leading down to the vaults by the entrance.'

'Jake – I'll take the door. You take the entrance stairs.' I checked my watch. 'The auction starts in ten minutes. Go!'

We separated and walked fast towards the respective doors.

'G-Force, patch in Hattie – he's going to need to be updated if we find anything.'

I walked up to the door marked 'Private' and, without slowing down or even looking round, went through. The combination of my black trouser suit and a confident air of belonging should be enough to stop anyone questioning me. Otherwise a flash of one of my police or Security Service IDs and talk of a confidential operation would ensure no one got in my way.

I got down one flight of stairs without seeing anyone; on the second there were two girls who looked not long out of school, on the landing whispering to each other and giggling. Interns catching up on last night's gossip. They went quiet as I came past, giving them a nod. I kept going. One more flight of stairs to the vaults. I came out the door and into a narrow corridor. The right led to the vaults, the left to the Ryder Street delivery door.

To my right was empty.

To my left there was a broad back in a pinstripe suit walking towards the exit.

'Eyes on Frederick,' I spoke softly.

'*Take him alive, Lex.*' Hattie's voice came in through my earpiece. '*You can't risk firing. If there's a bomb he could be wearing a trigger vest.*'

I took a deep breath and walked towards him.

He stopped. And turned around slowly.

'Hello, Lex.'

'Frederick.'

'Now, let's not make a scene. Lots of innocent people around here. And let's face it, I could crush you without even really trying. Although I don't usually hit women. It's just not—'

I punched him in the face before he could finish.

He may have been bigger than me. He may have even been stronger. But he didn't have the training. He hadn't spent a year at the Farm. Learning how to fight. Learning how to kill. He thought he could beat me. The trained Rat. Because he was a boy. And I was a girl.

Before he had time to recover from the blow to the face I struck again with three sharp jabs to his lower torso. He bent over and dropped to the floor, winded.

Laughter and voices were coming up the corridor from the Ryder Street entrance.

I roughly pulled Frederick off the ground and propped him up against the wall. He clutched his stomach.

A couple of porters entered the corridor, pushing a trolley with several boxes on. One was regaling the other with his antics from the night before.

'Why, Frederick? All this just to get rich?' I spoke quietly. We needed to talk. We needed to be written off as two suited colleagues having a conversation.

Frederick shrugged. 'I was bored of my life. I wanted a better one. With nicer things.'

'Thatcher knew you were the Snake, didn't he?'

The porters passed right by us; they didn't even look at us as they continued their conversation about a girl with a frightening amount of facial hair.

'It was my fault. I got lazy. Letting four missions from the same department tank was too much. It was always going to draw attention. Our business model was always for Tenebris to be a high-income earner for a year and then disappear. And now we get to go out with a bang.'

The porters kept going down the corridor with the trolley towards the vaults.

A door slammed. I looked to my right. The interns I had passed on the way downstairs were now making their way down the corridor towards us.

'Don't get me wrong, this has been fun. Playing the part of helpful colleague. You liked me, didn't you? I think you did. I can do likeable very well. And you're nice. You're strong. You're impressive.' He reached a hand out and cupped my chin. 'It's a shame we didn't get to fuck.' He said this a little more loudly. The interns must've heard – they both turned to us briefly and smirked.

I waited until they'd passed us before pushing Frederick's hand off my chin.

Frederick shook his head. 'I just don't understand why you Rats are called the elite. You've proven to be a worthy adversary. Just not good enough to beat me.'

'We have beaten you. I could kill you right here.'

'If you do that everyone dies. Forty pounds of C-4 are set to go off the minute the auction starts.' He looked at his watch. 'That gives you eight minutes. Eight minutes isn't long to find and locate a bomb. Eight minutes isn't really long enough to evacuate. Or is it?'

Hattie crackled into my ear, '*G, join Jake on the vault search. Bring a defuser.*' A defuser was a crack device of Geraint's that was able to mimic the frequency of the bomb and reconfigure the detonator. It had an eighty-nine per cent success rate in testing.

'Just think about what you're doing. I saw you after you killed that Ghost at the Platform. You couldn't fake that kind of horror.

You don't want the deaths of that many people on your conscience.'

Frederick laughed. 'I was horrified not because I'd killed someone but because that dirty little man bled all over my shoes. It was disgusting.' He grimaced. 'I don't care about killing people. I just don't like being the one that does it. It's so messy.' He shuddered.

I remembered how he made the same grimace at his daughter's bleeding. He was happy for people to die just as long as their bodily fluids didn't touch any part of him.

'Let me go. You need to find the bomb.'

'You could be bluffing.'

'Yesterday morning, at 10.03 a.m., I came to Christie's flashing my MI6 card with a large ornament of significant international importance that we have asked them to keep safe while we negotiate the terms of its sale. Check with whoever you have listening in there.' He motioned towards my earpiece.

'*I'm on it, hun,*' said Pixie. '*I've already set up the SigBlock.*' The SigBlock stopped remote detonation through a mobile or wireless network. It was only effective outside a radius of twenty feet. Within that range and the bomber could still detonate.

'This bomb might kill Peng. It might not. It's always the gamble with explosives. But one thing is for sure. It will kill Robin.'

I let in a sharp intake of breath.

'Robin. Yes, your nice little friend. The one you were so sad about being taken. We didn't kill him. He was a good failsafe. Just in case we needed him. I can't guarantee he will still be alive by the time you get to him as he's in a bit of a state. But don't you think you should check?'

'At 10.03 a.m. Frederick enters Christie's at the Ryder Street entrance with a trolley that has a crate that's about six feet by four feet on it. He goes in with it and emerges empty-handed fourteen minutes later.'

'I can see by your face you've had confirmation. The bomb's there. Strapped to Robin. I just set the detonator. So it will go off in, let's see . . .' he looked at his watch, 'seven minutes from now.'

Jake crackled in. *There are twelve vaults. We've searched half so far.*

Frederick leaned towards me and spoke louder. 'Hattie, you'd better call off your attack dog. I see that look in her eyes. She wants me dead. And that would be bad for all of us. My heart stops beating and it will detonate immediately.' He patted his chest. 'Little remote back-up I've got connected. Remember the greater good here, Lex. If I die, you die. Robin dies. Peng dies. Hundreds of people die. Let me go. You go find the bomb. Be the hero.'

'*Lex – let him go.*'

'Hattie, I—'

'*There's no time, Lex. He could be wearing a detonator. We need him out of range. You need to help G and Jake find that bomb. Pixie will track Frederick's exit.*'

Fuck. I let go of Frederick. He smirked, gave me a little wave and ran down the corridor.

I set off for the vaults.

Hattie came in again. '*I'm evacuating the whole area using Protocol 324. Demon initiating now.*'

I turned the corner and ran straight into Jake. 'We're doing Protocol 324? Again?'

'You and Geraint do the vaults up the other end, I'll start here.' Jake ran back down the corridor as I entered the vault next to me.

Half the vault was full of crates, the other half had removal blankets, packing materials and a few lone pots and empty frames propped against the walls. I rushed round, peering in pots, lifting up crate lids and pulling back paintings.

I wanted to believe Robin was here and still alive.

I wanted to believe it.

But it could just be a bluff.

And the bomb could be hidden anywhere.

The fire alarm starting ringing. *Ding ding ding*. Red lights were flashing down the corridor. Protocol 324 had been activated.

I headed to the next vault. Works of art were piled round the edges. Even on the floor. Organised chaos. There were small sculptures lined up along the shelves and at the back was a large crate on its side. It was about the same dimensions as the crate Frederick had taken into the vaults on the trolley.

I ran to it. The crate was nailed shut. There was a small sliding lid within the top of the crate. It was fastened with a combination padlock. This had to be it.

If there was a bomb counting down inside this crate, I couldn't risk smashing it open. Too big a jolt could set it off. I looked round the room. It was a cheap padlock, designed to put off nosey porters rather than really keep anyone out. There was a screwdriver on one of the shelves. I ran over to it and picked it up. Just a few well-placed taps should . . . And it was off.

I took a deep breath and slid back the lid.

I let out a cry. A crumpled, unconscious Robin was curled up inside. Strapped to him was a black box with a series of red flashing lights attached to blocks of C-4.

'Vault four. I've found them. Robin and the bomb.'

Breaking the crate wasn't an option. The motion could set it off. The only way to do it was climb in. I peered down. The timer was reading three minutes.

Jake and Geraint arrived at the vault.

'Robin's inside. The bomb is strapped to him. Three minutes. G-Force, give me the defuser.' He reached over to me with it but Jake stopped him.

'Forget it, I'm doing it.'

'Jake, you won't fit.' I motioned towards the small opening. 'Only I can.' I took the defuser out of Geraint's hands.

'Now both of you go. Help with the evacuation.'

Geraint obliged, knocking over a picture on his way out. Jake didn't move.

'That fucker knew what he was doing. He knew it would have to be you.' Jake slammed a hand against the wall.

'Jake. Just get out of here. If it goes bad you know what you need to do.'

The benefit of having a partner who was also godfather to my only child meant one evening over several whiskies I had shown him exactly where on my laptop my post-mortem goodbye to my beloved daughter and husband were.

'I must be able to do something, I must—'

'Get the hell out of here. You know your job. Now do it. Speed up the evacuation. Save lives. I've got this.' I stared him down.

He nodded. 'Get our boy back.' And ran out.

I climbed into the crate. My feet slowly touched the bottom, just up against Robin's side. I gingerly lowered myself in, defuser clutched in one hand.

Inside the crate was stuffy, the air thick. The heavy smell of sweat and wood chippings. I looked at Robin's cut and bloodied face. I couldn't see if his chest was moving.

The bomb beeped.

59 seconds.

The final countdown.

The defuser had three different-sized cable heads coming out its side – the hope being one of them would slot into the bomb. There was a small port on the side of the flashing red incendiary device.

My hands shook as I tried to attach the defuser.

The first two cable heads didn't fit.

The third did.

I let out a breath.

20 seconds.

'Defuser attached.'

I gently leaned over and felt Robin's neck. A very faint slow pulse.

'Robin's alive. But barely.'

15 seconds.

I looked at the defuser screen and pressed the 'start' button. Numbers started scrolling across the screen as it got to work, hacking the bomb's detonator.

Eighty-nine per cent success was a great result when in the testing lab.

Not so much in the field.

Not so much when an eleven per cent failure rate meant being blown apart and never seeing your husband and daughter again. The defuser screen went blank and then started counting down in sync with the bomb's timer. Thoughts flew round my head.

10

This could be it. Fuck, this could be it.

9

What did I last say to Will?

8

Did I tell him I loved him?

7

Or was it to have a go about the bins?

6

God, I think it was about the bins.

5

Gigi.

4

She'll be broken.

3

I love you, baby girl . . .

2

So much . . .

1

Gigi.

'DISARMED,' announced the screen on the defuser.

The lights on the bomb all went green.

I let out a sob.

Christ.

It was going to be OK.

I cleared my throat.

'OK, everyone. The bomb is disarmed.'

'*Good work, Lex. Good work.*' I heard Hattie let out a long breath. '*G, get back in there and clear the device. Medics are on their way for Robin.*'

I felt Robin's skin. He felt very cold. 'It's OK, Robin, you're going to be OK. Just hold on.' I patted his cheek.

Jake crackled in. '*This way, sir, this way . . . Come on, people, let's speed this up! . . . Lex. Thank fuck.*' I heard the smile in his voice. '*I would've made a shit step-mum. Peng has left the building. Just getting the last few people out now.*'

Chapter Thirty-Two

*S*KY NEWS REPORT: *Piccadilly evacuated upon discovery of an unexploded WW2 bomb.*

My phone had pinged with a news update on our way to the Platform. Protocol 324. Rolled out whenever we wanted an area cleared for reasons we didn't want to explain. Robin had been whisked away in an ambulance straight to the Chelsea and Westminster. The Kensington Wing had already been briefed to give us constant updates as to his condition. His vitals were very weak but we were all hopeful.

Hattie was still at Heathrow. Peng and the delegation had gone straight from Christie's to the airport to wait for their flight. He reported they were currently enjoying fine wine in Suite One of the Windsor Suite and that their plane, due to take off in two hours, had passed all the extensive additional security checks that he'd been able to order using his Security Services ID.

'Any leads on Frederick?' Jake leaned round from the driver's seat to call back to Pixie and Geraint, whose fingers were flying across the keyboards of the computers built in to the back of the van.

'Nothing,' said Geraint. 'He's on CCTV leaving Christie's and then appears entering Fortnum and Mason's. No other sightings. He could've changed what he was wearing and merged into one of the crowds of people leaving. I'm looking further into his background, CV, known associates, for any clue as to what he could do next.'

'I've got alerts out for him at all airports, train stations, even ferry crossings,' added Pixie.

'Problem,' said Geraint. 'He's got a PPL.' A private pilot's licence meant Frederick could head to one of the small private airports; with less security and fewer people, he could hire a plane and be over the Channel pretty much unnoticed.

'You need to widen the search. If he's trying to get out to the BVIs to pick up his art shipment, he could use a light aircraft to get to any country in Europe and fly from there. You need to check passenger manifests on every incoming flight.'

We had to find him. I needed him secured. The memory of him seated next to Gigi still made me sick to my stomach.

Kenny, my commando on Gigi and Gillian watch, had confirmed everything was fine at Gillian's flat – she'd taken Gigi back there for a sleepover as I'd said our heating was on the blink. A lame excuse for a mild October day. Gillian may have questioned it if she didn't feel the cold so much she'd wear cashmere jumpers even in summer.

By the time we screeched past Leicester Square, Pixie had found a potential sighting of someone matching Frederick's description at Elstree Aerodrome. We'd been promised the CCTV shots within the hour. As soon as we confirmed it was him we could track where he flew to from his flight plan.

'I've got a ping on Hedge Fund Boy's Ferrari number plate,' Geraint shouted to us. 'It's now parked in front of Cipriani's.'

Pixie was already on the phone. 'Hello there, this is Mark Somersby's PA.' She seemed to have acquired a posh voice. 'I need to get some urgent documents to him for signing. Pray tell, has he arrived with you yet?' She paused. 'Brill. Cheers. I mean . . . how wonderful. Thank you, sir.' She looked up at us. 'Mâitre d' confirmed that Somersby and his guest are there.'

Jake screeched to a halt on Shaftesbury Avenue and turned back to Geraint and Pixie. 'You two get back to the Platform. Keep on the leads for Frederick.'

We pulled up right behind Somersby's Ferrari. It was illegally parked. His type would rather pay the parking fine than face the inconvenience of walking too far.

'How do we play this?' I asked Jake as we got out the van and walked up to the restaurant. 'Local police? Scotland Yard?' We each had wallets with an array of genuine IDs for any one of the law enforcement agencies.

'You choose. I'm just looking forward to humiliating him by dragging him out in handcuffs. Here's to hoping he knows plenty of people inside.'

'Now, remember. Don't get too enthusiastic with your inter-rogation. We need to get out of him who his partner is. Miss Jenna only knew he was a business associate. We need a name.'

'And I'm going to really enjoy getting one.'

We walked in and flashed our police IDs to the mâitre d', who was all too quick to point out Mark Somersby's table and look both excited and terrified as to what was about to take place.

As we approached the table Somersby looked up. He was a slight man, with glasses and thinning hair. Did he know who we were? Was he going to run? He sat perfectly still, watching us get closer, his face slowly losing colour. His dinner companion had his back to us and clearly hadn't noticed as he continued to talk animatedly with big hand gestures.

Jake went straight to Somersby and roughly pulled him to his feet. 'Police. You're coming with us, Mark Somersby.' Jake raised his voice further to announce his name, before turning him round and clipping a pair of handcuffs onto him.

The restaurant quietened, apart from the clink and clank of cutlery hitting plates as everyone strained to hear what was going on.

Somersby's companion turned around to face me, his eyes widening in recognition.

I looked over at Jake. 'I hope you have another set of handcuffs.'

The man stood up. 'Now, look here, you've got this all wrong.'

'I always carry a spare.' Jake threw a pair at me across the table and I snapped them firmly onto Charles Wycombe's wrists.

There were no such thing as coincidences in this industry and there was no doubt Wycombe was the third partner in Tenebris.

Charles Wycombe and Mark Somersby were officially the easiest subjects to get talking in all of Platform Eight's long, bloody history.

Blindfolded and handcuffed and thrown into the back of our van, they remained completely silent the whole drive back to the Platform. Yet as soon as they were alone in separate interrogation rooms they each started talking before Jake and I had even sat down in our respective chairs. Frederick may have told them enough about Platform Eight to be rightly terrified by exactly what we were capable of.

Charles Wycombe blamed it all on his great big castle. It didn't matter how much money he made at his hedge fund, it wasn't enough to keep the place running. Breaking the law, betraying your country and getting our agents killed were clearly acceptable collateral when trying to keep the family seat.

Mark Somersby had no excuse other than Frederick had come to him and Charles with what looked like a genius business plan guaranteed to net them each tens of millions. He admitted he hadn't troubled himself with all the details and that yes, it probably was 'terribly out of order', but when he saw the margins it was impossible to say no.

Jake escorted Mark to his St James's office to retrieve his laptop, and with a push of a few buttons the Tenebris Network was taken offline for good and we were given access to their whole server of data. In our possession were the names of everyone who had registered as an Employee, and the bank details and contact details for each organisation who had registered as an Employer. It would take weeks to work through but our Security Services were going to be reaping the benefit of their databases for years.

Cameron arrived back from guarding Miss Jenna and relayed what she had learned from her. I tried to imagine Miss Jenna's sing-song voice as she detailed just how deeply involved she'd been with such dark people. She had been due to start at the nursery Little Lambs, which Frederick had Florence down for. Due to Dugdale's insistence that Frederick switch Florence to Yvonne's so we could use the school run to communicate, they'd had to improvise – by running over a nursery school teacher. It meant a lengthy hospital stay for the unfortunate woman and a panicked Yvonne having to find a last-minute replacement in order to meet health and safety teacher-child ratios. A teacher with a missing qualification was a better option than closure.

Somersby, Wycombe and Miss Jenna were all very clear in pointing the finger at Frederick being the mastermind behind it all. He had killed his boss, Thatcher, when he started digging into Tenebris. And he had been the one to shoot Y. Y. – Peter Yan – really was a waiter at the Phoenix Palace restaurant. He had never worked for the Chinese Embassy. Frederick had just paid him to tell me information about Peng that the Chinese People's Alliance had discovered from one of their sources. Yan was the disposable face of an inside man. Frederick killed him when he needed to make it look like he was the leak who had told Tenebris about the Dictaphone. He was just another pawn in the carefully constructed game Frederick had set up. I wondered if his plan was always to abandon Camilla and his kids. To leave them behind so he could enjoy his riches abroad without fear of capture.

I wanted to do more to find Frederick.

The sighting at Elstree Aerodrome wasn't him. Having analysed the CCTV both at Elstree and at Avignon where the plane landed, it was clear it couldn't have been him. There was a facial similarity but no one could fake being six inches shorter than their recorded height.

I tried voicing my concerns with Jake and Cameron. Cameron was going to stay on for a few weeks to help us work through all the data from the Tenebris server. We were in the meeting room, waiting for Hattie to arrive back from Heathrow. Peng and the delegation had taken off and were now safely en route to Beijing.

Peng may still be at risk from the Chinese People's Alliance, who had ordered the hit on her, but at least it would be harder for them to get her back in China. Peng's safety was no longer part of our remit – that responsibility was, as it should be, back with her own country. I hoped they looked after her. Everything she had achieved was admirable and I believed her when she said she still had so much more to do.

'Come on, Tyler. Cheer up,' said Jake. 'Today was a good day. Robin is still alive. Only just but he's going to make it – I know he will. Peng is officially no longer our problem. We've just crushed a multi-million-pound underworld recruitment website, saved the Security Services, and two greedy, self-serving city boys are headed for the Box.'

'Frederick is still out there.'

'He'll be out of the country by now. He'll be lying low, thinking of a way to get to the BVIs and his stash of precious paintings.'

'Jake's right,' said Cameron. 'Frederick will know it's crazy to hang round here with a pack of Rats on the hunt for him.'

The lockdown had officially ended. Platform Eight was now back up and running.

'Wow. You and Jake agreeing. That's new.'

'Jake and I had sex.'

I looked over at Jake. 'Really?'

He shrugged. 'She seduced me. I was helpless.'

'You're really making yourself at home here, Cameron. Using my desk. Sleeping with my partner.'

'You don't own him. He can do what he wants.'

'Of course he can do what he wants. I'm allowed to have an opinion on it, though. Are you going to do it again?'

Cameron pondered. 'I think I will. He's good.'

'He's not that good.' I wrinkled my nose.

Jake got up. 'I'm right here. You're both talking about me and I'm right here.'

'It wouldn't interfere with my work,' she added.

'Of course.'

'I'm still here. Do you not think I get an opinion in this? I might not want to have sex with you again, Cameron.'

Cameron and I looked at each other and both laughed. 'Come on, Jake, who are you kidding?'

'Fucking great. You guys are friends now? I liked it better when you hated each other.' He stalked out of the room.

'You did a good job, Lex.' Cameron looked at me with what seemed like a half-smile.

I shook my head. 'I should've caught it earlier.'

'Perhaps. But let's face it, we could all beat ourselves up about every job we do, but we need to take a win when it's a win. Maybe the kid hasn't ruined your career after all.'

All this niceness from Cameron was disconcerting. This wasn't us.

'You do look like shit, though.'

And we were back.

The Platform was buzzing again. Back to how it should be. Rats and technicians scuttling through the corridors. The occasional flicker of the lights, the sizzle of bacon in the canteen, the slam of punch bags being pounded. We were open for business again. Another enemy defeated. We lived to fight another day and take down another target.

I came out the meeting room to find Mrs Moulage waiting for me, resplendent in a fitted tweed coat with fur collar.

A flower-shaped diamond brooch glinted on the lapel. She was holding a red box.

'Siew-Yong asked me to give this to you. A token of her thanks for keeping her safe.'

Mrs Moulage handed the box to me and I lifted the lid. A beautifully carved jade rat nestled inside. I touched the cold stone.

'It's very kind of her. But really it was a team effort.'

'Don't do that.' Her tone sharpened. 'Take the credit. When you've done well you shout about it. No one else will. Take it from this old Rat; things haven't changed that much since my glory days.'

I tilted my head. 'What was it like back then?'

'Darling, it was wonderful.' Mrs Moulage beamed. 'I can forget now all the rubbish I had to put up with. And just think about the fun I had. The day they realised I wasn't just decoration. But an equal. An agent. A Rat. It felt like coming home. To a place where I belonged. Where I could shine.'

'Being the very first woman, the only woman' – I shook my head – 'I can only imagine how tough it was.'

'To do a job like this takes a certain type of person. Even the most Neanderthal of men eventually realise what sex, colour, religion you are is irrelevant. It may have taken a little time but soon enough I was just one of the team, one of the pack. After every successful mission, we'd let loose down here. Good music and hard liquor. We all smoked, we all drank, we all didn't think about tomorrow. The world was just as frightening then as it is now.' Mrs Moulage cast a glance down over my jeans and T-shirt. 'Except everyone was better dressed.'

'Did you not always feel you had more to prove? More to lose?'

'Back then none of us could afford to make any mistakes. My old chief, before every mission, he'd say, "DD, you get one shot. Make it count."' She shrugged. 'And I did. I always did. I had a near perfect success rate. Just like you.'

She held up her hand before I could speak.

'Yes, of course I've followed your career. I've felt proud watching each of you girls come through.'

I smiled. 'And I'm proud to be here. It's not easy but I can't imagine doing anything else.'

'Quite right. What we do is too important. *This* is our life.' She touched my shoulder. 'We get one shot. And we make it count.'

'Goodbye, Mrs Moulage.'

'Goodbye, my dear.'

I watched her walk down the corridor. The nods she got from everyone she passed. The Dior Dame, the Rat Queen.

It was nearing 1 a.m. by the time I finally got home. After we'd debriefed Hattie on everything we'd learned, we focused on chasing down any leads we could find with Frederick's location. There had been another potential sighting at a small airport in Yorkshire. If he was trying to leave the country undetected, travelling north before trying to hire a plane was a clever move.

The house was quiet. I wished Gigi was home and not staying with Gillian so I could go check on her. There was no better antidote to a long, stressful day at work than tucking her in and watching her sleep.

I dropped my bag on the floor and hung up my coat. I checked my phone: a goodnight from Will, safely in Chicago, and an update from Kenny, confirming all was quiet at Gillian's flat. I wondered how long I was going to need him for. How long it would take for me to believe that Frederick was really gone.

I needed a drink to unwind. A drink to shut my mind down so I could drift off to sleep. One glass of red wine and I could retreat to bed and hopefully a good night's sleep.

I walked into the kitchen and stared at the item on the middle of the kitchen table.

A small figurine of Snow White.

It was missing its head.

Part Six

Hug

hug, *v.*
1. Squeeze (someone) tightly in one's arms, typically to express affection.
2. Congratulate or be pleased with oneself.

One Month Later

Chapter Thirty-Three

*I*T'S DONE, WAS all the message from Jake said. I let, a long deep breath out.

It was over.

'Gigi, darling, time to pack our bags – we're going home.'

The Committee had wanted Frederick alive. They wanted us to track him down and bring him in so he could undergo interrogation at the Box. They believed that for him to be the successful mastermind of a plot like Tenebris, there could be other things he might be hiding. Other information that could be helpful. He had had direct contact with many of the Employers listed on the Tenebris Network – he would know things that weren't on the databases.

We had always respected orders. Always respected directives from the Committee.

But the minute I saw headless Snow White, I knew there was only one way I'd ever feel safe again.

Jake and I had both requested blowers and both packed a bag.

I'd picked up Gigi immediately and retreated to the wilds of a remote island off the Scottish coast, having Will join me the moment he landed, in what he thankfully took to be a sponta-neous gesture of reconciliation. Jake had gone hunting. Tracking down every lead he could. Guided by me and Geraint with remote access. We'd scour the online intel and lead him to places. A sighting here. A clue there.

While we were away Hattie had sorted through the mess Tenebris had left behind. Going through their records, it seemed Wycombe, Somersby and Miss Jenna had been telling the truth. The Tenebris Network was Frederick's brainchild. Gaining an understanding of how much enemies would pay for privileged security information had sent his entrepreneurial skills in motion. Wycombe and Somersby had bank-rolled Tenebris, hiring a few top-level IT experts and hackers to set up the website and the unhackable algorithms.

Cameron and Jake had never managed to identify the hackers working for Tenebris as they were all based abroad. Frederick's intel's claim that Tenebris's technological set-up was run from London was obviously faked. There were apparently a team of five of them working remotely from different international locations. Geraint was confident he would be able to find them all eventually. Having access to Tenebris's internal records had given enough clues as to ways he could find their online footprint.

Wycombe and Somersby were now incarcerated in the Sweat Shop – a prison we sent all individuals the Security Services deemed valuable or high-risk enough not to be contained in the normal system. At the Sweat Shop, prisoners' individual skills were put to use in specially allocated assignments. It was run just like any large corporation – except longer hours, no pay and serious micro-management. Not so much Golden Handcuffs, just handcuffs.

Those who completed their time without burning out were released back into the world, some even to the same job they'd had before. The majority became model citizens, now appreciative of a place of work that gave such civil liberties as days off and lunch breaks. Those who ended up back in the Sweat Shop for a second time didn't get out again.

The millions these two men had in the bank were directed to worthy causes, while they continued to do what they did best: hedging bets, making money – but this time it was all for the State. And if they didn't reach their quarterly targets, their punishment was a little more upsetting than not receiving a six-figure bonus. Wycombe's impressive castle had been taken over by the Security Services. It was rented out for company away days during the week and on the weekends the public were given castle tours and tea in the gardens. Allowing the common people full reign of his beloved family seat was apparently more upsetting than his incarceration.

Eight were able to get the names of every Employee and Employer registered on the Tenebris Network. Those for whom matches had been made and information sold were also sent to the Sweat Shop. Those who had just signed up but never actually committed a crime were fired immediately and black-marked for any future intelligence work. We distributed all the information gleaned from the Tenebris databases to our international counterparts. Cameron was particularly looking forward to bringing back to the States the list of US operatives who'd chosen to register as Employees. I had a feeling there would be no mercy for any of them.

We all benefitted from being able to freeze the assets of all the Employers' registered bank accounts. It wouldn't hold them back for long, but for all of us in the intelligence services, knowing who wanted what information for what purpose was a massive win.

Robin had been in the Kensington Wing for three weeks before he was well enough to be discharged. He'd taken numerous hard beatings from the Ghosts and had nearly overdosed on the sedatives he'd been pumped full of to ensure he was in a comatose state for being unceremoniously dumped in a crate with a bomb strapped to his chest. As soon as he was well enough to come back in to the Platform, Jake and I had approved his transfer to Jagger, to take over from a retiring Rat. As Jake said, 'If you can survive having the crap kicked out of you and becoming a human bomb, it probably is time you got to decide your own destiny.'

Will had only stayed with us in our beautiful Hebrides cottage for the first two weeks because of his work, but it had been pretty blissful. No arguments. No loaded comments about not really knowing me. We were back to being us. Able to finish conversations without one of us having to rush off or falling asleep as we were so exhausted.

But then it was a holiday. It wasn't real life. There was no Platform Eight, no outside pressures, just our little family fishing for our dinner and early nights by a crackling fire.

And now we could go home.

Now it was safe.

It was going to be back to real life. The real test, when the demands of the Platform were back in my life.

'We're nearly home, Gigi. We just need to make one stop first.'

I pulled up outside the large house with the Savills 'For Sale' sign outside and parked the car.

I rang the bell.

Camilla opened the door. Arthur was in her arms in his pyjamas, holding a bottle of milk.

'I've been expecting you,' was all she said.

Camilla had been right. Frederick had never come after them. He had walked out of their house, leaving Florence alone, and never once tried to make contact.

'Hello, Gigi. Florence will be so happy to see you. She's through there, building a fort.'

Gigi ran ahead of us into the kitchen, where Florence was piling up empty cardboard boxes. Gigi joined in with a series of giggles and squeals from them both.

I sat down at the table with Camilla. Arthur was on her lap drinking his milk.

'You don't need to worry anymore. He will never bother you again. He will never bother anyone again.'

Camilla let out a long breath. 'Are you sure?'

It's done.

'Positive.'

She stared down at the table. 'They haven't asked for him.' She looked over at the girls playing. 'Not once. We're all getting on with life as before. Just . . . happier.' She smiled.

'Mama, mama, mamaaaaaa.' The bottle was now empty and Arthur was wriggling. 'I'd better take him up to bed.'

I watched her leave the room, Arthur in her arms. She was dressed down in jeans and a baggy sweatshirt, her hair up in a messy ponytail. No Frederick forcing her into immaculate clothing. No Frederick overtaking every part of her life. It hadn't been a marriage, it'd been a dictatorship. And she was now free.

I thought of Peppa, George and Daddy Pig. All had planned covert meetings. All had things they wanted hidden. Real life came with its own set of challenges. But the people we went into battle with should be the ones that lifted us up. We needed to stand side by side and feel like there was nothing we couldn't do together. You didn't want to have to worry they were working for the other side. That they were keeping secrets from you. That they had found another teammate.

I loved Will. I wanted to be with him. There might be times when I didn't appreciate him. And he didn't appreciate me. But we were still good together. I was happy with him. He was my family. And if having my head briefly turned by a charming but ultimately sociopathic colleague had showed me anything, it was: don't ever underestimate what you have at home.

Camilla came back downstairs holding the monitor. The strains of a lullaby could be heard playing through it.

Naomi and Camilla were both now going it alone and they were better for it. I thought of Kate. Of her and George Pig walking down the street, hands clasped. That's what it was about. Finding someone who put your happiness above theirs. It wasn't about the big gestures and the grand declarations of love. It was fighting unseen battles for them. Knowing what was better for them than they did. When the lights went out and before sleep came, you wanted the person next to you to be on your team. Rage, fear, hurt, loneliness. They shouldn't be in the marital bed. A partnership was meant to make your life better. It was meant to give you more joy than pain.

We bid Camilla and Florence goodbye at the doorway.

As we reached the car, I turned back and saw Camilla pick Florence up in her arms. The girl nuzzled into her neck as she closed the door. They were going to be OK. It was only going to get better from now on.

Kate, Naomi and Suze had all come through for Camilla. They'd been coming round to see her, to commiserate over the bastard husband who'd just run off and left her. I thought of the WAF initiative; it may have started out as a farce but it had proven to be a huge success. Flicking through the reports from the other WAF groups, there was nothing but effusive praise from everyone involved. All had voted for it to continue. Everyone needed support. And not just from the person they lived with. I thought of my female friends. Of all the times I had turned to them when I wasn't sure what to do. Reassurance whenever I questioned a decision. Help when childcare was an issue. Laughter at a time when otherwise it would be tears. Us women relied on each other. We understood each other, sometimes better than the men in our lives. We could build each other up in a way only we knew how. Tell each other we were doing brilliantly, when husbands forgot to, or didn't even notice. We needed each other just as much as the man we may live with, sometimes even more so, as friends would still be there, even if the man no longer was.

As we drove the short distance home, I realised that Frederick had only turned my head as he'd reminded me of what the beginning of a relationship could be like. The getting-to-know-each-other thrills. It wasn't real life and daily logistics. It wasn't remembering to take the bins out. Sitting through dinners with their colleagues, friends, relatives who bored you. It was easy in the early stages. You were being your best self. Nice underwear. Not the comfortable kind. Engaged conversation, not checking your phone. You were making an effort. He was making an effort. Everything was shiny and new. But then, like all nice new toys, they grow dull. The gloss and sheen of a new flirtation eventually gives way to the mundane of familiarity.

But being reminded of the early days. Being appreciated. Feeling special. Getting those moments was important. Remembering us as a couple and not just us as parents. I might never be able to be fully honest with Will about my job. But I could at least be more open about what I was feeling.

Maybe, just as with my work, I needed my home life to have that spark. And if it was missing now, I needed to bring it back.

'We're home!' I opened the door and Gigi went running through the hallway and into Will's arms.

'Dada!'

He looked at me over her head as she clung to him. I walked up to them and gave him a kiss.

'Back at last.'

'Bed now, Dada,' said Gigi. It was no wonder she was tired. It had been a long day of travelling.

'Come on, sweetheart. I'll take you up.'

I went to the kitchen and got out a bottle of wine. I opened it and poured a large glass. I listened through the monitor as they talked and he read her a story.

I loved him. I loved our life. I didn't want to be with anyone else. It was him I wanted to come home to. It was him I wanted to grow old with. We had our problems. But then everyone did. It couldn't always be all flowers and rainbows and mini-breaks and over-the-top declarations of love. We were a team. We were married. Wed. Together. And that's the way it needed to stay.

Will came downstairs and took a seat at the kitchen table.

'I need to talk to you.' I smiled at him and handed him the glass of wine.

'I do too.'

He reached behind his back.

And placed my gun down on the kitchen table.

'Just who the hell are you?'

Everything was spinning.

I felt like I'd been punched in the stomach.

I dropped down into the chair opposite him.

'I . . . I'm your wife. Mother of your child.' I took the long, thin object out of my pocket and placed it on the table next to the gun. 'Mother of your children.'

The two of us sat there staring at the gun.

And the positive pregnancy test.

Acknowledgements

I think all acknowledgements should be written a little bit drunk. It allows you to really gush in proper Oscars acceptance speech style.

So whoooop here goes . . .

Me standing on stage, clasping a copy of this book, looking out at a packed applauding audience.

A huge thank you to my editors of dreams, Katherine Armstrong and Eleanor Dryden, for loving Lex from the very start and for only ever giving me edit notes which had me nodding in agreement. You guys get me. So thank you!! And to all the very talented people at Zaffre for their hard work in bringing *The Nursery* into the world.

Alice Lutyens, my Superagent. A big sparkly thank you for the hand-holding and endless good advice.

I continue to be forever grateful to Tom Bromley and Faber Academy for giving me the guidance and start that helped me get published.

To my BESTIE FOREVER Rebecca Thornton. *Camera pans to beautiful, dark-haired woman, who can't be more than thirty-two, and is the only person in the audience standing and still clapping manically.* I don't think I could write at all without you to ask advice from and have therapeutic EAC chats with. Let's keep doing this together, as together there is NOTHING we can't do *dramatic air punch* . . . (except drive and cook).

To Caroline Barrow, Lara Smith-Bosanquet and Georgia Tennant. THANK YOU *hands clasped to chest* for the endless support and reading and rereading and basically being wonder women and wonderful friends.

To others in my girl gang of favourites: Alicia Grimaldi, Suzannah Lockwood and Debbie Macey White. Thank you for 'killing it' with your help for my first book *Killing It*. *Audience collectively eye-roll.* To the rest of the godparents – sorry couldn't squeeze you in as characters for this book too (that was my ingenious way of testing which of you actually read it . . . I KNOW WHO FAILED). *Three people in the audience look very sheepish.*

Andrew Trotter. This book is dedicated to you as you're awesome, etc. but mostly to let people know that, despite writing about marriage problems, ours is clearly ROCK SOLID. High fives for that and forever may it continue. *Camera close up of handsome black-tied Cumbrian looking very awkward at the attention.*

A big thank you to my parents for, as always, being my biggest cheerleaders. *Camera pans to elderly (sorry) dapper bald-headed man and glamorous Chinese woman beaming with pride.*

To my very beloved children: Tavie, Arlo, Gus and Silva. *Pause for people to absorb that I have FOUR children.* You are wonderfully inspiring and inspiringly wonderful. *Blow kisses.*

And not to sound too sucky but a big final thank you to everyone who read *Killing It* *arms outstretched to audience* and took the time to leave (nice) reviews. I know it's not cool to admit to reading reviews but I do. And there is no bigger kick than seeing kind words people you've never met have written about something you tapped out at your kitchen table. It makes my day EVERY TIME. *Talking louder over sound of orchestra starting.* SO THANK YOU THANK YOUUUU AND GOOD NIGHT!!

Dragged off stage still effusively waving and smiling.

If you enjoyed *The Nursery*, you'll love
Asia Mackay's first book . . .

'Witty and original' CLARE MACKINTOSH

KILLING IT

MOTHER. WIFE. ASSASSIN.

'Will keep you
gripped . . . and rooting
for a rather wonderful heroine'
SUNDAY MIRROR

ASIA MACKAY

AVAILABLE NOW